DE BOHUN'S DESTINY

BOOKS BY CAROLYN HUGHES

THE MEONBRIDGE CHRONICLES

Fortune's Wheel

A Woman's Lot

De Bohun's Destiny

THE THIRD MEONBRIDGE CHRONICLE

De Bohun's Destiny

CAROLYN HUGHES

Riverdown

Published in 2019 by Riverdown Books

Riverdown Books
Southampton, SO32 3QG, United Kingdom
www.riverdownbooks.co.uk

ISBN 978-1-9160598-0-1 (paperback)
ISBN 978-1-9160598-1-8 (eBook)

British Library Cataloguing in Publication Data
A CIP catalogue record for this book is available from the British
Library

Cover design by Avalon Graphics www.avalongraphics.org

CAST OF CHARACTERS

PRINCIPAL CHARACTERS ARE IN BOLD

MARGARET, LADY DE BOHUN, mistress of Meonbridge manor
Sir Richard, lord of Meonbridge, her husband
Agatha, Margaret's maid
Piers Arundale, squire

SISTER DOLOROSA, or **SISTER ROSA**, of Northwick Priory, formerly Johanna, daughter of Sir Richard & Lady de Bohun

MATILDA FLETCHER, Lady de Bohun's companion
Libby, her daughter

JACK SAWYER, carpenter
Agnes, his wife, mother of the de Bohuns' grandson
Dickon, Agnes's son by Sir Philip de Bohun
John atte Wode, Agnes's brother, the Meonbridge bailiff

Sir Morys Boune, of Herefordshire, cousin to Sir Richard de Bohun
THORKELL, Morys's younger son

Gunnar, Thorkell's brother
Alwyn, Morys's wife

Sir Giles Fitzpeyne, of Shropshire, once suitor of Johanna de Bohun
Earl Raoul de Fougère, of Sussex, liege lord of Sir Richard de Bohun
and Sir Giles Fitzpeyne

Sir Hugh de Courtenay, of Surrey, once father-in-law to the de Bohuns'
son, Sir Philip
Hildegarde, his wife
Baldwin, their son

Simon Hogge, Meonbridge's barber-surgeon
Sire Raphael, Meonbridge's priest
Nicholas Ashdown, a freeman
Susanna Miller, a widow
Maud, Susanna's adopted daughter

PROLOGUE

S ir Giles Fitzpeyne raised his wooden mazer and knocked it robustly against that of his drinking companion, spilling a little of the rich red wine onto the table.

'To my fair Gwynedd,' he said, grinning.

The other man guffawed, waggling his head, then reciprocated with such vigour that liquid spewed from both their cups, spraying the table and their hoary beards. The spilt wine trickled and merged into a run of blood-coloured pools, which slowly travelled to the table's edge and dripped down onto the already rancid rushes strewn beneath.

Neither man took any notice of the mess.

'To the uniting of our houses,' cried Sir Morys Boune, lifting his mazer aloft, then he downed the entire cupful in a single gulp.

Giles grinned again. 'And especially to the uniting of Gwynedd's loins and mine...'

Another father might take exception to such an indelicate allusion, but Giles was certain Morys would take it in good part. For he suspected, although he did not know for sure, that his soon-to-be father-in-law had illicit progeny scattered the length and breadth of

1

Herefordshire and perhaps across the hills and valleys of Wales, and that the union of his aged loins with those of any woman who would let him was ever on the old man's mind.

Not that Morys needed illegitimate offspring when his licit unions were evidently so fruitful. For Gwynedd's mother, Alwyn, had borne him seven children, all dark-haired and dark-eyed, of whom four had survived, though admittedly they were all girls. But, before Alwyn, Morys had sired two sons upon the daughter of a Danish count. As little boys, Gunnar and Thorkell had been, by all accounts, as golden-haired and meek as cherubs, but now, as men, they were handsome yet seemingly as fond of barbarity and pillage as their mother's long-dead ancestors. And, curiously, it seemed that Thorkell, the more angelic-looking of the two brothers, had the greater penchant for obtaining what he wanted through violence rather than negotiation.

And, in this, Thorkell was no different from his father.

In truth, Giles disliked Sir Morys, knowing him to be a villainous caitiff, no worthier of his knightly title than the lowest cur. Morys was a few years Giles's senior and, like Giles, bore the scars of battle. But, whereas Giles had won his during decades of knightly service to his king and country, most of Morys's wounds had been gained less honourably, in his private pursuit of other people's property. When Morys inherited his knighthood from his father, he had, it seemed, not felt obliged to honour his position by giving service to his king.

Yet Giles had decided to overlook the unsavoury character of the father of his bride. Tomorrow he would marry Gwynedd, take her away from this dark and comfortless castle, back to Shropshire, and set about the founding of the Fitzpeyne clan. And not before time. Giles had spent far too many years *not* finding himself a wife and, at forty-nine, he could afford to wait no longer. Gwynedd was something of a beauty, with her black hair and dark brown eyes, her olive skin more like that of girls Giles used to plough in Italy and Spain. But her beauty was an unlooked-for blessing, for it was Gwynedd's ability to bear him sons that was important, and at fifteen, she was ripe for motherhood.

Improbably, Giles thought, there had been tears in Morys's eyes earlier when he was relating how his lovely Danish wife had died soon after birthing the second of their two sons.

'She was an angel,' Morys said. 'Too delicate to squeeze out such another lusty boy.' He took a gulp of wine. 'But my Gwynedd's dam's quite different. Local girl, strong Welsh border stock.'

'You make her sound like a brood mare,' said Giles, laughing.

'Indeed.' Morys's eyes had glinted. 'And she's borne me many a fine filly. You're marrying into a robust family, Giles.'

Giles emptied his mazer and leaned back in the rough-hewn oak chair, wishing it was a little less unforgiving against his aching spine. A simple cushion would help, but Morys seemed oblivious to the need for comfort in his vast but cheerless hall. Giles hoped that the chambers set aside for Alwyn and her daughters afforded at least some small touch of luxury.

Morys raised his hand and an elderly serving man slid silently from the shadows beyond the fire and candlelight and came to his master's side.

'Sire?'

'More wine,' growled Morys, and the man hobbled away and at length returned bearing a flagon, gripping it with both his gnarly hands. He poured the wine, his hand quivering, first into his master's cup, then into Giles's.

'Leave it,' said Morys, and the man bowed and, putting the flagon on the table, withdrew.

Morys gulped down his wine and poured himself yet more. Giles thought he should ease off a little, reminding himself of the need for vigilance when talking to Sir Morys Boune, not saying more than he intended. So he shook his head when Morys waved the flagon in his direction.

Morys shrugged, then belched a few times before turning to Giles and grinning. 'Why don't you tell me about your gallant deeds in the service of the king?'

Hearing a tone of mockery in the request, Giles doubted the old man had any real interest in his knightly exploits. But he was always happy to recount his battlefield adventures and decided to spare Morys none of the heroic details. Yet, for the most part, Morys's face looked surprisingly rapt.

At length, Giles arrived at the telling of the great victory at Crécy ten years before. Giles shook his head as he told of how the French were routed. 'It made no sense, for they fielded three times our number of men-at-arms. Yet our archers easily overcame them, and the French were gripped by such confusion and incompetence that at length thousands were left dead.'

Morys smirked. 'And did you get yourself a hostage, Giles?'

Giles laughed. 'Indeed, a fine French knight. Although I shared the bounty with Sir Richard.'

'Sir Richard?'

'De Bohun, my oldest friend and comrade-in-arms.'

Morys raised his eyebrows. 'I'd no idea you and Richard de Bohun knew each other.'

Giles nodded. 'Since we were boys, in the service of the then Baron de Fougère, in Sussex. We've seen much action at each other's side, in many countries, and survived.' He grimaced. 'Although Dick came through more or less intact, whereas I...' He raised his left hand to his face and ran a finger along the silvery scar that extended from his eyebrow to his chin, then flapped at the loose fabric of the half-empty right hand sleeve of his tunic. 'I lost this a year later, in an unfortunate incident during the siege of Calais, just before the French surrendered. Vexing, after all those years on the battlefield.'

Morys grimaced. 'So, how do you manage to fight with only one hand?'

Giles's smile was rueful. 'I don't. Since I lost the hand, I have had to stay more or less in the rear, letting my retainers do my fighting for me. I tried once or twice to fight one-handed, but it's a quick route to suicide, so I submitted to my fate.'

'And how is Richard now?' asked Morys. 'Did you know that we are cousins?'

Giles's eyebrows shot up and he guffawed. 'I'd no idea. But, in truth, Morys, you and I have not known each other long.' He accepted more wine from Morys's proffered flagon and took a swig. 'As for Richard's health, I must confess I've not seen him for nearly seven years. When I left him, he was as hale and healthful as he had ever been, but much time has passed since then.'

Morys raised his hand again and, when the serving man tottered forward, his master pointed to the fire in the huge hearth in the middle of the hall floor, where the logs had largely burned away and the guttering flames were weak and emitting little warmth. The man

4

heaved more wood into the fireplace and, crouching down, poked feebly at the embers with a stick to try and revive the flames. Morys rose from his chair and paced about a while. As the fire continued to struggle, he advanced towards the old man and cuffed him around the head.

'It's your job to keep the fire going, you decrepit old fool. You don't have to wait for me to signal.'

The man cowered as Morys lashed out again towards his head but, as at last the new logs caught and flamed into life again, he hauled himself to his feet. He muttered something Giles could not hear and, bowing, retreated once more into the shadows.

Morys took his chair again and put his mazer to his lips for another long draught. 'So what's kept you away from my cousin when you were such comrades? A quarrel?'

'Not at all. Merely the passage of time. And no reason for us to meet, for I no longer offer my services to the king. Or perhaps it was what happened all those years ago...'

'Which was?'

Giles was curious about what lay behind Morys's sudden interest in his cousin, given that he had, presumably, had no contact with him for even longer than he himself. Something made him question if he should be telling Morys the story but, unable to pin down what the "something" was, he decided to proceed.

'You know, I suppose, that Richard had two children, although I suppose Margaret might have birthed one or two others that died in infancy. Anyway, a son, Philip, and a daughter, Johanna, survived to adulthood. Philip was with us at Crécy. He was only seventeen but had the makings of a fine young knight.'

Giles was just going to tell Morys about his meeting with Johanna when a painful spasm shot through his foot and up his lower leg. He was forced to get up and hobble around the room until the cramp had passed. Giles was well accustomed to pain, but these cramps came too frequently these days and their intense sharpness always made him sweat. He silently cursed what he presumed must be a sign of advancing age. What he needed was young Gwynedd, and the prospect of fatherhood. If only events had taken a different turn all those years ago and he had married Johanna, he might by now have sturdy sons,

5

and maybe some lovely daughters. He sighed at the memory, then, realising that the pain had eased, resumed his chair.

'I met Johanna for the first and only time three years later,' he continued, 'some months after the end of the Mortality, when I travelled to Meonbridge for us to be betrothed. Ungallant as it is of me to say so, I must admit the lady was no beauty, unlike the divine Gwynedd.' He grinned and raised his cup again. 'And Johanna was probably too studious for my taste, for by all accounts she spent most of her time with her nose between the pages of a book, and those mostly books of prayer.' His eyes twinkled. 'And she was clearly less than enthusiastic about me and my battle scars, *and* about moving to Shropshire. Nonetheless, I was happy enough with the match. I needed heirs...'

Morys guffawed. 'And now you are about to get them, Giles. So what happened?'

'It all came to nothing when young Philip was found dead on that very same day—'

Morys's jaw dropped. 'Dead? God's eyes! How?'

But Giles just shrugged. 'I'd already wondered why I had not seen Philip, and no explanation had been given for his absence. But, as I was there for Johanna, I thought little more about it. However, the discovery caused such an uproar, and Johanna was so much beside herself with grief, I saw no point continuing my suit. I left Meonbridge, having learned nothing of how Philip had died, and I'm ashamed to say I never sought to find out what had happened. Nor did I ever discover if Johanna married another. For I was, in truth, so disappointed at my thwarted plans that I did what I always do in moments of regret: find a battle to fight. I went abroad and became a mercenary, if not a very useful one, with only one hand. Nonetheless, I did not return to England and my beloved Shropshire until two years ago. Since then I have been trying to bring my estates back into shape and looking for a bride. I scarce understand why it took me so long to realise my bride was living just a few miles away.'

'You did have to wait until she was of beddable age,' said Morys, winking. 'After all, you do admit it's for begetting that you want my little Gwynedd.'

Giles choked slightly. He could hardly deny the truth of it, for he had already said so. 'Well, I am keen to create a dynasty like yours, Morys. But I do not consider Gwynedd merely a brood mare.' Then he reddened, in case the comment offended Morys, but the old man just laughed.

The next day Morys Boune gave his daughter Gwynedd to Sir Giles Fitzpeyne, and the knight rode home to Shropshire with his new young wife as soon after the wedding as he could honourably escape, asserting with a grin that he was eager to embark on married life.

Morys slapped his new son-in-law cheerfully on the shoulder. 'Of course you are, Giles. Who wouldn't want to bed my little Gwynedd?'

Indeed, Morys often fancied bedding the girl himself, for she was quite a beauty, but he managed to quell any urge to betray his paternal duties. He was glad the little wench was now gone, temptation removed. There were plenty of other maids in Herefordshire ripe for tupping.

But even they could wait.

For, right now, Morys had quite another matter to consider: the status of his cousin Richard. Giles seemed not to know who was heir to the de Bohun estates. He assumed it was Johanna, unless the murdered Philip had produced heirs of his own. But Giles did not know if the boy had even married.

When Morys revealed this information to his sons, at first they showed no interest, for they knew nothing of this cousin of their father: he'd never mentioned him before.

'So why have you had no contact with this Sir Richard, Pa?' said Gunnar. 'And how is it you've not heard about what happened? Odd, isn't it, no one's even mentioned it?'

'Perhaps we've always had our minds on other matters – our own private *business* matters?' Morys smirked, and his sons reciprocated.

Thorkell stroked his pale beard. 'So who *is* Sir Richard's heir? If Philip had no spawn and Richard had no more sons, then surely the daughter would inherit.'

'Though, if she's married,' said Gunnar, 'her husband's poised to inherit the estate on Richard's death.'

Thorkell nodded. 'But if she isn't—'

'Then *you* could marry her,' said Morys, turning to Thorkell with a grin. 'And secure *my* claim as the next rightful heir, which of course I am.'

Thorkell frowned. 'Hampshire's a long way away, Pa. Is it worth the effort, with so many more estates around here for us to win?'

Morys guffawed. 'You've no idea, Thorkell, just *how* worth it. Meonbridge is only one of the many manors Sir Dicky holds across the south of England, but it's the best one, in good farming country, as good as here. You and Gunnar can't both inherit my Herefordshire estates, so why don't we try and bag Meonbridge for you? And in good time you could be master of all the de Bohun estates.'

Thorkell nodded. It all sounded propitious enough. But what about the de Bohun daughter? Giles reckoned her no beauty, and fond of books, and maybe even pious. That didn't sound the sort of woman Thorkell would want to marry. On the other hand, if she came with vast estates, what did her beauty or her disposition matter?

1

In the bright and airy solar of Meonbridge's graceful manor house, Matilda Fletcher was sitting with her lady, Margaret, as they did every morning in the hour or two before dinner. Both were sewing, taking advantage of the sunlight streaming through the open window, a rare event in this wet and gloomy summer. Although, as ever, Matilda wondered why she even bothered, when her embroidery was always such a dreadful botch.

At the far end of the room, little Elizabeth was playing with her dolls, or rather she was shouting at them and throwing them around the floor.

Margaret tutted at the noise the child was making, and Matilda sighed.

'I'm so sorry, my lady. Libby's only misbehaving because she wants to go outside and play with Dickon.' She glanced over at the window. 'Especially when it's such a lovely day for once.'

Margaret nodded. 'I realise that, my dear. But Dickon's mother has made it clear she does not want them playing together too often, and I suppose you must respect her wishes.'

Matilda snorted. 'Agnes is always saying they "run wild" when they're together, and insists it's Libby who gets Dickon into mischief, which is laughable, as he is just like his father.' At once she bit her lip. 'I'm sorry, my lady, that was tactless. But Philip *was* a lively boy, by all accounts.'

'My son was certainly as boisterous as any village lad. In truth, I found him difficult to control when he was Dickon's age.'

Her face softened and Matilda knew she was thinking about her murdered son, as she often did, even after so many years. And Matilda thought yet again how painful it must be to lose a child – even one who was unruly and ill-tempered, as Philip evidently had been, and as both young Dickon and even her own Libby often were.

'It was your father who found the way to tame him,' Margaret continued, tears glistening on her bottom eyelids. 'Which is why I never understood—'

Matilda leaned across and touched her arm. 'I'm so sorry,' she whispered, words she found herself repeating often, as the memory of Philip's murder, committed by her own father Robert and her husband Gilbert, and their henchman Thomas Rolfe, surfaced yet again in Margaret's thoughts, a dreadful and incomprehensible spectre from the past.

In fact, Matilda was quite resentful that the murder of the de Bohuns' heir, and the subsequent ignominious deaths of all his killers, had left *her* not only with the taint of being both a Tyler and a Fletcher, but also with no property and no funds and, shortly afterwards, a baby daughter to care for. Yet, despite her connection to their son's murderers, the de Bohuns – or, at least, Margaret – had felt sorry for her. Margaret declared herself so saddened by the cruelty Matilda had suffered at the hands of Gilbert and her father, she had offered Matilda a home until she found herself another husband.

Matilda put down her clumsy needlework and wandered over to her daughter. She picked up two of the discarded dolls and, smiling, crouched down by the child's side, putting the dolls together in a gesture of embrace. Libby held out her hands, retrieved the dolls and cuddled them. Matilda pulled the girl gently onto her lap and, cradling and rocking her in her arms, rested her chin upon her daughter's curly head. Libby was not a pretty child, and she was more often tetchy than sweet-natured, but Matilda loved her dearly – of course she did. For Libby was all the family she had, apart from her older sister Margery, whom she never saw, because of the way she had betrayed her years ago.

Whilst grateful for Margaret's kindness at giving her a home, Matilda was lonely.

She had lived here in the manor house since before Libby was born – more than six years past. She was twenty-five and was still living essentially as a lady's companion – a servant. The husband the de Bohuns had undoubtedly hoped would soon take her off their hands had not materialised.

To Matilda, her failure to make another marriage seemed ridiculous, and she recognised that it was mostly her own fault. She was certainly to blame for rejecting John atte Wode, after their long courtship, and then the various suitors that Sir Richard had found for her. She hated all the suitors, but now she sometimes wondered if she'd been foolish not to find something good in one of them.

She thought Margaret was still happy enough to have her company, but she was surprised that Sir Richard continued to put up with her and Libby – and indeed to fund them. She put it down to his mixed feelings about her father, who had been his bailiff for many years, as well as Philip's guardian and tutor, and whom his lordship had once much respected and admired, until he apparently lost his wits and betrayed his lord in the cruellest possible act of revenge.

Moments passed as Matilda thought about lost opportunities, then Margaret's maid, Agatha, appeared at the entrance to the chamber, and Matilda twisted around, eager not to miss any scrap of news the maid might bring.

Agatha curtsied, then announced that Sir Richard had two visitors.

'His lordship will be back soon, for dinner,' said Margaret, 'so ask them to wait for him in the hall.' Agatha nodded and turned to go, but her mistress called her back.

'Do you know who they are, Agatha?'

To Matilda's great amusement, Agatha, despite her advancing years, blushed from her cheeks up to her wimple. 'Two most handsome young men, my lady. Such golden hair... They said they're cousins of Sir Richard.'

Matilda's heart leapt a little, for visitors here of any sort were rare enough, and handsome young men almost unimaginable.

After Agatha had gone, Margaret looked across at Matilda, her eyes wide. Matilda pushed Libby gently off her lap and, because one leg had gone a little numb, somewhat lumbered to her feet. She took the child by the hand and led her over to the chair by the window.

'Do you know them, my lady?'

Margaret ran her hands over the skirt of her blue gown, then did it again. She nodded. 'They might be the sons of Sir Morys Boune. How strange...'

Matilda shook her head, not recognising the name.

'Morys is Richard's first cousin,' continued Margaret. 'He lives in Herefordshire, I believe.'

'So why would his sons come here today?'

Margaret did not answer. She stroked at her gown again, then fingered the golden crucifix hanging on a long chain around her neck.

Then, all of a sudden, she sprang up from her chair, with an energy unusual in Margaret in recent years. 'I must find Richard,' she said, her voice tight, 'so I can warn him.' Smoothing her skirt yet again, she adjusted her already perfectly positioned wimple, but for moments did not move.

'Margaret?' said Matilda, coming over and taking the lady's hand in hers. 'You were going to find Sir Richard...'

Margaret gave a start. 'Yes, yes, I must.' She squeezed Matilda's hand, and hurried from the room.

Intrigued by the prospect of two "handsome young men" visiting the manor, Matilda imagined herself slipping quietly down the narrow staircase that led to the hall, so that, hiding behind the screen at the bottom of the stairs, she could take a peek at the visitors as they waited for Sir Richard to arrive. But she also imagined Margaret coming back and catching her there; such a demeaning possibility that she resisted the temptation. It would be time for dinner soon enough, and she could go down with Margaret and Richard, as she usually did, dignified and aloof, and spy on them discreetly from behind the edge of her veil.

Indeed, Margaret did return only moments later, a faint smile on her face confounded by a continuing air of agitation. 'I have seen them,' she said, 'and they are indeed most handsome. One of them in particular...' She let the smile blossom for a moment, but then it vanished, and she frowned. 'But then I met Richard in the yard, returning from his ride, and he was most displeased with the news of their arrival.'

Margaret paced to and fro whilst Matilda sat in the chair and, encouraging Libby to return to playing with her dolls, she picked up her embroidery again.

It was not long before Sir Richard burst into the chamber, and Margaret at once hurried over to him. Matilda glanced at them, and thought he looked even more disquieted than Margaret. He did not acknowledge Matilda's presence; she thought perhaps he had not realised she was in the room, as she was hidden by the tall chair's solid back. So, she continued to sit quietly, apparently attending to her sewing.

Margaret's agitation erupted into a torrent of questions. 'What's wrong, Richard? Who are those young men? Why have they come here?'

He paced a while, then took Margaret's arm and drew her towards him. 'Calm yourself, Margaret, but we must treat their presence here with caution.' Then he lowered his voice a little, so that Matilda found it difficult, but not impossible, to hear.

'Their visit is not purely sociable, you can be sure of that. It will relate to Morys's claim on my estates.'

'Morys has a *claim*?' Margaret's voice was tremulous.

'Of course.' He sounded vexed. 'You must surely realise, Margaret, that he is next in line after Johanna.'

'But Johanna is no longer *in* line. Surely Dickon is your heir?'

Sir Richard did not answer, and Matilda peeked around the upright of her chair. His lips were pressed together. 'Indeed,' he said at length. 'Johanna has put herself beyond inheritance, and young Dickon *is* my nominated heir...' He paused. 'But he is a bastard, and bastards, as you must know, are not legally entitled to inherit—'

Margaret let out an audible gasp, and Matilda was astonished but managed to keep silent whilst his lordship carried on.

'You might well gasp, my lady, for those boys may look like angels, but I can tell you they are malefactors, if they are anything like their father, and why would they not be?' He paced up and down the chamber. 'But you can be sure they know the law.'

'But why have they come *now*?' said Margaret, wild confusion in her tone.

Richard grunted. 'I have no idea, wife, what has prompted it. Perhaps we shall discover the answer shortly?'

'At any event,' said Margaret, 'we must be civil to them. No matter what their intentions, they are still guests here in our house.'

'Indeed, but be wary of what you say, Margaret. Do not *mention* Dickon. Nor even Johanna. I must think out what to do to send them away without any expectations.'

As Margaret gave her agreement, Matilda got up and came across. Sir Richard seemed startled to see her.

'I suppose you heard all that, young woman?' Matilda nodded, and a scowl of frustration crossed his face. 'Same applies to you. Keep your mouth *shut* on family matters. Just stick to pleasantries.'

Richard and Margaret took their places at the centre of the high table, and Matilda sat, as usual, on his lordship's other side. The other customary diners, mostly Sir Richard's retainers and, on this occasion, two of their wives, occupied the benches at the two tables set at right angles to their lord's. A few moments later, Alexander, the manor seneschal, came forward with the two fair-haired young men behind him, and introduced them to their host.

Matilda was intrigued by what she heard, for the Bounes bore the most curious of names. The first brother was called Gunnar. He stepped forward and knelt before Sir Richard, then his brother did the same. And Matilda had to suppress a gasp as she watched the taller and more slender brother, Thorkell, kneel and then look up, for his face was the most handsome she had ever set eyes upon. His nose was straight, the bones of his cheeks were set high and his eyes glowed with the pale blueness of a summer sky. His hair was lighter than his brother's, the colour of wheat shimmering in the sunshine, and he wore it long. Matilda's heartbeat thrummed a little faster at the sight of him, and she was sure her face was flushed.

Richard rose from his chair and acknowledged the obeisance of the brothers with a rather thin-lipped smile. 'Come,' he said, 'join us at the table.'

He gestured to Gunnar to sit at one end of the long high table, three chairs' distance from Matilda, and Thorkell at the other, the same distance from Margaret. Matilda was at first surprised they were not invited to sit next to Margaret and herself, as was usually the way with honoured guests. As it was, the gap between them would make conversation a little strained, so she could only assume that Richard was determined to minimise the chances of any incautious revelations. He clearly did not trust her, or his wife, to be close-lipped.

But Matilda did not mind. At least she could now gaze upon Thorkell from a distance of half a table's length. And gazing upon Thorkell, discreetly from behind her veil, was exactly what Matilda did for the duration of the meal. If the food was delicious, she did not notice, and put no more than a morsel or two into her mouth, although she saw that the Bounes helped themselves eagerly from every dish.

'And what brings you to Meonbridge?' said Richard, addressing Gunnar somewhat inopportunely whilst he was chewing upon a leg of capon.

Gunnar choked a little and reddened in the face as he tried to wash down the mouthful of poultry with some wine, and Thorkell spoke up instead of his brother.

'We're on our way to London, doing business for our father.' His voice was deep and smooth, with a lilting accent Matilda had never heard before but assumed must be that of a Herefordshire man. 'But Father bid us make a detour to Meonbridge, to offer commiseration for the death of your son—'

Margaret gasped and put her hands up to her face, whilst Sir Richard straightened his back and raised his eyebrows.

'Commiseration? But Philip has been dead nearly seven years.'

Gunnar, recovered from his choking fit, held up his hands in a gesture of apology. 'Our expression of sympathy does indeed seem much belated, my lord, but, in truth, we learned of Sir Philip's demise only recently, from our neighbour, Sir Giles Fitzpeyne.'

'How extraordinary,' said Margaret, 'that you had not learned of it before.'

'Indeed, lady,' said Gunnar. 'But we are glad at last to be able to offer our condolences.'

Margaret inclined her head, and Gunnar helped himself to more capon.

Richard had become a little quiet, perhaps, Matilda thought, at the painful memory of the murder of his only son. But, after a few moments, he poured himself more wine, and enquired after his old friend, Sir Giles.

Gunnar nodded. 'He recently became our brother-in-law. Married our little half-sister Gwynedd.'

Margaret clapped her hands. 'So Giles has found himself a wife at last. I am glad of it, for he is a good man, and a noble knight.'

'He is,' said Richard, his eyes glazing over. 'Or he was, at least. It has been years since we have seen him, indeed since Philip's death. Yet, for so long before then, we spent years in each other's company, as comrades-in-arms.'

Gunnar nodded. 'Sir Giles told our father of your many heroic exploits. He also expressed his sorrow that so much time had passed since your last meeting.'

Richard agreed it had been too long, then embarked upon a long-drawn-out tale of the two knights' adventures in the king's wars, and of Philip's prowess at Crécy.

Matilda's attention drifted; she had heard his lordship's tales many times before. She tried not to stare at Thorkell, who also seemed uninterested in Richard's rambling saga. Gunnar looked genuinely rapt, but Thorkell twisted his head this way and that, apparently viewing the high rafters of the hall, and the fine woven hangings on the walls.

But then Thorkell turned back to the table and his eyes fell upon Matilda. His tight smile broadened a little. She felt herself blush and lowered her own gaze to her plate, scattered as it was with uneaten scraps of food. She could scarcely believe that someone as attractive as Thorkell was smiling at her. She was afraid to look up, in case he was staring and caught her eye, so she contrived to drop her napkin onto the floor, then glanced up and across the table from her bent position.

He *was* staring at her. Matilda was certain that her blush was deepening and spreading down to her neck, mortifyingly on show above the low cut of her kirtle. Picking up the napkin, she sat up with a corner of it pressed to her lips, the remainder fanned out across her throat and chest. But when she raised her eyes again, Thorkell's gaze had shifted away from her towards Blanche Jordan, the wife of one of Sir Richard's retainers, a woman of little beauty who made up for it by flaunting her body in revealing gowns.

Thorkell's eyes remained upon Mistress Jordan.

Disappointed, Matilda lowered her napkin to her lap and picked at the unappetising morsels on her plate. She was relieved when, at length, Sir Richard downed the last of his wine and rose from his chair, declaring the meal over. Matilda slipped away, muttering an excuse to Margaret about a sauce stain on the sleeve of her kirtle.

Back upstairs, Matilda found herself a little breathless. It was the first time she had felt so attracted to a man since Philip de Bohun, and Thorkell was far more handsome. And, she thought, witty and cultured too. Before Sir Richard had started on his heroic tales, Thorkell had leaned across the table towards Lady de Bohun, trying to engage her in some merry discourse about French troubadours, and Margaret had appeared enchanted, until her husband interrupted and changed the topic of conversation.

Margaret, startled at Richard's sudden intrusion, had blushed a little. She caught Matilda's eye, and Matilda responded with a little shrug: his lordship presumably thought any conversation between his wife and Thorkell might lead to indiscretion. But, if Margaret understood this at that moment, she soon seemed to forget her husband's earlier warning.

'Must you rush away,' she said to the brothers, 'or can you stay a night or two here in Meonbridge, so we can get to know each other a little better?'

Matilda saw Richard's face darken when Gunnar immediately accepted the invitation, if only for one further day, but his lordship too used his napkin to conceal his irritation and, after a few moments, threw the napkin down again and applied a smile to his lips. 'A splendid idea,' he said.

However, when Margaret returned to the solar a short while later, she was red-faced, and her chin was trembling. She paced a little, plucking at her skirts, before coming to sit down by Matilda.

'I do not know what I was thinking of,' she said at last. 'And Richard is so angry with me.'

'For inviting the Bounes to stay?'

Margaret nodded. 'How foolish of me. It was the last thing Richard wanted me to do. But they were both so charming, it is hard to think of them as anything other than the most delightful guests.'

Matilda leaned across and touched Margaret on the arm. 'It *is* hard to believe they can be malefactors, as Sir Richard said.'

Margaret shook her head. 'I do not know what to think. But Richard scolded me most cruelly and said it will be my fault if any indiscretion in our future conversations gives even a hint to those young men of our situation.' She took Matilda's hand. 'So please, dear Matilda, I beg you to be more discreet than I have been. Richard will blame me entirely if the Bounes learn either of Dickon's existence, or Johanna's confinement in the priory.'

Matilda promised not to say a word. Nonetheless she was thrilled that she would once more be able to gaze across the table at the handsome Thorkell Boune. Even if he did not gaze back at her.

2

From the discreet darkness of the space beyond the great bed he'd made in modest imitation of those up at the manor, Jack Sawyer stared across at his wife, Agnes. She was bent over the hearth in the middle of the hall, stirring listlessly at their supper simmering in the pot.

When Jack had first met Agnes, seven years ago, she'd seemed to him like a fay in human form with her golden hair and lovely ever-smiling face. He was so smitten he married her despite her carrying another man's bastard child. He'd thought her brave to leave her home, to birth the baby all alone, to save bringing shame upon her own family and that of her baby's father. In accepting Jack's offer, she'd been modest and even grateful; though it did seem she loved him in return. She promised to be a constant and helpful wife, supporting him in his trade and giving him sons of his own. She'd seemed happy enough in Chipping Norton and had agreed to settle there. But, a few months after baby Richard's birth, she began to hanker after Meonbridge.

'I just want Ma and Pa to see how happy I am,' she'd said, her eyes a little moist. 'And to see the baby.'

Jack wasn't so sure it was a good idea. 'What about the de Bohuns?'

She shook her head. 'I don't think we'll tell them. Richard's young enough, don't you think, for us to pass him off as our own?'

Her eyes were wide and her lips parted slightly. But Jack turned away, unwilling to be swayed by her female wiles. He thought her idea risky, for the boy looked naught like him.

'So why d'you call him Richard?'

Agnes giggled. 'To honour his pa's father, I suppose.' Then she pouted. 'Perhaps I should've picked a different name.'

He'd agreed. 'Let's change it now. Dickon, perhaps?'

Agnes pursed her lips, then nodded. 'Anyway, Isabella will've given Philip a child by now, so the de Bohuns won't be interested in our boy.'

Yet Jack sensed danger, and still tried to talk Agnes out of visiting Meonbridge. But she wore him down.

'Just for a visit, mind,' he'd said at last, 'and just to your atte Wode family, then we come back home to Chipping.' And she'd agreed.

But the visit didn't work out at all as Agnes, or indeed Jack, had imagined. For they found her father and eldest brother had perished in the Death, as had Philip's wife Isabella, taking their unborn baby with her. Worst of all, Philip had been murdered by his father's former bailiff and his henchmen.

The murder itself was shocking. But it led to more revelations. For, despite their plan to claim Dickon as their own, Jack and Agnes couldn't deny the truth when Agnes's brother John, a mischievous twinkle in his eye, declared how much the boy looked like Philip, and their mother Alice nodded. Agnes blushed, and Jack lifted the child higher against his chest trying to hide his own disquiet. But Agnes couldn't stop herself from blurting out the truth, and John guffawed.

Alice looked both disappointed and relieved. 'So, Sir Richard and Margaret have a grandchild after all,' she said, almost to herself. 'The only one they'll ever have, since Lady Johanna decided to take the veil.'

John sniggered. 'Though who knows, Ma, how many other bastard brats Philip left behind him.'

Alice tutted. 'Hold your mischievous tongue! No such children have been born in Meonbridge.'

'But maybe somewhere else?' persisted John.

Agnes began to fret and Alice cuffed her enormous son around the ears. 'Stop it, John. Just stop.' She put her arm around her daughter's shoulder. 'Ignore your brother. He's no evidence at all for such a wicked claim.'

Agnes nodded and wiped her nose against the sleeve of her kirtle.

Jack was angry with his brother-in-law for upsetting his beloved wife but could see John's assertion might well contain at least a grain of truth.

But then Alice suggested Agnes might show the de Bohuns their grandchild. Agnes nodded, but Jack felt a tightness in his chest. He went over to the women, with baby Dickon now sleeping in his arms.

'Do you think that's wise, Mother?' he said to Alice, who tipped her head a little. Then he addressed his wife. 'We agreed to come to Meonbridge just to visit your family, then return home to Chipping. We *agreed* we'd not talk to the de Bohuns.'

Agnes raised her eyes to him and Jack wasn't sure what to read in them.

'But, Jack, I'm sure they'd be delighted to know they've a grandchild after all,' said Alice.

'An *illegitimate* grandchild? You really think so?'

In truth, Jack had no idea what people like the de Bohuns might think of bastard children even if, in his world, they weren't always openly accepted.

'I think they might, Jack,' said Alice. 'The Death has changed so much. Losing Philip, then Johanna – for she *is* lost to them as a daughter – means they have no heir. It saddens Margaret greatly to think she'll never dandle a grandchild on her knee.'

So Agnes did introduce Dickon to his lordly grandparents, and they were, as Alice had predicted, delighted to accept him as their own, and Sir Richard suggested Jack take on the vacant carpenter's shop in Meonbridge. Jack wondered then at Agnes's motives for gainsaying their original agreement. But it was soon clear enough she saw the chance of a better future for her son. If Sir Richard accepted him as his grandson, Dickon's destiny would be no longer the life of a carpenter, but that of the inheritor of Meonbridge and all the other de Bohun domains.

His lordship had said as much. 'You raise him as a Sawyer until he is seven or so,' he told Agnes, 'then I'll send him off to train to be a page.'

He'd not have said that unless he intended to follow through with a knightly education.

Jack had thought it odd Sir Richard didn't simply hire a nurse and then a tutor for the child, but Agnes was, unsurprisingly, thrilled to be allowed to raise her baby until boyhood. Though, seven years later, she seemed no longer quite so pleased.

Indeed, she now seemed a different woman from the one he'd married all those years ago.

Jack stared across at her again. Did she *look* any different? Her lovely yellow curls were still the same, though these days she mostly kept them hidden beneath her wifely wimple. Her figure too was hardly changed, just rounded out a little after the birthing of four babies. But where were those soft pink lips, once so often slightly parted, awaiting his kiss? Now they seemed always to be pressed together in disapproval or dismay, expressing the change in Agnes's demeanour, along with her frequently furrowed brow and sharpened tongue.

He sighed. His lovely Agnes had become something of a shrew.

And why she had wasn't hard to understand – wasn't it entirely because of Dickon? For, if she'd imagined spending a few years cosseting her first-born son – as she surely had – she found out soon enough that Dickon refused even a hint of cosseting. She – indeed Jack himself – found the boy impossible to control.

Now, though still only seven, he was always running wild, joining the more unruly of the village boys in mischief and, sometimes, worse. If Agnes attempted to constrain him, he fought and broke free from her grip.

'You can't stop me,' he would yell at her, and she wondered out loud to Jack if the boy somehow *knew* he was a de Bohun.

But Jack shook his head. 'How can he?'

Then there was, in Agnes's eyes, the problem of Libby, Matilda Fletcher's daughter, only a few months younger than Dickon, who clearly adored him. For Agnes considered Libby a "bad influence" on her son. 'She's inherited bad blood,' she'd said.

Jack thought her carping ridiculous. It was clear enough that Dickon was the image of his father, not only physically, but in his arrogance and wilfulness. Agnes's brother John had told him of Philip's reputation as a boy and as a man. Jack doubted Libby could teach Dickon anything about misbehaviour.

Jack was back in his workshop, shortly after dinner, when a dark shape filled the doorway, cutting off the stream of sunlight shining onto his carpentry bench. Jack looked up to see Sir Richard, blinking as his eyes adjusted to the indoor gloom. His lordship scanned the modest workshop, the wall of tools, the benches set up for different tasks, cutting, planing, chiselling, the floor of beaten earth ankle deep in wood shavings. Apart from the floor, the room was a model of order and control.

Sir Richard nodded as he came in. 'You keep a tidy workshop, Jack. A credit to you.'

Jack grinned. 'And to young Christopher. My 'prentice is a stickler for neatness.'

'Good lad, then?' He stroked his beard. 'Is Agnes here?'

'She doesn't come to the workshop nowadays. Shall I send for her, m'lord?'

His lordship nodded. 'Something to tell you both.'

Jack went to find Christopher and told the boy to send Agnes here, then stay in the house himself to mind the children. Back in the workshop, Jack found Sir Richard pacing up and down, inspecting the chisels, saws and adzes, then examining a stack of small decorated lidded chests at the far end of the room.

'They're Agnes's work,' said Jack. He'd insisted three years ago she gave up trying to use the lathe. She'd so wanted to be a craftsman, but none of her turned pieces were fit for sale and, when James arrived to be Jack's journeyman, it was the perfect excuse to force her to give up the lathe. Nonetheless, she'd begged him to let her continue making small things. He didn't want her to: she had three boys to mind and he was keen for her to have another child. But arguing with Agnes was exhausting and he decided to give in, for a while at least.

So she continued making the chests and little boxes, and trays and whittled spoons. Small stuff. With only the little market in Meonbridge in which to sell them. He'd never admitted it to Agnes, but in truth he missed going to Wickham's market to sell his furniture.

Indeed he quite missed making the furniture, but manufacturing frames and beams and posts and doors for the building trade was where his future lay.

Sir Richard picked up a little chest and turned it over. 'Well enough made. For a woman.'

Jack waggled his head. 'Well-made regardless, m'lord.'

But his lordship demurred. 'She hardly has your skill, Jack.'

It was true, of course, but Jack was loath to belittle Agnes's craft. She had become quite skilful in her way, and the simple carved decoration on the chests had been well done. 'But she made those more than a twelvemonth ago. She gave it up entirely when little Alice was born.'

Moments later, Agnes appeared at the door. Blinking away the brightness of the afternoon, she stepped inside and almost collided with Sir Richard.

'Oh, m'lord,' she cried, but he laughed and patted her lightly on the arm.

'No harm done,' he said, then resumed his pacing a few moments longer. When he stopped, his lips were pressed together and Jack wondered what his lordship's concerns might have to do with them.

'Sit down, m'dear,' Sir Richard said at last. Perching on a stool, Agnes threw a glance of puzzlement at Jack, who shrugged.

His lordship took a commanding stance, his legs astride, but he softened the sternness of his face with a smile.

'This afternoon, Agnes, I want you to bring young Dickon to the manor. He is to meet his cousins.'

Agnes nodded happily.

'I have decided to make it clear to them that Dickon is my heir – my *legitimate* heir.'

Agnes beamed, but Jack was curious.

'What d'you mean, m'lord?'

Sir Richard cleared his throat. 'What I mean, Jack, is that, from now on, Dickon will be regarded as *Isabella's* son. She died in childbirth, rather than from the Mortality—'

Agnes sprang to her feet. 'No,' she cried, 'he's mine!'

Jack moved swiftly to her side and grasped her arm. 'Stop it, Agnes. You mustn't question—'

24

But Sir Richard laid a hand upon Jack's shoulder. 'No, no, Jack, she's entitled to be upset. But you must understand, dear Agnes, that I have no choice.'

Agnes's brows knit together and her lips trembled. 'Why?'

'Because yesterday the sons of my cousin Morys Boune came to Meonbridge, ostensibly to offer their belated condolences for Philip's death, but actually, I am certain, to discover if he had a son to succeed him.'

'You think they suspect the truth?' said Jack.

'I cannot tell how much they know. We have just finished an entire meal without mentioning either Dickon or Johanna – or rather, Sister Dolorosa.' Sir Richard raised his eyebrows. 'I had hoped the Bounes would now be on their way, none the wiser for their visit – or perhaps assuming that, with Philip dead, Johanna was now my heir – but her ladyship took it upon herself to invite them to stay longer.' He lifted his eyebrows even higher. 'So we shall surely be unable to avoid the inheritance conversation for much longer.'

His lordship's face grew dark, his mouth turned down, his jaw slack. He looked a worried man. A rare sight, Jack thought, in one normally so confident of the rightness of his own position.

'I think the Bounes are bound to enquire about Johanna,' Sir Richard continued, 'and will soon realise that she gave up her claim to inherit Meonbridge when she entered the priory. If they also discover that Philip's only child is a bastard, Morys will stake *his* claim to the de Bohun estates, and I shall have no case to answer.'

'*His* claim?' said Agnes, wiping her sleeve across her face.

'Indeed, Agnes. Morys will take everything if he can. Your son may be half a de Bohun but, as a bastard, he has no entitlement in law.'

Agnes gasped, but Jack pressed down upon her shoulder. 'Which is why you want to say Dickon is Isabella's son, and your *legitimate* appointed heir.'

'Precisely,' said Sir Richard. 'I have always reckoned that Dickon will succeed me, illegitimate or not. I expect at length to have to argue my case before the law, but I am confident that I will win. But I have also assumed that my cousin, living so far away, and with such vast estates of his own – that he is, I understand, relentlessly expanding by diverse villainous means – would not trouble himself with Meonbridge, or my other domains.'

Jack was mystified about the Bounes. 'What prompted your cousin's sons to come here now? Have they truly only *just* learned of Sir Philip's death?'

'So it would seem. His sons said they heard it lately from my old comrade Sir Giles Fitzpeyne, who lives up that way. It does indeed seem puzzling that, in seven long years, the news did not somehow travel as far as Herefordshire. But we must believe it.' He pulled on his beard. 'It is unfortunate indeed that Giles let slip the information, but he was not to know it would cause me such embarrassment.'

Jack nodded. 'And now you have no choice but to show the Bounes that you do have an heir?'

'I had hoped I would not need to, but circumstances have changed.' Sir Richard grimaced. 'This afternoon, I will let the Bounes meet Dickon, but not talk to him beyond initial pleasantries. I will make some excuse for the boy not to stay.' He raised a quizzical eyebrow. 'But, Jack, I want to ensure that Dickon himself does *not* know who it is he is meeting today or understand his status as my heir, until he is a little older. It must remain a secret between us, you and Agnes, and Margaret and myself. The Bounes will know, of course, but my plan is to dispatch them home to Herefordshire as soon as maybe after I have told them what they undoubtedly came here to discover. And my hope and expectation is that we shall not see them again in Meonbridge.'

When Sir Richard bid Agnes and Jack farewell, Jack walked with him out of the shop.

'I apologise, m'lord, for Agnes's earlier behaviour.'

But his lordship waved his hand. 'It is only to be expected. But she has to understand my position.'

Jack nodded. 'I can see the difficulty of your situation, m'lord, and I'll try and make Agnes see it too. Anyways, she'll bring the boy up to the manor shortly.'

But when Jack went back inside the shop, Agnes flew at him, beating at his chest with her hands.

'How could you, Jack,' she cried. 'You agreed he could pass Dickon off as Isabella's. It's not fair!'

He held her arms. 'What's fair got to do with it, Agnes? You were glad enough, all those years ago, to show the de Bohuns their grandson, to associate yourself with them.'

Agnes whimpered. 'That's not fair either. You knew we weren't going to tell them. And I was worried when Ma suggested it.'

'Only in case they didn't accept him.' Jack frowned. 'But once you knew Isabella and her unborn babe were dead, you were only too happy to think your son might be heir to Meonbridge.' Agnes shook her head, but Jack continued. 'You didn't consider he had to be *legitimate* to inherit—'

'No more did you.' Agnes's eyes were sparking. 'And Sir Richard was so pleased to find he had a grandson after all—'

'So, in your dreams, you imagined everything was fine. But it isn't the way of things, is it?'

Jack felt his body stiffen, his shoulders set. He rarely lost his temper but was close to it now. And when Agnes started to cry, he lost patience.

'Calm down, Agnes. I'm going to fetch Dickon home. You get yourself ready to go up to the manor.'

For once, Jack found his stepson easily enough. He was down by the river, fishing with a couple of village boys. Village people weren't allowed to fish the Meon, for all the river creatures – trout, eel, pike, grayling, perch and salmon – belonged to Sir Richard. But Dickon seemed to think he too had the right to fish. Or he was simply being disobedient, which Jack thought more than likely. But his lordship, who must know Dickon was misbehaving, didn't complain. He should have taken the boys into custody and whipped them, but he never did.

Jack waded through the water meadows, knee-high with flower-filled grass, rustling gently in the breeze, until he reached the part of the river bank where he knew Dickon often went. He was not in the habit of shouting for his children from a distance, unlike some cottar parents whose bellowed "Ivo" or "Joanie" carried far across the fields. He preferred a quiet approach, trying to encourage – albeit not always with success – civility and calm. So he was only a few feet away from Dickon when he called his name. At first, Dickon ignored him, though

Jack couldn't be quite sure he'd heard. So he spoke a little louder and the boy turned, scowling at his stepfather.

'You must come home, Dickon,' said Jack.

Dickon said nothing and, turning back to his friends, sniggered.

'*Now*, Dickon.'

Jack heard the boy mutter something – a curse, he suspected. But then Dickon sprang to his feet and glared, his face dark with frustration. In that moment he reminded Jack somewhat of Sir Richard in one of his blacker moods.

'You can't *make* me,' Dickon yelled.

At times like these Jack wished he could beat Dickon for his insolence, but the boy wasn't his own son, and he always felt he had no right to punish him, especially as he was his lordship's grandchild. But leaving discipline to Agnes had proved hopeless, for she doted on the boy, despite his obstinacy and rudeness.

'You're right, Dickon,' he said, 'I can't force you against your will. But I'd like to think you are grown up enough to make the right decision, especially when it's his lordship asking for you.' He grinned to himself – the boy was only seven but appealing to his sense of manhood always worked.

The darkness on Dickon's face faded and, leaning towards his friends, he whispered something to them Jack couldn't catch, then scrambled up the bank.

'What's he want?' he said, when they'd walked a few paces away.

'Not sure. He has some visitors.' He hesitated, loath to lie. 'I think mebbe they've a boy your age, and his lordship wants you to go and play.'

It was just as well Sir Richard didn't want Dickon to know about his cousins, or the proposed announcement. Despite his age, Dickon was surprisingly aware – if he understood the situation, he would almost certainly ask awkward questions. Jack knew Richard was planning to send the boy away before too long to start his training. Yet he was going to do so without giving Dickon any preparation for a future very different from what the boy might be expecting. The whole situation seemed dangerously risky, yet he knew he had to trust Sir Richard knew what he was doing.

Dickon pouted. 'That sounds boring.'

'Nonetheless, that's what his lordship wants you to do,' said Jack, itching to thump the boy. 'Let's go home and get you tidied up.'

But, when they arrived home, they found Agnes had done nothing at all to get ready Dickon's clean clothes, or her own.

She ran to Dickon and clasped him to her breast. 'It's not right,' she cried. 'It's not fair.'

Jack knew that, if Dickon saw her anxiety, he might ask one of those awkward questions. But the boy just pushed her away.

'Don't be stupid, Ma. I'm only going up to play.'

Agnes looked at Jack, confused, and he glared at her and nodded, willing her to understand. She turned away and slumped down onto a stool.

Dickon ignored his mother. He quickly washed his face and hands, and Jack helped him put on his best clothes, kept clean in a special chest. Agnes didn't move from the stool, and it was clear to Jack that *he* was going to have to take Dickon up to the manor.

'Come on, lad, let's go,' he said, and Dickon nodded, going to the door.

Jack glanced over at Agnes, still sitting on the stool. 'Wait for me outside,' he said to Dickon, and the boy ran out. 'And don't get yourself dirty.'

Once he'd gone, Agnes looked up. 'Is he really just going up to play? Is Sir Richard not going to say he's Isabella's son?' Her cheeks were streaked with dried tears, and more were leaking from her eyes.

Jack sighed. 'Yes, of course he is, Agnes. But he said Dickon mustn't know, so I assume he won't say it in the boy's hearing. But he wants these cousins to *see* Dickon does exist.'

Agnes shook her head. 'So who's Dickon going to play with?'

'Libby, I expect. Though I told him mebbe the visitors had a son, and Sir Richard had invited him to play.'

'You lied to him?'

Jack shrugged. 'To persuade him to leave his fishing.' He stepped across to Agnes and placed his hands upon her shoulders. 'We're at Sir Richard's mercy, Agnes. We have to do what he asks of us, even if we don't like it. If this is what his lordship wants, we can't gainsay it.'

3

MEONBRIDGE

JULY 1356

'And here is Dickon.' De Bohun beamed, coming forward with a boy Thorkell thought looked about six or seven, although his stiffly held back and the grave expression on his face gave him the air of an older child. A young female servant followed close behind.

Thorkell had been sitting with Gunnar at the long table at one end of the hall, making polite conversation with Lady de Bohun and her companion, Matilda. But the only topics Lady de Bohun seemed to permit were the weather and the difficulties it was causing the Meonbridge tenants, something Thorkell could not care less about. Yet Gunnar seemed to be finding enough to say for both of them, and Thorkell could concentrate on trying to get the Matilda woman to look him in the eye. Moments ago, he had succeeded, causing a healthy blush to bloom upon her face, spread quickly down her throat and settle on her pretty breasts, which just peeped above the neckline of her gown. And then the old man came forward with his grandson.

Frustrated, Thorkell clenched his teeth, but stood up with his brother nonetheless. As they did so, he noticed Lady de Bohun's face had drained of colour, and that Matilda's bright blue eyes were wide.

'Dickon, these gentlemen are the sons of an old acquaintance of mine,' de Bohun said.

Thorkell was surprised at "old acquaintance". "Cousin" would have been the truth. Behind him, Lady de Bohun audibly sighed.

But her husband continued grinning. He stood behind the boy, holding on to his shoulders. Then he gave him a little nudge. 'Come, boy, shake the gentlemen's hands.'

The boy took a step forward and, bowing his head slightly, took first Gunnar's hand, then Thorkell's. Thorkell was struck by the firmness of the child's handshake.

'How old are you, boy?' asked Gunnar.

'Seven,' said Dickon, rolling his eyes, and Thorkell recalled how tiresome he too had found it as a child when people asked him pointless questions.

But when the boy seemed about to ask a question of his own, de Bohun stepped forward and, grasping the child's shoulders again, spun him around and pushed him towards the servant girl. She nodded and, gripping the child's hand, marched away and back through the door that, Thorkell presumed, led to the de Bohuns' private quarters. As he was being led away, the boy protested, tugging against the girl's hand, and turning several times to look back at the visitors.

The old man laughed. 'Ha, boys! Always hate missing any excitement, eh?'

Gunnar joined in the laughter. 'Indeed. But why can't he stay?'

'Ah, well, despite appearances, my grandson is quite a timid little boy, readily alarmed by strangers.'

Gunnar nodded, but Thorkell thought the claim was ludicrous, given the strength of the child's handshake. He wanted to say as much, but even he recognised that arguing with his host would be ill-mannered. However, Gunnar couched his own apparent disbelief in a question. 'And why is that, Sir Richard?'

The old man shrugged. 'I don't rightly know, for his father, our son Philip, was not at all timid, was he, my dear?' He turned to Lady de Bohun, who laughed lightly in response, but still looked pale.

Then Gunnar guffawed. 'That's true enough,' he said, and de Bohun looked surprised. 'Do you remember, Sir Richard, when Philip and I first met?'

The old man shook his head and frowned.

Gunnar continued. 'Philip had just started as page with Baron de Fougère, in Sussex, whilst I, although the same age as him, had already been two years with Sir Henry Blandefordde, in Dorset. I teased Philip that, because he'd begun his training later than most boys, it might take him longer to become a knight.' Then Gunnar grinned broadly. 'But I was wrong about that, wasn't I?'

Thorkell knew his brother had, in fact, been irked by de Bohun's bragging about his son, covering himself in glory when he was only seventeen. For Gunnar had been denied a chance to prove himself. Although his father sent him and, later, Thorkell himself, to Sir Henry Blandefordde to train to be pages and then squires, Sir Henry had discharged both boys when Thorkell was fifteen, claiming they were no longer "suitable" for training. Their father had contested Sir Henry's outrageous allegations, but the old fool was adamant, and the boys had no choice but to return home to Herefordshire. Gunnar ranted at his brother for, as he put it, damning his reputation as well as his own, but Thorkell just thought Sir Henry a decrepit old clodpate who didn't understand the impulse of young squires for pranks and mischief-making.

In truth, Thorkell had been glad to be rid of his squire's duties, waiting at table, running errands and looking after the knights' clothes, which he thought demeaning. Though he did regret being denied his knightly training, for he loved riding and learning to fight with bow and sword and had been looking forward to accompanying Sir Henry's men-at-arms to tournaments and even war.

But Morys ensured his sons engaged in battles of a different kind.

Thorkell knew his father was much aggrieved by the insult to his status implicit in Sir Henry's dismissal of his sons, and resolved upon a campaign of terror throughout the border counties and the whole of Wales, to best his swell-headed knightly neighbours by the power of his stratagems and his sword, and those of his "unsuitable" sons.

But Gunnar seemed to have forgotten about lost opportunities, or perhaps he was simply ingratiating himself with the de Bohuns. 'You arranged a jousting contest, do you recall, Lady de Bohun?' he continued. 'Our lords brought along us pages and squires, to serve the competing knights. How excited we all were. It was the first time I'd been anywhere since I started training, and Philip was pleased to be coming home for a few days.'

The old man appeared confused for a moment, but Lady de Bohun laughed lightly.

'Oh, surely, Richard, you can't have forgotten? It was a wonderful occasion. Philip was nine.'

De Bohun tugged on his greying beard. 'Ah, yes. So it was here that you and Philip met? I'd no idea.'

'Although it was the only time,' said Gunnar. 'Despite my teasing him, we made friends at once. But with so much going on, and our lords insisting we stay with our own retinues, we didn't spend much time together.'

Thorkell was already bored with Gunnar's tedious story. His brother seemed to have forgotten too that Thorkell had never been to a proper knightly joust – had been denied that particular excitement. Thorkell jerked his chin up and glared at him, and Gunnar at once seemed to understand, for he nodded. There was no further talk about the joust.

But the short silence was soon broken by the old man. 'Anyway, I have always thought that Dickon's frailness might be because he never knew his mother...'

Thorkell heard Lady de Bohun draw in her breath, then saw her waft her hand in front of her face. But her husband ignored her and continued. '...the Lady Isabella de Courtenay.'

'Lady Isabella?' repeated Gunnar, exchanging raised eyebrows with Thorkell. 'I knew her brother Baldwin. He trained with me at Sir Henry's. So, Baldwin's sister was married to Philip?'

De Bohun sighed. 'Indeed she was but tragically she died giving birth to Dickon. It was a dreadful, dreadful time – just as the Mortality was coming to an end in Meonbridge, and the future was beginning to look a little brighter.'

Gunnar nodded, looking grave. 'How tragic indeed. So young Dickon has something in common with his cousin Thorkell. For he too didn't know his mother—'

Thorkell bridled. Gunnar should keep his mouth shut about their mother. Nonetheless, he was about to remark upon the commonness of motherless children, when he saw Lady de Bohun's face was no longer pale but had become quite florid. And Matilda was turning away, fanning herself.

'Ladies, are you hot?' he said.

Matilda turned back briefly, and her face was flushed and shiny. 'Indeed, sir. I must get some air.'

She hurried over to the door that led out onto the bailey. Regardless of her sudden unbecoming glow, the woman really was quite handsome. Much more so than Blanche Jordan, he thought, whose principal assets had been her lovely breasts, which she allowed to spill so prettily from the top of her gown, and her eagerness to take him to her bed. Matilda, he suspected, would not be such an easy lay but, given the way she'd gawped at him all through dinner, she would surely not take too much persuasion.

Lady de Bohun smiled wanly. 'It *is* very warm in here. Perhaps I shall join Matilda for a few moments by the door.'

Her husband laughed. 'Ladies, eh? Always either too cold or too hot.'

Thorkell thought it unlikely Lady de Bohun was too hot, as the hall was large and airy, and the door had been left wide open to let in the summer breeze. Though he supposed her ladyship was quite old, and he'd heard that women of her age sometimes became a little flushed for no apparent reason. Perhaps that was the truth of it?

Nonetheless, he wanted to return to de Bohun's ludicrous explanation for not allowing the boy to stay and talk to them. 'Your grandson didn't seem unduly shy. I thought he was about to engage us in conversation?'

But de Bohun shook his head. 'Oh, I doubt it. He quickly gets excited, then takes fright soon after.'

He was clearly talking nonsense, but Thorkell could hardly say so. He tried a different take. 'But if the boy is seven, I assume you'll soon be sending him away?'

De Bohun frowned. 'Sadly, yes. We have allowed the boy to enjoy his childhood for as long as we are able but soon, of course, we shall have to let him go. Though it will be hard for us to part with him, eh, my dear?' He looked towards his wife, still languishing at the door, who nodded feebly. 'Our only grandchild, you see.'

Gunnar murmured understanding. 'So where will you send him?'

The old man shrugged. 'Perhaps Sir Giles would be a good choice? Or the de Courtenays, Dickon's other grandparents?'

A sigh came from the direction of the door and Thorkell turned just in time to see Lady de Bohun appear to stumble as she moved back towards the table and almost collapsed into a chair.

Matilda hurried to her side. 'Are you all right, your ladyship?'

'Yes, yes, child, merely overcome a little by the heat.'

Thorkell had had enough. Their visit had been a waste of time. They'd learned that de Bohun did have an heir, albeit a very young one. But the old man looked plenty fit enough for a man of his age – a good deal healthier than his own father – and might well survive until the boy became a man. There was nothing more to learn. They might as well go home and tell their father what they knew.

He locked eyes with his brother, who nodded and took a few steps towards Lady de Bohun, still flapping at her glowing cheeks.

'It's time we took our leave of your generous hospitality, your ladyship,' said Gunnar. 'Glad to have met your grandson, Sir Richard, albeit briefly. If he proves anything like his father and grandfather, I'm sure he'll make a fine heir to your estates.' Then he bowed to Lady de Bohun and Matilda, and clasped Sir Richard's hand.

Thorkell, repelled by his brother's fawning, bowed his head briefly to each de Bohun.

'No doubt we'll come to Meonbridge again,' said Gunnar to Lady de Bohun, 'now that we've made acquaintance.'

In truth, Thorkell couldn't think what reason might bring them for a second visit apart, perhaps, from seeing Matilda Fletcher again. And, just to confirm what he already knew, he contrived to catch Matilda's eye. She was handsome, with what he could see of her hair a glossy black, and her mouth so soft and inviting. She blushed and dropped a curtsey, and he licked his lips.

That was all he had to do.

Some hours later, Thorkell and his brother were dining on stewed mutton and red wine in a grimy, smoke-filled inn near Andover, some thirty miles from Meonbridge, on their way home to Hereford. The inn was uncomfortable, the mutton tough and the wine sour, but the brothers didn't care. They'd been accustomed to discomfort all their lives, and right now all that concerned them was how to tell their father their disheartening news.

For if de Bohun *did* have an heir to his vast estates, Morys's ambition of claiming them for himself, in order to pass them on to Thorkell, was untenable. It was disappointing, particularly for Thorkell, but their father would be more than merely disappointed, for he couldn't stomach being thwarted.

Thorkell was relieved, however, that Philip's sister Johanna was no longer a contender.

Gunnar laughed. 'Did you see Sir Richard's face when he told us she'd become a nun?'

Thorkell nodded, putting a piece of mutton in his mouth. He tried to grin, but his mouth was full.

'Strange to think Fitzpeyne was going to marry her,' continued Gunnar, 'but had to give up his suit when Philip was murdered and she went to pieces. Our little sister's good fortune.'

'Thank God *I* don't have to marry her,' said Thorkell, swallowing. 'She's best off in a nunnery, where a dearth of men won't cause her any heartache.' He smirked. 'Unlike Blanche Jordan.' He started to chew another piece of meat.

'Was that her name?' said Gunnar. 'The one showing everyone her tits?'

Thorkell nodded and moved his mouth to speak, but the mutton was tough and gristly, and he tried to wash down the half-masticated lump with some of the foul wine. But suddenly he was choking and tears came to his eyes. For a few moments he couldn't breathe, and his face became red and sweaty, until Gunnar thumped him hard upon the back and the vile lump flew from Thorkell's mouth and landed in the noisome rushes on the floor. Thorkell gulped more wine and, puffing out his cheeks with relief, wiped his sleeve across his eyes. Then both men threw back their heads and guffawed.

'That was a close one, little brother,' said Gunnar. 'Thought I'd lost you there, just when things are getting interesting.'

'I swived her yesternight,' said Thorkell, grinning. 'Blanche. In a tumbledown old house. God's eyes, she's a minx. But barren, she claimed, so spared the risk of accidental spawn.'

36

'That's lucky.'

Thorkell grimaced. 'But too strong-willed for my taste.'

Gunnar's eyes twinkled. 'Haha! Can't have the woman on top...'

Thorkell pressed his lips together, ignoring Gunnar's jibe. 'The Matilda woman's more interesting—'

'And clearly besotted with you, the way she was making puppy eyes.'

'I noticed. And, because of that, she'll probably be more, shall we say, malleable than Blanche. Could be useful.'

'She's handsome enough. But "useful"?'

'As a source of information. She must know a good deal about the de Bohuns.'

Gunnar nodded. 'I wonder if she'd tell you about herself? That she's the daughter and the wife of villains who murdered their lord's son, then got themselves killed, buried at the crossroads and forfeited all their property to the king.'

Thorkell snorted. 'Philip was *murdered*? How do you know that?'

'I asked one of Sir Richard's retainers who she was.'

'Even better. If she has such an *interesting* heritage, her usefulness is strengthened. If I woo her, the penniless widow of a felon and daughter of a felon, she'll surely think she's everything to gain by helping us.'

'What sort of help?'

'Don't know yet. But I *want* Meonbridge, Gunnar – and I'm damned sure Pa does too. Old man de Bohun might have an heir, but he's a very *small* heir, and I'm thinking Matilda might – unwittingly, of course – help us work out how we can make him disappear.'

'You're the Devil himself,' said Gunnar, 'the Devil in angel's form. Isn't that what everybody thinks?'

Thorkell smirked. 'But wasn't Satan Heaven's greatest angel?'

Gunnar nodded. 'Till he fell into the abyss.'

4

M argaret had always looked forward to the regular visits of her grandson. Even though the boy didn't *know* he was her grandson. At first, she and Richard had been delighted to find that they had a grandchild after all, albeit illegitimately born. But they thought it wise to keep the knowledge of the boy's true parentage a secret, and the Sawyers and the atte Wodes had readily agreed. The Sawyers would bring the boy up as their own, and none of them gave much consideration to what would happen in the future.

But, once Dickon passed babyhood, Margaret found herself longing to see him, and Agnes and Jack agreed to him coming to the manor once a week, supposedly to spend time with Matilda's daughter, Libby, but mostly to give Margaret the chance to watch him play and hear him talk.

Why Dickon had been chosen as Libby's playmate was never explained to him and, perhaps because he was still so young, he never asked. And, if anyone in the village asked themselves why he had been chosen from amongst the village children, no one asked the question. Margaret sometimes wondered why no one seemed to have even noticed how much Dickon looked like Philip, and not at all like Jack. Or maybe many had noticed but decided not to mention it.

However, as the years passed, Margaret became increasingly anxious about the situation in which she and Richard had placed themselves. For if Dickon was, thus far, ignorant of the reason behind his weekly visits, Margaret knew he would not remain so for much longer. Surely he would soon demand to know. Dickon was nothing like the timid, fearful little boy that Richard had painted for the benefit of the Bounes but was most definitely his father's son – brave and boisterous, and, above all, curious. Indeed, Margaret could hardly believe that he had not already guessed the truth. Moreover, if Richard soon sent the boy to begin his knightly training – a plan Richard had not discussed with her – then that, if anything, would alert not just Dickon himself, but everyone in the village, that he was not Jack Sawyer's son.

And now there was the added worry of Richard's declaration to the Bounes. For he had said not only that Dickon was their grandson – which was true enough, if not widely known – but also that he was their *legitimate* grandson, the son of Isabella and not Agnes – which was a wicked lie. A lie that could be easily uncovered, for did not most folk in Meonbridge *know* that Isabella had died in the Mortality?

Perhaps she always knew that Richard would, in due course, formally nominate the boy his heir, despite his illegitimacy. Bastards did not always find it easy to inherit, especially large estates, but she thought that somehow her husband, who invariably succeeded in whatever he undertook, would find a way. But she always assumed that the way would be honest and undisguised.

In retrospect, however, maybe this – the lie – was always what Richard had in mind, and she had simply been too naïve to recognise it. Of course he had had to say something yesterday to warn off the Bounes. She just wished it had not been such a falsehood. For everyone in Meonbridge knew that the boy was *Agnes's* son, even if they did not realise that he was also Philip's. It would only take one person who held a grudge against Richard – and surely there must be one or two – to speak out.

He had made an already difficult situation much, much worse.

Margaret felt quite helpless with anxiety. She had dismissed

Matilda and Agatha, so that she could be alone in her private chamber to think. But the wave of heat and nausea that had come over her yesterday, when Richard was spinning out his web of fabrication to the Bounes, had returned. Carefully tipping the pitcher of cold water that stood on the table by her bed, she moistened her kerchief and wiped her face. Then she slumped into her chair and closed her eyes. The megrim was returning too.

The last person she wanted to see right now was Agnes Sawyer.

Although yesterday it had been Jack who brought Dickon up to the manor, it was usually Agnes who came, leaving the boy with Margaret for a few hours. But today Agnes was in bad humour, and she lingered, wanting to unburden herself, though she waited until she and Margaret were out of Dickon's hearing before she did so.

Margaret soon learned that Richard had told the Sawyers of his plan, whilst keeping it from her. And Agnes was clearly much offended by his untruthful assertion that Dickon was Isabella's son and not hers.

Margaret often found Agnes unreasonably cavilling and critical, about Jack, her three energetic boys and even her mother. Baby Alice, at least, could so far do no wrong. But in today's particular complaint Margaret agreed with Agnes entirely.

For Agnes was not only angry but afraid, and full of questions that Margaret could not answer.

'Why did Sir Richard feel he had to lie to the Bounes?'

'Suppose they find out Dickon isn't legitimate?'

'Is my son in danger?'

Margaret shared Agnes's disquiet about the Bounes. Richard had said that all the Bounes were knaves; that his cousin Morys had, for years, used violence and intimidation to extend his domains.

'And yet Sir Giles Fitzpeyne, the most honourable of knights, has married one of this so-called miscreant's daughters?' Margaret had countered.

'The daughter is not the father.'

'And yet the sons are?' Margaret shook her head, confused. Thorkell and Gunnar were such handsome young men; Thorkell in particular looked quite saintly with his fair hair and light blue eyes.

40

But, perhaps, if Richard was right, he was the Devil in an angel's form?

She found it hard to comprehend.

'And Dickon was so confused by what happened with the Bounes,' continued Agnes.

'Whatever do you mean, my dear?'

'Jack had told him he'd been asked to come and play with the children of some visitors.' She pursed her lips. 'He knew it wasn't true of course but he didn't know what else to tell him.'

Margaret nodded. 'It was a difficult situation.'

'But, according to Dickon, his lordship just brought him in to meet the Bounes, made him shake their hands, then hurried him away before he had a chance to say anything. Then all he did was go and play with Libby, as usual. He was confused about what was going on. And really rather cross.'

As was I, thought Margaret, but wouldn't say as much to Agnes. 'I can understand that what Richard did must have seemed very strange. But he had his reasons, Agnes – the best of reasons – and I think we must not question them.'

Margaret felt the bile of anger rising, as once again she was covering up for, trying to justify, Richard's inexcusable behaviour.

When Richard returned later in the day, after Agnes had taken Dickon home, Margaret suggested they take a stroll in the garden, citing the balmy air and sweet-smelling roses as the reason for her desire to walk. But, in truth, she wanted to take advantage of the privacy of being outside, away from Matilda – whom she was fond of, but knew to be an incorrigible gossip – and away from the servants' flapping ears.

'Do we have to, Margaret?' he said. 'I've had a long day, and I'm more interested in taking some wine and a little nourishment.'

But Margaret could still flirt, withal her incipient wrinkles and greying hair. She reached out to touch her husband's cheek. 'Please, Richard. It is such a lovely evening.'

And, as he invariably did, he acquiesced.

He might have regretted his decision, she thought later, when they were standing together in the arbour, admiring the yellow roses and breathing in their heady fragrance, and she asked him the question she knew very well he would not wish to hear.

'Please, Richard, I beg you, can you not retract your statement about Dickon's legitimacy?'

He stepped back from the roses. 'So that's why you've brought me here, you vixen. Mischievous of you, Margaret.'

She blushed. He used to call her "vixen" years ago, when sometimes she beguiled him into her bed – not that he ever needed much persuading. But it was a merry game they played together when they were young, and it brought back happy memories of the affection they once shared. Yet, despite the happy memories, Margaret was trembling. Richard hated his decisions being questioned. Even when they could be easily reversed.

Which, in this case, seemed unlikely.

He knit his brow and shook his head. 'How can I, Margaret? Tell me, *how*? It is too late. You know why I said it. I made the statement in *all* our interests, and I can hardly now say I made a mistake.'

Margaret felt her eyes pricking. 'But it was a lie, Richard,' she said, her voice a whisper, 'and lying is a sin.'

He shook his head. 'It was a lie uttered from the best of motives. I will atone for it, but I cannot unsay what I have said. We must all live with it, right or wrong. And I shall find a way to ensure that my wishes are fulfilled.' Then he took Margaret's hand in his and, raising it to his lips, kissed it gently. '*Our* wishes.'

5

Little Sister Juliana opened the door of the prioress's private chamber and tiptoed inside. Coming close to the chair where Mother Prioress Angelica spent most of her days, the young nun bobbed a curtsey.

'Dear Reverend Mother,' she said, her voice barely above a whisper, 'Sister Dolorosa has a visitor.'

Sister Dolorosa was sitting a few feet away, at a table strewn with documents and ledgers, poring over the priory's accounts. Hearing Juliana's message, she rose and came across.

'It will be John atte Wode, Reverend Mother, come to discuss the estate with us.'

The old prioress slowly lifted her head and cast her rheumy eyes at her deputy.

'Ah, yes, Rosa, our new bailiff,' she said, and winked.

Sister Dolorosa smiled. The Reverend Mother might be old, and she might be ailing, but she had not lost her sense of fun. For John atte Wode was not "their" bailiff at all, but her father's at Meonbridge, on loan every month or so for consultation about the priory's domains, in an arrangement she had made a year ago, when their last bailiff was discovered to be a thief and had to be dismissed. As a result of the man's misdemeanours, Northwick Priory had become somewhat short of funds, despite the generous dowry that Sir Richard had provided when she, his daughter, Lady Johanna de Bohun, became Sister Dolorosa.

The "old" bailiff, who had served Northwick faithfully and efficiently for twenty years, had died, a victim of the Mortality, not long before Johanna entered the priory. The prioress had taken on a new man but, some years later, it came to light that he was not only failing to run the estate with any degree of efficiency but had been stealing from Northwick's coffers for most of his tenure.

And it was Sister Dolorosa who discovered the man's transgressions.

She had been assisting the Reverend Mother ever since the prioress realised that she was becoming not only old but frail and needed help with the management of the extensive priory estate. She had asked her latest novice to assist her in her day-to-day administrative duties. But, as time passed, and the novice progressed to the full status of a nun – and the prioress's health declined yet further – she found herself more and more in charge, and the prioress seemed to consider her as her deputy, a role that had not existed in the priory before.

It was a demanding job.

Northwick's estate included a large farm, worked by a small group of tenants who lived in a rundown five-house hamlet. Since the bailiff's dismissal, the tenants had been getting on with their work unmanaged, but it soon became clear that they were working for themselves more than for the priory. The new "deputy prioress" took only a few weeks to discover why Northwick's profits were disappearing, but she had little idea of how to deal with the problem. Which is when she decided, with Mother Angelica's agreement, to ask John atte Wode for advice.

'Please ask Master atte Wode to join the Reverend Mother and myself in here, Sister Juliana,' she said, and the young nun bobbed another curtsey and left the room as quietly as she had entered it.

'Do you need anything before Master atte Wode arrives, Reverend Mother?' said Sister Dolorosa.

Mother Angelica shook her head. 'Just help me sit up a little more, and straighten my wimple. I feel somewhat dishevelled.'

She did as she was asked, then rearranged the blanket wrapped around the old prioress's legs, gently tucking it down either side. The weather was unusually wet for August and the priory was chilly and damp from both the present rain and the years of underfunded neglect. Yet the prioress insisted that, if there was insufficient money to provide the other nuns with the comfort of a fire, she too would go without.

'A small glass, Reverend Mother?' said Sister Dolorosa and, when the old lady's eyes twinkled, she went over to a cupboard and poured a glass of tonic wine. She put it in the prioress's bony hand. 'To revive your spirits.' But in truth the prioress's vitality was flagging and it was difficult to imagine that she would survive much longer.

When Juliana returned, John atte Wode was with her. They both entered the room with the deference due to a lady of Mother Angelica's age and dignity, and when John approached the prioress's chair, his hat in his hand, he bowed his head. Then he nodded briefly to Sister Dolorosa, whom he still regarded, her status as a nun withal, as a familial sister, for they shared a nephew – young Dickon de Bohun – and a sense of responsibility for his welfare.

The prioress and her deputy spent an hour with their adviser, discussing what, at this season, needed to be done on the estate. Both women knew little of farming practices, and Sister Dolorosa, in particular, was eager to learn as much as she could from John, not because she wanted to join her tenants in the fields, but so that she understood what it was they should be doing.

But, this year, what they should be doing was being hampered by the incessant rain. Spring had been dry enough but, since July, the skies seemed to need to empty themselves almost every day. Haymaking last month had been a miserable affair, with much of the crop too wet to cut, and some of what had been cut was now rotting in the barns. Then the tenants had tried to shear the sheep out in the fields, as they were accustomed to, but, if their sturdy Hampshire sheep could bear the damp and cold, the shearers grumbled constantly at the difficulty of shearing in the pouring rain. John had suggested they move the sheep into the barns, ramshackle as they were, for, even with rafters missing from the roofs, they did at least provide a little shelter. The tenants still complained, but did as they were told, and the shearing did proceed more efficiently than before.

One of the most important, if disliked, tasks was, John told her, weeding the field crops, especially when the weeds were spiky thistles. But, this year, with the fields so claggy, the job of moving down the rows of barley, wheat or rye to snip the weeds off at ground level with their long-handled tools, was even more disagreeable than usual. For the workers' soft boots sank into the mud and, by the end of the row, had accumulated a heavy clump of sticky earth, almost impossible to clean away. John recommended the use of some sort of overshoes but there was no money and, this year, the tenants would just have to manage as best they could, which meant going to the fields unshod.

Sister Dolorosa noticed the prioress's eyelids fluttering and, touching John lightly upon the arm, she gestured towards the old lady with her chin. He grinned and nodded, and Dolorosa rose and opened the door to speak to Sister Juliana, whose job it was to wait there to run errands for the prioress and her deputy.

'Please fetch Sister Amata,' said Sister Dolorosa, and Juliana scurried away with almost soundless steps.

Sister Amata, Northwick's almoner and, for the past few years, also the prioress's particular carer, arrived within moments. Dolorosa did not know how old Amata was, although she thought, from her delicate wrinkling skin and the wisps of greying hair that escaped often from her wimple, that she might be as old as the prioress herself. But she was nonetheless robust, despite her frequent stifled groans as she straightened from a bending to an upright stance – as now, when she gently helped the prioress to her feet and escorted her over to her bed at the far side of the chamber.

The oaken bed was unusually wide for a nun's resting place. Many years ago, this priory had been wealthy, and a former prioress had invested in the trappings of a manor's mistress for herself – whilst still keeping the nuns in the discomfort appropriate to their order. She installed wall hangings and rugs in her private chamber, and heavy oaken furniture, including the magnificent curtained bed. Mother

Angelica was the reluctant beneficiary of her predecessor's unseemly extravagance but, these days, Sister Dolorosa suspected, she was grateful for the comfort the bed afforded her frail and failing body.

When the prioress was settled down to rest for a couple of hours and the almoner had returned to her usual duties, Sister Dolorosa and her "brother" strolled to the refectory, where they would eat together – in full sight of, but separated from, the other nuns – and discuss her family and the news from Meonbridge.

When she first entered the priory more than six years ago, she had embraced with enthusiasm and relief the idea that she was about to be sequestered from the world. She would no longer need to concern herself with her family or the ghastly possibility of marriage. And she settled quickly into Northwick's routine, which in truth was hardly onerous, for Mother Angelica presided over her little community with the love of a natural mother. Yet the novice was hard upon herself, spending more time upon her knees, or prostrate before the altar of the tiny chapel, than any of the other nuns, including the prioress herself.

She would sometimes reflect upon her disposition all those years ago. She was such an unhappy young woman, who chose the religious life to escape what she considered a repugnant and alarming world. And, more seriously, to atone for the sins she believed she had committed in the name of sensual passion, an atonement she had expected to occupy a lifetime.

But the kindly Mother Angelica had rescued her from the profoundest depths of her distress. For, when she asked for her help in administering the priory, she had given her a diversion as well as work. It had proved, as Sister Dolorosa never failed to acknowledge, the making of her, for it had meant she had to look outside herself and give attention to matters that were not entirely selfish.

The prioress had also tried to persuade her to choose a different religious name before she took her vows. 'Dolorosa is such a sad name, child,' she had said. 'Can you not think of a more joyful one?'

But she could not – or would not – do so. 'I want to spend my life meditating on the sorrows of the Holy Mother,' she said, 'and atoning for my own sins and my brother's. I think the name "sorrow" is most fitting.'

Mother Angelica had shaken her head. 'Oh, child, you can do those things, but there is more to the life of a nun – in our order, at least – than meditation and the search for forgiveness. You must also praise God for His love, and to praise you must be joyful.'

But the novice was stubborn and took her vows with her gloomy name. Yet, more recently, she had come to agree with the prioress that saddling herself with such a miserable, even faintly ridiculous, designation had been a step too far. It was too late now to change her name, but she allowed the prioress, and her sisters, to call her "Rosa", and was beginning to think of herself as "Rosa" too.

For Sister Rosa was a very different woman from Johanna de Bohun. Her work, and the support and affection of her religious sisters, had changed the unhappy, whey-faced girl into a sunny-tempered, energetic woman. A woman for whom "Rosa" *was* a fitting name. The deep melancholy of her girlhood had passed away, not because she had either forgotten her former sadness or had fully atoned for her sins, but because she had found a purpose in her life.

And that purpose included engaging with the world outside Northwick Priory. Or at least some of the world: in particular, the priory's estate and its workers, and those she invited to Northwick as advisers, tradesmen or suppliers. Rosa had no reason to deal with the much wider world, but Northwick did not embrace a strict religious order, and Mother Angelica encouraged all her nuns to keep in contact with their secular families, although a few of them no longer had any living relatives. So, if Rosa had once wanted to estrange herself entirely from her family, she was now glad to learn of the lives of her parents and her little, albeit illegitimate, nephew Dickon, gleaned from her meetings with her father's bailiff.

But what John atte Wode had to tell her on this occasion brought her not pleasure but disquiet.

'Do you know of your father's cousin, Sir Morys Boune?' he said, between mouthfuls of tasteless boiled salt fish.

Rosa shook her head. 'I don't think so. Where does he live?'

'In Herefordshire. Not all that far from Sir Giles Fitzpeyne.' John's brow was creased.

Rosa wiped her fishy fingers on her napkin. 'Sir Giles?' She laughed lightly. 'How badly I once thought of him. And how unjustly, for I am sure he is, or was at least, a most honourable and worthy knight.'

John nodded. 'It was Sir Giles who set in motion a visit from Sir Morys's sons.'

Rosa raised her eyebrows, but John continued. 'I hardly want to tell you why they came, for I know it will upset you.'

'You have to tell me now.'

'Yes, I do, I'm afraid.' He hesitated a moment. 'They came supposedly to offer condolences for Sir Philip's death—'

Rosa gasped and made the sign of the cross upon her breast, but John held up his hand.

'But, in truth, it seems they really came to discover whether Philip had had a son, an heir to Meonbridge.'

Rosa nodded slowly. 'And they discovered that his only son was illegitimate?'

John shook his head. 'No, they didn't. For your father presented Dickon to them as the son of *Isabella*, rather than my sister Agnes—'

Rosa's hand flew to her mouth. 'And therefore his *legitimate* heir?' she said, her voice a whisper.

'Indeed. Your lady mother is most distressed about it all.' When Rosa frowned, John bit his lip. 'Her ladyship did ask me to tell you that.'

Rosa gave John a thin smile of understanding. 'Poor Mama, she must be devastated that my father would lie about such a thing.'

'She considers it a sin.'

'As indeed it is.'

Rosa gestured towards the plain-looking frumenty, enlivened, she knew, by only a very few almonds and currants. John nodded and she passed him the dish and a serving spoon. John served himself, then passed it back to Rosa, but she declined it, and sat with her head bowed, unspeaking, for a long while, until John coughed.

'Sister Rosa?' he said, and she looked up.

'What was my father thinking of?' she said at last. 'To compromise our family's honour and reputation by claiming such a falsehood, and in public.'

'And in *what* public,' John said, grimacing. 'Her ladyship understands well enough that Sir Richard had to divert the Bounes,

49

and had to do so quickly, before they discovered the truth by chance. But she's afraid that somehow the lie will be revealed for what it is.'

Rosa narrowed her eyes. 'Lying is always wrong – and dangerous. But what do we do now?'

'Her ladyship asked Sir Richard to reverse his claim.'

Rosa splayed out the fingers of both hands upon the table, then retracted them and clasped them together. 'Which he can hardly do. What has been said cannot be unsaid.'

She rose from the table, and all the other nuns, sitting at a long table further down the room, got up too. 'You may return to your duties,' said Rosa, raising her voice a little, and the nuns filed out of the refectory.

'Should we be alone?' said John.

Rosa smiled. 'Probably not. Let us walk in the cloisters. We shall find sufficient witnesses to our conversation there.'

As they strolled the chilly cloisters, the rain falling on the central grassy quadrangle eased, and the sun must have emerged from behind the clouds, for a beam of sunlight shone down making the raindrops on the blades of grass sparkle.

'That's better,' Rosa said. 'The sun always brightens the gloomiest thoughts.'

She fingered the set of keys hanging from the chain she wore around her waist. Her mother wore a set of keys just like these. When she first came to Northwick, Rosa did not imagine she would ever be in charge of a great household, having given up the chance to marry. But here she was, responsible, in part at least, for the running of this household and its estate, not great perhaps, but more than large enough for a young woman with no worldly ambition. Despite her as yet imperfect knowledge of estate matters, Rosa did feel quite in control here at the priory. Whereas, if she had once believed her father to be in full mastery of Meonbridge, and his other vast domains, she was now afraid that he no longer was. And she did not know what she could do to help him.

'What should I tell her ladyship?' said John. 'Can I take her a message from you, Sister Rosa?'

Rosa stopped walking and faced John, her hand upon his arm. 'Yes, John, you can. Tell her that we must support my father in his rash

50

decision to declare Dickon his legitimate heir. I can see no alternative.'

'Are you sure? Supposing the Bounes decide to test Sir Richard's assertion by taking the case to court?'

Rosa shrugged. 'We shall have to meet that test when it arises.' Then she turned to face the quadrangle and the beam of sunlight. 'I can hardly believe that I am saying this. Corroborating a lie.'

When she turned back to John, she blinked away some tears. 'But we have to, in order to safeguard our nephew, and the future of the de Bohuns.'

John nodded. 'Reluctantly, I suppose I must agree. Yet, like her ladyship, I'm most concerned that someone in the village might let slip the truth, deliberately or otherwise.'

'Do you have any idea whether there might be such a person?'

'Not really. Maybe I need to make it my business to find out?'

John left Northwick shortly after their cloister conversation, allowing himself time to reach Meonbridge before darkness fell, not wanting to risk the dangers of being abroad at night.

When Rosa bade farewell to John, she felt confident at least that she and the bailiff were in agreement about both her father's recklessness, and their immediate response. How to manage the problem longer term, when the Bounes might make matters even more difficult, was something she would consider later. But, in truth, despite her apparent fortitude and poise when speaking to John, as soon as he had gone, and she was left alone, Rosa felt as if her heart might break.

She hurried from the cloisters to her cell and shut the door, then sank to her knees at her *prie-dieu*. At first she wept, and could not even whisper any prayer. But at length she let the words of a psalm run through her head, and gradually a calm enfolded her.

Have mercy upon me, O God... Cleanse me from my sin. For I acknowledge my transgressions...

She was angry with her father for forcing her to compromise her own sense of right and wrong, for she had no other course but to support him and, at the same time, seek God's forgiveness for being party to a lie.

Rosa neither took supper nor slept that night. She spent all evening and the hours of darkness in prayer, either in her cell alone, or in the chapel alongside her sisters, reciting the offices of Vespers, Compline and Matins. But when dawn brightened the sky and a shaft of pale light seeped through the tiny window of her cell, she knew she had to rise and meet the day, and whatever the future might hold for her and her de Bohun family.

6

CASTLE BOUNE
AUGUST 1356

Morys was pacing up and down his gloomy hall. Thorkell gazed around, comparing this dark, damp and disagreeable chamber with the well-lit, warm and richly furnished hall of Meonbridge manor. He had never cared much about comfort – he had simply become inured to the austerity of his father's castle. But, seeing the warmth and luxury of the de Bohuns' residence made him realise it was what he wanted too, indeed what he *deserved*.

As Thorkell had foreseen, his father was not pleased with the news he and his brother brought back from Meonbridge.

'So we can't just walk into the title,' Morys said, grimacing. 'A pity. Given that the de Bohun filly decided to lock herself away, it would've been simpler if her brother had died childless.'

He came back to the table and sat down, signalling to his ancient servant to pour him some more wine, then sending him away. 'Leave the flagon on the table. We'll serve ourselves.'

The serving man did as he was told and, bowing stiffly, left the room.

'But I'm damned if I'm going to give it up,' continued Morys. 'I *want* Meonbridge and all of my vainglorious cousin's other domains.'

Thorkell laughed. 'Me too, Pa. The others in Dorset and Sussex might not be quite as good, but Meonbridge is a prize all by itself.'

Morys thumped his mazer on the table. 'So let's win it. You're right, what danger can a seven-year old present?'

Gunnar frowned. 'What you thinking, Pa?'

'We'll spirit him away.' He waggled his fingers.

'Won't the de Bohuns suspect us, if we then claim the inheritance?'

His father scoffed. 'Don't be such an idiot, Gunnar. We won't make our claim till the boy's been lost a good long while. And we'll be clever about exactly *how* the boy is lost.'

'You're going to kidnap him?'

Thorkell exchanged a grin with his father. 'Maybe not just kidnap?'

'You're going to *murder* him?' Gunnar's face went quite pale.

'What's wrong with you, brother?' said Thorkell, in a mocking tone. 'You're not usually squeamish about murdering people if it means we win more land.'

'I've never murdered a child before, and certainly not a cousin.'

'Not strictly true,' said his father, scratching at his unkempt beard. And he reminded them of a raid a couple of years back when, between the three of them, they had killed every member of a Welsh family whose land they coveted, including the women and children.

Gunnar reddened, and Thorkell remembered how furious his stepmother, Alwyn, had been when she found out what they had done.

'My own kinsfolk,' she'd screamed at Morys, but he just beat her for her insolence and hauled her off to bed.

Thorkell had always known his father was a knave. And he knew that, in principle, he was himself cut from the same cloth. Gunnar was not so heartless, but rather collaborated with their father's plans in the interests of the family. It had always been Morys's strategy to expand his domains by whatever means were necessary, and if that meant violence and bloodshed, as it invariably did, Gunnar generally just went along with it.

His brother was not, thought Thorkell, a man of much imagination or ambition. He hardly had to be. As heir to their father's vast and remote hill estates, he was quite content with his lot in life. He'd lined up the young daughter of a Welsh nobleman to be his bride and hoped to marry her soon and settle down in Herefordshire to await his father's passing. Not that he necessarily wanted that to happen yet.

Thorkell, on the other hand, had to establish himself as lord of some estate or other. It was true that his father's strenuous, if mostly unlawful, efforts to expand his domains were at least partly intended to provide property for him to inherit. Yet Thorkell thought he deserved more: a substantial estate of his own, and the opportunity to hold a respected position in society – or outwardly so, at least. In truth, the latter seemed largely unachievable, the reputation of the Bounes being as it was, but at least the de Bohun domains *could* perhaps be his, in time.

Thorkell was enjoying the conversation. He shared his father's fondness for causing mayhem. He quite liked the idea of kidnapping the boy, who, despite de Bohun's claim that he was a timid little lambkin, was more likely an arrogant little turd just like his father. Perhaps arranging for an "accident" would be even better? Indeed, he'd rather they claimed the de Bohun domains with some impression of eligibility, so whatever "accident" befell the brat needed to appear to be exactly that, an unfortunate and unavoidable misadventure.

His father was still laughing, recalling the havoc they'd caused amongst some of the remoter Welsh communities, but Thorkell wanted to get on with planning their campaign. He raised his mazer and brought it down onto the table with a bang. Gunnar jumped but Morys just looked up in surprise.

Thorkell frowned. 'We need a plan of action, Pa.'

'And what do you suggest?'

'You were right when you said we needed to be clever. We can't just walk into Meonbridge and kidnap the brat. Whatever accident befalls him, suspicion for it must not fall upon us.'

Morys held up his hands in a gesture of impatience. 'Obviously. So, as I've already asked you, boy, what do you suggest?'

Thorkell bridled. He loathed it when his father called him "boy", as he did from time to time, though he never belittled Gunnar in that way. Nonetheless, he controlled his rising temper.

'I've already told you, Pa, about the woman, Matilda Fletcher, Lady de Bohun's companion. And her connection to the death of Philip de Bohun.'

Morys nodded curtly.

'She's close to the de Bohuns, close to the boy,' continued Thorkell. 'She knows what goes on in the manor. I thought she could show us – without meaning to – a natural way for the brat to meet with an accident.'

'And you plan just to ask her?' said Morys, rolling his eyes.

'Of course not, Pa.' Thorkell rolled his eyes in return. 'I need to woo her, to win her confidence, so she'll – spontaneously, and in the natural course of things – tell me everything I need to know.'

'And you think she will?'

Gunnar guffawed. 'The woman's so itching for him, Pa, she'll probably do *anything* he asks.'

Thorkell leered. 'You know me, Pa, I can win any woman round, one way or another.'

'And when do you plan to carry out your raid upon Mistress Fletcher's heart?' said Morys, his eyes twinkling now.

'Not yet. I'll let her stew a little in her own delightful juices. Then, when I turn up at last, she'll be so desperate, she'll throw herself at my knees and beg.'

But, later, when Thorkell was alone in his chamber – a chamber that was bitterly cold, the walls glistening in the candlelight, the blankets on his unforgiving bed damp and musty-smelling – he thought of the comfort of Meonbridge manor and smashed his fist against the bedpost.

The plans he'd been discussing with Gunnar and their father meant only that they'd deprive Sir Richard of his heir, so that they could claim the de Bohun domains when Richard died. But when would that be? God's eyes, it might be years before the old man croaked…

Why wait? It would surely not be hard to hasten de Bohun's end? Then, after a "decent" interval, they could carry out Morys's plan to get rid of the boy, and the domains would automatically fall to Morys, and to him. Easy…

He lay down on his uncomfortable bed. But sleep did not come quickly. Nor did he want it to. He had a plot to devise, a plot that he at once decided he would keep from his father and brother. It would be his secret. He laughed into the darkness. And, by the time sleep overcame him, he was a happier man.

7

MEONBRIDGE

SEPTEMBER 1356

M atilda was bored. Of all the women of her age in Meonbridge, she was the only one with nothing to show for her twenty-five years on this Earth. Her friend Eleanor Nash was a successful sheep farmer, as well as married to the man she loved – even if he was only a cottar. Agnes Sawyer was not only happily wed to her gallant carpenter, with a brood of handsome, healthy boys, but had even become a craftswoman in her own right. And Lady Johanna, or rather Sister Dolorosa – what a ridiculous name! – was almost a prioress, for Heaven's sake.

Whereas Matilda didn't have a husband, had just one difficult daughter who wasn't even pretty, and was merely a companion to an ageing lady.

Her life was just a waste...

It was only two months ago that Thorkell Boune had come here with his brother, yet it seemed more like a year. He was so very handsome, even more so than Philip de Bohun, and so fashionable. And he seemed most cultured and refined, not at all the brutish knave Sir Richard claimed he was.

And Thorkell had *looked* at her...

Of course, he'd looked at Blanche Jordan too, but any man would, with her breasts hanging out of her gown like that. And everyone knew Blanche was a slut, and Matilda would like to think the divine Thorkell wouldn't sully himself on a body so well used.

Although some men didn't mind — like her disgusting, and thankfully long-dead, husband Gilbert. He was vile, with his greasy hair, sour expression and horrible bony fingers. She supposed that "soiled goods" — which is what her father had said *she* was — were probably all that he could get. She shuddered at the memory of him.

She recalled a conversation she had had with her best friend Eleanor, just before she married Gilbert. Matilda, whose father was keeping her from her friends, hadn't seen Eleanor for weeks. But then Eleanor came calling, saying she was worried for Matilda's safety. With good reason, though Matilda didn't tell her then about the baby. Instead, it was her latest misery that she shared.

'My father insists I marry that odious Gilbert Fletcher,' she said, breaking down into sobs.

Eleanor was aghast, not understanding why Matilda *had* to marry Gilbert if he was so horrible.

'Because he's a freeman, and heir to great domains.'

Eleanor joked with her. 'You always did want to marry a rich man, Matty.'

And Matilda tried to smile. It was true. 'But I'd never have chosen Gilbert Fletcher. He's old, and ugly, and ill-tempered. And he doesn't care for me at all.'

What she told Eleanor then was only half the truth. She implied her father wanted the marriage as some sort of useful alliance, but in fact he was forcing her into it to punish her for sleeping with Philip de Bohun and getting pregnant with his child. And, in Gilbert, he had found a man more than willing to take on his "soiled" daughter, driven by both lust and the pursuit of power.

It was not until much later that Matilda told Eleanor the uncut truth, and the horror of Philip's murder, and of her father's and her husband's guilt, finally unfolded.

But Thorkell Boune was hardly Gilbert. Thorkell could surely have his pick of any women he wanted, and didn't have to resort to other men's rejects? In this respect, he was much more like Philip.

She had fond memories of her few weeks as Philip's leman.

In truth, she didn't really love him, and went with him simply because he asked her to. His wife Isabella was getting fat around the middle with the child growing inside her, and Philip's eyes were wandering. They alighted on Matilda and she couldn't have been more excited to be chosen.

She'd been courted by John atte Wode for many months but, although he was a kind and honourable man, he was a villein, and she'd always hoped she might win someone more well born. Not that she believed that Philip *loved* her, and obviously she knew he couldn't marry her. Nonetheless, she contrived to shut her eyes to the risks of getting with child for the sake of a few tumbles with a handsome and noble knight.

Philip did at least pretend to love her and was everything as a lover that Gilbert would prove not to be. For Philip was the master of the gentle caress, so tenderly and carefully placed that, by the time he was ready to take her, she was almost begging him to do so. Not so with Gilbert, who had no idea at all of how to arouse a woman, and each time he ploughed her it was simply an assault that left her bruised and weeping.

But her relationship with Philip ended in disaster. When she discovered she was with child, which must have happened only the second or third time they lay together, it was a shock as well as some sort of delight. She wondered for a short while if she could somehow keep the child or run away like John's sister Agnes was rumoured to have done. But if Matilda had fantasised for a few days on possible happy outcomes for her shameful state, she was brought unpleasantly down to earth when it turned out her father knew of her condition.

Matilda had been in the garderobe, the tiny closet located in the middle of the long wall of the solar chamber, where her father's great bed stood at one end, and the bed she shared with Margery was at the other. She was crouched over a basin, vomiting. Suddenly there came a light knocking on the door, and Margery called out to her.

'Are you all right in there, Matilda?'

Matilda groaned. She thought Margery had gone out to the market, although there was no way Matilda was going to be able to keep this from her sister, as the sickness came too often for her to hide.

'Well enough, thank you, sister,' she called back. 'Leave me be.'

And it seemed that Margery had gone back downstairs. But when it happened again the following morning, Margery would not be dismissed. She opened the door of the garderobe and entered.

Matilda thought it served her sister right for interfering, when she saw her gag on the vile smell arising from the basin.

'Oh, my goodness, Matilda,' said Margery, 'what on earth is happening?'

'Isn't it obvious? I'm sick.'

'But why? Something you've eaten?'

Matilda brightened a little. 'Yes, perhaps so.'

Margery nodded, but then she frowned. 'But hasn't this been going on for days? And aren't you only nauseous in the mornings?'

Matilda looked up at her sister, wishing she'd just disappear – down through the hole in the garderobe floor, perhaps, onto the stinking mound of shit.

But it was clear that Margery had guessed the truth. 'I wondered why you haven't washed out any rags the past few weeks.' She smirked.

'Don't tell Pa,' said Matilda, a slight panic rising in her chest.

'How will that help you? Do you imagine you can keep your sin and shame from him?'

'Damn you, Margery, you're such a prig!'

Margery sniffed. 'But not a slut. Nor some man's disgusting whore. Nor a vile *sinner*.'

'Oh, do shut up,' cried Matilda. Her sister was right, of course, but she wasn't helping. And there was no point at all in denying her sister's conjecture, for time would soon enough prove the truth of it. But Matilda refused to tell her the name of her lover.

Margery certainly did tell their father about her sister's pregnancy, but Matilda suspected that she told him too that she thought Philip was the culprit. Because soon afterwards, for reasons that at the time Matilda didn't understand, her father, who had been Sir Richard's respected bailiff and, before that, Philip's tutor and guardian when he was a boy, took against Philip, declaring him a blackguard and a whoremonger.

And he forced Matilda to get rid of the child.

Only a few days after Margery had discovered her in the garderobe, quite late one evening, when it was already dark, her father left the house and returned with Alys Ward, one of Meonbridge's midwives, and not the one with the best reputation. Alys was a hard-bitten cottar woman, whose long life had been one of almost constant poverty and suffering, and who resented those better off than her. She hadn't been asked to attend a birth for years, for the last few deliveries she'd overseen had all resulted in dead babies, and in two cases a dead mother. Since then, she was only called upon to get rid of inconvenient babies, and the families always tried to keep her intervention secret.

For what Alys did was both witchcraft and a mortal sin.

Matilda was in the solar with her sister, both preparing to go to bed. Their father and Alys Ward came up the narrow staircase and appeared at the solar entrance. Matilda glanced at her sister in alarm, but Margery simply moved away. Damn her! She must have known this was going to happen.

Her father gestured to Alys to come forward. Her face bore no expression, neither compassion nor indifference. She nodded and opened a grubby scrip that was tied around her waist.

'Father?' said Matilda, her heart pounding.

He was standing with his legs astride, his big arms folded across his chest. His nostrils flared and his eyes narrowed as he shook his head at her. 'You've no choice. I won't have our family's honour besmirched by your debauchery. You'll drink what Alys gives you and be done with it.'

He had never been an affectionate father but, now, Matilda felt that he must *hate* her.

She quailed, terrified of what Alys's potion would do to her. She began to cry, but her father's angry expression did not change. She raised pleading eyes to his, but he shook his head again.

'Drink,' he said, as Alys handed her a small bottle.

'What is it?' said Matilda, her voice a whisper.

Alys raised a questioning eyebrow at Robert, who nodded. 'Pennyroyal,' she said.

Matilda blenched. 'Will it hurt?'

'Of course,' said Alys, smirking. 'No more'n you deserve for such wantonness.'

Robert tutted. 'Thank you, Mistress Ward, your opinion's not required.'

Alys snorted but said no more.

'You may go,' Robert said to her. 'Margery will take care of her sister now.'

Margery spun around. 'Why me? It's nothing to do with me—'

But her father roared. 'You'll look after your sister because I say you will. And you'll say nothing of any of this to anyone outside this family. Is that quite clear?'

He glared at his older daughter and with good reason, for Margery had a tendency to prate amongst the gossips in the village. But Matilda suspected that, in this case, her sister would keep her mouth firmly shut, for Matilda's shame would be her shame too and, with her lack of either beauty or any charm, Margery could ill afford to risk any further opprobrium spoiling her chances of finding herself a husband.

Once he'd satisfied himself that Matilda had swallowed the contents of the bottle, her father took Alys back downstairs and presumably walked her home, for he was gone for a while. When he returned, he came back up to the solar, looked in on his daughters, shook his head, and retreated to his end of the chamber, pulling across the thick dividing curtain. It seemed he wanted nothing more to do with this evening's unhappy enterprise. Matilda was left to her own suffering, in the dubious care of a sister who both disliked and envied her. Even though Matilda's affair had ended in disaster, she knew that Margery was much aggrieved that she never would be "chosen", and perhaps would never even experience the delicious pleasure that a man could give a woman.

Matilda sat on the edge of the bed she shared with her sister and waited for something to happen.

But, when it did, it seemed that the potion had failed. For Matilda had to fly to the garderobe as nausea again surged into her throat. Throwing herself down upon the floor, she pressed her cheek against the wooden bench atop the stinking hole, and vomited and vomited until she felt she might be expelling her baby through her mouth.

Margery left her to it.

After a while, the vomiting eased a little, but then a great wrenching pain tore at Matilda's belly and she screamed so loudly that her sister ran to her side.

'What's happening?' said Margery, actually wrapping an arm around her sister's shoulders.

Matilda shook her head, and let out a terrible groan, as she doubled over. Matilda was briefly grateful for her sister's comfort, but she wanted to be left alone.

'I'll call out if I need you,' she said feebly, as another wave of pain ripped through her belly.

And so it continued for most of the night, with pain and nausea taking turns to wrack her body. Sometimes she sensed the room was spinning, or bees were buzzing inside her head, and she curled up on the hard, cold floor to try to dispel the dizziness. Sometimes, she presumed her suffering was God's punishment for her sins, her two terrible, *mortal* sins, having lain with Philip de Bohun and, now, murdering their unborn child. And her physical agony was compounded by an agony of terror of what God's intentions were for her, perhaps already the Devil's handmaiden.

It was not until she could see dawn's light beginning to brighten the ground beneath the hole in the garderobe floor that she realised how much time had passed. And it was at that moment that her body's agony reached its terrible conclusion.

With a final savage spasm, her body expelled a torrent of blood and mess from between her legs. Weeping and fragile, Matilda lifted her chemise, already wet and filthy from her night-long labours, and she saw the red stickiness on her thighs and the pooling on the garderobe floor. She touched it, and wept some more. It was still quite dark in the garderobe, for there was no window, but as light seeped up from below the hole in the floor, she could just see that some tiny *thing* was mixed in with the blood.

And the sight and touch of it caused Matilda to cry out for her long-dead mother.

Matilda's thoughts returned to Thorkell Boune. She took advantage of Lady de Bohun's temporary absence – she'd gone down to the garden to inspect her herber and had taken Libby with her – to let her fantasy take flight.

Remembering how it had been with Philip – for, despite the ghastly outcome of their affair, she still looked back on those few weeks with pleasure – she replaced in her imagination the lover she had then with the one she wanted now. She imagined a strong muscular body beneath his clothes. And she thought about him touching her, stroking her skin with gentle fingertips, kissing her with tender lips...

Matilda played this game with herself for the best part of an afternoon, realising she was behaving like a lovesick girl, instead of a twenty-five-year-old widow.

But surely it did no harm to dream.

Although, in truth, Matilda suspected she never would see Thorkell Boune again. Didn't he and his brother leave Meonbridge believing that Dickon was Sir Richard's legitimate heir? What reason would they have ever to return?

Except that Matilda knew very well that Dickon was *not* legitimate at all, but Philip's son by Agnes Sawyer. Matilda had been astonished, and Lady de Bohun clearly horrified, when Sir Richard declared to the Bounes not only that Dickon was his grandson, but that he had been birthed by *Isabella*. It seemed his lordship had not warned his wife that he would be making such an announcement. Perhaps with good reason, else her ladyship would surely have tried to stop him.

It did seem extraordinary that he would utter so blatant an untruth.

She wondered how many other folk in Meonbridge knew the truth about Dickon's father. She soon began to suspect it when Dickon started coming up to play with Libby. Seeing him close at hand, watching him play, and hearing him talk, she realised how much he was like Philip, and how very unlike Jack Sawyer – not just in looks, but in temperament and attitude. How could it possibly be that *no one else* in Meonbridge had noticed it. Or maybe they had, but had decided to keep it to themselves?

When Agnes returned to Meonbridge, a few months after the Mortality had passed on, Matilda had been confined to her chamber, having given birth to Libby only a week before. So she wasn't amongst the crowd of folk who apparently had gathered outside the atte

Wodes' house when Agnes presented her mother Alice with her baby grandson. And Matilda was *still* in her chamber, waiting to be allowed back into the world, when – as she only found out much later – Agnes came up to the manor and presented the baby to the de Bohuns as *their* grandson. As Matilda also learned long afterwards, from overheard conversations, the de Bohuns had been thrilled to find they had a grandchild after all but agreed with the atte Wodes and the Sawyers to keep the boy's true parentage a secret between them – to save any awkwardness. Dickon would be brought up as Jack Sawyer's son.

Whether – and how – the de Bohuns would eventually claim the boy publicly as their own was, as far as Matilda knew, not then discussed. And didn't have to be, until the Bounes arrived in Meonbridge, asking awkward questions.

So the Bounes had gone away with one untrue version of Dickon's parentage, and the villagers of Meonbridge held another. But how many knew the truth, apart from the boy's immediate family and herself?

Maybe no one. Or maybe many. And what would happen if someone *did* speak out, and somehow made it known – and especially to the Bounes – that Dickon was neither Jack's son, nor Isabella's, but a bastard?

Matilda sat down in her usual chair by the window and picked up her sewing. But she could not concentrate.

Suppose Thorkell discovered that Dickon was a bastard, and not entitled to inherit? Lady Johanna was no longer a contender, since she'd become a nun, and Thorkell's father was next in line. Sir Richard had said so. And if Sir Morys did claim the estate, perhaps he would at length pass it on to Thorkell, as surely Gunnar would inherit the Herefordshire lands? And if she could somehow win Thorkell's heart...

Matilda found herself warming to the delightful possibilities of what *might be*. She got up and went to stand by the open window, where she gazed across the vast expanse of fields and woodlands.

How wonderful it would be to be mistress of all of this.

8

MEONBRIDGE
SEPTEMBER 1356

M argaret was walking in her garden, inspecting the flowerbeds
for damage after the past two days' torrential rain. As if the
summer had not been wet enough, autumn was already proving worse.
Some of the climbing plants that covered the pergolas, the
honeysuckle and rambling roses, had been partly wrenched from their
supports by the ferocity of the wind. And many of the roses' fairest
blooms had either dropped their petals or were spattered with black
specks. But some flowers had survived, and there were buds yet to
open, if only the weather would relent.

Despite the disarray, it was peaceful in the garden.

No gardeners were working here today, for every hand was
required, either in the fields to finish the delayed harvest of the last of
the wheat and barley or to pick the peas and beans for drying, or in the
barns to thresh the grain already gathered in. Richard had said the
grain harvest would be poor this year, for the rain had caused such
damage that much of the crop had to be abandoned in the fields, to be
dug back in at the next ploughing.

But Margaret's peace was intruded upon when she heard the clatter of horses cantering along the road that led towards the manor precinct. She knew it could not be Richard because he was out in the fields with John atte Wode, overseeing the various works being undertaken, in an effort to ensure it all happened as fast as possible.

Margaret squinted across towards the road, and saw perhaps seven or eight horses, although she could not be sure, for her eyes were not so good these days. She moved in the direction of the manor gate – she wished she was able to run but had to be content with her briskest walking pace. When she arrived, perspiring a little and rather short of breath, the horsemen were already there, and one of them was in conversation with the gatekeeper.

As she approached, the man riding the finest of the horses, a black mare, her head erect and proud, dismounted and came towards her.

'Margaret,' he said, holding out his hand.

She stopped, trying to make her poor foggy eyes see the man more clearly. But then she realised who he was.

'Giles!' she cried. 'You have returned at last to Meonbridge.' She moved a little closer, and he dropped to his knee before her and bowed his head.

'It has indeed been far too long,' he said. 'And entirely my fault.'

She shook her head and gestured to him to rise. 'Ours too, I am sure.' She smiled. 'And are you proposing to stay?'

'If you will honour me by giving me and my retainers a space in your fine hall.'

'Of course we will. And Richard will be delighted to see you, Giles. He is out in the fields at present, but will return before too long.'

Giles's eyebrows shot up. 'In the fields? That doesn't sound like the Richard de Bohun I used to know.'

Margaret gave a tinkling laugh. 'Ah, Richard became almost a different man after the Mortality. For the world changed then, did it not, and so did my noble husband.'

Giles nodded. 'Indeed the world did change, although I confess I did not observe it here in England for, after my failed betrothal to the Lady Johanna...' He paused. 'I am afraid I left the country for the battlegrounds of France and Italy. It was not until two years ago that I returned to Shropshire—'

Margaret held up her hand. 'Stop, Giles,' she said, laughing, 'you must save your news until Richard has joined us. Why don't you come in, stable your horses and take some refreshment?'

Giles grinned. 'Splendid, Margaret, splendid.'

Richard was not in the best of tempers when he returned from his long day in the fields. It had been a frustrating day, with evidence of the damage the weather had been wreaking everywhere to be seen. Richard had come straight upstairs to the solar, declaring that he needed to change his shirt and warm himself a while beside the small fire in their private quarters. But Margaret was giddy with excitement, and although she found him a clean shirt, she could not allow him to sit down until she had told him her news too.

'God's eyes, Margaret, what can be so important that a man can't rest his aching bones a while?'

But when she told him, he rolled his eyes. 'Why didn't you say so earlier, woman?' He took two long strides towards the solar door, but Margaret called him back.

He turned to her, frowning. 'What *is* it, Margaret?'

'I know you are delighted that Giles has come but I do wonder, Richard, how open you should be with him...' She hesitated. 'Given his alliance with the Bounes?'

'What are you talking about, woman? He is my oldest friend and comrade-in-arms.'

'I know that, husband, but remember he has just married Morys's daughter. His loyalties might be divided. And I did say "might", not "will".'

'You're saying I shouldn't trust Sir Giles Fitzpeyne, one of the finest knights in the entire kingdom?' Richard's eyes narrowed, and he swatted at an invisible fly.

Margaret sighed. 'No, husband. I am simply suggesting that we might want to be a little *cautious* about what we say to him. About the Bounes.'

Richard stared at her, almost as if he thought her mad, then shook his head. But he said nothing more and, leaving the solar at a run, clattered down the narrow staircase to the hall.

Margaret sighed again. He could be most insufferably stubborn and obtuse at times. Nonetheless she smiled to herself and followed her husband at a more leisurely pace. When she arrived in the hall, Richard was clasping Giles to his breast, and both men were laughing.

Margaret approached them. 'I told you he would be pleased,' she said to Giles.

'We are both delighted,' said Giles. 'I cannot think why either of us left it so long.' He rubbed at his greying beard. 'It was a dreadful business... Philip's death, Lady Johanna's deep distress – indeed yours. And I was a coward to leave you all. And no friend at all not to return.'

'Where did you go?' asked Richard.

'Abroad, as I always do. To try to support King Edward's continuing meagre efforts in France. But in truth I was of little use without my sword arm. I had to let my retainers do any fighting, whilst I kept to the rear as some sort of adviser.'

'I am sure your advice was greatly valued, Giles,' said Margaret, but he rolled his eyes.

'Kind of you to say so, Margaret, but sitting on my arse out of the way of all the action is not my idea of knightly service.'

Richard nodded sagely. 'Galling, but what else could you do?'

'I could have come back here.' Giles shrugged.

'But you are here now, Giles,' said Margaret, 'and Richard and I are truly delighted that you are. Come, let us take some supper.' She pointed to the long table at the far end of the hall, which, whilst they had been talking, had been laid with trenchers, spoons and goblets, and a variety of dishes. 'It is only a cold collation—'

'But nonetheless most welcome after our long ride,' said Giles, and Margaret took his proffered left arm to walk down to the table.

Margaret wished she was not sitting between her husband and his friend, for Richard constantly leaned across her to offer Giles more wine or some reminiscence of their exploits on the battle fields of France. And, as the number of mazers he emptied grew, so did the coarseness of his tongue.

'And how is that young bride of yours?' he said, waggling his head, and smirking most indecorously, Margaret thought.

Giles grinned. 'Ah, she's a beauty, Dick – black hair, deep dark eyes. And already carrying my son.'

Margaret clasped her hands together. 'Oh, Giles, how wonderful. Although it might not be a *son*, of course...'

Giles pushed out his lips, but his eyes were twinkling. 'I am quite sure it is,' he said, then roared with laughter, and she and Richard joined in.

Then Richard changed the subject. 'I see you have brought a fine courser with you, Giles,' he said. 'In anticipation of a little hunting perhaps?'

'Indeed. The mare is new, a gift from my father-in-law. A pair, in fact, sire and dam. Came with their own groom.'

Richard raised his eyebrows.

'Morys told me the groom could not bear to be parted from the horses,' Giles continued. 'Which sounded unusually soft-hearted for Morys, but I thought I could not refuse.'

'Tomorrow, then?' said Richard. 'And hounds not hawks, agreed?'

'Splendid. I have not hunted for many months. Indeed, I've not ridden for pleasure for almost as long. A most agreeable prospect, Dick.'

'Up betimes then, in the morning,' said Margaret. 'I shall not join you, Richard, if you are taking the hounds.'

Giles frowned. 'You do not hunt, Margaret?'

'Only when we take the hawks. Sadly, my capacity for galloping through the forest and across the heath has long since diminished.' She sighed. 'I used to enjoy it, but my feeble body no longer allows it.'

Margaret thought she would take her time this morning preparing for the day. When Agatha had come earlier to help her dress, she dismissed her, saying she could manage by herself. Not that she could take too long, for she had to ensure the cook was making headway with the feast to be provided when the hunters returned.

Richard, Giles, their retinues of retainers, grooms and pages, the horses and the pack of hounds had left the manor early. Richard's chief huntsman would have left just before dawn, taking his special dog, the lime-hound, with him to scent out the quarry. The dog had a particularly remarkable nose and could follow the scent of a hart over a great distance. The huntsman reported his findings back to Richard, and the hunting party was by now in pursuit of the chosen beast.

Still clad only in her night chemise, Margaret went over to the window and gazed out towards the forests where the hunters would be riding. How she wished her body was not so often stiff, her legs not so given to collapsing under her after the mildest exertion. It really was most vexing. When she was young, she had so loved to race with Richard across the fields, riding her courser like a man – most shockingly – with legs astride. It was awkward with her skirts bunched between her thighs, but she had found it wonderfully invigorating. Although it was not something she did often and, by the time she had become a mother, she abandoned it for sitting sideways atop a docile palfrey. Scarcely as much fun, but undoubtedly more seemly.

She had been energetic and almost impetuous when she first married Richard. It was true that, initially, she had been afraid to leave her parents and travel south to Hampshire to live with a man she had met only weeks before. But it was the lot of young women of gentle and noble families to leave their homes, and she considered herself fortunate to have bagged such a handsome, wealthy knight. And, for the first two years or so, Richard had proved a most loving and attentive husband, and she had reciprocated by joining him, whenever she could, in those activities he particularly enjoyed, like hunting. He seemed to appreciate her lively nature and encouraged her to play her part.

But then times, and Richard, changed. He often went, alongside Giles and their liege lord, Raoul de Fougère, to support the king in his battles against the Scots and then the French, leaving her in charge of the estates, which was no burden. Although, when he returned from battle, he often undid some of the policies she had implemented, considering them too "merciful", as he put it, to their tenants. It was frustrating. Their relationship became less one of collaboration, and more one of conflict, arising from their differing perspectives on how tenants should best be managed. In those years Richard became more frequently morose, and occasionally he treated her unkindly.

Margaret left the window and stepped over to the bed. She sat down and stroked the pillow where Richard's head had earlier been resting. Despite everything, she still loved him. He rarely went away these days and, since the terrible travails of the months following the Mortality – when their tenants rebelled so ferociously against their working conditions – Richard did, as Margaret had said to Giles, once more become a changed man. And so he had remained. A man who was much happier with running his estates, and who had learned how to manage both his property and his people. He and Margaret had settled down again into a comfortable companionship.

Although it was true that, years ago, there had been times when Margaret wished that Richard might not return from the king's wars, leaving her to manage their estates entirely alone, she could not now imagine life without him.

She stood and pulled the chemise up and over her head. Then she leaned forward to the garments that Agatha had laid out on the end of the bed before she left the chamber: a clean chemise, a simple woollen kirtle and a warm surcoat, proof against autumn's chilly draughts.

Margaret propped her small silver-backed hand mirror against a pitcher standing on the coffer and, peering into it, undid and then re-plaited her thin greying hair. Despite its fogginess, she loved her mirror. Richard had bought it for her soon after they were married and, stowing it carefully in his saddlebag, had borne it safely home over the hundreds of miles from – where was it? She could not recall the name of the faraway city where he had found it.

Wherever it was, Richard and Giles had been there together, the comrades-in-arms they had been since boyhood. She smiled to herself: how very pleased Richard was to have his old comrade back by his side. And how foolish it was that both he and Giles had let so many years pass by without sending at least a message of friendship each to the other.

Winding the two plaits together in a coil at the back of her head, she tucked them into a netted snood. Then she took the fresh linen barbet that Agatha had laid out and, wrapping it beneath her chin, pulled the two ends up over her head and pinned them. Finally, she selected a plain cap and, positioning it carefully over the barbet and the snood, pinned that too. She took a final look at herself in the little mirror. It would have to do.

As she made her way down to the kitchens to speak to the cook,

Margaret recalled what she had said to Richard yesterday afternoon, about being wary of what they discussed with Giles. She had always considered Giles the most honourable of men, even more so than her husband, yet she still felt the need for caution. Though, predictably, Richard had dismissed her fears.

Yesterday evening, after supper, Margaret had suggested that the three of them take a stroll in her flower garden, as the autumn air for once was warm.

'Ah, yes,' said Giles, 'I could do with some advice on the garden at Fitzpeyne Castle. It has become much neglected – with my gross lack of attention – and I fear my little Gwynedd knows nothing of the art of cultivating plants, flowering or otherwise.'

Margaret laughed. 'Neither did I when Richard first brought me here to Meonbridge. It takes time to learn. And a good teacher is most beneficial. Do you remember old John Greenfinger, Richard, our gardener?'

'Do I?'

She tutted and shook her head. 'He died in the Mortality, husband. Anyway, Giles, John was an expert in all things horticultural, and I learned a great deal from him, until he died, and I had to look after the gardens on my own.' She sniffed, and looked askance at her husband. 'For Richard refused to provide me with any help, saying that every hand was needed in the fields.'

Richard harrumphed. 'Quite right too. We had few enough workers as it was.'

'Yes, yes, I know,' said Margaret, throwing a sidelong glance at Giles. 'Anyway, the result of all my efforts lies here before you.' She spread her arms wide, for they had arrived at her favourite part of the garden, with its pergolas and flowerbeds, and the tinkling fountain in the middle of a patch of bright green lawn.

Giles cheered. 'Well, Margaret, this is splendid. You must be proud of your lady's skills, Dick.'

Richard harrumphed again, then allowed a grin to brighten his face. 'I am. And I will admit it is a haven of tranquillity after a busy day, with its sweet-scented blooms and many birds and butterflies.'

73

Giles laughed heartily. 'Can this truly be Richard de Bohun speaking? So lyrical, my friend? You are indeed a changed man.'

Richard glanced across at Margaret, his eyes wide, and she could not help herself but blush.

But then he proceeded, against her earlier advice, to tell Giles about the Bounes coming to Meonbridge in July. 'It was after you mentioned to Morys that Philip had died.'

'Ah, yes, Morys and I were talking, and I was telling him of my exploits in the king's wars. And, of course, I mentioned you, and I learned that you and Morys Boune were cousins.'

Richard nodded. 'My only cousin. No others have survived.'

'I did not know they had paid you a visit,' said Giles.

Richard nodded again. 'Just the two sons, Gunnar and Thorkell—'

'Unusual names, don't you think? And it's said they have the appearance of their mother, with their good looks and flaxen hair – and she was, by all accounts, an angel.'

Richard grunted. 'I warrant *they* are anything but angels. Rather more akin to their father—'

Margaret caught her breath and laid a hand on Richard's arm. 'Husband! Giles has married into Morys's family – you should not speak so disparagingly of your cousin.'

But Giles shook his head. 'Do not concern yourself, Margaret. I quite understand Dick's disquiet about Sir Morys Boune. I believe him to be a less than honest man. I don't yet know the extent of my new in-laws' misdeeds, but they are certainly much talked of in the border counties, and I am well aware that they have increased their domains many-fold in ways that were, shall we say, not entirely legal.'

Richard nodded. 'I have heard the same, and I know no more than that.'

'However,' continued Giles, 'I intend to have as little as possible to do with the Boune family in future. I have taken my little Gwynedd away to Shropshire, and in truth she seems to be more than happy to be distanced from her father and stepbrothers.' He grimaced. 'Especially Thorkell, whom she finds most disquieting.'

'So you might not think me overly suspicious,' said Richard, 'when I say that I fancy that the principal motive for the Boune brothers visiting us was not to offer their condolences for Philip's death, but to discover if he had an heir.'

Giles frowned. 'But why would they want to?'

'Simply because, if Philip did not have a son, and if Johanna was, for some reason they knew nothing of, no longer a contender, Morys is next in line.'

'I see... How interesting. I had not realised. Who is your heir, then, Dick?'

Richard grinned. 'When you came to us, Giles, seven years ago, to be betrothed to our Johanna, you perhaps wondered if Philip had a wife?' Giles nodded. 'In fact, his wife, Isabella de Courtenay, had died some months before, giving birth to their son, Dickon. Poor girl, she died not knowing that her husband would also not live much longer but die at the hands of vicious knaves.'

'And young Dickon lives?' said Giles, and Richard nodded. 'So you have a grandson. My congratulations to you both.' He thumped Richard on the shoulder. 'Tomorrow I must meet him.'

Margaret had moved a little distance away from the men and was dabbling her fingers in the fountain, enjoying the cool spray of the water on her skin. When she heard Richard repeating, even to his oldest friend, his claim that Dickon was *Isabella's* son, she might have gasped, but managed to keep silent.

Giles had no reason to disbelieve what his old friend said, and it seemed that he accepted it, not even enquiring as to Dickon's whereabouts.

Nonetheless, Margaret was heavy-hearted that Richard and, by implication, she herself, had to lie to Giles so soon after renewing their friendship. She hoped that if, one day, Giles learned the truth, he would understand the reason for their falsehood and forgive them.

Richard went on to tell Giles about Johanna, who was so beside herself with grief at Philip's death that she decided to become a nun. Giles at first expressed astonishment, but almost immediately changed his mind.

'In truth, the Johanna I knew, and I certainly did not know her well or for long, did seem a very studious young woman – pious, even. I hope, Margaret, you are not offended by my saying that?'

Margaret faced Giles and shook her head. 'Not at all, Giles, for it is true. Johanna was already an unhappy girl, although Richard and I were unable to discover why. And Philip's death pushed her deeper into despair. She said the only way she could find peace was to enter the priory. We did try to dissuade her, but she insisted.'

Margaret turned back to the fountain, anxious that her face might have become a little flushed. She was glad the evening was advancing, the light fading. For, if she herself had not exactly lied, she had nonetheless told Giles only a part of the truth about Johanna. She could hardly tell him of her daughter's desperate need to atone for her own sins and those of her brother. Richard had considered Johanna's avowed guilt just the mewling nonsense of a girl who needed bedding, as he put it. But, in the end, even he did not prevent his daughter doing as she wanted, albeit it might put in jeopardy the future of the de Bohun estates.

Margaret had been grateful that Richard had not forced his daughter into marriage, as many another father would have done. He was furious with her for refusing to marry and ensure he had an heir, but Margaret eventually persuaded him to accept Johanna's decision.

'She will make a devout nun,' she had said. 'Perhaps even become prioress?'

Richard was not convinced but he was distracted by the chaos going on around them and, by the time he had resolved the rebellion on the manor, Johanna had made arrangements to enter the priory and to take her dowry with her. To renege on the agreement would have been dishonourable.

One evening Margaret had suggested to Richard that perhaps they should leave all their domains to Northwick Priory, but he bridled, scorning the ability of nuns to run such a substantial estate. Of course she pointed out that most priories ran estates, and sometimes very large ones. And it would surely be preferable to letting ownership pass to Richard's cousin, a man they hardly knew, who might care little for the place? He scoffed, but allowing the priory to inherit did briefly become their unspoken strategy.

Until the day that baby Dickon arrived in Meonbridge.

Despite Margaret's embarrassment at her less than honest explanation, Giles did not question either of them further about Johanna, but simply wished her well.

76

Margaret beamed. 'In fact, Giles, Johanna is happier than she has ever been. She is not yet a prioress herself but is acting as the Reverend Mother's deputy. She has a purpose, and her life is full of busyness, as well as prayer.'

'That is good to hear,' said Giles. But then he turned back to Richard. 'So, how old is Dickon? When will you be sending him for his page training?'

Richard nodded. 'Seven, so soon.'

'And where to? Shropshire, perhaps?'

'Perhaps, or to Dickon's other grandparents, the de Courtenays in Surrey.'

Margaret had thought it almost ridiculous to suggest that the de Courtenays would be willing, for Dickon was not *their* grandchild at all. And now Richard was suggesting it again.

Margaret felt quite queasy, her horror of the sticky web they were weaving growing by the moment.

'I'd always hoped I might raise your grandsons, Dick,' said Giles. 'Do give it your consideration.'

'Of course I shall, my friend. But it is still some months away.'

Yet, given the truth of the de Courtenays' likely lack of interest in Dickon, Giles might be their only option.

Margaret was pottering in the garden again when, as yesterday, her peace was disturbed by the sound of horses' hooves on the road leading to the manor. But this time the sound was thunderous and accompanied by clouds of dust.

She threw down her gardening tools and gloves and walked as fast as she was able back to the house. When she arrived in the hall, all was chaos and confusion, with retainers, pages, grooms and household servants all crowding together, surrounding the long trestle table where she and Richard dined. With sudden apprehension, she recalled the day when Philip had been brought back home, a lifeless body, his good looks disfigured by his murderers' blades.

'Let me pass,' she cried, as she pushed her way through the throng of people. Had there been an accident at the hunt? Was someone injured?

Then Giles was at her side. 'No, Margaret, come no further.' His face was dirty and streaked with tears.

At the sight of it, Margaret was gripped by panic.

'Giles?' she said in a whisper, her throat constricted with dread at what she was about to see.

He shook his head and held her arm, but she pulled away and darted towards the table. And there lay her beloved husband, life evidently draining from him. His face was white, and his shirt and tunic were soaked in blood, although a thick pad of cloth had been placed upon his chest.

Margaret looked around her wildly. 'What happened?' she cried, her voice almost a scream. 'Tell me!'

Giles hurried towards her and held her shaking shoulders. 'It was an accident, Margaret. Somehow Dick took an arrow in his chest—'

'How?' said Margaret, but he shook his head.

'No one saw it happen, and no one's come forward to confess to letting the arrow fly.'

'But someone must know—'

'Perhaps, but now's not the time to discover it. I have sent for Simon Hogge – he should be here shortly.'

And, at that moment, Simon arrived, the man who had served Richard as his barber-surgeon so many times during the king's wars. He ran to the table and, removing the pad of cloth, ripped Richard's shirt away. Someone had already brought a basin of water and some rags, and Simon gently dabbed at Richard's bloody chest, although Margaret could see blood still flowed freely from the wound. But, moments later, Simon stopped dabbing and bowed his head.

Margaret gasped. 'Is he dead?' she said in a whisper, but Simon shook his head.

'Not yet, my lady, but soon. The arrow entered close to his heart—' He began to weep. 'I'm so sorry, m'lady, but I can't save him.'

Margaret could scarce believe what he was saying. But the truth of what his words implied was confirmed as a solemn, pale-faced figure in black slid silently forward and came to Margaret's side.

'Your ladyship?' said Sire Raphael. 'I have been called to offer Sir Richard the last rites. Shall I proceed?'

Margaret thought that she might faint, but Giles was still standing close and she grasped his arm for support. 'What should I do, Giles?' she whispered.

'Comfort your husband,' he said, a tear trickling over his long silver scar.

Margaret nodded and, whilst Raphael stood on one side of Richard, she leaned over the table and cradled her husband's head on her arm.

The priest recited the Latin words of the confession, asking Richard to join in. But, although Richard appeared to hear him, for his eyes flickered, he did not answer. So Sire Raphael continued, saying the words on his behalf.

Margaret placed her mouth close to Richard's ear, and whispered. 'Can you hear me, my love?' And, when he gave the slightest of nods, she let her tears fall onto his face, then gently kissed them away.

Richard slowly lifted his bloody hand and put it against the side of Margaret's head, and she folded her own fingers around it. 'Richard?'

'Margaret, beloved wife,' he said, in the smallest of voices.

Sire Raphael leaned over the table. 'Do you think his lordship can make his own confession, my lady?'

But Richard moved his head just once from side to side, and the priest sighed and continued to recite the prayers alone.

Richard's fingers then pressed lightly upon Margaret's head, and she leaned in closer to him, putting her ear right against his mouth.

'Promise to fulfil my wishes, Margaret,' he whispered. 'Dickon—' But a shuddering groan cut off any further words, and Margaret thought she had no time to say that she would.

She sought the face of Simon Hogge. 'Is he gone?' she said to him again, and Simon stepped forward and pressed his fingers against Richard's neck.

'No, m'lady. His lordship is still with us.'

Margaret nodded in relief and again put her lips to Richard's ear. 'Yes, my love, I shall carry out your plans. Dickon will follow you as lord of Meonbridge.'

Richard gave another small nod. 'Beloved wife.'

The priest leaned across again. 'May I anoint his lordship, my lady, and administer the *viaticum*?'

For answer, Margaret lifted her head, uncovering her husband's face, so that Sire Raphael could touch Richard's forehead with a drop of holy oil, making the sign of the cross. Then, with more recitations, he took the host from the little silver pyx he carried with him and held it against Richard's lips. Richard seemed to murmur something, but Margaret could not hear the words. She took his bloody hand in hers and brought it up to her face. She laid it against her cheek and then her lips.

But Richard, for all his frailty, managed to turn his hand so that he could clasp hers, and he continued to grip it whilst Sire Raphael gave the final blessing. At which point, Richard let out a long breath and his chest was still, and the hand holding Margaret's slid away. Margaret rested her head upon his chest and wept.

And the crowd of retainers and servants, who had been murmuring, fell silent and most dropped to their knees and bowed their heads.

Giles had left Margaret lying across her dead husband. She heard him bid everyone leave and let her be alone with Richard. They all shuffled away, until the vast hall was silent.

At length, Margaret lifted her head and dabbed at her eyes with her fingers. She was sure she must look a dreadful mess, with her face and barbet undoubtedly all bloodied from the gore on Richard's chest. But she did not care. Indeed, she thought for a moment that she could not bear to wipe away the blood, for it was the blood of her beloved husband.

Had he truly left her? It was hard to countenance. How many battles had Richard fought? How many times had he faced death upon the fields of war? And yet, he had survived. It was such a foolish, ignominious death, to be shot by a stray arrow on a *hunt*.

Margaret slumped onto one of the benches that stood alongside the table and, putting her hands together, she uttered a prayer for strength and courage. But then she heard a shuffling just behind the table and, looking around, she saw Giles standing beside the open arras that led through to the solar staircase, his eyebrows raised in enquiry.

She nodded. 'Come in, Giles. Let us comfort each other in our grief.'

He came and sat down next to her and placed his hand upon her arm.

'Tell me what happened,' she said.

'In truth, I don't know, Margaret. Perhaps one of our party was over enthusiastic, for we had caught up with the hart, and were preparing to shoot it down. Indeed, Dick himself was excited, and only feet away from the beast. It did seem like a dreadful accident. But no one has confessed to it.'

'Would they confess?'

He shrugged. 'Maybe not. But one of my pages did say he thought he saw someone running away immediately afterwards, so perhaps it was not one of our party at all?'

'Only *thought* he saw? He might have imagined it, in the confusion.'

Giles nodded. 'Maybe we'll never know.'

They sat together in silence for a while. Margaret felt drained of tears for now, although she knew that she would weep again. But, when she looked up at Giles, she could see his silver scar was glistening in the shafts of sunlight piercing the high windows of the hall. What right had the sun still to cast its rays, she thought, when the light of my life has been snuffed out?

'Giles?' she said, touching his hand. 'We must take care of Richard's body.'

'We must. But I keep thinking, if I'd not come to Meonbridge, this terrible misfortune would not have happened.'

'You cannot blame yourself. You must not. It was, we must presume, a dreadful accident. Someone did shoot the arrow, but it was not you.'

'But if Dick had not gone hunting today, and he went only because of me, he'd still be alive—'

'Stop it, Giles.' Margaret took his hand and squeezed it. 'What you say may well be true, but what is done cannot be undone.'

He let out a heavy sigh. 'Nonetheless, I bear some of the responsibility, for which I'll remain forever in your debt.' Then he rose from the bench. 'Come, Margaret, let us make a start on our sad obligations.'

9

MEONBRIDGE
SEPTEMBER 1356

Rosa was sitting in the arbour in her mother's garden where, as a
girl, she had spent so many hours alone reading a breviary or a
book of hours. The arbour was a circular tunnel of climbing plants, and
half way round the circle was a hidden archway that led into the
fragrant, flowery interior of a little enclosed herber with a seat. She
remembered sitting here on hot summer days, when the coolness of
the arbour was a welcome relief from the heat of the sun, and the
roses' heady perfume was caught inside the herber's enclosure,
hovering in the warm stillness of the air.

But it was autumn now, and the roses were mostly faded, and no
longer sweet-smelling, and the air was chilly. She shivered and rose to
go back to the house. She had asked her mother and John atte Wode to
meet her in the solar, to agree the arrangements for her father's
funeral. Then Agnes and Jack Sawyer would join them to discuss
Dickon's future.

It was strange being here, in the house that had been her home for
so long. She had not been back for nearly seven years. Indeed, this was
the first time she had been outside the boundaries of the priory's

estate. For, although the prioress encouraged her nuns to maintain contact with their secular families, travel outside the priory was not often undertaken, unless the circumstances were exceptional.

Such as now.

Rosa walked back to the house, along the familiar paths. When she first entered the religious life, she thought she might never see her family again, expecting to – hoping to – sequester herself away from the world forever within the priory's walls. But, since John atte Wode had been visiting Northwick to give her advice on the estate, and also bring her news of her parents and little nephew, she had begun to imagine that perhaps the day might come when she *would* return to Meonbridge for a short visit. But she had always supposed the occasion would be a happy one.

Her grief at her father's death was confounded by distress at the difficult position in which he had placed the family with his falsehood about his grandson. She wanted to be angry with him, but anger was not an emotion that sat well with her calling. She resisted the intemperate feelings that threatened to bubble up from time to time and concentrated on using her new-found organising skills to help her mother arrange the funeral, then guide the decision about how best to protect the boy.

When Rosa arrived back in the solar, her mother and John atte Wode were already there. 'I am sorry if I have kept you waiting,' she said. 'You must have much to do, Master atte Wode.'

John shook his head. 'This is more important, Sister Rosa.'

Rosa saw her mother's eyebrows rise a little. She supposed it was still difficult for her mother to accept that she was now "Sister Rosa", and no longer "Johanna". 'It is most important, John,' she said. 'For I believe that Dickon may be in danger now that my father is dead.'

Her mother gasped. 'Danger? From the Bounes, you mean?'

Rosa nodded. 'It is not his life that is at risk, but his position as Father's heir. We have to decide how best we can protect it. Though any plan we make will not be infallible, because of the risk of the falsehood being revealed. In the event of someone disclosing the truth, we might have to prepare ourselves to face the Bounes in court.'

Margaret coughed. 'My dear, should we not wait for Jack and Agnes before we talk any further of the child's future?'

'Yes, Mother, you are quite right. Let us three finalise the funeral arrangements. Have you already sent messages to all those who might attend?'

They had only a short while in which to agree the arrangements before Margaret's maid, Agatha, appeared at the entrance to the solar and announced that the Sawyers had arrived.

'Bring them up, Agatha,' said Margaret and, moments later, John's sister and brother-in-law entered the chamber.

As she looked up to greet them, Rosa sensed that a shadow had crossed the threshold of the room.

She had only met Jack Sawyer once, seven years ago, and he seemed to present as calm a demeanour now as he had then. But Agnes appeared so very different from the happy young woman she had been when she returned to Meonbridge with her baby. As Johanna, Rosa had not been much interested in the baby or his mother, for she was still consumed with grief over her brother's murder. Indeed, Agnes's return only served to reinforce the unhappy Johanna's conviction that she was somehow responsible for her brother's sins, and therefore herself a monstrous sinner. Her only interest was in going to the priory. But she did recall that Agnes was then still the pretty, lively, girl who had been her playmate when they were small, when Agnes's mother, Alice, often visited the manor house, to bring the clothes and furnishings that she made for the de Bohun household.

Now Agnes appeared quite different. She looked much older than Rosa might have expected. It was not that Agnes's skin was wrinkled like her mother's, but that the lines on her brow seemed fixed, and her lips stayed pressed together as if she could not smile. Agnes seemed melancholy and distracted. Perhaps it was just the worry about Dickon? Rosa knew nothing of the feelings of a mother for her child but guessed that Agnes must be fearful of what the future held for him.

'Let us all sit down,' said Rosa, and gestured to the others to take a seat alongside the small table that her parents used when they dined together privately. 'We must make our plans for Dickon.'

Jack nodded. 'Do you accept Sir Richard's pronouncement about the boy, Sister Rosa?'

Agnes at once began to sniffle, and Rosa could not help her body tense with irritation. Agnes's weeping would not provide the answer. She decided to ignore her.

She clasped her hands together. 'I think we have to, Jack. The boy *is* my father's chosen heir—'

John gave a small snort. 'Though, of course, you are now the *rightful* heir, Sister Rosa. You could leave Northwick and take on the estate yourself.' He slapped his hand upon the table.

Rosa thought she heard murmurs of approval from Jack and Agnes, perhaps even from her mother, but she was more than horrified at John's words. She felt suddenly light-headed and, for a brief moment, thought that she might faint. But she breathed deeply and, closing her eyes, uttered a silent prayer for calm. She unclasped her hands and pressed them against the table, drawing strength from the solidity of the oak. After a few moments, Rosa sensed her agitation ease and she lifted her face.

'John, how could you say such a thing?' she said, her voice quiet and a little quavery. 'The priory is my *destiny*, my chosen path...'

John blushed crimson, and Rosa could see that he understood he had offended her. 'I apologise, Sister Rosa. I'm a fool even to think it.'

She forced herself to smile and clasped her hands together again. 'No, we must uphold my father's wishes and support Dickon's claim to the Meonbridge domains.'

John, Jack and her mother all murmured their agreement.

'But,' Rosa continued, 'we shall not openly declare Dickon to be the son of Isabella, for that is a lie, and I cannot be party to such a sin—'

Margaret held up her hand. 'But, my dear, your father was adamant that he made his declaration with the best of motives, and that therefore it was not a *mortal* sin.'

'Yes, Mother, I do understand the reason behind Father's decision, but I am afraid that what he said was nonetheless a falsehood.'

Her mother's face crumpled a little. 'He said that he would atone for it—'

'But he does not now have the opportunity,' said Rosa, 'so I shall have to do it for him.' She frowned, conscious that she might be sounding sour. She did not wish to bring her mother more grief than she was already suffering. She reached across and laid a hand upon her mother's. 'But now, Mother, we must be practical.'

She and her mother had agreed how Meonbridge would be managed for the next few years. They would make it clear to anyone who asked that Dickon *was* Richard's nominated heir but, as he was too young to inherit, Margaret would manage the estates, as she had done many times in the past, with the help of her bailiff, John atte Wode. Dickon would soon go away for his knightly training and, in due course, perhaps ten years or so, he would take his place as lord of Meonbridge.

Rosa expected no disagreement and none came. She had thought that John or Jack might question her mother's fitness to run the estate, though it would have been ungallant and they did not. Rosa had considered it herself but chose to keep it private. After all, her mother was, what, forty-five? Not a young woman, of course. But Mother Prioress Angelica had been managing the priory's estate until only a few years ago, and she was seventy now, and Sister Amata was surely at least sixty, and how energetic she still was. But perhaps they were exceptional. Nonetheless, Rosa persuaded herself that, with the de Bohun estates, they should take each year as it came.

'We shall not,' she continued, 'openly claim Dickon's legitimacy, unless the Bounes somehow discover his true status and take the matter before the courts.'

'Is there anyone you know, John, who might reveal the truth that Agnes is Dickon's mother and not Isabella?' Jack asked.

John shook his head. 'I've asked around discreetly amongst the tenants but haven't learned of anyone who might. Though what we don't know is who in the village knows that Philip is his father. It would be surprising if no one did, the way gossip gets around.' He grimaced.

Jack nodded. 'Though that's not the secret we now need the villagers to keep.'

'No, indeed,' said John. 'But the danger is if someone who knows that Dickon's parents are Philip and Agnes, and realises he is illegitimate, decides to pass *that* information on...' He bit his lip. 'We must just hope there's no one in Meonbridge who would want to betray Dickon and her ladyship.'

'Indeed,' said Rosa. 'But I suggest that Dickon is sent away soon to do his knightly training, just as my father always planned. He's already seven and would have soon begun his training anyway. So, why do we not let him go at once?'

Agnes let out a cry. 'No! He's too young. Still a baby—'

Jack grasped her arm. 'Stop it, Agnes. Dickon's *not* a baby. And I'm sure the training will do him good. He needs a bit of discipline.'

Agnes whimpered. 'But I'm so afraid. I can't bear the thought of him leaving me. And, anyway, he doesn't know anything about all this. He thinks he's a Sawyer. So how can we send him away?'

Jack sighed. 'You're being ridiculous, Agnes. You have to let the boy go. You're not in charge of his destiny. Lady de Bohun and Sister Rosa are. But you're right about him thinking he's my son. He doesn't even know it's his grandfather who's died. We must tell him, mustn't we?' He turned to Rosa.

Rosa nodded. 'With everything that has happened, I had completely forgotten that my father had insisted the boy was kept in the dark. He is very young but, from what Mother has told me, quick to understand, so you are right, he must be told everything, and soon.'

'How foolish of us not to think of it,' said Margaret. 'Please, Jack, bring him to the manor soon, so that we can explain.'

Jack bowed his head. 'Then you must decide where he's to go.'

'Only two days ago,' said Margaret, 'Richard and Giles were discussing the possibility of the boy going up to Shropshire—'

'But isn't that a risk?' said John. 'Sir Giles being married to Morys Boune's daughter, mightn't he have divided loyalties?'

'How can you say that, John?' cried Margaret. 'Giles is the most honourable of men.'

'I'm sorry, your ladyship, but we don't know if his marriage has altered his allegiances. He may even be acting for the Bounes—'

Margaret gasped, but John held his hands up in a gesture of apology.

'I'm sorry, my lady,' he said again, 'but consider what's happened. Sir Giles hasn't been to Meonbridge for seven years. A few months ago, he marries Sir Morys's daughter. Sir Giles tells his new father-in-law about Sir Philip's death, and his brothers-in-law turn up here for the first time ever, probably – assuming Sir Richard was right – to find out who's going to inherit his estates. Then three days ago, Sir Giles turns up, quite unexpectedly, and the very next day our lord's killed, from an allegedly stray arrow.'

'It might all just be chance,' said Jack. 'After all, Sir Giles did say it was an accident—'

'But there was also talk of some fellow letting fly the arrow, then vanishing into the woods.'

'But why would Giles want to kill my father?' said Rosa. 'Or, indeed, why would the Bounes?'

'To put Dickon in a dangerous position,' said John, 'without his grandfather's power behind him.'

Agnes wailed. 'Oh, my poor baby,' she cried, and Jack exchanged an expression of despair with John.

'So where could Dickon go, if not to Shropshire?' said John.

'To the de Courtenays?' said Jack.

'But would they want to take him?' said Rosa. 'My father's claim that Isabella was Dickon's mother purported that the de Courtenays were his grandparents, but of course they are not.' She turned to Margaret. 'Do you think, Mother, that they could be convinced to help us in this crisis?'

'In truth, I am doubtful they will want to. On the other hand, they might be charitable. I shall ask them – I am sure that they will attend the funeral.'

After John and the Sawyers had gone to their homes, Rosa and her mother were left alone in the solar. Margaret sat in her chair next to the hearth, where a fire had just been laid and was beginning to take hold. She was shivering, Rosa noticed.

'Are you cold, Mother?'

Margaret shook her head. 'Just fearful.' She plucked at the fabric of her gown. 'Do you think John could possibly be right about Giles?' She turned towards her daughter, her eyes damp.

Rosa sighed. 'I doubt it, for I believe, as you do, that Giles is an honourable man. But I agree with John that we cannot take the risk of allowing Dickon such close proximity to the Bounes.'

Margaret nodded. 'What John said, about Giles coming here, then Richard being killed—' She dabbed at her eyes with a kerchief. 'Could it be true? I wonder if my faith in him might be misplaced?'

'Again, I doubt it, Mother,' Rosa said. 'Anyway, Giles is still here. We could ask him again about the man who shot the arrow.'

But her mother slowly moved her head from side to side. 'I do not think so. Let us bury your father tomorrow, then make arrangements for the child.' She looked up again. 'Not that I am certain that the de Courtenays will agree.'

'You believe they will resist?'

'Hildegard can be very *difficult*.' Margaret almost smiled.

'So who else is there?'

Margaret gave a little shrug. 'I really cannot think.'

10

MEONBRIDGE
SEPTEMBER 1356

L ady Hildegard de Courtenay's face was purple, her fashionable headdress quivering. Sir Hugh felt almost cowed by his wife's indignation, as if it was somehow his fault that they had fulfilled their duty as former relatives of the de Bohuns by agreeing to come to Sir Richard's funeral. For Hildegard seemed to think he had brought her here against her wishes. It was true that, when their daughter Isabella died, together with her unborn child, the de Courtenays' association with the de Bohuns was fractured. But, in his wife's opinion, when Isabella's husband Philip, Sir Richard's son, was murdered, it was broken altogether. They no longer had a duty to fulfil.

'Can we not just leave?' said Hildegard, her face pinched with agitation. 'All the formalities are over. What need is there for us to linger?'

Her husband patted her arm. 'Hildegard, my dear, can you not be a little more understanding? We came to show respect for Richard, and to give Margaret our support at her time of grief. Surely it is not too much to ask for us to stay a while longer? After all, we have had little chance to speak to Margaret herself, and I do think we should.'

Hildegard harrumphed and shook her shoulders. 'If you say so, husband. I shall go and speak to Johanna – or what is it that she is called now?'

'Sister Dolorosa—'

'What a ridiculous name. Why could she not choose something less overtly melancholy? That girl always was too much preoccupied with her own overwrought and fanciful musings—'

'Hildegard, my dear,' said Hugh, 'please try to be a little *kind*.'

The lady harrumphed again and swept away towards Sister Rosa, hailing her when she was still several feet away. Hugh saw the nun – whom he had always considered an intelligent, prayerful young woman, unlike his vain and silly daughter – turn, and he was sure he observed a furrowing on her brow. He tutted to himself. His wife's tongue was becoming increasingly acerbic, and he always felt quite sorry for anyone who found themselves trapped in conversation with her. It would invariably be a one-sided discourse.

He moved towards Giles Fitzpeyne and Giles's liege lord, Raoul de Fougère, sitting together at the far end of the manor's great hall, seemingly engaged in quiet, courteous, conversation. Raoul stood up as Hugh approached.

'Sir Hugh, do join us,' said the earl. 'Giles has been telling me of the tragic circumstances of Richard's death. When you think of all the times he and I and Giles fought together in our support of the king, and how close Richard so often came to succumbing on the battlefield, to lose his life in a hunting accident is lamentable.'

Hugh nodded. 'Indeed, my lord. A wretched end to such a noble knight.'

'I had thought, my lord,' said Giles at length, 'that I might move amongst the Meonbridge tenants for a while. Discover if anyone's heard anything to help us understand how Richard died.'

'You think they would tell you?'

'Maybe not, but worth a try.'

'I believe that the tenants here became surprisingly loyal to

Richard following the mayhem that so rent the manor after the Mortality,' said Hugh.

Raoul nodded. 'And they were always loyal to Margaret, or so I understand.'

'I will make discreet enquiries.' Giles bowed to Raoul. 'My lord.' Then, nodding to Hugh, he strolled towards the door that led from the hall out onto the bailey, where the tenants were gathered, consuming quantities of ale.

But whom should he approach? He recognised few of the men and women clustered together in small groups, most in noisy conversation. But then he noticed Simon Hogge, whom he'd known for years as Richard's barber-surgeon, and who was with them on many of their campaigns abroad.

Giles strode towards him, a large man whose head stood a little above those of his companions. Simon turned just as Giles approached and hailed him. His face was strained, and Giles thought the man must be distraught that, this time, he couldn't save his master's life, when he had, in direr circumstances, so many times before.

'Sir Giles,' said Simon, 'this is John atte Wode, Sir Richard's...' He faltered. 'Or rather Lady de Bohun's bailiff.'

John bowed his head to Giles. 'Your lordship.'

Simon did not introduce any of his other companions, who muttered their excuses and drifted off. 'Did you want a word, Sir Giles?'

'Only to enquire if you'd heard anything about Sir Richard's accident?'

'Heard anything?' said John.

Giles nodded. 'Lady de Bohun wishes to understand what happened. How it was that Sir Richard lost his life.'

John shrugged. 'There's been talk of some fellow letting fly an arrow, then making off under the cover of the trees.'

'Yes, I heard that,' said Giles, 'from one of my pages, but neither he nor anyone else seems to know who the fellow was. Perhaps I hoped such knowledge might have found its way into one of Meonbridge's ale-houses.'

Simon shook his head. 'I've not heard of any stranger here the past few days, apart from yourself, Sir Giles, and your company. And I can't think why any of the tenants would want Sir Richard dead. If you're suggesting, sir, it were done deliberate?'

'I do not know, Simon. Perhaps it *was* an accident, but I should like to be sure of it, as would her ladyship. And it is for her, as well as in memory of my oldest friend, that I wish to learn the truth. Any help you can give me would be most welcome.'

Both Meonbridge men frowned a little. 'I'd like to help, m'lord,' said John, 'but I've heard nothing, and if the fellow were a stranger, he'd be long gone, don't you think?' He narrowed his eyes, and Giles felt suddenly uncomfortable.

'Nonetheless,' he said, 'do keep a heedful ear for any information.'

But, although John and Simon agreed, they were mostly pessimistic, and Giles was disappointed. But he did wonder what to make of the errant bowman. If Simon was right that he was unlikely to be a Meonbridge tenant, was he then indeed a stranger? Or perhaps a member of the hunting party?

After Giles had gone to discover what he might from the Meonbridge tenants, Hugh exchanged a few further words with Raoul de Fougère, and then excused himself. He was watching his wife and Sister Rosa from a distance and became anxious to relieve the young nun from the burden of her inquisitor. As he approached them, he could see her wilting under the onslaught of whatever Hildegard had chosen to assail her with. He came up behind his wife and grasped her arm, at the same time nodding to Sister Rosa.

'My dear girl, will you forgive me for withdrawing Lady de Courtenay from your conversation? We must speak to your mother before we leave.'

Sister Rosa gave a brief nod, and Hugh was certain he saw her shoulders lift and her eyes brighten. 'Of course, Sir Hugh.'

Tightly clasping Hildegard's arm, Hugh marched across to Lady de Bohun, who for once was sitting quite alone. 'Margaret,' he called. 'A word?'

Margaret turned, but the smile she quickly applied to her face seemed tinged with anxiety. 'Ah, Hugh, Hildegard, how opportune—'

'We are leaving shortly, Margaret,' said Hugh, 'and wished to bid you farewell.'

Margaret gasped and shook her head. 'Oh no, not yet, I need to speak to you both.'

Hildegard frowned and tutted. 'What about, Margaret? It is time that we began our journey home to Surrey.'

All at once Margaret seemed short of breath and her hands were agitated. 'But I have something to discuss with you. Would you please join me in the solar, for a little privacy?'

Despite his wife's evident irritation, Hugh did not see how they could refuse. Moments later, the three of them were seated at the table in the solar, and Margaret had visibly composed herself, with her hands clasped together as if in prayer.

'I need to tell you both,' she said, 'that, a few months ago, Richard presented our grandson, Dickon, to the sons of his cousin, Morys Boune – do you know Sir Morys?'

Hildegard shook her head, although Hugh raised his eyebrows. But Margaret seemed not to notice and continued. 'He presented Dickon as his legitimate heir, the son of Philip and...and Isabella—'

Hildegard let out an explosive gasp. Hugh too was astonished but managed to contain his shock, whilst signalling to his wife to do the same. But she ignored him. 'That was untrue,' she cried. 'A bare-faced lie! Our daughter died in the Mortality and was no more than six months pregnant. That was what you told us, Margaret, and we had no reason to doubt your word.'

'Indeed,' said Margaret, her face grey. 'It was true. Poor Isabella did die, together with her unborn child.'

'So why change the story now?' said Hugh.

'It was...necessary,' continued Margaret, little beads of moisture forming on her upper lip, 'to secure the future of the de Bohun estates.'

'Pah!' cried Hildegard. 'So now you are claiming – what? – that Isabella died giving birth to this boy? When in fact he was birthed by some *peasant* girl, one of Philip's whores.'

Hugh saw Margaret wince. 'Agnes was no whore,' she said, her voice a whisper. 'We know that Philip cared for her—'

Hildegard sniffed. 'You think that makes me feel better?'

'No, of course not, Hildegard. But can you understand why Richard said what he did? Dickon is our *only* heir. With Johanna in the priory, the other claimant to the estates is Richard's cousin. And surely you must see that we could not let the de Bohun domains fall into the hands of such a...a stranger?'

Hugh nodded. He and Hildegard had been distraught at Isabella's death, but they had another daughter and two sons, and several thriving grandchildren. To ensure the future of the de Courtenays in Surrey, they did not "need" a grandson in the same way that Margaret de Bohun did.

Hugh leaned forward and lightly touched Margaret's clasped hands with his fingers. 'We do see your difficulty, Margaret, but did it justify such manifest deception? How can you live with the knowledge of your falsehood? How will you justify yourself to God?'

Margaret lifted her eyes to him, her face twisted with evident concern.

'And what if you are challenged?' said Hildegard, her headdress quivering. 'Supposing someone who *knows* the boy is not Isabella's comes forward and denounces you – what then? Will you maintain your lie in the face of the conspicuous truth?'

Margaret's shoulders slumped. 'Richard made the claim without consulting me, and, now he is dead, *I* am left with the problem of maintaining his claim or refuting it. And I know that, if I did refute it, I would be leaving the door open for Morys Boune to take the de Bohun estates away from us.'

Hugh felt sorry for the predicament in which Richard had placed his wife. 'I do understand, Margaret, but you have not answered Hildegard's question. Supposing someone who knows the truth about the boy's mother betrays you?'

'How many people *do* know that truth?' said Hildegard, her voice rising.

'No one outside Meonbridge, apart from you.'

'Very well, how many inside?'

Margaret blanched. 'Many of the tenants saw Agnes atte Wode come back to the manor with a baby in her arms. But how many realised that the child was Philip's son, and not her husband's, I cannot tell.'

'So any one of fifty people know that this Agnes is the child's mother, and might betray you?' Hildegard almost shrieked. 'Really, Margaret, this is absurd. To run such a risk of discovery and dishonour. Richard was an utter fool.'

Simon Hogge nudged John atte Wode's arm. 'Her ladyship,' he said, and pointed across the bailey to the door that opened into the manor hall. Lady de Bohun had appeared at the top of the short flight of steps leading up to the door, with Alexander, the ageing seneschal, standing at her side. John could see a group of manor servants and retainers gathered together beyond the door. But then he saw Sister Rosa come forward to stand on her mother's other side, with her head bowed and her hands placed palms together.

'D'you think she's going to make a speech?' said Simon.

'Mebbe.' John gazed across at Lady de Bohun, thinking how grey and drawn she looked, the strain of the past few days evident in her bearing.

Alexander tried to call for quiet, but his voice was no longer strong enough to rise above the din. John noticed and, because as bailiff he was used to commanding folks' attention, he jumped up onto a nearby mounting block and raised his arms. Then he bellowed 'Quiet for her ladyship!' and all the people in the bailey turned and looked, and silence fell.

Lady de Bohun nodded to John, who melted back into the crowd, then she drew herself up tall and clasped her hands together at her waist.

'My friends,' she said, her voice strong. 'This has been a dreadful day. To lose our lord, still in the flower of his youth...'

'Dunno about "flower",' muttered a fellow standing close to John, and received a clip on the ear from the bailiff's stout fingers for his insolence.

But her ladyship seemed not to have heard the remark and continued. '...is a great tragedy for us all, for you men and women of Meonbridge, as much as for me and my family.'

A general murmur of agreement hummed around the crowd.

'But I want you to know that, despite our great loss, life in Meonbridge will continue as before. I shall once more pick up the reins of authority over this manor – and indeed all our other manors. And, with the help of our bailiff, John atte Wode, and the steward, Adam Wragge, and all of you…,' and she unclasped her hands and spread her arms wide before her tenants, '…I shall ensure that the de Bohun domains grow ever more bountiful and productive.'

The appreciative hum grew a little louder.

'And, God willing, I shall continue until my grandson, young Richard, comes of age and takes up his position as the new lord of Meonbridge.'

At this, the insolent man standing close to John guffawed and shook his head, his eyes alight.

'Yer *what*, m'lady?' he bellowed. 'Didn't know you 'ad no grandson, yer ladyship.' And he guffawed again.

John again hit out at the man, trying to stop him talking. But the man ducked, and astonished laughter was already sweeping across the bailey like a forest fire. Surprised comments were being tossed into the air.

''Er grandson?'

'"Young *Richard*"?'

'Be that Jack Sawyer's lad?'

'Din't I always say as much. 'E looks jus' like young Philip.'

'Who'd 'ave thought it?'

John looked across at Lady de Bohun, expecting to see her quailing under the villagers' verbal onslaught. But she was still standing tall and straight-backed, one hand now touching the chain of keys hanging from her waist. She seemed just to be waiting for the clamour to die down.

John leapt up on the mounting block again. 'Silence! Let her ladyship speak.'

Mutterings continued but, once most villagers were looking at her expectantly, Lady de Bohun spoke again.

'I know this has come as a surprise, indeed shock, to many of you, but the time has come for all of you to know the truth. The boy Richard – Dickon – whom Jack and Agnes Sawyer have been raising as their own son is, in truth, half a de Bohun. His true father is my dead son, Philip.'

'Told yer.'

'Obvious, innit?'

John stared at her ladyship, full of admiration. Had she alone made the decision to make this announcement, or had she agreed it with Sister Rosa? Either way, he thought the Sawyers hadn't been consulted for, a short distance away, he could see his sister Agnes leaning into Jack, whose arms were wrapped around her, as her body shuddered, presumably with sobs.

Lady de Bohun lifted her hands up in a gesture of supplication. 'Sir Richard and I have known Dickon was our grandson since he was a baby. But we agreed then with Jack and Agnes that they should bring him up, to give him a normal village childhood, until the time arrived when Dickon had to take on the mantle of his responsibilities.' She paused, closing her eyes briefly. When she resumed, her voice was quieter. 'But, of course, we did not imagine that time would come so soon. We thought that Dickon would grow to be a man before he was called upon to take his grandfather's place as lord of Meonbridge.'

But, at that moment, her ladyship faltered a little and the elderly seneschal put out his arm to steady her. She smiled at him and nodded, but then Sister Rosa moved forward and whispered something to her mother. Lady de Bohun seemed as if she might deny her daughter, but acquiesced and allowed her to step to the front of the platform.

Comments and exclamations erupted from the crowd as, John realised, none of the Meonbridge tenants had seen "Sister Rosa" before, and word was quickly spreading that this nun must be the Lady Johanna, returned almost from the dead.

Rosa raised her arms, and John almost laughed at the speed with which the clamour ceased.

'This has been a most distressing day,' she said, 'for her ladyship, and for me, and indeed for all of you. To lose her husband, my father, and our lord so untimely is hard to contemplate or bear. But it is God's will, and we *must* bear it, and praise Him for the life of Sir Richard de Bohun.' She bowed her head, and everyone in the bailey did the same. 'Sir Richard nominated little Dickon as his heir, and the boy will take on my father's mantle in due course. Until he is old enough to do so, my lady mother will manage the estates, whilst Dickon will go away from here to start his knightly training. It will be difficult for him, being such a little boy, to leave everything and everyone he knows, but it must be. It is the way things are.'

If anyone in the bailey disagreed or considered it a sudden move to send the boy away from Meonbridge, no one said so.

John grinned. 'I'm glad folk have accepted my little nephew,' he said to Simon.

But Simon frowned. 'I wouldn't put it that way out loud, if I were you, John,' he said, in a low voice. 'Even if most folk are willing to accept Dickon *is* Sir Richard's heir, you can't forget the truth about his blood.'

John coloured slightly. 'He's my sister's—'

Simon raised his hand and put it on John's shoulder. 'I know. And so does everyone else in Meonbridge. That Agnes is the boy's mother has never been in question. But it means young Dickon's not the *legitimate* heir. Even Lady Johanna – Sister Rosa – said "heir", and not "legitimate heir".'

John nodded. 'She's a stickler for the truth.'

'But the fact is, John, your nephew's position is not secure. If everyone keeps their mouth shut then, in due course, he *will* become the lord of Meonbridge. But it's a long time till then.'

Hugh de Courtenay had persuaded his recalcitrant wife that they should stay another night in Meonbridge, in order to consider the proposal that Margaret made to them, to acknowledge Dickon as the de Bohun heir and to provide for the first stages of the boy's knightly training. Hildegard wanted neither to stay nor to discuss the proposal, but even she would not openly defy her husband.

It was a difficult conversation.

'Do remember, my dear,' Hugh said, 'that, when our beloved Isabella died, she took the de Bohuns' grandchild with her, and then Philip was murdered by a villain. The de Bohuns suffered terribly—'

Hildegard grunted. 'No more than we—' she began but, when Hugh raised his hand and narrowed his eyes at her, she gave her shoulders a little shake and closed her mouth.

'And the discovery,' continued Hugh, 'of an, albeit illegitimate, heir clearly gave them hope that the de Bohun line was not entirely lost.'

Hildegard could not contain herself. 'But the boy's mother is a *peasant*,' she said, unable to stop her voice from rising, 'so the line is severely sullied.'

Hugh did not respond to his wife's taunt. He himself had fathered two bastard children, and in truth he thought of them as fondly as he did his legitimate offspring. Moreover, he had made provision for them, both now and after his death. Although Hildegard knew nothing of either the children or the provision.

'My dear,' he said, 'I think we can afford to be generous towards the boy.'

'But he is *nothing* to us, Hugh. The de Bohuns became nothing to us once Isabella died. Why should we care what happens to them?'

'You are right in principle, my dear,' said her husband. She simpered but he shook his head. 'But *most* uncharitable.'

Hildegard sniffed but said nothing.

'Consider also,' Hugh continued, 'the alternative. The Bounes might take over the de Bohun estates, and surely we do not want the likes of them in our part of the world? Meonbridge might be some distance, but one or two de Bohun manors are no more than twenty miles from Courtenay Castle.'

'Why? What do you know of these Bounes?'

Hugh rolled his eyes. 'I had forgotten, but my memory was prompted by a conversation earlier with Giles Fitzpeyne. Do you remember the older son, Gunnar?' Hildegard shook her head. 'He was a squire at Sir Henry Blandefordde's at the same time as our Baldwin. The boys were the same age. But when Gunnar's younger brother, Thorkell, also began his training there, I recall Sir Henry saying how much he regretted taking the younger Boune boy on. For the boy was violent, Hildegard, a dangerous prankster, and Baldwin loathed, indeed, feared him. And I have heard that the father, Morys, is as callous and intemperate as his younger son.'

'I admit, husband, that they do not sound like the kind of people who should inherit Sir Richard's estates.'

Hugh nodded. 'Anyway, Hildegard, do you really want to see Margaret ejected from her home? Surely that would be an ignominious end for such a noble lady?'

When Hugh had bidden Lady de Bohun good night, he thought that she looked most despondent, for the way Hildegard had left it, Margaret would have assumed it unlikely that they would accede to her request. But, next morning, he was able to greet Margaret with a cheerful grin. He had persuaded Hildegard to agree, albeit his ill-humoured wife had done so only under protest.

'I am certain,' she had said to her husband at the end of a tiresome and tiring evening, 'that all of this has no more substance than a milk pudding, which will collapse as soon as anyone pokes it with a spoon.'

Hugh was amused by his wife's peculiar analogy but could not disagree that poor Margaret was attempting to hold together a most delicate and risk-filled situation. Not wishing to make the lady's task any more alarming than it already was, he led Margaret to believe that he, at least, was content with his decision. Which again was only partly true but, in the face of an unconscionable dilemma, it was made with the most honourable of intentions.

However, when Dickon arrived at Courtenay Castle, Hugh would have to bolster his decision by ensuring that the boy's true parentage was kept a secret. Margaret had not asked him to lie, not to say explicitly to anyone that *Isabella* had birthed the boy, but simply not to volunteer the truth of his mother's identity. He agreed that most gentlefolk of his acquaintance were unlikely to enquire into the boy's parentage – why should they? And few, if any, would know the truth. It was undoubtedly a risk maintaining such a falsehood, albeit tacitly; a risk that Hildegard really did not want to take. What he would answer if, one day, someone did ask the question, was a problem Hugh decided he would deal with when – if – it happened.

But his son Baldwin, who was responsible for the younger squires and pages in their charge, and therefore Dickon, would have to be told – both the full truth, and the unspoken falsehood that Hugh had agreed with Margaret to maintain.

Hugh speculated on how his son would take the news, especially when he learned that his dead sister was being misrepresented. If Baldwin's heart was usually in the right place, his head was not always as fully engaged as it might be. And, if Hildegard got into one of her flusters and declared in public that the de Bohun boy was in fact a bastard, Baldwin could easily enough forget what he had been told and uphold his mother's view.

Hugh closed his eyes, imagining the scene. Then he sighed and trudged off to gather up his wife and her ridiculous number of travelling boxes for the journey back to Surrey.

The decision had been made, and he could not change it now.

11

'The time's come, Agnes,' Jack said, placing a gentle hand upon her shoulder. She lifted her eyes to his. They were already pooled with tears.

'Why're you crying?' he said. 'This is what you wanted.'

She bit her lip but didn't answer.

'Seeing how ill-behaved you always find him,' continued Jack, 'you should be pleased he's going away.'

But Agnes whirled away from him. 'How can you say that, Jack?' she cried. 'He's my baby, my first born—'

'But Dickon wears you out, Agnes, with his rudeness and disobedience.' He grimaced. 'Now he'll have some discipline and good manners beaten into him.'

He didn't truly think it right that children, even rebellious ones, should be thrashed. But, as soon as it was out, he saw it was a mistake to goad Agnes like that, even though he'd meant it as a jest.

She flew at him. '"*Beaten* into him"? No, Jack, no!'

He grasped her wrists and pulled her towards him, so her face was resting against his chest. 'Don't be foolish, Agnes. Surely this is what you hoped for?' he said again. 'For Dickon to be Sir Richard's heir and train to be a knight?' He jiggled her wrists and, as she raised her eyes, he dropped a kiss onto her forehead. 'Discipline's bound to be part of it, Agnes, and he'll learn to accept it. If not at once, then certainly in time.'

She nodded against his chest. 'But I'll miss him so...' she whispered in a plaintive voice.

'And so will I, despite the little tyke driving me to distraction. He's been our boy for seven years, Agnes, but he's not ours any more. He's a de Bohun now, and you – we – must accept it. We always knew it was going to happen.'

Agnes pulled away. 'Geoffrey and Stephen will miss him too. They've always looked up to him, as a sort of hero.'

'And now he's got the chance to become a real hero, like his father and grandfather.' He took Agnes's chin in his hand. 'Hasn't he?'

He grinned, and she responded as he'd hoped she would, with a smile. 'Yes, I suppose he has.'

She seemed placated for the moment, and her ease continued whilst they found Dickon, dressed him in his good clothes, directed Christopher to mind the other children and set off for the manor.

Her ladyship greeted them in the hall. Dinner had just ended, and the servants were clearing away the debris and dismantling the trestles.

'Ah, well met,' she said, coming forward and patting Dickon on the head. 'I was just thinking of taking a turn about the garden, as it is such an unusually delightful autumn day...but maybe the garden, with its many distractions, would not be the ideal location for our conversation?'

Jack laughed politely. 'Indeed, your ladyship. I think we might be in danger of losing the most important member of our party.'

Margaret joined in his laughter. 'So let us go upstairs.' She moved towards the solar staircase, then stopped. 'Jack, you three go up. I just want to have a quick word with Matilda...' And she hurried away, to where Matilda was in conversation with the wife of one of her ladyship's retainers.

Not long afterwards, Margaret joined them in the solar. 'Matilda will stay downstairs for a while,' she said, her eyebrows slightly raised.

Jack nodded. 'Is anyone else joining us, your ladyship?'

'Your brother-in-law, of course. And Alice, too, perhaps?' She leaned forward and whispered. 'I asked them both. As they have always shared the secret of Dickon's true parentage, I thought they should also share the moment when Dickon learns of it, and of his future.'

Jack hadn't seen Alice for a while. Agnes had reported that she'd fallen sick again. Alice was a woman who generally scorned giving in to illness. But she'd become quite ill three years ago, her belly paining her for months. For a while then she had looked almost old, even a little frail, when she wasn't even forty. But, the following spring, she recovered much of her old strength and spirit. Yet it seemed her recovery was not to last.

When Alice arrived with John, her face was pale and rather drawn and, although she squeezed Jack's hand quite firmly, the brightness of her eyes seemed to have dimmed, the usual vigour of her body once more faded.

Margaret came forward and took her old friend's arm and drew her over towards the fire. 'Would you like to sit here, in one of the cushioned chairs?' she said, but Alice shook her head.

'Thank you, Margaret dear, but no,' said Alice, her voice still strong. 'The pains have returned a little, that's all.' She placed a hand upon the rounding of her belly. 'Why don't we all sit together around the table? It will be easier for us to talk.'

Margaret patted Alice's hand. 'Indeed.' She stepped over to the table and gestured to the others to sit down. Then she turned towards the end of the room to which Dickon had scuttled the moment he'd arrived. Jack assumed it was where Libby usually played, for toys were strewn across the floor. Dickon had one of Libby's cloth poppets grasped in either hand and was beating the head of one against the other, crowing and grunting all the while. Jack hoped the poppets would survive unscathed.

'Dickon,' called Margaret, 'will you join us at the table, dear?'

Jack glanced across at his stepson. Dickon neither responded to her ladyship, nor even showed he'd heard her, but simply continued his savagery with the dolls. Jack stood up and went over. Looming over the boy, he leaned down and tapped him on the shoulder.

'Dickon, didn't you hear her ladyship asking you to come?' he said quietly.

Turning round, Dickon screwed up his nose and shook his head. 'Didn't 'ear,' he said and resumed his violence with the poppets.

Jack would have liked to box Dickon's ears. Instead, he took hold of the boy's arm as gently as he could and pulled him to his feet. 'Nonetheless, it's for your benefit we've all come here, so put down the poppets and come over to the table.' He tightened his grip on Dickon's arm and the boy didn't resist, letting the dolls drop to the floor, though he did throw Jack a scowl. He ran over and scrambled onto a stool next to his mother. But, when Agnes hissed something into his ear that Jack took to be a chiding, he rolled his eyes and pouted, then, slumping his elbows onto the table, pushed his chin between his folded arms.

Jack exchanged a raised eyebrow with his brother-in-law but, if Margaret noticed her grandson's bad behaviour, she ignored it.

'Thank you, dear,' she said to Dickon. 'We have a lot to talk about. And it is important that you both listen and tell us what you think.'

Jack and John raised their eyebrows again and, this time, Margaret noticed. 'Dickon has much to learn today, and one of those things is how to be master of his own future. I simply recommend that we involve him in our discussion.' She tilted her head slightly.

Jack nodded. He could hardly gainsay her ladyship's opinion. 'Please, your ladyship, do continue.'

'Dickon,' said Margaret, 'do you know why we are all here today?'

He shrugged, not even bothering to lift his head. But Margaret continued to disregard his rudeness.

'It is to discuss your future.'

Dickon wrinkled his nose. 'What's "fewcher"?'

'It is what is going to happen to you, Dickon, now that you are growing up.'

He wriggled his nose again. 'What d'you mean?'

'"*Your ladyship*",' prompted Agnes, nudging him with her elbow.

'Your ladyship,' he added, and pouted.

'Dickon,' said Margaret, 'look at me.' He lifted his face from his arms, and she smiled down at him. 'Now, please listen, dear, to what I have to ask.' He gave a single nod and sat up.

'Can you tell me who your mother is?' she said.

Dickon giggled and rolled his eyes, then poked Agnes in the arm. '*She* is.'

'And your father?'

He looked at Jack. 'Him?' The question in his voice was clear.

'Are you not sure, dear?' Margaret said.

He pressed his lips together. 'He's like my pa and yet...'

'And yet?'

'My friends...'

Margaret nodded. 'Your friends...?'

'...say he isn't. They say he can't be 'cos he's got fair hair and mine is black.'

Margaret laughed lightly. 'Lots of people have different colouring from their parents. But, Dickon, if you are not Jack's son, then whose son do you think you are?'

He reddened and stared down into his lap. 'Dunno.'

'I think perhaps you do,' she said, 'but feel you should not say?' He shrugged again.

'So let me tell you,' she went on. 'Jack is assuredly the father who has cared for you since you were a baby, but your friends are right that he is not the man who gave you life. That man was *my* son, Sir Philip de Bohun, and you do indeed look much like him.'

'Why've I never met him?' said Dickon.

'Because he died before you were born. He died young, but he had already gained great honour on the battlefield and was considered likely to become one of the king's most brilliant and illustrious knights.' Her eyes gleamed as she spoke, and Dickon's eyes were wide.

'A knight?' he said. 'But—'

'A knight indeed,' she said, still beaming. 'And if you were about to ask, Dickon, how such a man could be your father, I will tell you that, long ago, he and your mother, Agnes, were...' A light flush brought colour to her ladyship's cheeks, until she found the word she wanted. '...were *known* to each other.' She chewed her lip a moment. Perhaps she wasn't sure it was the right word after all? But then she gave her shoulders a little shake and carried on. 'But poor Philip died, Dickon, without ever knowing that he would be blessed with such a fine strong son as you. It was much later that Agnes met and married Jack, and Jack agreed to raise you as his own.'

Jack glanced across at John and lifted his eyebrows once again. Her ladyship's story was not quite the truth, obscuring somewhat the exact nature of what had happened between Agnes and Philip, and when. Nonetheless, it was a sort of truth and would serve well enough for now.

'I wish I'd known my pa,' said Dickon, his expression pensive. Then he looked up sharply. 'How'd he die?'

Margaret blanched, yet she must've realised Dickon would likely ask that question. How would she respond – tell the truth, or again skirt around what really happened?

A few moments passed before she answered and, when she did, she held her kerchief to her face, covering her cheeks a little. 'Through a dreadful misadventure, dear.' This time, it was John who raised an eyebrow at Jack, whilst her ladyship's eyes clouded briefly. 'I shall tell you all about it another time,' she continued. Then she let a broad smile part her lips. 'But *now*, Dickon, I want to tell you about the exciting world that awaits you, as Philip's son, and *my* grandson.'

Dickon seemed to take in his stride the news of his father's true identity – and, indeed, his own. It was clear he'd already had an inkling Jack wasn't his birth father. But had he also known he was a de Bohun all along? Did he somehow *remember* the day Agnes first brought him to the manor to meet his de Bohun grandparents? When Sir Richard had taken Dickon into his arms and carried him around the great hall, introducing him to his ancestral home, as he had put it. The boy was only six months old, but had those few moments with his grandfather somehow lodged inside his being?

And when, three years ago, Dickon started visiting the manor, supposedly to play with Libby Fletcher, the boy might have wondered why *he*'d been chosen, yet he behaved almost as if he knew it was where he belonged.

Jack laughed to himself. The boy could not possibly have *divined* his heritage: that surely made no sense. Yet, when her ladyship told

Dickon who his father was, and what that signified for his future, the boy seemed not at all surprised. Of course he was still only seven, so some might say he scarcely understood what he was being told. But Jack was certain Dickon was much wiser than most boys of his age. So perhaps, indeed, he *had* divined his situation well before he was told of it?

Whatever the truth of that, it was clear the boy was greatly pleased to hear her ladyship confirm he was indeed the son, and the grandson, of an illustrious knight.

On the other hand – and perhaps somewhat unexpectedly – his cheeks leeched their colour when Margaret then explained what was to happen in a few months' time.

Jack assumed Dickon would leap at the chance to train to be a knight and, at first, he did. As Margaret described the nature of the training he would undergo – telling him rather more about the horsemanship and sword skills than the duller aspects of his new life – Dickon's eyes shone with excitement.

But when she went on to explain that, to undergo this training, he would be leaving Meonbridge, to live somewhere far away amongst people he didn't know, it was then the boy's eagerness and anticipation faltered.

And, as her son's eyes moistened, so once more did Agnes's.

Before Sister Rosa returned to Northwick, she had agreed with Margaret that Dickon would go to the de Courtenays in early March, allowing him, and Agnes, a few months to adjust to the impending change. And Jack surprised himself by realising he too needed a little time to come to terms with Dickon's leaving.

Ever since he and Agnes came back to Meonbridge, and the de Bohuns found they had a grandson, Jack had known Dickon would never follow him – as sons usually did – into his craft. But he had two other sons who would. And Dickon was destined for higher things: for a noble future to which Jack sometimes felt such an ill-behaved and ill-tempered child had no right. Though John said often enough that Philip was just the same – choleric and arrogant, as much so as a boy as when he became a man.

'Perhaps,' said John, holding forth about the nature of the man it seemed he had argued with fiercely over Agnes's disappearance, but with whom at length he found a form of friendship, 'that arrogance is the essence of what made him a great knight.'

Jack had nodded. 'Sir Richard also. And, as Dickon shares their temperament, perhaps he'll follow in their footsteps, and make a fine knight too.'

If the date of Dickon's departure was not a matter for discussion, neither it seemed was *where* he was to go. When at length the de Courtenays had agreed, Lady de Bohun was delighted, and didn't invite Jack or the others to approve or censure her decision.

Nonetheless, John continued to act the sceptic. He'd already said Sir Giles couldn't be trusted any longer, since he was married to a Boune. But he also questioned the dependability of the de Courtenays, given, he said, he'd heard they'd had to be persuaded to take the boy.

Now Margaret bit her lip. 'What Sir Hugh agreed to was to say *nothing* about Dickon's parentage, hoping that no one would ask outright. In truth, Hildegard was more chary. She hates duplicity of any sort. As do we all.' She briefly wrung her hands. 'So I admit it is a risk, but where else could I send the boy? Much as I honour and admire Sir Giles, I am much warier of sending him to Shropshire.'

John agreed wholeheartedly with that.

'I suppose,' said Jack, 'it's unlikely anyone will ask about the parentage of a little page. Why should they?'

'Exactly,' said Margaret. 'That is also Sir Hugh's opinion. It is possible that someone will either know the truth or be suspicious enough to ask, so there *is* a risk, but perhaps it is not a great one.'

'And it's surely better to keep Dickon reasonably close to home than send him all the way to Shropshire,' said John, 'within striking distance of the Bounes?'

And everyone agreed to that.

Even Dickon himself, whose eyelids had been drooping and who probably – Jack suspected, indeed hoped – hadn't been following the discussion about what would and wouldn't be said by all and sundry about his parentage, sat up straight and nodded knowingly at the notion that he wasn't going to be sent too far away from home.

. . .

But, if Dickon had been pleased to find he was heir to Meonbridge and all the other de Bohun estates – though Jack presumed he had no true understanding of what "heir" or "estate" in practice signified – the boy remained anxious about the looming consequences of his new position in life.

Margaret had – somewhat belatedly, Jack now realised – tried to help prepare him by giving him into the charge of Piers Arundale, one of Richard's young squires. Piers's job was to introduce Dickon to his role as a page in the de Courtenay household, and to teach him something about horses and handling weapons – knowledge most boys in Dickon's position would presumably already have. And he also offered him a little grounding in etiquette and manners, and even tried instructing him in his letters – topics, Jack now discovered, usually taught to a young gentleman by his mother. Poor Dickon, it turned out, had much to learn, and little time in which to learn it.

'D'you enjoy your lessons with young Piers?' he'd asked Dickon one evening after supper, and the boy had nodded.

'And you're looking forward to going away and learning properly with the other boys?' Jack put his arm around Dickon's shoulder. He hoped the fear the boy had first shown when he found he must leave Meonbridge would by now have eased. But, unusually, his son wriggled closer into him, mumbling something he couldn't hear.

Jack held him closely for a moment, squeezing his shoulder and ruffling his hair. But then he pulled back and, gently taking Dickon's arms, held him away from his chest, so he could see his face. His heart turned over when he saw the trembling on Dickon's lower lip. '*Are* you looking forward to it?' he said again.

'Some of it,' said Dickon, his voice a whisper, then he swallowed hard.

Jack pulled him to his chest again and hugged him tight. 'Oh, son, you'll surely enjoy it, once you're with the other boys, taking your first step to becoming a great knight like your pa and grandpapa.'

Dickon sniffed against his chest. 'But the other boys will scoff...'

'Why'd you say that?'

''Cos I'm not like them, am I? I've never ridden a horse, or...'

Jack knew nothing of the lives of gentry boys, but imagined they climbed into the saddle almost as soon as they could walk. He should have thought of it all before but, more importantly, why hadn't Sir Richard and her ladyship been preparing their grandson for his future *ever since he was a baby*? By letting Dickon stay with him and Agnes, growing up as an ordinary village boy, he'd missed out on all the learning his fellow pages would have had. Agnes had done her best, and he too had tried to play his part. But the boy had hardly been receptive to any of their efforts, preferring to run wild with the sons of cottars. And he, and the de Bohuns, had let it happen.

Jack hugged the boy again. Perhaps Dickon did after all have cause for feeling nervous about his future.

But he wouldn't say as much, not to Dickon, nor to Agnes.

12

'Our little Gwynedd is most happy in her new home, husband,' said Alwyn, whisking off her hood and cloak and sending a cascade of raindrops onto the floor of the hall. 'Giles's castle is quite delightful. Comfortable, warm, and full of light. How fortunate our eldest daughter is.' She tilted her head at her husband.

Thorkell glanced at his father out of the corner of his eye. The old man's face was gloomy, and Thorkell deduced he was sensing criticism in his wife's report. Nonetheless, Morys applied a smile to his lips. 'I'm glad to hear of Gwynnie's joy, my dear. I knew Fitzpeyne would do the business.'

Alwyn frowned. 'What can you possibly mean?'

He winked. 'She's with child, isn't she?'

'Really, Morys.' She swept across the hall and, handing her cloak and gloves to a servant, took a seat close to the fire. She shivered.

Morys grunted and took a few steps towards the door that led outside, gesturing to Thorkell to go with him. But Alwyn called him back.

'Don't go yet, Morys, I have more to tell you. Unhappy news.'

113

Morys stopped and strode back towards his wife, his eyebrows raised. 'What?'

'Giles returned only yesterday from Meonbridge. His visit was prolonged by the need to attend a funeral.' Morys's eyebrows rose higher. 'Sir Richard's funeral.'

When Morys laughed, even Thorkell thought his father's response was inappropriate. But Alwyn gasped at her husband's loud guffaw and sprang to her feet. Thorkell was unsurprised that his stepmother was shocked, for she knew nothing of her husband's – and his own – ambitions.

'Morys,' she cried, flapping her hands at him. 'How can you laugh? Your cousin is *dead*, killed in a dreadful accident—'

'What sort of accident?' said Thorkell, interested.

His stepmother pursed her lips. 'When he and Giles were hunting. A stray arrow or some such, Giles said.'

Thorkell hid a smile but his father guffawed again, clearly elated by the news. 'A *stray* arrow, eh? A likely story—'

Thorkell was frustrated that his father was being so openly callous about his cousin's death, instead of at least *feigning* sorrow and respect. Even though de Bohun's death of course made their plans easier to achieve, he didn't think it wise to display such lack of feeling in front of Alwyn. It might arouse suspicion. And his stepmother was no fool.

He sidled up to her. 'So do you know what's happening to the estate?'

Alwyn nodded. 'Apparently Lady de Bohun will manage the estates, as she's done many times in the past, according to Giles, together with her bailiff. They'll do so until her grandson comes of age.'

Thorkell stroked his beard. So the boy was still the heir. He looked across at his father and caught his eye. Morys nodded and turned to his wife.

'My dear, why don't you go up to see the girls. They've been looking forward to your return all day.' He stepped forward and took her arm, pulling her towards the solar steps.

'You want me out of the way?'

'Not at all,' said Morys, affecting merriment. 'But I do have some business to discuss with Thorkell.'

Alwyn sighed. 'Of course you do.' She pulled her arm free from her husband's grasp and strode towards the door that led to their private quarters. 'Will I see you for supper?'

Morys grunted agreement, then she was gone.

Thorkell waited a few moments more, to give Alwyn time to be beyond overhearing their conversation. Then he gestured to his father that they move to the far end of the hall, away from any other prying ears.

'Well, Pa,' said Thorkell, 'what do you make of Lady Alwyn's news?'

Morys smirked. 'Most surprising, to be sure. And much to our advantage...'

Thorkell frowned. 'You shouldn't seem so gleeful, Pa. It might give your wife the wrong impression.'

'Or rather the *right* impression, but not the one we want her to have?' Morys's eyes twinkled.

'Exactly. So, what now?'

Morys scratched his nose. 'With Richard dead, the de Bohuns are dangerously weak. They might think Meonbridge is in safe hands but, from what you said, Margaret's too old, and that bailiff of hers far too young and inexperienced, to run such a great estate.'

'Not just Meonbridge, but all the other manors. And it'll be years before the brat inherits.'

Morys nodded. 'Ten years. And, in the meantime, if the estates aren't given strong direction, they'll go to wrack and ruin. What Meonbridge needs is us.'

'So we need a plan to lay our hands on it.'

'And how hard can that be, with only a boy and his old grandma standing in our way?'

'We shouldn't underestimate the de Bohuns, Pa. And it would be better if our claim bore at least some suspicion of eligibility.' Thorkell grinned. 'So whatever we do to spirit the boy away needs to be carefully planned.'

'And you have such a plan?'

'Not yet. As I said before, I thought I'd get some inside help.' Thorkell's eyes glinted. 'So the time's come at last to pay a visit to the bewitching Mistress Fletcher.'

13

M atilda threw her embroidery onto the floor. It was the petulant behaviour of a child but, for Heaven's sake, she *felt* petulant.

Libby was playing with her little family of cloth dolls – somewhat unkindly, as was her wont. She tutted. 'Mama, is your 'broidery being naughty?'

Matilda couldn't help but smile. 'Yes, poppet, it is – *very* naughty, just like your dollies.'

Libby giggled. 'I have to smack them when they're bad.'

'Sadly, my sewing won't get any better if I smack it.' She got up from her chair and went across to her daughter. Hitching up the hem of her gown, she crouched down on the floor. 'It's a bit like you.'

Libby giggled again. 'I don't like being smacked.'

'Nor does anyone, poppet.'

Neither does it work, she thought. It doesn't with Libby, and it hadn't with Dickon, who, according to his grandmother, behaved much better now he was more often away from his doting mother.

Matilda gazed fondly at her daughter. She'd miss Dickon when he left Meonbridge to start his training. Not that she played so much with Dickon these days. For even though, since Sir Richard's death, Dickon spent more time here at the manor, he didn't come to play with Libby.

Margaret had assigned Piers Arundale, one of Richard's squires, to keep in more or less constant attendance on Dickon and prepare him for his page training. Libby was still allowed to spend a little time with him, but no more than two or three times a week.

Matilda knew Agnes had declared – though never to Matilda's face – that Libby was a bad influence on Dickon, that she encouraged him to "run wild" as she put it. But it seemed that Margaret was willing enough to ignore Agnes's preposterous claims and allowed the two companions a little time together before Dickon left Meonbridge for good.

As if Libby was reading her mother's thoughts, she looked up. 'Is Dickon coming today, Mama?'

'I don't know, poppet. He may be busy getting ready to go away—'

Libby pouted. 'Why does he have to go?'

Matilda got up from the floor and went over to the window. It wasn't open, because of the cold and rain, but she knew well enough what lay beyond the cloudy horn infills of the panes. Because Dickon's going to be lord of Meonbridge, she thought, but did not say out loud. And yet, he's not *truly* entitled...

'*Why*, Mama?' repeated Libby, slapping the head of one of her dolls against the floor.

Matilda turned. 'Because his grandmama wants him to train to become a knight.'

Libby gave a nod. 'Dickon will like that.'

And Matilda could not but agree.

Dinner was, as usual, a dull affair. The cook undoubtedly did his best but, Matilda knew, Margaret had lost all interest in food since Sir Richard's passing, and was perhaps not giving the kitchen as much direction as she used to. For Matilda, a tasteless meal was just another moment of tedium to add to the succession of tedious moments that made up her days. Today, she couldn't even go outside for a walk, with the rain lashing against the walls and windows. But at least Margaret returned to the solar for the afternoon. Not that, these days, she often wanted Matilda's company, preferring, it seemed, to sit silently with her own thoughts or doze away an hour or two – as she was doing now, snoring and restless in her chair.

Matilda picked up a small book of hours that Margaret had loaned her in an attempt to provide her with some occupation other than the sewing she so much loathed. She turned the pages and read a few lines of a psalm but, although she *could* read, she didn't find it easy, or of much interest.

She lifted her eyes and glanced across to where Libby had been playing this morning. The child at least was happy now, for Dickon had come for dinner and, afterwards, they stayed together down in the hall, under Piers's watchful eye, to race up and down on their stick horses, yelling and laughing, pretending to be jousting knights.

Matilda's eyes flickered back to the book resting open in her lap. She reread the lines of the psalm, then managed another two or three lines before Margaret snuffled in her sleep, and Matilda's attention was again diverted, and she looked up.

This life was almost unbearable…

But moments later there came a knock upon the solar door, and Agatha, Margaret's maid, entered the room. Seeing that her mistress was asleep, she clicked her tongue softly, then glanced over at Matilda. 'What d'you reckon, missus, can I wake her?'

'Oh, I should think so,' said Matilda. 'She's only dozing.'

Agatha nodded, and tapped Margaret lightly on the arm. 'M'lady?'

Margaret grunted, but did not wake up until Agatha had repeated both her question and the tap. Then Margaret awoke with a little start and looked around her in an apparent daze. 'Oh, my goodness, was I asleep?'

'You do still need your rest, m'lady.'

Margaret nodded. 'Perhaps I do.' She looked up at her maid. 'Am I needed, Agatha?'

'Yes, m'lady, Missus Fletcher's got a visitor.'

Margaret told Agatha to ask Thorkell Boune to await them in the hall. 'We shall be down shortly. Mistress Fletcher needs to compose herself.'

She raised her eyebrows at Matilda, who was already light-headed with excitement, and found herself grinning like an imbecile. She couldn't believe that this moment had come, that Thorkell had actually come back to see her when, in truth, she'd thought he never would return.

Although it was true that Thorkell had paid her *some* attention during his first brief visit, Matilda had since persuaded herself that it had meant nothing. Yet she had still harboured longings, both for Thorkell the man, and for what he might be able to bring her...

And here he was. Come, Agatha said, to visit *her*.

Margaret became a little flustered, perhaps because, Matilda noticed, her wimple had come adrift from her greying hair during her restless dozing. Agatha fussed around her, helping to put the headdress straight. But Matilda was so excited that she ignored Margaret's plight. She ran from the room, along the solar passage that gave onto a number of small sleeping chambers and entered the one she shared with Libby.

She would have liked to change her kirtle from the rather old and faded blue one she was wearing, but there was no time. She decided to make do with covering most of it with her new green sideless surcoat. Throwing open the lid of the chest where her clothes and Libby's were kept, she lifted the surcoat out. It was not too crumpled, and the rich emerald would enhance the pale blue. And, if Sire Raphael was to be believed, it might also enhance her attractiveness to Thorkell.

Raphael wasn't unkindly like the previous priest, the odious Hugo Garret, but she had heard him proclaim a while ago in church that the new style of surcoat encouraged wantonness, as the wide side openings, he claimed, inspired men to peer beneath the outer garment, to stare at the shapely curves clad in a tight-fitting kirtle. But what did Sire Raphael, of all men, know of fashion, or indeed of women's curves? Whilst Thorkell, surely, would admire her sense of style and, if the priest was right, might also stare at her and, she hoped, find her utterly beguiling.

When Matilda was satisfied with her appearance, she crept down the staircase that led from the solar into the hall. Margaret and Thorkell were standing together next to the hearth, Thorkell warming himself with his back to the fire. Margaret was speaking, but Thorkell's face seemed to be creased into a frown. But, as Matilda approached, he turned towards her, and his face unfolded into a smile, which he held as he watched her cross the hall to join them.

Margaret, too, turned, but Matilda thought her face looked troubled. 'Master Boune,' said Margaret, 'has been offering his, and his father's, condolences for Sir Richard's death.'

Thorkell nodded, frowning again. 'It's distressing, your ladyship, that my visits to Meonbridge have been in the wake of two such tragic losses.'

'Indeed,' said Margaret, and held her hand out to Matilda, who took it and stepped forward. 'But I am sure that Matilda is delighted to see you again, even if your visit must be brief.'

Matilda couldn't help but blush, and she dropped a brief curtsey to hide her discomposure. When she looked up again, Thorkell was smiling at her.

'I would suggest a stroll in the garden,' said Margaret, gesturing vaguely to the door that led outside onto the bailey, 'but that would hardly be suitable in this dreadful weather.' She laughed lightly but Matilda could tell that she was troubled by Thorkell's return to Meonbridge.

'Instead,' continued Margaret, 'I shall leave you two young people here, so that you can talk. You will be quite private, at least until the servants come in to set out supper.' Her lips widened into the briefest of smiles, then she hurried away towards the kitchens.

'Shall we sit?' said Thorkell, gesturing towards a cushioned bench. Matilda nodded and, gliding across, sat down.

So, Margaret had placed no ban on conversation. Surely she hadn't already forgotten Sir Richard's concerns? Matilda couldn't help but smirk at the thought, and Thorkell noticed.

'Is something amusing you?'

Matilda's hand flew to her mouth. 'Oh, no. I am just so happy to see you again.'

'As I had anticipated.' He grinned and, if Matilda thought his comment arrogant, she didn't care.

Sitting side by side with Thorkell on the bench, Matilda found it awkward to look at him. She wished now she had suggested they sit opposite each other at the table. But, turning her head, she was able to glance at his face, and saw again the pale blue eyes and gleaming flaxen hair, the strong mouth and fine straight nose.

Then, feeling her face aglow, she quickly turned away again, and let her gaze fall upon her lap. Her heart was thumping, and she wanted to speak, but couldn't think of anything to say. The only thought in her head was how very handsome Thorkell was, but that was hardly a suitable topic for conversation. Mortified by her unaccustomed shyness, Matilda kept her face averted, hoping that Thorkell would be bolder.

And indeed, his next action was to shuffle closer to her and take her hand. He lifted it to his lips and kissed each of her fingers lightly. 'How very lovely you are, Matilda,' he said, leaning his face close to hers and whispering in her ear.

The kisses sent a thrill of excitement surging through Matilda's body. Then, when Thorkell put his other hand through the side opening of her surcoat and placed it on her narrow waist, Matilda thought that she might faint.

'Do you like my new surcoat?' she gasped, feeling foolish the moment the words were out.

Thorkell grinned again. 'It's quite revealing.' Matilda caught her breath, wondering if the priest had been right after all, and she'd already encouraged Thorkell to overstep the mark.

'But delightfully so,' he continued, and lightly squeezed her waist, before withdrawing his hand and easing himself back away from her. He crossed one knee over the other and, resting his elbow on his thigh, put his chin into his hand and stared at her face.

'So, Mistress Fletcher, I would know everything there is to know about you. What can you tell me?'

Matilda was at first quite flummoxed by Thorkell's request, at once thinking there was nothing of any interest in her life to tell. Yet she soon found herself relating tales about herself that were not entirely within the realms of reality. Of course, she started with the truth – the simple fact of her widowhood, and the birth of her beloved daughter, then the great kindness and generosity of Sir Richard and Lady de

Bohun when they gave her a home and an occupation. But exactly *how* she lost her husband, and *why* the de Bohuns felt they needed to be generous, and how *tedious* she found her role as Margaret's companion – all of that she either ignored or found a way of embellishing the basic truth with some colourful invention.

And, if Thorkell suspected she was not quite telling him the truth about herself, he did not show it. He nodded and expressed sympathy in all the appropriate places, and Matilda thought he must have accepted the picture she had painted of her life.

So now it was her turn to ask.

'My life's not so genteel as your own,' he said, 'but you'd hardly expect it to be so. I spend most of my time helping my father and brother manage their estates.'

'Which I suppose are vast?'

'Indeed. The domains are principally in Herefordshire, but some extend far beyond the border country into Wales.'

Matilda had no idea where either Herefordshire or Wales might be, though she thought Margaret had said that Castle Boune was several days' ride north of Meonbridge. However, not wanting to seem stupid, she affected an air of understanding.

'But they are, of course, not mine,' Thorkell continued. 'They're my father's and will, in time, pass to my brother Gunnar.'

Matilda grinned. 'Fortunate Gunnar.'

Thorkell returned her grin. 'But my father will ensure I do have estates of my own, albeit small ones. I'll not go without.'

She thought how phlegmatic Thorkell seemed about his position, not minding that his inheritance would be small, when his brother Gunnar's was apparently so large. It was the way things were – the eldest child always claimed the main prize, leaving his younger siblings to make good marriages, or earn themselves a living, or simply settle for less. But she'd have thought Thorkell was not the sort of man to be content with less, if *more* might somehow be available, one way or another.

She tilted her head. 'But it will be a while before you come into your inheritance?'

Thorkell shook his head. 'My father's already assigned two of his smaller Herefordshire manors to me, with Gunnar's agreement, so I could establish my own domain before too long.'

Matilda nodded, but then Thorkell leaned towards her. 'But before I do, I've been thinking I should marry, and establish a dynasty as well as a domain.' His handsome mouth widened into the broadest of smiles. 'Gunnar's betrothed already to a Welsh princess and intends to settle down with her quite soon.'

'A princess?' said Matilda, her eyes wide.

'Well, the spawn of a nobleman.' Thorkell snorted. 'Gunnar likes to call her a princess.'

Matilda laughed. 'I see.' She tilted her head again. 'So you'd like to settle down as well?'

Thorkell's expression became instantly charming and boyish, and Matilda felt her insides turn to liquid, and her head was full of cloud. Was he really suggesting that he might want to marry *her*? Did Thorkell want her, as much as she wanted him?

And, if he did, well, that was wonderful, of course, because at least she'd have Thorkell *the man*. But two small manors, somewhere far away in the north of England, did sound rather disappointing. Not the wealth and status she'd imagined Thorkell bringing her. And hardly a substitute for Meonbridge.

Wondering if she should say what she was truly thinking, Matilda sprang up from the bench and strolled in a small circle about the room. When she came back towards the bench, she smiled at Thorkell, but remained a few paces away from him, running her hands up and down the skirts of her gown and surcoat, as if trying to smooth out the creases.

Thorkell's cheerful face was frowning a little. 'Do you wish to walk, Matilda?'

She shook her head. 'I would, if we could go outside. I do so love to walk in her ladyship's delightful gardens. But no, I'm happy to sit here with you.' And she sat down again, her hands clasped together in her lap.

If Matilda looked calm enough, her mind was in a whirl. Should she speak out or not? Thorkell believed that Dickon was the legitimate heir to Meonbridge, but *she* knew the boy wasn't truly entitled to inherit. Whereas Thorkell's father was. And, if Thorkell knew the truth, he'd surely be delighted to discover that Meonbridge – and all the de Bohun estates – were really *Boune* domains.

She turned to face him and smiled again. His eyes were bright now, as if he was waiting for her to speak. She gave a little cough, still undecided, but then launched into a paean of praise for the place she'd lived in all her life, disregarding the fact that, for her, it had actually been a most unhappy place for much of the past seven years or more.

Thorkell seemed to enjoy the charming picture that she painted and agreed that Meonbridge was not only undoubtedly a pleasant place to live, but was certainly a magnificent estate, one of many, he understood, amongst the de Bohun domains.

Matilda nodded. 'I've not visited any of the others, but Sir Richard surely would have kept them all well-managed.' She paused. 'But isn't your father heir to Meonbridge?'

'Only after young Dickon, and any sons he might produce when he's grown.'

'But, if Dickon *couldn't* inherit,' continued Matilda, 'your father would be first in line?'

Thorkell's eyes widened. 'Well, yes. But why might the boy be unable to inherit?'

Matilda laced her fingers together, then unlaced them again. 'I'm not sure I should tell you. Yet it *is* the truth—'

'What is?'

She didn't answer and stared down at her lap. Surely she'd already gone too far to turn back now? And, if she told Thorkell the truth, wouldn't that convince him she'd be honest and loyal as a wife?

'Matilda?'

She faced him again. 'The truth is,' she said, keeping her voice low, 'Dickon can't be Sir Richard's *legitimate* heir, for he isn't legitimately born. He's Philip's son, for sure, but not his wife's. Poor Isabella died in the Mortality, taking her unborn baby with her. Dickon's real mother is Agnes, the wife of the carpenter, Jack Sawyer.'

As her explanation unfolded, Thorkell nodded slowly, and his eyebrows arched. When she had finished, he leaned forward and took her hand.

'Thank you, sweet Matilda, for being so candid. It seems that, first, Sir Richard, and now, Lady de Bohun, have perpetrated a wicked lie.'

Matilda nodded. 'With the *best* of intentions,' she said, pleased with his response, yet already uncertain if she'd done the right thing.

'But a lie nonetheless...' Thorkell leaned closer. 'In truth, Matilda, Gunnar and I both suspected that what Sir Richard told us was not quite right. For when he said the boy was his *rightful* heir, both you and Lady de Bohun looked astonished, and we noticed.'

'So is it true that bastards can't inherit?' said Matilda.

'I believe so.'

'Nor nuns?' She smiled and Thorkell reciprocated. 'And do you think your father would press his claim to Meonbridge?'

'He has many domains already, but I daresay he'd consider it. After all, the de Bohun estates are highly valuable.'

Matilda realised that her heart was thumping, and it wasn't because Thorkell's leg was pressing against hers. She knew she had just upset Sir Richard's plans, *and* put Margaret in danger of eviction from her home. She wondered what would happen to Lady de Bohun if – when – the Bounes took over Meonbridge, but she had no answer to the question.

14

NORTHWICK PRIORY

FEBRUARY 1357

I n all the seven years that Johanna had been sequestered in the priory, Margaret had never visited her there. As much as she would have liked to see her daughter, Margaret had relied on John atte Wode to take and bring back any news. But when Johanna – Sister Rosa – visited Meonbridge following Richard's death, she seemed to have changed her mind about her need for absolute seclusion from the world.

In fact, Margaret thought her daughter was altogether changed from the girl who had left home in order to become a nun. Then she had been melancholy, self-deprecating, miserable and fey, a girl who wanted to hide herself away from the world and spend her life in prayer. But now she was cheerful, self-confident and assertive. Still most prayerful, surely, but perhaps her prayers these days would be full of joy instead of guilt? But Johanna's – Rosa's – change of demeanour most strongly showed in her decision to involve herself in her family's concerns, despite her no longer having any claim to the estates, and to support her mother in the difficult task ahead of her.

Margaret knew that Johanna – no, she really must learn to call her

Rosa! – was angry with her father for placing his family in such a difficult position. Yet, despite her horror at Richard's overt lie, Rosa seemed determined to remain calm and manage the situation as best she could. Seven years ago and more, Margaret had believed her daughter almost despised her, reckoning her judgement lacking, especially in her attitude towards their tenants, which she considered too soft-hearted. Margaret recalled how dismissive the girl had been of her attempts at reconciliation with the tenants during the riots that followed the Mortality. Instead, she revered and honoured her father and even more so, her long-dead brother. Yet now, Margaret supposed, Richard's judgement had been called into question, even in the opinion of his doting daughter.

When, on the day of Richard's funeral, Margaret had told Rosa of her intention to throw herself upon the mercy of the tenants – as she put it – and bring the supposed secret of Dickon's heritage out into the open, she might have expected that her daughter would, at best, consider it a risky proposition.

Margaret had mentioned too her conversation with Lady de Courtenay, and her fear of the consequences of the secret simply slipping out. For Hildegard had hinted, quite reasonably, that everyone in Meonbridge might already *know* that Dickon was Philip's son and not Jack Sawyer's.

'But the tenants do not know that Richard accepted Dickon as his grandson,' said Margaret. 'And I would prefer to tell them of his decision to make the boy his heir.' Rosa shook her head, but she continued. 'Surely they will want to support us, after all the decades that de Bohuns have been at Meonbridge?'

Rosa bit her bottom lip. 'I appreciate your reasoning, Mother, but I do not share your confidence in the tenants' affections for our family.' She gave her a wan smile.

Margaret nodded feebly. 'If not affection, then, perhaps a recognition of where their own advantage lies? Surely they would wish to know that their future here is safe in my hands, and then in Dickon's?' She frowned. 'As I think it would not be if Morys Boune became the lord of Meonbridge.'

Rosa had shrugged. 'I agree with that, despite having little knowledge of our cousins. But Dickon is so young, Mother, and has so much to learn, that I do not believe that offering *him* as the future saviour of Meonbridge will bear much weight. That he is also only half a de Bohun and therefore not a *legitimate* heir cannot be gainsaid.'

She was right, of course. Yet, in the dreadful position she found herself, Margaret wanted the support of the tenants, many of whom she had known since they were children. She had always thought of the Meonbridge people as part of the de Bohun family. Richard and, even more so, Philip, considered her deluded and sentimental. And she imagined her daughter had thought much the same. And when the tenants rose up against Richard after the Mortality, it had seemed that they were all quite right that, far from feeling affection for their lord, the tenants *hated* him. Yet, after Philip's murder, and then when Richard at last resolved the villagers' complaints, Meonbridge did settle down once more into relative contentment.

Rosa remained doubtful of the wisdom of Margaret's plan, but she agreed at length that, if her mother was determined upon it, she would support her. When Margaret made the announcement to the tenants gathered in the bailey after the formalities of the funeral were over, she discovered that many of them seemed surprised by the news that the Sawyer boy was in fact her grandson, even though it was also clear that some others, if just a few, did already know the truth. Whether everyone was pleased at her announcement, she could not tell. But, all the same, she felt satisfied that, at least, she had told them the truth. She had been honest with them.

Or, perhaps, not completely honest.

For what she had not said was that, because of that very truth, the lives of everyone in Meonbridge could now be in danger.

Given her daughter's change of attitude towards her family, Margaret thought she might not object if her mother paid her a visit at the priory. Her excuse for the visit was finalising the matter of Dickon's future and their estates. She wanted to ensure that her daughter fully understood and was in agreement with her plans.

So Margaret sent a message to the priory requesting permission from both Sister Rosa and Mother Angelica, and was delighted – and perhaps just a little surprised – when they suggested that she accompany John on his next visit.

The journey was not very long – only ten miles – but, at this time of year, the roads became indefinable, ankle deep in mud, and the potholes, already full of rainwater, were gouged even deeper by relentless rain and careless wheels. If he had gone alone, John would have ridden, as he always did. But, when Margaret suggested she did the same, he scoffed.

'What would Sister Rosa think of me, if I allowed her lady mother to make such a disagreeable journey on horseback? No, my lady, I've already ordered up the carriage. Even that will be uncomfortable, given the condition of the roads, but at least you will be dry.'

Margaret held up her hands. 'You are right, John. My poor old body would hardly bear such a long, unpleasant ride.'

As it was, by the time she reached Northwick, Margaret's head was throbbing so badly that she had wrenched her wimple from her hair to relieve the pressure of the fillet band against her brow. And, when John opened the rain-soaked flap at the end of the carriage and held out his hand to help her climb down, she could hardly rise from the seat, for her back seemed to be locked into a painful spasm, and her legs declined to shift at all.

Even once she was settled in the priory's comfortable, if somewhat narrow, guest chamber, Margaret still felt wretched and collapsed into the single softly-cushioned chair. Had she been unwise after all to attempt the journey, when it really was not necessary? John could easily enough have relayed the information to and from Johanna. But Margaret had long harboured a wish to see precisely how her daughter was faring in her newly elevated position in the priory, and she chose to ignore her inner warnings.

Foolish old woman! She thought it, and suspected that her daughter would think it too.

It had been agreed that she and John would stay for two nights at the priory. Margaret might have wished it could be longer, to give her poor body more time to recover, but John had to get back to Meonbridge, for his bailiff's responsibilities were arduous and many. So, despite the stiffening in her limbs, Margaret forced herself to get up from the chair, and smoothed down her gown. She replaced her headdress, wishing that the megrim would stop pounding in her temples. But she had to ignore the pain and go to see her daughter.

She found little Sister Juliana outside the door of the tiny chamber, waiting to escort her, and Margaret followed the young nun along a maze of corridors to the room that served as Northwick's administrative office.

When Sister Juliana ushered Margaret into the room, Rosa came forward to greet her mother. She asked Juliana to fetch John and then bring a little watered wine. Then she took Margaret by the hand and drew her over to another cushioned chair.

'John tells me that you found the journey wearisome, Mother,' said Rosa, adjusting the cushion behind Margaret's back.

Margaret smiled thinly. 'I had forgotten how very uncomfortable our carriage is. I find the prospect of the return journey quite dispiriting.' She gave a little laugh. 'Perhaps I should just stay here as your permanent guest?'

Rosa let out a gasp. 'But, Mother—'

Margaret tittered despite her aching head. 'Oh, my poor girl. That was only my little jest, Jo...Rosa. I apologise if I alarmed you.'

Rosa then joined in her mother's laughter, although her cheeks were a little flushed. 'Of course not, Mother. I was just surprised.'

'Nonetheless, I hardly *could* stay here,' continued Margaret, 'when I have so much work to do in Meonbridge.'

Rosa nodded and, at that moment, Juliana returned with John and the wine. Rosa dismissed the young nun and poured three cups of the diluted Burgundy.

'Here, Mother,' she said, handing her a cup, 'this should help you to revive a little.'

John accepted a cup as well. 'So you've moved out of the Mother Prioress's chamber, Sister Rosa?'

'Yes, I had begun to realise that carrying out all my work in her private chamber placed too great a burden on the Reverend Mother. So I found this little room, to which I can retreat when Mother Angelica needs to rest.'

John grinned. 'So this is *your* domain, Madam Deputy Prioress.'

Rosa tutted and shook her head. 'I do not think of it that way, John. I simply wanted to do what was best for the Reverend Mother.'

At which John nodded, then turned to Margaret. 'My lady, shall we tell Sister Rosa the details of our plans?'

Margaret agreed and gestured to John to speak. He told Rosa that he, with an escort of armed men, would accompany Dickon to Courtenay Castle in eight days' time.

'And the de Courtenays are happy with this arrangement, Mother?'

Margaret beamed. 'Oh, yes, they were thrilled to have the boy.'

'Despite not one drop of their blood running in his veins?' Rosa's eyebrows arched towards the edge of her crisp white wimple.

Margaret felt her cheeks flush a little. Hugh and Hildegard had agreed to take the boy, but they – or at least Hildegard – were hardly happy with the arrangement. She was lying once again – to her own daughter, and to a deputy prioress. She took a sip of her wine. 'I have not asked them to say that Dickon is their grandson. Just not to say openly that he is not. To keep the truth of the boy's mother simply unstated, in the hope that no one in Surrey will be any the wiser.'

Rosa's eyebrows were still arched.

'In truth,' continued Margaret, 'Hildegard is not entirely content, but Hugh has convinced her that they should help us in our time of tribulation.'

'A messenger has been sent to the de Courtenays to warn them of Dickon's arrival,' said John.

'Good,' said Rosa. 'I am glad that the child will at least be well out of the Bounes' reach. I remember how well fortified Courtenay Castle is. I assume the Bounes know nothing of the de Courtenays?'

Margaret flushed again. They did, of course. She recalled the conversation with the Bounes, when Gunnar had told them he had once known Isabella's brother. Perhaps they were still in contact with each other? She took several more sips of wine, drained the cup, then held it out for more. John sprang forward and poured.

'What is it, Mother?' said Rosa. 'You look troubled.'

Margaret had to tell her about Gunnar. Rosa became a little agitated and paced the floor of the small chamber. She stopped in front of her mother. 'Well, I suppose we must hope that they have lost touch since boyhood.' She frowned. 'Do they know that Dickon is going to Courtenay Castle?'

Margaret shook her head. 'I do not believe so. What is your view, John?'

'Not sure, m'lady.' He turned to Rosa. 'They've not been told – but they might've heard somehow.'

Rosa pursed her lips. 'Very well. There is nothing we can do about it now. We must trust in God to keep the child safe from harm.'

After imbibing four cups of watered wine, Margaret felt a little drowsy, and accepted Rosa's suggestion that she rest a while in her chamber. 'John and I have much to discuss,' said Rosa. 'I have some ideas for making changes to the way the priory estate is run and need his advice.'

Margaret was glad of the opportunity to lie down. The journey – and perhaps a little too much wine – had left her feeling quite exhausted.

When she awoke to find Sister Juliana gently tapping on her shoulder, Margaret learned that it was already time for supper, and felt ashamed that she had slept so long.

'You were sleeping so deeply, your ladyship,' said Juliana, 'that I didn't want to wake you. But Sister Rosa said we couldn't let you miss supper.'

She smiled sweetly, and Margaret held out an arm for the young nun to help her up from the hard, narrow bed. Margaret straightened her wimple as best she could, before following Juliana along a different maze of corridors to the refectory. The priory's permanent residents were already seated at the single long table, with Mother Angelica at one end and Rosa at the other. John was seated on Rosa's left, and Margaret could see that there were two empty places to her right, presumably for herself and Juliana. As Juliana led her to the table, the other nuns were talking amongst themselves, merrily enough but quietly. Juliana helped Margaret to slide onto the end of the bench that stretched the length of the table, and then she dropped a brief curtsey towards the Mother Prioress before lifting the hem of her habit a little in order to climb over the bench into her place between Margaret and a rather stern-faced, scrawny woman, who, alone amongst the group, was silent, with her eyes closed and her hands clasped together in her lap.

As soon as the latecomers were seated, Rosa uttered a brief prayer then nodded to the waiting servants, who promptly served the meal.

Margaret leaned towards her daughter. 'I am so sorry to have kept you all waiting. I had no idea that I had slept so long.'

Rosa shook her head. 'No matter, Mother. We have only just finished reciting Vespers. And it does us no harm to wait.'

The stern-faced nun must have overheard her, for Margaret saw her open her eyes and knit her brow at Rosa, who merely returned the scowl with a sunny smile.

As the simple meal proceeded – just dry bread, with a little cheese, and plenty of weak ale – Rosa whispered to her mother, telling her the names of all the nuns and their roles in the priory.

The stern-faced nun was Sister Evangelina, the sacrist, whilst a portly, rather pretty woman with a merry laugh was Sister Beatrice, the cellarer. 'She loves her food,' whispered Rosa, leaning close to Margaret's ear and, when she leaned back again, her eyes were bright.

It seemed to Margaret that her daughter was very happy here. As she looked around the table at Rosa's fellow sisters, she thought that Evangelina was the only one who appeared at all ill-tempered. Two of the younger nuns seemed somewhat dull-spirited, but the others, including the aged Mother Prioress, and two rather bent and wrinkled ladies who were clearly even older, had shining eyes and smiling mouths.

And Rosa herself was bright-faced and vigorous, and Margaret thought that her nun's habit seemed to frame her joy with life rather than conceal it. For a moment, she wished that Richard had seen how satisfactory their daughter's decision had proved to be.

Rosa linked her arm through Margaret's as they strolled around the cloister for a while after supper, before returning to Margaret's little chamber. Margaret's heart lifted at her daughter's touch. She would have liked to take the young woman in her arms and hug her to her breast, as Johanna used to permit many years ago, when she was still a child. But she marshalled her emotions and urged herself to be contented with this small gesture of her daughter's affection.

When they arrived back at the guest chamber, Margaret lowered herself into the cushioned chair, whilst Rosa perched on the hard edge of the meagre bed. She leaned forward and patted the back of Rosa's hand.

'Do tell me, my dear,' she said, almost in a whisper, 'a little more about the rather dour Sister Evangelina. Everyone here seems so full of joy, all except for her.'

Rosa pursed her lips. 'Ah, you noticed, Mother, that dear Evangelina seems not quite as content with her life at Northwick as the other sisters.'

'Why is she so unhappy?'

'I regret to say that it is my fault that she is so.'

Margaret gasped. 'Your fault? But how can that be?'

'Because, Mother, Evangelina has been at Northwick for thirty years. She has held many of the priory's offices and, for the past six or seven years, has undertaken what has recently proved the most arduous role of sacrist—'

Margaret raised an eyebrow. She knew nothing of priory administration.

'She is responsible,' continued Rosa, 'for every aspect of our church. All the valuables inside it and the vestments are hers to care for but, most important and, lately, most burdensome, she has been attending to the building itself. The tower fell into serious disrepair several years ago and has demanded much money and effort for the restoration. It has been the most onerous of tasks.'

'But you said it was *your* fault that she is gloomy...'

Rosa sighed. 'And I was coming to the reason for it. For, until the Reverend Mother asked me to assist her in her daily duties, three years ago or so, Evangelina thought herself the most likely of the senior sisters to step into the Reverend Mother's shoes when...' she crossed herself, '...when our dear Angelica passes into Paradise.'

'But she now thinks that you have usurped that position?'

Rosa nodded. 'Though it was never my intention, or desire, to wrest the role from her. It must be so vexing for her, a woman in her fifties, to see one more than twenty years her junior apparently taking from her what she considers rightfully hers.'

'But you are not—'

'No, indeed, Mother, I am *not*. And, in truth, I *will* not – when that sad time comes – lay claim to the role of prioress over Evangelina. Except...'

'Except?'

'I am afraid that the other senior sisters, Amata, Beatrice, and the others – and even more so the younger nuns – find Evangelina brusque and overbearing and I think they are most unlikely to choose her to replace our patient, gentle, warm-hearted Reverend Mother.'

'But they would choose you?'

Rosa shook her head. '*Evangelina* thinks so. But, unless dear Mother Angelica lives for many more years, I will still be too young to accept such a position. No, Amata or Beatrice would be much better suited.' Then she let a smile blossom. 'It is a difficult situation. One that I neither sought nor know how best to deal with.' Then she laughed. 'It is hardly a cause for merriment, but Evangelina has so convinced herself of something that really is not true that the other sisters giggle about her behind her back. Most uncharitable behaviour, I know. I try to talk to her about it but she always spurns my approaches. So my only recourse is to pray for her, that God might soothe her resentment, and reveal to her that I am not the rival to her heart's desire that she imagines.'

Rosa's good spirits dissolved when she asked Margaret for some brief snippets of news from Meonbridge.

'I cannot stay much longer,' she said, 'as it will soon be time for Compline.'

Margaret at once felt flustered and could not think what "news" might interest her daughter. And, with little time in which to consider what to say, she found herself talking about Matilda and her visit from Thorkell Boune. But, as soon as she had begun the story, she realised it was a mistake for, before she had even explained what happened, Rosa's smile had faded and she had flown into a temper – not unlike those she had displayed as a young girl back in Meonbridge.

'Mother, how could you let that man back into the manor?' she cried. 'Especially to see Matilda.'

Margaret quailed, upset by the swift change in her daughter's humour. 'But what was I to do? Of course I was worried when he turned up unannounced. I went down to meet him ahead of Matilda, thinking that I should tell him to leave, yet I could not think of a polite excuse for sending him away.'

Rosa tutted, and Margaret plucked at her skirts. 'Then he offered his condolences for Richard's death—'

Rosa shook her head and Margaret wrung her hands. 'I did not welcome him warmly,' she said, feeling foolish. 'But I did not know what else to do.'

'Surely, Mother, you knew it was dangerous for him to return to Meonbridge?'

'But he was so charming—'

'The serpent in Paradise was charming, Mother.'

Margaret nodded. Rosa was right. But it was always easier to realise later that you could have handled something better, than it was to handle it well at the time.

'When Matilda came downstairs, she was so thrilled to see him that I could not help but be pleased for her. Poor Matilda has been so miserable. I think she regrets not accepting any of the suitors your father found for her. I have always felt rather sorry for the girl, for she had such an unhappy life, with her overbearing father and cruel husband. Which is why I persuaded your father to let her stay with us until she found another husband. Although I did not imagine that it would take so long.' She raised her eyes to Rosa and gave her a wry grin.

'In truth, Mother,' said Rosa, 'I never understood why you and Father were so generous, given that it was Matilda's father who murdered Philip. Although I will admit that I have become much less bitter towards her, as I have come to learn the blessings of mercy and forgiveness.' She paused. 'But, now, I simply have a great sense of unease about her interest in Thorkell Boune.'

Margaret slumped back into the cushioned chair, feeling weary once again.

'I suppose I thought that it could not hurt, to let Matilda spend a few hours with him, if it would bring her a little happiness.'

Rosa nodded. 'I do understand that, Mother. But the Bounes are dangerous, can you not see? If they find out the truth about Dickon, you can be sure they will press their claim to Meonbridge. And I am afraid I do not trust Matilda not to tell Thorkell.'

Margaret gasped. 'You think she would *deliberately* betray us?'

Rosa shook her head. 'Not necessarily, but I am certainly fearful that the truth might just slip out. You know how Matilda loves to gossip. She might simply forget that it is something that should be kept a secret from the Bounes.'

Margaret was now both bemused and worried. She had not thought of Matilda as in any way a threat. But Rosa was right that she was much prone to gossip, for Margaret had often spotted her hiding behind an arras or a door, presumably eavesdropping on some conversation.

Rosa sat back down upon the bed and took her mother's hand. 'So why do you think Thorkell came, Mother?'

Margaret hesitated a moment before she answered. 'To woo Matilda?'

Rosa laughed. 'You truly think that? Surely Thorkell Boune would not be interested in marrying Matilda, for she has nothing to offer, neither status nor money. He would surely hope for a much better match?'

Margaret did not answer. Rosa was of course quite right about that too.

'He must be using her,' continued Rosa. 'And who knows what she might tell him, whilst she enjoys his undoubtedly accomplished attentions?'

'Really, daughter, what do you know of a man's "attentions"?'

'All I need to.' She let go of her mother's hand and stood up. 'But that is not important. What is important, Mother, is that Matilda knows the truth about Dickon, and that she might reveal that knowledge in conversation with the man she will presumably think of as her suitor.'

Margaret nodded feebly. She felt overwhelmed by Rosa's argument. Why had she not considered all of this herself? She knew *something* was not right about Thorkell's visit, but the unlikelihood of him coming to Meonbridge to pay genuine court to Matilda had not occurred to her. Nor had the danger of Matilda letting slip the truth about young Dickon.

137

Rosa took a few paces around the little room and then came to stand before her mother. Margaret looked up at her daughter, feeling anxious and dull-witted. But Rosa crouched down before her and took her hands again. 'Mother, you must not allow that man to visit Matilda again.' Then she squeezed her mother's hands. 'I suggest that you marry her off to some wealthy old villein, and do it quickly.'

The journey back to Meonbridge was even more uncomfortable than before. Margaret was forced to keep grabbing at the struts in the wall of the carriage as it lurched from rut to rut, and she was thrown back and forth like kittens in a bucket. It did not help having to perch on the edge of the hard wooden seat, to relieve the agony in her back. Once or twice she had been almost tossed onto the floor, and the constant roll and weave was making her feel nauseous. Unsurprisingly, the megrim had returned and was throbbing at the left side of her head. She considered calling upon John to stop the carriage and let her rest a while but, as she had insisted on making this ridiculous journey, she thought it her duty to endure without complaint.

She tried instead to occupy her mind, thinking about her daughter's recommendation concerning poor Matilda. She understood Rosa's concern that it was a risk allowing Matilda to spend time with Thorkell Boune. Her own recent concern had been to ensure that all her tenants knew the truth about her grandson, but it was much trickier to determine how to ensure that the Bounes did *not* know that truth. For, once they did, her future and Dickon's would surely be undone. Yet she could see how easy it would be for Matilda to let slip the truth in conversation without intending to.

But how could she prevent Thorkell from visiting? What could she say to him? Perhaps she need not see him at all, but just leave instructions with the gatekeeper and seneschal that he was not to be admitted? Matilda need never know he had come to visit her again. If indeed he ever did.

In the meantime, she considered Rosa's advice to find a husband for Matilda from amongst Meonbridge's wealthier villeins. Not an "old" villein, as Rosa had rather uncharitably suggested, for there were surely at least one or two of middle age who might be suitable? Closing her eyes against the megrim's pounding, she tried to bring to mind those village men who were still widowed or unmarried. Two names emerged: Nicholas Cook and Adam Wragge, both prosperous men even before the Mortality. And, after the disease had killed half of Meonbridge's tenants, including Nicholas's and Adam's wives, each man took on many of the tracts of now untenanted land, and soon became two of the estate's most industrious and wealthy villeins. She pictured each man in turn, considering each as a potential suitor.

Although, in truth, the choice was obvious.

Nicholas had concentrated all his efforts on his land, much of it on the outskirts of the village, on the road to Middle Brooking, where the Gyffords used to farm. The entire Gyfford family had perished in the Mortality and it was Nicholas who annexed their substantial holdings to his own. But, if Nicholas had proved a successful farmer, he was less adept at caring for himself, and had allowed his person to deteriorate to the appearance of an unkempt and grubby vagrant. He had had a son, Margaret recalled, but the boy had died of a fever a year or two after the Mortality. Perhaps, she thought, Nicholas lost interest in his own person when he lost his only surviving child.

Adam, on the other hand, though the same age as Nicholas, was still a handsome man. He reminded Margaret a little of Matilda's long-dead father, Robert, in his upright bearing and well-groomed appearance, although Adam by no means shared Robert's unstable temperament or lust for power. After Robert's ignominious death, Adam, as one of the manor's wealthiest villeins, took over Robert's duties as bailiff. Then, last year, Richard promoted him to steward of all his estates, declaring him the most efficient and reliable of men. Margaret wondered now why Adam had not remarried for, despite his age, with his good looks, wealth and status there must surely be widows or even younger maids in Meonbridge who would welcome his advances.

But would Matilda?

15

CASTLE BOUNE

MARCH 1357

Gunnar grinned and their father guffawed when Thorkell told them Matilda's news. Thorkell shared their merriment. The brat's bastardy made their situation simpler. They wouldn't have to go to the trouble of disposing of him. If the boy had no entitlement to Meonbridge after all, the way was clear for Morys to make a legitimate claim.

Thorkell rewrapped his thick winter cloak about his chest and moved around the table to sit closer to the fire. Coming home again confirmed the desirability of winning Meonbridge. For Castle Boune was not a place of comfort. The hall was huge – his father had rebuilt it several years ago to be one of the largest, most impressive halls in Herefordshire. The four crucked arches soared high above the stone-flagged floor, higher than in any other hall he knew. But, if the room itself was impressive, the windows Morys had installed were tiny, leaving the hall dark even on a summer's day, and, in winter, bleak and dismal. And the single hearth, large as it was, failed to heat the vastness of the space. Today, as usual, the fire's warmth was pitiful. And intermittent billows of choking smoke wafted about the room before they found their way up to the rafters, whipped up by the draught whistling beneath the door that led in from outside.

Thorkell compared this gloomy place, which he now realised he'd *endured* for all his twenty-five years of living here, with the one he hoped would soon be his. The manor house at Meonbridge might be smaller than Castle Boune, but it was a model of comfort – lighter, warmer, with tapestries on the walls, and cushions on the chairs. He snorted: it was laughable that he might care a fig for cushions, but he'd recently discovered he had quite a taste for luxury.

After his initial happy outburst, Morys paced up and down the hall's stone floor, muttering to himself. Thorkell exchanged raised eyebrows with his brother, who shrugged. 'Maybe Pa's trying to keep warm,' said Gunnar, smirking.

'I heard that,' said Morys, swinging round and coming back to sit down with his sons. 'You milksops don't know the meaning of cold.' But he cackled and filled a mazer from the flagon of spiced wine standing on a trivet by the fire. 'So, Thorkell, why's this whore of yours blabbing de Bohun secrets?'

Thorkell winced. For the most part he held women in low esteem but, for some reason he didn't understand, he found Matilda sufficiently bewitching to resent his father calling her a whore.

But he said nothing and Gunnar guffawed. 'I told you, Pa, she's got a powerful itch for him. I reckon she's hoping that letting slip this little secret will give him some encouragement.'

'But can we trust her?' said Morys. 'Or is the wench just making mischief?'

He'd thought that himself. 'It's true I planned to woo her first, then ask her what she knew. So I did the wooing, but I didn't need to ask – she came right out with it. Perhaps we need to check that what she said is true?'

Gunnar nodded but Morys shrugged. 'Why bother with the truth, if we can win Meonbridge by our usual methods?'

Thorkell grunted. 'Because, Pa, if we win Meonbridge by *legal* means, I'll be able to hold the estate with integrity and honour—'

Gunnar almost choked, spraying a mouthful of wine across the table. 'Integrity! *You?*'

Thorkell glared at him. 'You've a problem with that?' Gunnar was snorting. 'Wouldn't you like to thwart them, Gunnar, those turds who said we didn't "fit"?'

He wasn't surprised when Gunnar stopped snorting and agreed, but even his father nodded.

'It's a shame Sir Dicky's no longer with us. I'd have enjoyed showing my pompous cousin he can't have everything his own way, just because he always has.'

'I'm sure you would, Pa. But, if we take our claim to court, you can be sure the de Bohun women will argue the brat's case. So we need to be certain of our position. If we fail and have to resort to our usual methods in the end, so be it. But let's try this first, eh, Pa?'

Morys nodded but was scratching at the coarse hair underneath his beard. 'Very well, but if your wench knows this secret, I might ask who else in Meonbridge knows?'

'Good point, Pa,' said Gunnar. 'Perhaps we could arrange for some questions to be asked.'

'And we could ask your old friend Baldwin de Courtenay,' said Thorkell, sneering.

Gunnar frowned. 'Why him?'

Thorkell grunted again. 'Because Matilda let slip another secret. Courtenay Castle's where the brat's been sent. And, if he *isn't* the de Courtenays' grandson, don't you think they'd show it in some way, under reasonable enquiry?'

'But we can hardly just turn up and ask them.'

'No, so we need to think of a good reason to pay him a visit.'

Despite his seeming confidence, Thorkell couldn't immediately think of a viable reason for him and Gunnar to visit Courtenay Castle. Of course, they could just ride down to Surrey, in the "usual" way, with a fully armed and belligerent retinue of followers, and do whatever they had to do to get an answer out of Baldwin. But if, ordinarily, Thorkell was impatient and pugnacious, this time he wanted to proceed with caution and prosecute his father's claim to Meonbridge in a measured way. He wanted to ensure that, when the Bounes at length presented their case to court, they appeared to be honourable and fair-minded, pursuing an inheritance that was *rightfully* theirs, and not improperly usurping it.

However, after several days devoid of inspiration, and frustrated at his own impotence, he was almost ready to give up his pursuit of dignity and honour, call out the company of men-at-arms, and ride hard to Surrey. It would be a risky venture, for Courtenay Castle was noted for the robustness of its hundred-year-old fortifications. The Bounes rarely launched a raid against a strongly-defended target, choosing rather to attack weak, unfortified manors that would fall easily to an unexpected and well-armed assault. Indeed, since Christmas, they'd made two such raids on lesser estates in Herefordshire and Wales, but the elation Thorkell used to experience when they acquired a new manor, or simply a tract of land, was wearing thin.

It was Meonbridge he wanted – nowhere else would do.

But, when Gunnar returned from a trip to Oxfordshire, a journey he made every few months to spend a couple of days with an old friend of his, he had an idea that cheered Thorkell up immensely.

It was a fact that Thorkell had few companions besides his brother Gunnar. His reputation, not only as a ruffian, but as an arrogant one, went before him, and the only men who'd drink with him were in his father's pay, together with a couple of young Herefordshire sons of gentry who shared his penchant for what he thought of as simply "making mischief".

Gunnar, on the other hand, was not short of friends, including Benedict Farrington, a fellow squire from his years at Sir Henry Blandefordde's. It was true Gunnar had been forced to leave Sir Henry's, only a year or two before he expected to be dubbed a knight, and all because of Thorkell's misdeeds – or rather, his criminality. And it was true too that, at first, he was rancorously bitter that his brother had ruined his career. But Gunnar was not one to harbour resentment and, as time passed, his rancour eased, aided by his continuing friendship with Benedict, who also failed to win his knighthood. This was not for any ignominious reason, but simply because he didn't make the grade. Both men regretted their failure, but chose not to let it trouble them unduly. For Benedict was, like Gunnar, an eldest son who would inherit his father's wealth and vast estates with or without a knightly title.

Gunnar rarely told Thorkell about his visits to Farrington Manor, but this time he had something of interest to relate.

'Remember,' he said, 'Baldwin de Courtenay was at Sir Henry's the same time as us—' Thorkell let out a snort, and Gunnar grinned. 'Yes, stupid of me.'

'What about him?'

'Just that Farrington has kept in touch with him. God knows why, but Ben always was an amiable sort of chap.'

'Can't imagine why he'd bother with a loser like de Courtenay.'

'Well, Baldwin didn't make it beyond squiredom, either—'

'Though, in his case, it was because he was a pathetic milksop, with no skills and fewer wits.'

'That's unkind of you, little brother, but you're probably right. Anyway, I thought I could ask Ben to invite de Courtenay – and a couple of others – up to Oxfordshire, for a Blandefordde squires' moot, so to speak. What do you think?'

Thorkell laughed and slapped Gunnar on the shoulder. 'Good plan, brother. I'm coming too.'

But Gunnar shook his head. 'You know how scared of you de Courtenay was. He'd probably run a mile if you turned up.'

Although Thorkell agreed that might be true, he wanted to see de Courtenay's face when Gunnar asked him about the de Bohun brat. If Thorkell went, he'd have to go in some sort of disguise, so de Courtenay wouldn't know it was him. He'd always found satisfaction in mischief-making, and this would be a very *mild* sort of mischief. When he suggested it, Gunnar was reluctant but, by the time the "moot" had been arranged, he'd agreed that when he next travelled to Farrington Manor, he'd be accompanied by a servant, as well as his squire.

FARRINGTON, OXFORDSHIRE
APRIL 1357

When Baldwin de Courtenay turned up at Farrington Manor, in the pitch dark and hours late, the rest of the moot was already thoroughly inebriated, though not yet maudlin. Despite travelling with both a servant and a man-at-arms, de Courtenay claimed to have lost his way. Thorkell, standing at the shadowy edges of the manor's ample hall, to all appearances awaiting orders, considered the man a halfwit. But Ben Farrington was, as Gunnar said, affable and uncomplaining, and simply welcomed de Courtenay to his table and gave instructions for his travelling companions to be fed.

De Courtenay had some catching up to do, but Farrington insisted that he ate something with his first two or three mazers of wine and urged his other companions to refrain from refilling their own cups for a while. De Courtenay looked aghast that he was the only one still eating. Scanning the remnants of the feast left scattered across the table, he grabbed a leg of cold capon, pierced some slices of roast meat with his knife, and tore a small maslin loaf in half. Then he stuffed the food, one large morsel after the other, into his mouth and chomped. As Thorkell watched, de Courtenay was clearly forcing himself to swallow half-chewed mouthfuls, so he wouldn't keep the others waiting. It was a revolting spectacle. As well as a pathetic and even faintly amusing one.

Nonetheless, by the time drinking was resumed, Thorkell was no longer amused but bored. He'd engaged in this tedious impersonation with the express purpose of overhearing de Courtenay's answer to Gunnar's question. But he hadn't thought he'd have to wait so long. Standing around for hours, yards from the fire, not having eaten, and without a mazer of red wine in his hand, was not what he'd expected. He willed his brother to get on with it, then he could at least join the other servants and retainers in a few cups of ale before bedding down.

And, at length, Thorkell's discomfort was rewarded.

Once de Courtenay had gulped down three or four mazers of strong Burgundy wine, his anxiety fell away and, after six, he was laughing heartily at Farrington's feeble jokes and apparently enjoying the boisterous company. So, when Gunnar dropped the subject of Isabella into the conversation, de Courtenay was sufficiently relaxed to respond with nostalgia rather than indignation.

'I discovered a few months ago,' said Gunnar, 'when I visited Meonbridge, that your sister was married to my cousin, Philip de Bohun.'

'Which sister was that?' said de Courtenay, quite drowsy from the surfeit of wine.

'Isabella,' said Gunnar, exchanging a grin with Farrington.

De Courtenay's face, already flushed and soft, then crumpled, and it seemed that he might weep. 'She died in the Mortality.' Then he shook his head. 'Isabella was not my favourite sister – she was silly and too vain – but it was a horrible way to die.'

Gunnar and Ben, and their other drinking companions, all grunted their agreement of the grimness of a plague death.

'And she was with child,' de Courtenay continued, 'so the poor little baby died too. That's what the de Bohuns told us.'

Then he did begin to weep, and Gunnar rolled his eyes at Farrington. They shared another grin, and Thorkell thought what they must too be thinking, that de Courtenay had always been a milksop.

Farrington refilled de Courtenay's mazer yet again, whilst Gunnar patted his shoulder.

'That's what I thought, too. But there's a boy at Courtenay Castle, one of your father's pages, who comes from Meonbridge.'

De Courtenay's brow furrowed and his eyes scrunched almost shut.

'And Sir Richard de Bohun,' continued Gunnar, 'before he died – did you know he'd died?' De Courtenay nodded. 'He put it about that this boy was *Isabella's* son, and that she died in childbirth.'

De Courtenay shook his head. 'Tha's not true,' he said, his words slurring together a little. '"Cause, if it was, my parents would've known about it.'

Gunnar nodded. 'You're right about that, Baldwin. For, in fact, although the boy *is* Philip de Bohun's son, his mother is a Meonbridge wench – a common peasant. The boy was born well *after* your sister died.'

De Courtenay frowned again a moment, then scratched his head, and a thin smile stretched his mouth. 'What was it Pa said?' he muttered, almost to himself. He took a few sips of his wine, and then his smile widened. 'Yeah, tha's right. It's a secret. He's my nephew, but he's not my nephew. He's my parents' grandson, but he's not my.... He's...'

He tailed off, and the frown returned.

'So, if your parents were asked in a court of law,' continued Gunnar, 'do you think they'd say he *was* their grandson, or he wasn't?'

De Courtenay sat quiet for long moments, grasping his mazer in both hands, his head nodding like an imbecile's. He seemed to be trying to work out the answer. But at length he looked up.

'They'd say he wasn't.' He banged his mazer on the table. 'Well, Mother would. She'd never tell a lie before a judge, or in any public place.'

'And Sir Hugh?'

De Courtenay shrugged. Perhaps his father was warier of the truth, thought Thorkell. But if they could get a court to call Lady de Courtenay as a witness, surely the brat's bastardy could be proven?

But then de Courtenay belched and brought his mazer down again. 'And *I'd* say he wasn't. I don't like that little tyke – wha's his name...? Yeah, Dickon. Just like his father, *arrogant*.' He snorted. 'Hard to believe his mother's a peasant – he's got no humility at all.'

Gunnar smirked. 'Maybe he's already growing into the role his grandfather has laid down for him?'

Back home at Castle Boune, Gunnar resumed his banter about Matilda. 'She must be getting desperate to have her itching scratched...'

Thorkell grinned. 'When I left her back in February, she did seem very eager... Now, with Meonbridge within our sights, I'd enjoy another chance to see the place and make some plans.'

'And enjoy Matilda too?' said Gunnar.

MEONBRIDGE

APRIL 1357

When Thorkell turned up at the gates of Meonbridge manor, having spent four gruelling days on the road, changing horses at the end of every day, he could hardly believe his ears when the old gatekeeper told him that Matilda was away visiting relatives. Thorkell leapt down from his horse and lunged at the old man, grabbing the front of his tunic and shaking him like a cloth doll.

'How can she be?' he cried, letting go of the tunic and pushing the man away so hard that he fell backwards against the gate. 'Matilda Fletcher doesn't have any relatives.'

The gatekeeper cringed. 'Dunno 'bout that, sir,' he mumbled. 'Tha's what I were told.'

Thorkell roared his displeasure and frustration. He lunged again at the old man and raised a fist to strike him, then checked himself and, shaking his head, turned back towards his horse.

Four days in the saddle, and four nights in stinking inns, for nothing.

He lifted his foot into the stirrup, to remount the horse, then twisted round again. 'When's she coming back?' he growled at the gatekeeper, but the old man shrugged.

'Weren't told,' he said, and stepped back inside the gatehouse.

Thorkell considered asking to see Lady de Bohun but decided against it. So should he just go home? Surely he could find something else to amuse him now he'd come all this way?

Pulling roughly on the reins and kicking at the horse's sweating flanks, he urged the animal forwards and trotted down the road from the manor towards Mistress Rolfe's recently refurbished inn, which now provided stabling as well as bed and board for travellers. Thorkell settled the horse with the ostler then went into the ale-house.

As he entered, Thorkell grinned at Ellen. 'Good day to you, Mistress Rolfe.' He gestured at the enlarged room and pointed at the new tables and benches. 'Business thriving?'

Ellen returned the greeting. 'Indeed, sir. Better times.'

He nodded.

'You visiting the manor, sir?' she said, pouring him a cup of her best ale without being asked.

He frowned but then thought better of it. 'No, no. Not this time, Mistress Rolfe. I've business of my own hereabouts and I thought I might look up one or two old friends whilst I was here.' He winked and Ellen smirked.

'And who might *she* be, sir?'

'She?'

Ellen was no longer a young woman, but she still knew how to flirt. She tipped her head a little.

Thorkell laughed. 'Very well. Perhaps you might know where I might find Mistress Jordan?'

Ellen righted her head and snorted. '*Mistress* Jordan could be just about anywhere. Her poor husband, such a fine gentleman, he don't know how to keep her under control.'

Thorkell sneered and took a few gulps of the ale. 'So, any suggestions?'

She nodded. 'As it happens, I do know where Blanche is this afternoon. Gone hawking with her *lady* friends.'

Thorkell raised his eyebrows. Everything Ellen said seemed to carry a sneer. 'Just ladies?' he said, draining his cup.

Ellen shrugged. 'What do I know about such things?' She took Thorkell's cup and refilled it. 'But I daresay she's taken a couple o' young gents along with her, as well as the falconer of course...'

As the afternoon drew to a close, Thorkell found a hiding place near to the manor gate and lay in wait for Blanche Jordan to return. Ellen had confirmed that Blanche and her husband, Alain, lived at the manor, although, as Thorkell knew very well, Blanche owned a ramshackle house on the outskirts of the village, where she would entertain her friends – perhaps with her husband's unspoken knowledge. When he saw Blanche enter the gate, he went to find a boy to take her a message telling her to meet him at the house around the hour of Compline.

He went back to Mistress Rolfe's to await the boy's return but the lad told him Blanche's husband was annoyed with her for some reason she didn't understand, and she might not manage to get away.

Frustrated, Thorkell decided to go to the house and wait. He could not believe that Blanche would pass up the chance of a few hours in bed with him. But it was quite dark and well beyond Compline before he concluded that she had.

Thorkell thumped his fist down on the rickety table, making it rock, then kicked out at the single chair in the room, cracking one of its legs so that it fell over. He turned towards the bed, thinking he might rip up the bedding, but then questioned why he cared so much that Blanche hadn't come. He thought back to the time before with Blanche, how pushy and demanding she'd been. So why was he waiting here for her? No, what he needed, if he couldn't have Matilda, was more malleable fare, like one of the girls who moped about at Ellen Rolfe's.

By the time dawn's light began to tease its way through the flimsy, half-broken shutters, Thorkell felt both rested and mostly recovered from his choler. He got up from the bed and quickly dressed. He gazed at the young girl still sleeping beneath Blanche's less than pristine blanket. How sweet and biddable she'd been. He smirked. How easy it was to find pleasure in a woman, if she let you. He could do without the likes of Blanche Jordan. But he did wonder just how biddable Matilda might be. And he really wanted to find out.

He threw a coin on the bed and let himself out of the house. It was almost light and he could see the manor's tenants already tramping towards the fields. They looked quite keen, for peasants.

And one day soon they'd all be his.

16

'G'day to ye,' said a stranger, tipping his hat to the men sitting outside Ellen Rolfe's ale-house, drinking and munching on Ellen's hot meat pies.

Roger Stronge, his brow still black with soot and sweat from his morning's labours in the forge, looked up at the man. 'Fare you well. New to Meonbridge?'

The man inclined his head. 'I be, sir.' He strolled into the ale-house, emerging a few moments later with a brimming cup. He gestured to Roger and his two companions. 'Awright if I join ye?'

The companions exchanged quick glances and shrugged agreement, and the stranger, whipping off his shabby cloak to reveal a long workman's tunic and threadbare hose, sat down. When he took off his hat, they saw he had a grubby coif tied around his hair.

'Pies good?' he asked, sniffing the steam rising from the pastry crust Roger had just sliced into with his knife. Then he tipped his head towards the ale-house door. 'I jus' ordered one.'

Roger nodded, his mouth full of hot meat and gravy.

'Best in Meonbridge,' said Nick Ashdown, and sipped at his ale. 'You travelling through?'

The stranger shrugged. 'I were in the area, on business—' He winked. 'An' I thought to look up an ol' friend I've heard lives 'ereabouts.'

'Who?' asked Simon Hogge.

'Jack Sawyer.' The man gulped some ale. 'Y' know 'im?'

'Of course,' said Simon. 'Everyone knows everyone in Meonbridge.'

'Who's that man?' said Maud Miller, pointing across the green.

Sitting cross-legged on the grass under the light spring shade of the green's great oak, she was making flower garlands with her little cousin Joan, Libby Fletcher, and Jane Cole. The girls' mothers sometimes let them spend the afternoon together, at least till it was time for their evening chores. When it was warm enough, the girls liked to sit together underneath the tree, where they could gossip and giggle out of their mothers' hearing, and watch folk come and go.

Libby and Jane gazed in the direction of Maud's pointing finger. A man she didn't know was talking to a group of men she did. They were all sitting outside the ale-house in the warm spring sunshine, clutching pots of ale.

'That's your new pa, Maudie,' said Jane, smirking.

'Nick Ashdown's not my pa,' said Maud, prodding at Jane's shoulder. 'Anyway, not him. And not Master Stronge or Master Hogge neither...'

'Ma will tell Nick off if she catches him in the ale-house,' said Joan, giggling.

'Don't be silly, Joanie,' said Maud. 'Nick can do what he likes.'

Joan pouted, hating to be called "silly" by her cousin, but Maud jiggled her pointing finger.

'No, *that* man,' she said. 'The one with the coif.'

But when the others looked again, they all just shrugged and went back to their garlands.

Maud pursed her lips. 'I'll ask Nick later,' she said, almost to herself, and, picking up her garland, continued to weave together the primroses, celandines and bluebells they'd gathered earlier from the hedgerows.

'You can tell me where 'e lives, then?' said the man.

'You in the same line of work as Jack?' said Roger, casting a sideways glance at Nick, who nodded.

The man drank more of his ale. 'Nah! I never 'ad Jack's clever 'ands.'

At that moment, Ellen Rolfe came over, in her hands a hot pie on a wooden platter. 'Yer pie,' she said to the stranger, not looking at him, and fairly slammed the platter down onto the table. Then she darted back indoors without another word.

Roger, Nick and Simon exchanged raised eyebrows, and the man grunted. 'Don't like strangers 'round 'ere then?'

'Just wary,' said Simon.

Maud thought herself a skilful garland-weaver but, when she snatched a sidelong glance at Libby's garland, she was disappointed to see it was neater and prettier than her own. But then she realised Libby was gazing across the green again.

'That man's coming over,' said Libby. Maud looked and there he was, striding across the grass towards them.

Joan's eyes widened. 'Is he coming to talk to us, Maudie?' she said, her voice all quavery.

Maud rather hoped he was. But then she saw that Nick and the other men had left the ale-house, and the green was empty now of folk apart from her and her friends, and the stranger marching over. She felt a flutter of excitement, tinged with fear. He certainly looked as if he was coming to talk to them.

As he approached, the man called out. 'G'day to ye, young maids.'

Maud looked up at him, squinting because the sun was in her eyes. She could see the man was quite nice-looking, though his clothes were grubby.

'What ye be doing this fine spring afternoon?' he said.

'Making flower garlands,' said Libby, rolling her eyes.

'And right pretty they be,' he said.

'Ma says we shouldn't talk to strangers,' said Joan, her voice a whisper and refusing to look the man in the face.

'Quite right, little one, so I'll soon be on me way. But afore I go mebbe ye can answer me a question?'

Maud nodded. She liked answering questions.

'I'm looking for an ol' friend o' mine. Mebbe you maids know 'is lad, young Dickon? Dickon Sawyer?'

The girls looked at each other and then Maud nodded. 'We know him.'

The man grinned then rubbed at his chin. 'But wha' d'ye think, I clear forgot the name o' Dickon's ma... Mebbe ye know it?'

'Agnes Sawyer,' said Maud, though she thought it was a funny thing to ask.

The man laughed and cuffed his forehead with his hand. 'Agnes! 'Course it is. I'll be forgetting me own name next, eh, young maid?' His eyes twinkled and Maud was pleased she'd been able to help.

But the man had another question. 'Mebbe you know too where the Sawyers live?'

Maud pointed back across the green and explained that the carpenter's shop was on the road back up towards the manor. She was surprised Nick and the other men hadn't already told him that. But she liked it when the man bowed low to her and thanked her for her kindness, before turning and striding back the way he came.

Nick didn't go back to work at once. After he bid farewell to Roger and Simon, he headed for Susanna Miller's cottage. He might have his supper with her later, as he sometimes did, but he didn't want to wait till then to tell her about the conversation at the ale-house. And to warn her.

He hurried, hoping to catch her before she went out for the afternoon to discuss supplies with Thomas down in the mill, or talk to Ivo Langelee, who ran the bakery next door. But it was now well after the usual dinnertime and, when Nick arrived, Susanna was just closing the cottage door.

'Susie, wait,' he called out to her. 'Got summat to tell you.'

Susanna tutted and shook her head. 'I need to go. I can't keep Elly waiting—'

'Eleanor Nash?'

She nodded. 'I'm helping with the lambing.' She tilted her head. 'Surely you knew that, Nick?'

'No, I didn't. Since when?'

She giggled. 'Since the ewes started dropping their lambs...'

'I thought you'd have enough to do here at the mill.'

'It's only for the lambing. I enjoy it.' She turned to go. 'And I must be on my way.'

Nick took her elbow in his hand. 'This won't take a moment, Susie. Let's go back inside.' She wasn't keen, but he lifted the latch and ushered her indoors.

'What is it?' she said.

He began to tell her about the man asking questions in the ale-house, but she interrupted.

'Oh, him. Must be the same man spoke to Ann Webb and me, and some other goodwives too, when we was all at the well. He just come up and started chatting. Seemed friendly enough—'

Now Nick interrupted. 'You shouldn't talk to strange men, Susie. It's not seemly.'

But she rolled her eyes. 'Don't be daft, Nick. I wasn't alone with him, was I?'

Nick reddened a little. 'Anyway, what did he ask you?'

'Not much. Just if we knew where his friend Jack Sawyer lived. He said he came from Chipping Norton – you know, where Jack and Agnes met?' Nick nodded. 'So Ann told him, and then he asked if Jack had any children. And Ann said four. And what were their names, the man asked, and she told him. And she said how Agnes came home after the Death with baby Dickon in her arms, then set up home with Jack, and had more babies—'

It was Nick's turn to roll his eyes. 'I see. So he didn't ask much, but Ann blabbermouth gave him a right lot in return.'

Susanna nodded. 'She *is* a dreadful gossip.'

'Anyway,' continued Nick, 'they're the same sort of questions the man was asking us in the ale-house.' He rubbed gently at Susanna's shoulder. 'Did he look especially interested when Ann mentioned Dickon?'

'I didn't notice. I were drawing up the water. But he didn't hang about for long. He bowed his head, really polite, and went off down the street.'

'And did he go up to Jack Sawyer's workshop?'

'He went in that direction, but whether he got there, I couldn't say.'

Nick shook his head. 'I wonder if Jack's even *heard* of this so-called friend?'

'"So-called"? So you think he's not his friend?'

He shrugged. 'It just seemed... I dunno, unlikely somehow. He were a working man. What sort of business would a man like that have here in Meonbridge? It just didn't seem quite right. Roger and Simon thought so too.'

'So maybe you should go to Jack and find out if he knows him?'

17

MEONBRIDGE

APRIL 1357

I t was late afternoon, and Jack's day had been hectic and exhausting. A week ago, he'd received an order for several roof trusses, and he and his journeyman James had been working in the workshop without cease, cutting, planing and jointing the timbers. Back home, he'd hoped to relax a while with a cup of ale before it was time for bed.

As if repose was even a possibility with Agnes the way she was.

Ever since, two months past, Dickon had gone to Courtenay Castle, she'd been in such low spirits Jack sometimes thought with grief of Henry Miller. Henry, once the happiest of men, became so gloomy and downcast – for what reason, aside from the Devil's whispering, no one rightly knew – it seemed he might have longed for his own death. Though no one ever said so.

It was true too of Henry's sister-in-law, Joan, the wife of his older brother, Thomas. Joan fell into such a deep, dark melancholy after the loss of her children in the Death that, when she drowned in the mill race, most folk thought she'd thrown herself into the rushing waters. Though no one said as much.

And, now, when Jack looked at Agnes, his once-beautiful, golden-haired and gladsome girl, he saw a plain, grey woman, looking older than her years, who carried out her daily tasks without a scrap of contentment. Even their remaining children seemed to bring her little joy.

Yet he might have expected that, with Dickon gone, her sternness and disquiet – caused, Jack was certain, by Dickon's headstrong behaviour – might diminish. He hoped she might become once more his lovely girl, her soft lips sometimes parted and waiting for a kiss. But whilst the sternness had to some extent abated, the disquiet hadn't.

The day October last when Lady de Bohun had told Dickon he was her grandson was also when Agnes had realised her boy was finally going to be taken from her. Thereafter, Dickon spent most of his days with Piers, undergoing her ladyship's, now rather frantic-seeming, attempts to prepare him for his future. Jack urged Agnes to try to ensure the little time the boy now spent at home was happy. He'd never told her of Dickon's own anxiety about his future but had encouraged her to look forward with excitement to his new life, in the hope that her enthusiasm might rub off on him.

For a week or so, Agnes had been scarcely any more responsive to coaxing than her son. But then, one morning, for no reason that Jack could discern, she seemed to adopt a more relaxed and joyful manner. Jack could scarcely believe his eyes and ears: had his melancholy wife really changed back into the sunny girl she once had been?

On the few dry days of the remainder of a mostly damp autumn, Agnes had also spent time in the garden, picking beans for drying, collecting seed for next year's sowings, weeding cabbages, clearing ground of long-spent planting, and, when her exertions tired her out, she'd rested on the turf seat beneath the little arbour he had built for her some years ago.

He recalled one hot and airless midsummer afternoon, four years ago, when the arbour was rampant with sweet-smelling flowers, and Agnes had gathered the boys around her – Stephen and Geoffrey then scarcely more than babies – on a blanket on the ground, and she and Christopher, amid much giggling, had told ridiculous so-called midsummer tales of faeries, magic and evil spirits. At first the boys had enjoyed the stories, but Dickon became over-excited and dashed around the garden, squealing like a piglet. Then he tumbled his little brothers over when he threw himself back down onto the blanket, and they set up such a wailing that Jack had marched outdoors and reprimanded Agnes for filling the children's heads with ungodly notions. Yet, during those days, Agnes had seemed happy, and Jack regretted how pompous he had been towards her.

Then his thoughts returned to last October, to the moment when he, leaning against the frame of the garden door, watched Agnes, seated on the turf bench, despite the autumn chill. All her boys were once more around her, along with their little sister Alice, sitting on the blanket spread out upon the ground.

Dickon, young as he still was, seemed to understand the time had come to curb his misbehaviour, and was sitting straight-backed on the blanket, his two brothers, and even Alice, copying his pose. And all four were gazing up at their mother, eyes wide and mouths agape, as she told them tales again. But this time, Jack knew, they were not tales of faeries, but of knights. When she had begun to tell these tales, some days before, he'd asked her how she knew them.

'I suppose Ma must have told them when we were little...'

'And where might she have learned them?'

She had laughed, her lovely blue eyes crinkling at the corners. 'In truth, Jack, I can't imagine. But, perhaps, years past, in their long days together, Margaret told Ma tales of Sir Richard's noble deeds?'

'You must ask her about it,' he'd said, but he didn't think she ever had.

In those few months before Dickon was to leave, whether due simply to his own awareness, or to Piers's influence, or Margaret's, or indeed Agnes's, the boy's behaviour changed. At home, he did whatever his mother asked of him without complaint. He drew close to her, for the first time since he was a baby, seemingly *wanting* to spend time at his mother's side – and, to a lesser degree, at Jack's – whilst he still had the chance to do so.

And, when the cold February day arrived for him to travel to Courtenay Castle, Dickon clung to Agnes for a long while, and she to him, though neither cried.

'Remember who you are, my darling boy,' Agnes had said, unfolding her arms at length from his little body and holding him away from her. 'You'll always be our Dickon, but remember that you are also Richard de Bohun, son of Sir Philip, grandson of Sir Richard, and one day you too will be a knight.' She'd smiled her wonderful sunny smile, and he'd nodded.

'But you're still my ma,' he'd said.

She'd hugged him again briefly. 'But you must remember, sweetheart, not to tell your new friends your ma's a carpenter's wife.'

He nodded again. But Jack had felt a tightening in his chest. Did Dickon really understand *that* part of his new situation? He'd been told it several times, but it was surely hard for a boy of his age to make sense of the tangled web of lies that had been woven in an attempt to keep him safe. But no more could be done. They had no option now but to trust Hugh de Courtenay to manage Dickon's welfare.

Dickon rode pillion behind John, and three armed retainers and three squires, including Piers, had accompanied them to Surrey. As the procession wound out of the bailey, through the gate and down into the village where, Jack knew, the villagers were waiting to wish their little lord God speed, Agnes had stood watching from the bailey steps. Jack had his arm about her waist and, as Dickon disappeared from view, he'd felt a shudder jolt through Agnes's body and, shifting his arm to her shoulder, he'd drawn her towards him. Her head flopped against his chest, and he knew then she had allowed her tears to flow.

'I'm so afraid for him, Jack,' she'd said, her voice a whisper. He didn't deny it, for in his heart he sensed it too.

'I know this is his destiny and I know it is what I wanted for him but, now the moment has arrived, it feels as if he's being wrenched away from me.' She'd lifted her head and her damp eyes had looked into Jack's. 'I don't know why, but I feel our boy's in danger. I feel almost as if I'll never see him again.'

'But that's never been the plan, Agnes. You know that. Margaret has agreed he'll come home to Meonbridge every few months or so, to see her and to see us. It won't be long before he'll be back again.'

She'd nodded, then pulled back. 'I know you're right, Jack. I'm being foolish.' Then she'd turned and, as she stepped through the door into the manor hall, her sunniness of the past few days once more slid behind a cloud.

They had just finished supper and, although Jack was thinking it was time Agnes got up from the table and packed the boys and baby Alice off to bed, these days he tried not to press her or cajole. He had just lifted the flagon to pour himself another cup of ale when a loud knock upon the door roused Agnes from her lethargy. She pulled a face at him, but nonetheless shuffled over to the door.

'Nick Ashdown,' she said. 'What brings you here?'

'A word with Jack, if you please, Agnes,' said Nick, stepping inside the room.

Jack got to his feet. 'Nick? What's this about?'

Coming forward, Nick glanced at the table, still covered with bowls and cups and discarded scraps of bread. 'Have I interrupted—?'

'Just finished. Come, sit down. Agnes will bring you a cup of ale.'

Nick nodded and pulled up a stool, whilst Agnes poured some ale into a cup. She handed it to Nick, her brow creased into a frown.

Nick related the encounter he'd had at Ellen Rolfe's with the stranger claiming to be Jack's friend. 'Did you receive a visit, Jack?'

'No. I know no one from Chipping likely to look me up.'

'So why would a stranger be asking about Dickon and Agnes?' said Nick. 'It seemed queer to me and Roger and Simon. And the man spoke to Susanna too, and other women at the well.'

'What did he say to them?'

'Same as to us. Why not come and talk to Susie yourself?'

Jack turned to Agnes, who had slumped again onto a bench, her hand over her mouth. She was shaking her head. 'Why'd a stranger want to know about Dickon?' she said in a whisper.

Jack took hold of her hands and held them fast. 'I don't know, Agnes, but I'll find out. Stay here with the children and don't let them notice your concern.'

She nodded, but he could feel the tension in her hands. He raised his arms and, wrapping them around her shoulders, hugged her close. 'Try to keep calm, Agnes.'

. . .

At the mill cottage, they found Susanna in a pother.

'That man,' she cried, running to Nick the moment he stepped through the door, 'was talking to the children too. Maud and Joan, and Libby Fletcher, and Jane Cole, they were all together on the green this afternoon, and he marched across and spoke to them.'

Jack went over to Susanna's girls, sitting at the table playing with some roughly-carved wooden animals. A bowl seemed be standing in for Noah's Ark, for Joan was putting the animals into pairs and dropping them inside it.

Jack sat on the bench opposite the girls. 'Maud, Joan,' he said softly, 'can I ask you something?'

Joan stopped playing and stared at him with wide eyes, whilst Maud nodded.

'What did the man ask you, Maud?' said Jack.

'Just if we knew a lad called Dickon Sawyer,' she answered, 'and I said yes.'

'And was that all?'

Maud hesitated, but Joan piped up, 'No, it weren't. He asked what Dickon's ma was called. And Maudie said "Agnes Sawyer".'

'He asked about Dickon's ma,' said Jack, 'but not his pa?'

'He knew you were his pa,' Maud said. 'He'd just forgotten Mistress Sawyer's name...'

'I understand,' Jack said, and patted Maud's pale curls. Then he turned to Susanna. 'Nick says the man spoke to you too?'

She nodded. 'Not just to me. There were several of us at the well. But he said the same as what he asked the girls. Did we know where you lived. And Ann Webb told him and, then, when he asked if you had children, she told him that too. And how Agnes came back to Meonbridge with you and baby Dickon.' She chewed at her bottom lip. 'Was he a friend of yours, Jack?'

'I've no idea who he was.'

'So why'd he want to know all that, about Dickon and Agnes?' said Susanna, wringing her hands together.

Jack shook his head. Now wasn't the time to tell them about Sir Richard's assertion of Dickon's legitimacy to the Bounes. 'I don't know, Susanna. I really don't.'

He thanked Nick and Susanna and set off home. A chilly

breeze had sprung up and he pulled his hood snug around his head. He walked slowly, not wanting to have to tell Agnes what he'd learned. She'd demand to know who the stranger was, asking for her name. And she'd become distraught when he told her what he suspected.

But there was someone he did want to tell. And, as he reached the top of the track that led up from the mill towards the village road, he turned in at the entrance to the atte Wode croft.

John looked surprised when he found Jack on his doorstep. 'Summat amiss, Jack?'

'You know about a stranger asking questions in the village?'

'I'd heard, but I didn't see him myself. What was he asking?'

Jack repeated everything he knew and had been told by Nick, Susanna and Maud. 'Does that sound suspicious to you?'

John frowned. 'It does.' He got up and fetched a jug of ale and two cups.

He poured the ale and, pushing one cup across the table, sat down. 'For years there was unspoken acceptance that Dickon was your son, as well as my sister's. When Agnes came home with you and the baby, no one in the village had any reason to think the little one weren't yours. With the Death only just passed on, I doubt anyone thought much about Agnes and her boy.'

Jack nodded. 'That's true enough. It were a terrible time.'

'We all agreed,' continued John, 'it were for the best to keep the truth a secret between us and the de Bohuns.'

'We did.'

'But, as Dickon grew,' continued John, 'you might've thought his uncanny likeness to Philip de Bohun was obvious enough.'

Jack grimaced. 'I kept waiting for someone to say in passing "don't the Sawyer boy look like Sir Philip?".'

'Mebbe folk have thought it, but no one ever said. Yet, when her ladyship declared at the funeral that Dickon was her grandson, and Sir Richard had named him his heir, some folk were surprised, but many weren't.'

'But what would they think if they knew Sir Richard had claimed Dickon as his *legitimate* heir, Isabella's son as well as Philip's?'

'*And* that the Bounes are likely to claim Meonbridge for their own,' said John. 'Despite what his lordship said, with Sister Rosa in the priory, and Dickon illegitimate, Sir Morys *is* the rightful heir.'

'And now this stranger's come here asking questions... D'you suppose he was in the Bounes' employ? Come to... What? See what they could find out about Dickon's mother?'

'Mebbe. And now he's on his way back to Herefordshire, to tell his masters all he's learned.'

They fell silent and sipped at their ale. Then John got up to poke at the fire and add another piece of wood to the flames.

'What d'you think will happen now?' said Jack, his voice a sigh.

'If the Bounes are about to discover Dickon's not Sir Richard's *legitimate* heir, they'll surely challenge his claim in court.' John frowned. 'This has come sooner than Sister Rosa or her ladyship expected—'

'They *knew*?'

He shook his head. 'Suspected. Poor lady, Sir Richard left her in a dreadful pinch. She's not only had to maintain his lie about Dickon's mother being Isabella, but now she's got to deal with any challenge from the Bounes.'

'Who somehow got wind of Dickon's true parentage and sent that man here to test it?' said Jack. 'Is that what you think, John? But how might their suspicion have been roused?'

'I've no idea—'

But then John put his cup down with a bang, spilling what was left of the ale onto the table. 'I'm sorry, Jack, but I have to go. I must tell her ladyship and Sister Rosa what has happened.'

18

Dawn had barely broken; the air was damp and very chilly. The nuns were filing out of the chapel after Lauds, their heads bowed and their voices still reverently silent, when Rosa looked up, hearing a commotion at the gate. She hurried over to find out what was afoot, and found the gatekeeper debating with John atte Wode whether to let him through. She gently scolded the old man. 'You know Master atte Wode. Surely you cannot imagine that, if he has ridden all this way at such an early hour, he does not have urgent business here?'

The gatekeeper scratched at his hoary beard and grumbled, then took the great iron key from its hook on the gatehouse wall and made a fuss of inserting it into the lock, struggling to make it turn, all the while muttering to himself.

When John was at last permitted through the gate, leading his hot and sweating horse by its reins, Rosa gestured with her head towards the old man. John gave a small grin and nodded. Rosa then took the reins from him and led the horse the short distance to the stables, calling to the stable boy as she went. It took several calls before the boy emerged, rubbing his fists against his eyes, his hair spiked with straw and sticking up around his head.

As he glanced up at Rosa, his face crumpled. But Rosa smiled at him. 'Still sleepy, Rafe? Well, I am sorry, but Master atte Wode's horse needs a rub down and some hay and water. You can do that for him, can you not?'

'Yes'm,' mumbled Rafe, stumbling forward to take the horse. Then, clicking his tongue and pulling gently on the reins, he shuffled off into the stable's gloom.

'Rafe is most skilful with the horses,' said Rosa, 'and I am sure he will be wide awake before too long.' But then she realised that John seemed not to have heard her. His brow was creased, and he was fidgeting, running the edge of his hat through his fingers. 'John? Is something wrong?'

'Something I have to tell you, Sister Rosa. And urgently.'

'I suppose you would not have come so early if it was not important.'

John nodded. 'Shall we go inside?'

'The cloisters will be undisturbed,' said Rosa. 'And then you must break your fast.'

John gave a sheepish grin. 'I must admit I'm hungry. But what I have to tell is more important than my belly.' Then he coughed and thrust out his bottom lip. 'Forgive my manners, Sister.' But Rosa just smiled broadly.

They walked across the courtyard to a corner of the cloisters and sat down on one of the stone benches built at intervals along the outer wall. 'I've already told your lady mother,' said John. 'Last evening. I'd have ridden here right after, but her ladyship insisted I weren't to come such a distance in the dark.'

Rosa nodded. 'I am glad you took her wise advice, John. It would have been most dangerous, with all the villains there are abroad these days.' She rested a hand lightly on his arm. 'But you are here now, so what is it that you have to tell me?'

John told her about the stranger asking questions in Meonbridge, and about his own conversation with Jack, and Nick, and Susanna Miller. Rosa listened attentively, even though her heart was quickening.

She knew somehow that this would happen: that the Bounes would discover the truth about her nephew.

'So you think that this man left Meonbridge with evidence that Dickon is illegitimate?'

'Well, rumour, anyway.'

She nodded. 'But if, as you suspect, he was in the Bounes' pay, might he not also have somehow learned the names of those he spoke to? And might they not be called upon to speak in court?'

'You mean Nick Ashdown and Susanna Miller? Even little Maud?'

'I suppose it is possible. And, if asked, would they not feel obliged to tell the truth?'

Despite the chilly air, a sheen of perspiration was gathering on John's face, and he wiped at it fiercely with his tunic's sleeve. He did not answer at once. Perhaps he had not considered that his friends' honesty might be tested before a judge?

'If our suspicion is correct,' Rosa continued, 'and the Bounes have gathered sufficient evidence – even if it is only the say so of a few of the villagers – it is my view that they will soon start their legal claim. As I had thought they might. It may take them a while to arrange for the court to sit, but I think that we should work on our answer now, so that we are prepared.'

Despite her seeming steadfastness, Rosa was nervous of their position, and did not think she was capable of managing their defence on her own. 'But I am no advocate, John, and no orator. Nor is my mother.' She pulled a wry smile. 'Do you think we should engage a lawyer to speak for us? And, if so, how would we discover one who might defend us fairly?'

'I suppose, Sister, we'd fare better with some help.' Then a gurgling sound came from John's stomach and he grimaced.

'Your poor stomach is crying out for sustenance, John,' said Rosa, her eyes shining with merriment despite the seriousness of the moment. 'Come, let me take you to the refectory and see if I can find you a little bread and cheese.'

John nodded his gratitude but, as they walked, he told Rosa of her mother's recommendation. 'Lady de Bohun thought perhaps Sir Giles Fitzpeyne could advise you. You know she thinks most highly of his lordship.'

But Rosa frowned. 'Can that be wise, John? As he is so close now to the Bounes?'

John shrugged. 'He was your father's oldest friend. And her ladyship said Sir Giles felt responsible for your father's death. She believes he remains an honourable man, though I'll confess to you, Sister, I have my doubts.'

Rosa nodded. 'I want to agree with my mother, but the way my father died, in company with Giles and his retainers, did seem suspicious.' She turned to face John. 'Oh, John, what are we to do? Can we trust Sir Giles or not?'

MEONBRIDGE

MAY 1357

It was with much anxiety that Rosa finally agreed to send a message to Giles. She received his reply only a few days later, that he would come to Meonbridge, to speak with her and her mother. Yet it seemed that his support might after all be limited:

"I cannot avow to offer you direct counsel in whatever is troubling you but, for the sake of our past friendship and affections, I shall try to help you find someone who can."

Rosa was grateful that the fair spring weather was rendering the roads to Meonbridge a little less treacherous to travel and, despite her contentment with her new life in the priory, she enjoyed the opportunity to gaze across the fields and woodlands of Hampshire, and drink in the beauty of the landscape.

As a girl, Rosa had taken great pleasure in her horsemanship, but in those last two years or so before she left Meonbridge for the priory, her melancholy had led her to give up outdoor pursuits of any kind, as she increasingly turned in upon herself and her guilty imaginings. But now she rather relished the prospect of a small adventure so, as it seemed that the day was to continue warm and dry, she chose to ride on horseback the ten miles to Meonbridge. She was accompanied by young Sister Juliana, and Egbert, a grim-faced servant of the priory, noted for his willingness and ability to protect those he referred to as "me damsels".

Rosa arrived at Meonbridge manor well before the dinner hour. When she entered the hall with her small entourage, her mother came forward to greet her.

'Giles is still out with John,' she said, 'surveying the demesne. They will be back for dinner.' She gestured Rosa towards the staircase. 'Shall we sit upstairs a while, until they return?' Rosa nodded, then Margaret addressed Sister Juliana. 'My dear, would you care to play with my companion's little daughter, Libby?'

Juliana turned to Rosa, asking a question with her eyes. Rosa nodded agreement, and Margaret continued. 'Poor Libby has become such a lonely little girl since my grandson Dickon went away to Courtenay Castle.'

Juliana pushed out her lips, then widened them into a broad smile and lifted her shoulders. 'Oh, poor little thing. I'd love to play with her a while, your ladyship.' She looked so happy that Rosa reflected, not for the first time, on how difficult the privations of the religious life could be for a girl who entered a priory when she was barely out of childhood.

Rosa and her mother shared the usual pleasantries, about the weather, how well or otherwise the crops were growing on their respective estates, and Rosa was always interested in news of any marriages, births or deaths amongst the Meonbridge tenants she knew well.

But then she looked about her and raised an eyebrow.

'I should have asked you earlier, Mother, when you sent Juliana off with the Fletcher girl. Where is the child's mother?'

Margaret shook her head. 'Oh, poor Matilda is such a melancholy young woman.'

Rosa let her eyebrows rise a little higher. 'Yes, Mother, so you have said before.'

'So I suggested that, once a week, she pay a visit to one of her friends in Meonbridge, like Eleanor Nash—'

'Eleanor *Nash*?'

'Eleanor Titherige that was.' Margaret gave a little laugh. 'Surely you knew she married that shepherd of hers, Walter, no matter he was a cottar?' Rosa shook her head, wondering why she had not heard. 'It was two years ago now,' Margaret continued. 'And they have built up such a splendid flock together. One of the best in Hampshire, Eleanor says.'

Rosa was listening but at the same time recalling the discussion she and her mother had had a few months ago about Matilda Fletcher. But Margaret was still in full flight about Eleanor.

'What a remarkable young woman she has proved to be,' she said, her eyes alight. 'And so busy, yet she still makes time for Matilda. They were once the best of friends, you know—'

Rosa held up her hand. 'Yes, Mother, I do know that. And I must confess that it surprises me that a woman like Eleanor still considers Matilda suitable for a friend.'

'Really, my dear, that is a most unchristian thought,' said Margaret, sounding severe but letting her mouth turn a small smile.

Rosa sighed. 'You are right, Mother. Most unchristian, and most unworthy of my veil. I shall pray for forgiveness for such uncalled-for malice, and for the grace of a kindlier attitude towards my fellows.' She pursed her lips. 'But, as we are talking of Matilda, has anything come of our discussion about her future?'

Her mother frowned, and seemed confused for several moments. But then she threw up her hands and laughed. 'Oh, yes, of course,' she cried. 'We talked about trying to find her a suitor.'

Rosa had found herself musing recently about whether her mother was quite in control, for she seemed more often to forget conversations, or to babble as she had just been doing. She gazed at her, noting the strands of greying hair escaping from her wimple, but reminded herself that her mother was only forty-six. Surely, not *really* old?

Then her mother touched her arm. 'Rosa? Are you listening?'

She shook herself. 'I am so sorry, Mother. What were you saying?'

'That I have approached Adam Wragge about Matilda. You remember Adam?'

Rosa nodded. 'The steward? Quite a handsome man, I seem to recall?'

'Indeed. Still handsome, and trustworthy, and prosperous...' She paused.

'And...?'

'Well, he did seem interested, but said he would have to think upon it. He had always imagined he would remain unmarried since his wife died in the Mortality.'

'Matilda is handsome enough herself, but surely her heritage could put off a man like Master Wragge?'

'He did express some doubts. So I tried to convince him that Matilda is nothing like her father, and that Libby is nothing like hers. So we shall see.'

'And have there been any more visits from Thorkell Boune?'

Margaret shook her head. 'He did come in April. But, following your advice, I had already instructed the gatekeeper that, if he did come, he was to be told that Matilda was not in Meonbridge, but away visiting relatives.'

'He is unlikely to believe that story a second time.'

'That is true. I shall have to think of another reason for Matilda's absence.'

'Or maybe he won't come again. If he thinks he is going to win Meonbridge through the courts, he will surely not be interested in Matilda?' Rosa puckered her brow. 'What is his interest in her, anyway?'

Margaret looked almost grief-stricken. 'Only as another woman to bed, I fear.'

Dinner with Giles was accompanied by uncomplicated, amicable, conversation. The dry weather was discussed again, and the fine growth of crops in the manor's fields, but Giles also expressed his delight in the violets, periwinkles and irises blooming in Margaret's garden. But, when the meal was over, Margaret invited Giles to join her and Rosa in the solar where they could discuss their affairs in private. She had already asked Matilda to take Libby and Juliana out into the garden for a walk. 'A long walk, I think,' she had hinted.

'Should John not join us too, Mother?' said Rosa.

Giles nodded. 'Your bailiff has much wisdom, for all his youth.' His eyes twinkled. 'As indeed do you, Sister Rosa.'

Rosa acknowledged Giles's intended compliment with a slender smile and raised a questioning eyebrow at her mother.

'Very well,' said Margaret and asked her maid, Agatha, to send a boy to fetch the bailiff back from wherever he had gone.

Whilst they awaited John, Rosa told Giles of the recent happenings in Meonbridge and their suspicion that a so-called friend of Jack Sawyer was in fact in the pay of Morys Boune. 'We are troubled that what the man learned might prompt Morys to challenge Dickon's right to Meonbridge.'

A shadow fell across Giles's invariably cheerful face.

'I must tell you that my wife begged me not even to respond to your message, Sister Rosa. She pleaded with me not to go against her family, for she is, I know, fearful of what action they might take.' He grimaced at Margaret. 'I am in an awkward position now, with Morys Boune my father-in-law. I adore my little Gwynedd and would not wish our marriage had not happened. So it grieved me sorely to rebuff her pleas, yet I had to come and offer you what little help I can, for the sake of the comradeship I shared so long with Richard—' He paused, and bowed his head. 'And because I still feel somehow responsible for his death.'

Margaret laid her hand upon Giles's arm. 'We are most grateful that you came. We understand that you cannot stand for one side or the other in this dispute – if dispute it proves to be. For of course Morys has not yet issued any summons, despite our expectation that he will.'

Rosa nodded. 'It is possible that he will do no such thing, and that the man prying around in Meonbridge was truly just some long-forgotten friend of Jack's. But it does not seem that way.'

At that moment, John burst in through the solar door, red and shiny in the face. He dragged his hat from his head and bowed to Margaret. 'Apologies, m'lady. I'd not known I were needed here.'

'No, John,' said Margaret, 'it is I who should apologise, asking you to drop whatever you were doing. But we all agreed that your wisdom on this matter of the Bounes would be of value.'

Despite his already red complexion, Rosa was sure that a different kind of flush then bloomed upon John's face. She nodded. 'This is a matter for Meonbridge, not just the de Bohuns.' Although, the moment she had said it, she thought how strange and unlikely a comment it sounded coming from her lips. A de Bohun telling a *villein* that he might have a say in their deliberations. Her father would have considered it unthinkable – or at least he would have once. But, after all, he had always respected the opinions of John's father, Stephen, when he was reeve, and those of his bailiff, Robert Tyler, before the man went mad and murdered her beloved brother. 'And, after all,' she continued, 'you are Meonbridge's bailiff now. And you are Dickon's uncle as much as I am his aunt.'

John nodded and wiped the moisture from his face with the sleeve of his shirt.

'Come, let us all sit down,' said Margaret, gesturing to the chairs surrounding the small table. She then nodded to Rosa.

Rosa splayed her hands upon the table. 'Despite our present uncertainty about exactly what the Bounes will do,' she said, 'my mother and I agree that we must prepare ourselves for a potential court case. If it does not happen, we shall have lost nothing but time and effort.' Everyone nodded, and she continued. 'The Bounes may not be able to prove Dickon's illegitimacy—'

Giles made a sudden explosive noise. '"Illegitimacy"? The boy is *illegitimate?*'

Margaret's hands flew to her face and Rosa felt her cheeks grow hot. Did Giles not know the truth of Dickon's birth? She glanced at her mother, and her horrified eyes showed clearly that Giles had not been told.

'I am so sorry, Sir Giles,' said Rosa, 'you have evidently not been told the truth.'

He frowned. 'So it seems. But what is the truth? Is the boy not Philip's son?'

'Not Philip's?' Rosa was only momentarily confused. 'Oh, no, Sir Giles, you misunderstand. He is most certainly Philip's, but not *Isabella's*, child.'

'But Richard told me—' Giles said, addressing Margaret.

She lowered her hands. Her face was drawn and grey. 'I must add my apologies, Giles. It has been such a difficult time. If Richard had not died, I would have persuaded him to tell you the truth. But I did not have the opportunity.'

Giles seemed to be keeping his dismay under control. 'But why did Richard say that Isabella died giving birth to the boy?'

Margaret sighed. 'Because he had said that to the Bounes, in an effort to claim that Dickon was his legitimate heir. And...' She stumbled. 'And, having said it to them, it was almost as if he needed to repeat it often, to convince himself, as well as others, that it was true.' She looked up at him, her eyes almost wild with distress.

But Giles stood up and, stepping around the table, laid his hand upon Margaret's shoulder. 'I apologise for my sharpness, my dear. I can see the problem. And, even more so, I understand the difficult position in which Richard has left you. But, God's eyes, he was a fool to say something so outrageously untrue—'

She shook her head. 'He was not to know that the lie would so soon be tested.'

'And you suspect that it is going to be tested in court?' said Giles. 'That my father-in-law now knows of the lie and intends to arraign you for it?'

'It is only our suspicion,' said Rosa. 'But we must prepare ourselves to answer.'

Giles nodded. 'Indeed you must.'

'We fear that they may summon a number of Meonbridge folk to court and make them swear the truth of Dickon's parentage,' continued Rosa.

John frowned. 'And I think the folk that man questioned would find it hard *not* to tell the truth. I know them, and they're all honest folk, who believe in the right and wrong of things.'

'As indeed they should,' said Margaret. 'We could hardly expect them to lie on our behalf.'

'Especially before a judge,' said Rosa. 'Anyway, Sir Giles, we intend to counter with the truthful declaration that my father nominated the boy as his heir. If necessary, given the tragic circumstances of Philip's and Isabella's deaths, and indeed my father's, we shall appeal to the king's clemency.'

Giles said nothing for several moments, but at length he nodded.

'Do you intend to speak in court yourselves, or had you thought of acquiring an advocate to speak on your behalf?'

'Neither my mother nor I are orators,' said Rosa. 'We are both able to make some little speech before our tenants, but that seems a quite different matter from defending our position to a judge. I had considered hiring a lawyer to speak on our behalf, but I have no idea where I would find one.' She paused. 'Or, even if I found one, whether I could trust him truly to support our case, given what I assume is its tenuousness in law.'

'I agree,' said Giles. 'Lawyers, in my limited experience, are not always the men of probity you might expect. I wish I could speak for you myself, but I fear that it would be unwise – and unkind to my little Gwynedd – if I overtly took your side against the Bounes.' He stroked his beard. 'But there is a man of undoubted probity who might well be willing to lend his voice to yours in appealing to the king. And that is Raoul de Fougère, my lord and benefactor, and Richard's.'

Margaret beamed. 'Of course, Giles, why had I not thought myself of his lordship? Shall I go to him and beg for help?'

Giles leaned his elbows on the table and steepled his fingers together. Then he rested his chin on top of the steeple and closed his eyes. Rosa exchanged an anxious look with John and her mother, but all three stayed silent whilst Giles seemed to struggle with himself. But at length he opened his eyes and raised his head. He unclasped his fingers and spread his hands in a gesture of surrender. His eyes were smiling, if not his lips.

'I may regret my action, but I cannot, Margaret, let you go to see his lordship alone.'

NORTHWICK PRIORY

JUNE 1357

Rosa settled her mother into a cushioned chair with a small cup of reviving wine. 'And how was your journey, Mother?'

'The road from Meonbridge is improving nicely,' said Margaret, beaming through a wince as she shifted in her chair. 'The warmer weather makes such a difference.'

'Yes, of course it does. And I am glad that your travels this morning were so agreeable. But that was not the journey I was referring to.' Rosa smiled at her mother. 'Sussex?'

Margaret let out a tinkling laugh. 'How silly of me.' She nodded. 'It was *most* successful.'

'But why has Sir Giles not come here with you?'

'He said he should go home at once, for he thought his little Gwynedd, as he calls her, would be much troubled by his already lengthy absence.'

Rosa nodded. 'Best not upset his wife too much.' She paused. 'So are you going to tell me about your audience with his lordship?'

Margaret laughed again. 'Oh, such an honourable and noble man. And how grand is Steyning Castle. And her ladyship, the countess, is so charming and graceful—'

Rosa raised her hand. 'Yes, yes, Mother, but what of your conversation about Dickon and the Bounes?'

Margaret's pale eyes shone as she related the details of her meeting with the earl and countess. 'There was no need at all to plead. His lordship understood immediately the nature of our case.'

'Perhaps he has experienced such a case before?'

Margaret shrugged. 'He did not say so. But he did seem most eager to support the maintenance of the de Bohun line, for he declared your father an exceptional knight and loyal supporter of the king.' She paused, and beamed again. 'And he was most kind too about your brother, recalling his knightly adventures at Crécy.'

Rosa dropped her gaze and closed her eyes. She had been so proud of Philip when he returned from Crécy with their father, hailed a most extraordinary and valiant young knight, who was expected to go far as a warrior of the king. And how much he looked the part, with his noble stature, his dark mane of hair, and his bright and piercing grey-blue eyes. She could still see him in her head. What a handsome man he was. Yet only three years later, he was dead, murdered out of spite, for ignoble retribution, a promising career snuffed out almost before it had begun.

'Rosa,' she heard her mother say, 'are you listening?'

'I am so sorry,' she said, looking up. 'I was thinking about Philip.'

Margaret put out her hand and patted her daughter on the arm.

'Indeed. I too think of him often. And of your father...' She bowed her head, and Rosa did the same, and both women sat in silence for a few moments.

But then Rosa lifted her gaze to meet her mother's. 'I am sorry, Mother, you were saying?'

'Just that his lordship said he thought it only right that I, on Richard's behalf, should retain our estates through the medium of our grandson, as Philip had died in such exceptional and tragic circumstances, having already lost his young wife and unborn child. He said also that Dickon's illegitimacy might be overlooked in the light of Richard's long and faithful service to the king, in contrast to the dubious reputation of the Bounes.'

Rosa let out a deep sigh of relief and took her mother's hands in hers. 'So, he would come to court and speak for us?'

Margaret squeezed Rosa's fingers gently. 'He would. We simply have to send him word that the Bounes have brought their case against us. But he did also make a suggestion about the Bounes.'

'What was that?' said Rosa.

'He thought it might lessen the degree of Morys's disappointment for not winning Meonbridge if we made over, say, the Dorset lands to him, as compensation.'

'So his lordship did think we would win?'

'It seemed so. What do you think of his suggestion?'

Rosa pressed her lips together. 'It is perhaps a pity to break up the estates once we – or rather Dickon – have won entitlement to them. But if it lessens the Bounes' chagrin at losing their prize, it is undoubtedly wise counsel.'

'I agree,' said Margaret. 'So all we must do now is wait, to see if, or when, the Bounes make their move.'

19

The clamour in the manor hall was making Matilda's headache worse. The entire village seemed to have come, men, women and children, cottar, villein and free, and they were all talking at once, all fearful, she supposed, of the outcome of the proceedings if Sir Richard's cousin, the now notorious Morys Boune, succeeded in snatching the inheritance of Meonbridge for himself.

When the news had emerged of the Bounes' appeal to the court of pleas in London on the matter of young Dickon's right to inherit from his grandfather, the manor's tenants and servants were appalled. Small deputations of villagers came up to the manor house, one or two to harangue Margaret for allowing the estate to be put at risk of usurpation by such a knave, but most to offer their support in the crisis into which she had been plunged.

Margaret had been distraught when, two months ago, the sheriff of Hampshire, Sir Walter de Haywood, turned up at the manor and presented her with the writ that the London court had issued, summoning her to give answer to the Bounes. At first, Margaret had been most distressed at the thought that she would have to go to

London to defend herself and Dickon. But Sir Walter shook his head.

'In fact, your ladyship, the court of pleas has passed jurisdiction of this matter to me.' He sighed. 'I am expected to hold the hearing in Hampshire, before a Hampshire jury, and with myself presiding.'

'In Winchester, then?'

The sheriff puffed out his chest. 'Where we hold it is for me to decide.' He stroked his beard. 'We could, my lady, hold it here in Meonbridge, given the number of witnesses the plaintiff plans to call.'

Margaret gasped. 'Witnesses?'

Sir Walter nodded. 'Several.'

Her ladyship's distress had turned to shock at the notion of her tenants testifying against her. By the time the sheriff left, with assurances that he would consult her again soon on the arrangements for the hearing, Margaret had collapsed into her chair, and Matilda could not persuade her to take any supper.

But the next morning her spirits had revived somewhat, and she set off once more for Northwick Priory in order, as she had put it to Matilda, to plan the particulars of the family's defence.

This morning, Matilda had thought she'd rather not attend the court at all. She had slept little, spending most of the night worrying over her part in what was about to take place. She rose at dawn and, leaving Libby sleeping soundly in the narrow truckle bed, crept quietly along the solar passage, intending to go downstairs to the hall and thence outside. As usual when she didn't sleep well, Matilda's head was aching, and she fancied a stroll in the garden, perhaps to sit awhile and listen to the gentle sounds of early morning. But, as she approached the staircase, she heard the sound of movement a little further along the passage, in Margaret's chamber, and she went to see if her ladyship needed her help.

She found Margaret slumped in her chair, her head flopped forward onto her chest. But, as Matilda approached her, Margaret lifted her head up and gave her a weak smile.

'You are up betimes, Matilda.'

'I couldn't bear to lie there any longer, not sleeping.' Matilda guessed that Margaret too had not slept well, for her greying hair was awry, her nightcap slipped and hanging around her neck.

Margaret rubbed at her eyes. 'I feel the same. A dreadful night.'

'Can I help you with anything, my lady?' said Matilda. 'I'd thought to go into the garden for a while, hoping it might clear my aching head.'

Margaret shook her head. 'You go. I shall just sit here and rest my eyes.'

Downstairs in the hall, the servants were already bustling about, making preparations for the arrival of the sheriff and his jury. Matilda was heavy-hearted: it was all her fault that this was happening. She slipped out of the door that led onto the bailey, then ran lightly across the courtyard towards the ramp that led down into the gardens. She headed for an arbour that had a fine view across the fields towards the forest. The arbour was sheltered by an arch covered in cascading honeysuckle and climbing roses, both faded though the roses were still wafting their heady perfume into the early morning air. Nestled beneath the arch was a new turf seat that Margaret had had built last year.

It was Matilda's favourite place to sit and survey the broad expanse of Meonbridge's domain.

She shivered, despite the meagre warmth of the rising sun. She pulled her cloak more closely about her shoulders, but it wasn't just the chilly air. She was frightened of what today might bring, because it wasn't unfolding quite as she had expected.

Back in April, two months after she had revealed to Thorkell that Dickon was Agnes Sawyer's son, that stranger had come to Meonbridge pretending to be looking for his friend Jack. She had been horrified when Libby told her she was with Maud when the man came asking questions. John atte Wode said he suspected the man was in the pay of Morys Boune and would have told his master the truth about Dickon's parentage. At first Matilda thought John must have got that wrong, because why would the Bounes bother to send a man all the way to Meonbridge to discover what they already knew? But then she concluded miserably that perhaps Thorkell didn't trust her or her information, and that was why she hadn't heard from him again.

She really *had* thought he'd come back to see her. She thought they had an understanding. She even thought he might be falling in love with her. But now it seemed he had no interest in her after all.

Which was very disappointing.

When Matilda returned from her stroll, her headache, far from clearing in the morning air, was worse. She'd been worrying for weeks that Morys Boune might call her as a witness, to make her say in court, under oath, that Dickon's mother was Agnes, not Isabella, and so proclaiming Dickon as a bastard. Which was of course what Thorkell hoped to prove and what, surely, she herself had hoped for when she betrayed the de Bohuns to him? Yet, she was now terrified that somehow her evidence would show everyone in Meonbridge that she was a traitor, betraying the family who had so generously taken her in and given her and her daughter a home, despite her father's and husband's wicked crimes against them. But it occurred to her that, if she didn't even attend the court, if she slipped away from the manor for the day – where to, she hadn't thought – she surely couldn't be called upon to speak?

Back in her ladyship's chamber, Matilda had found Margaret asleep, apparently not having moved from her chair. When Matilda shook her gently awake, Margaret's mood was melancholy.

'I think I must have been dreaming of the court,' she said.

'What happened?' said Matilda.

'I cannot remember.' Her face puckered and, when she looked up at Matilda, her eyes were wet. 'I do not know if we won or lost.'

'It was just a dream,' Matilda said, and Margaret nodded. 'But you should get ready, my lady. To prepare yourself...'

Margaret put out her arm so Matilda could help her to her feet.

'Shall I fetch Agatha to help you dress?' said Matilda. 'I'm afraid my headache hasn't shifted.' She put one hand up to her brow and closed her eyes. 'Indeed, it is *much* worse.'

Margaret touched Matilda on the shoulder. 'Why not lie down for a while? I shall call you when it is time—'

'In truth, my lady, I'd thought that maybe I wouldn't come... I do feel so very ill...' She clutched at the back of Margaret's chair, as if she was about to faint.

'Not come?' Margaret stepped back and stared at her. 'You surely cannot mean that?'

She swallowed. 'I...' She *did* mean it but could hardly explain the reason to her ladyship. 'It's just that the megrim—'

Margaret shook her head. 'Oh, I do understand, my dear, how debilitating a megrim can be.' She stepped forward again and put an arm around Matilda. 'But, on this day of all days, I need everyone's support, including yours.'

'You will have Sister Rosa—'

'Of course, and the atte Wodes and the Sawyers, and Raoul de Fougère.' Margaret turned Matilda around to face her. 'But I would have thought, my dear, that you would *want* to show that you too support Dickon's claim to Meonbridge?'

Matilda bowed her head and stared at the floor. Now was not the time to arouse, or perhaps confirm, Margaret's suspicions about her loyalty.

Only two weeks ago, Margaret had taken Matilda into the privacy of her physic garden.

'I was wondering, my dear,' she had said, smiling broadly, as they strolled along the little pathways between the beds of medicinal herbs, still mostly in full bloom, 'if you might welcome a suit from Adam Wragge?'

Matilda gasped, for this had come quite without warning.

'Adam Wragge?' she stuttered. She hadn't set eyes on Master Wragge for months; perhaps at the last Christmas celebration here at the manor? He was away so often these days, overseeing the other de Bohun manors. Adam was an important man, as the de Bohuns' steward, and must be quite well off, she thought. But whilst she might admit he was still a handsome man, he was a villein and, what's more, he was *old*.

Margaret nodded. 'A fine man, Master Wragge, and prosperous. And assuredly far too lusty and vigorous to remain a widower.' She had almost smirked at Matilda, who at once felt queasy.

'Does he want to marry again?'

'Well, he did confess that he had thought he would not do so, as his children are now quite grown and do not need a mother.'

'So he doesn't want me?' Matilda had sighed with relief, yet it was quite vexing to think a man like that might spurn her.

Margaret had shaken her head. 'It was not exactly a refusal, although I shall give some thought to other potential suitors. For I have been thinking of late that, surely, Matilda dear, you would rather be the mistress of your own domain than keep on lodging here, almost as if you were a servant?'

That last comment had been hurtful, but Margaret was quite right. She certainly would rather be the mistress than the glorified lady's maid that she was now. But not the mistress of just any domain. And not the wife of just any man. Matilda was clear enough *whose* wife and *which* domain she hoped for. And, despite her worry that Thorkell might have lost interest in her, she wasn't going to give up that hope.

The last thing she needed now was to get palmed off onto some ageing villein before she had a chance to win over Thorkell Boune.

So, despite her headache and her apprehension, here she was, awaiting the arrival of the sheriff and the jurymen.

But, notwithstanding Margaret's insistence that she needed Matilda's support, her ladyship was not sitting with her, but in a chair at the front of the assembled company, facing the long table where the sheriff and the jurymen would sit. Alongside her were Sister Rosa, and a fine-looking man dressed in the most sumptuous black velvet cotehardie, who Matilda thought must be the earl who Margaret had said would speak for them. Just behind them sat John and Alice atte Wode, and Jack and Agnes Sawyer.

So Matilda had no special place, but at least found herself a seat to one side of the hall, with Alexander, the manor seneschal, and Margaret's maid, Agatha. She turned her head a little so that she could see the crowd gathering behind her. Most of the other manor servants and all the villagers were standing, a throng of people jostling each other for the most advantageous view. But the mood was very different from the last time Matilda had been in their company, last Christmas. Now, many folk had creased brows, or lowering eyelids, or were standing with their arms crossed tight about their chests; others *in* particular the women, were pale-faced, had trembling lips, or just stared into space. Matilda tried to pick out what people were saying above the clamour, and what she heard both disquieted and comforted her.

For most folk thought the Bounes were going to win.

And when she saw Thorkell, standing with his father close to the sheriff's table, a short distance from the de Bohuns, she saw that he must think so too. Then, when he noticed her looking at him, and gave her a brief nod, she was both thrilled and relieved. For his nod was surely accompanied by smiling eyes, and she now felt confident that she would not be called to speak.

Moments later, Matilda heard voices coming from behind the arras that led to the stairs up to the solar, and also to the cross-passage between the hall and the buttery and pantry beyond. Then someone drew the arras back, and the sheriff, Sir Walter de Haywood, and a dozen other men were ushered into the hall. Sir Walter sat down in the grand chair that used to be Sir Richard's, but today was placed at one end of the long table. A clerk sat at the sheriff's side, at a small writing table. He took from a leather scrip parchment rolls, an ink-pot and some quills and, putting them on the table in front of him, he began to write. The other men, whom Matilda presumed were the jurymen Sir Walter had appointed, shuffled along the long bench set behind the table and sat down. None of them were Meonbridge men.

The clamour amongst the villagers subsided, though some low mutterings and whisperings continued to shush around the chamber. But when the constable, Geoffrey Dyer, stepped forward, pulled himself up tall, puffed out his chest and called for silence in a booming voice, everyone fell quiet.

'Oyez,' cried the constable. 'The court of the sheriff of Hampshire is in session, on this Tuesday before Saint Matthew in the thirtieth year of our sovereign Edward the Third. Sir Walter de Haywood, the sheriff of Hampshire, is presiding. Be silent for Sir Walter.'

Sir Walter made a few comments then gestured to Sir Morys Boune to present his case. But it was Thorkell who stood up and bowed to the sheriff. Matilda couldn't see his face but, from the straight set of his shoulders, she guessed that he was looking proud and confident. He raised his voice to speak, ensuring that his deep, clear tones reached to the back of the hall. He spoke of his family's conviction that, despite the assertion of Sir Richard de Bohun that Dickon Sawyer was the heir of his body, the boy was in fact illegitimately born and therefore not entitled to inherit Meonbridge, and the other de Bohun estates. The true heir, he said, was Sir Morys Boune, first cousin to Sir Richard.

His speech concluded, Thorkell bowed again to Sir Walter, who asked him to present evidence of his claim to the court.

Thorkell nodded and whispered to the constable, and Master Dyer announced the name of William Mannering, a cottar. Grunting, William pushed forward through the crowd and stood before the sheriff, shuffling from foot to foot, and fidgeting with the hat he was holding in his hands.

Thorkell stood beside him. 'Master Mannering, will you please tell the sheriff and the gentlemen of the jury who is the mother of the boy called Dickon Sawyer?'

Matilda wondered why Thorkell had asked such a question of a man with no relation to the Sawyers, whilst William shuffled his feet some more and fixed his gaze upon the floor. Thorkell turned slightly to look at his father, and Matilda saw that a frown was creasing his handsome face.

'Well?' he said, his eyebrows arched, and William lifted his head. He turned a little too, and Matilda could see the misery on his face. 'Young Dickon's ma is Mistress Sawyer,' he said, in a voice so low it was hard to hear.

'Say that again, more loudly,' said Thorkell, and William repeated it, only a very little louder.

A good deal of muttering issued forth from the assembled villagers, and it continued as Susanna Miller took William's place before the sheriff and, despite her terrified face and the long pause before she answered, repeated what William had said. Then little Maud came forward, looking as if she might faint from fright, and some folk in the crowd cried 'Shame!'.

Matilda gulped. She'd been so afraid it might be her, standing before the sheriff, obliged to say what William and Susanna and Maud had said, too afraid to be anything but truthful. Then, as she thought it, Matilda felt sure her face was flushed, for suddenly she was very hot, as she wondered once more if Thorkell might still call her forward. Or did the others *know* they would be called? For, in truth, although they all looked frightened, none of them seemed surprised.

More witnesses quickly followed, including – cruelly, Matilda thought – John's mother, Alice. She'd become ill last winter and remained a little frail. Matilda remembered how kind Alice had been to her in that dreadful plague year, when her father and husband murdered Philip de Bohun, and she'd been in such despair to be carrying Gilbert's child. But, frail or not, Mistress atte Wode stood firm enough and upright, but of course she would – could – do no other than declare Dickon the child of her own daughter, Agnes.

And Agnes herself, trembling before Sir Walter, was unlikely to deny that Dickon was her own, after being so indignant when Sir Richard had proclaimed him Isabella's.

But when Nick Ashdown and Simon Hogge were called forward, both stood tall and proud, looking Thorkell in the eye. And when asked the question about Dickon's mother, both declared that, when Sir Richard said the boy was his true heir, he must have *believed* Isabella de Courtenay was his mother. So that must be the truth, else his lordship would not have said it.

A gasp came from the gathering, and Matilda could scarce believe that Nick and Simon would so boldly declare what everyone here surely *knew* to be untrue. Thorkell's shoulders were rigid, and she imagined his face must be black with anger that these two witnesses had denied him the answer he required. Yet she supposed they were simply expressing their support for Lady de Bohun. She wished she could see Margaret's expression, but her ladyship continued to face forwards, holding her back upright and her head high.

But, when Thorkell called his final witness, Margaret did turn her head to look at the woman who then rose from her seat behind the Bounes and moved at a serene and stately pace towards the sheriff's table. It was Lady Hildegard de Courtenay, and her face was dark, revealing what Matilda presumed was her indignation at being summoned to appear before a court. It was curious that the lady had come at all, for surely she could have refused? But perhaps the reason would be borne out in her reply to Thorkell's question.

'Our daughter, the Lady Isabella,' she said, 'the then wife of Sir Philip de Bohun, died in the Great Mortality. They were living here in

186

Meonbridge, and at the time Isabella was with child, but by no more than six months' duration. That was what the de Bohuns told us then, and we had no reason to doubt their word.'

'So, when Sir Richard told us, my brother and myself,' said Thorkell, 'that your daughter died giving birth to the boy now called Dickon Sawyer, it was not true?'

Lady de Courtenay's headdress quivered. 'When my daughter died, she took her *unborn* child with her.'

'So, your ladyship, Sir Richard lied when he said that Isabella gave birth to the boy whom he later claimed to be his grandson – his *legitimate* grandson?'

Her ladyship's eyes were glinting. 'Pah! You already know the answer. Of course Richard lied. No doubt for the best of reasons.' She glanced around the room then brought her eyes back to Margaret. 'I am sorry, my dear, but I cannot allow my darling Isabella to be implicated in such a gross deception. I have to lend my voice to the cause of truth.'

Thorkell thanked Lady de Courtenay, and the sheriff, and the jurymen, then sat back down next to his father. But, before he turned away, Matilda could see that he grinned at his father. And indeed, with so much testimony that Agnes was Dickon's mother it was hard to imagine that the Bounes' case was not entirely proven.

But then Sir Walter turned to Margaret and asked if she, or her daughter, wished to speak. At which, the earl stood up and, stepping slightly forward, nodded to the sheriff and the jurymen. 'Lady de Bohun and her daughter have requested that I speak for them.'

Sir Walter nodded. 'Your name, sir?' He smiled. 'For my clerk.'

The earl briefly bowed his head. 'Raoul de Fougère, Earl of Steyning. I will call no witnesses, sir, but simply make a statement, on my own behalf and that of Lady de Bohun.'

The sheriff nodded again and gestured to the earl to continue.

'I am not here to deny the validity of the plaintiff's claim, nor to refute the statements of the plaintiff's witnesses. It is clear enough that the boy whom Sir Richard de Bohun appointed as his heir is *not* the son of the Lady Isabella. But he *is* the son of Sir Philip de Bohun and therefore carries de Bohun blood.'

He paused. 'Despite the circumstances of his upbringing, the boy

187

Dickon *is* a de Bohun. And I, as lord and benefactor of Sir Richard, am most eager to support the continuation of the de Bohun blood line, for Sir Richard was an exceptional knight and loyal supporter of the king. As was Sir Philip, who, despite his youth and lack of experience, proved a most remarkable warrior.'

The earl then launched into an account of what he referred to as Philip's glorious exploits on the battlefield of Crécy, when he was virtually still a boy, two and half years before the Great Mortality.

Matilda had heard these stories many times before but, looking around her, she realised that most of the villagers had not, for they were listening in silence and with rapt faces. And her heart swelled with pride that she known such a man as Philip de Bohun, if only for a short time, and even though he had treated her rather badly.

She turned back to look across at Thorkell, whose shoulders were now hunched, and one of his feet was tapping at the floor. She recalled how Thorkell became quickly bored with tales of knightly adventures for, she supposed, he'd none of his own to brag about.

And, only a moment later, he sprang to his feet and addressed the sheriff. 'Do we have to listen to this interminable eulogy of the so very *valiant* Sir Philip?' He sneered, and the sheriff raised his eyebrows.

Even Matilda thought it very ill-mannered of Thorkell to interrupt the earl so rudely. And the sheriff seemed to agree, for he flapped a hand at Thorkell.

'You have had a good and lengthy opportunity to present your case, *Master* Boune. Please do his noble lordship the courtesy of allowing him to present his case, in whatever way he considers apt.' He lifted his eyebrows even higher and gestured to Thorkell to sit down.

Matilda could see from the stiffness of his shoulders how furious Thorkell was to be spoken to in such a way. But he did sit, and flicked his hand towards the earl, who inclined his head.

Matilda then noticed that each and every juryman was grinning and nodding at his lordship, and she wondered, with disappointment, if Thorkell had spoiled his chances by his outburst, despite the strength of his case.

The earl turned back to the sheriff. 'Sir, if I may continue. My view is that, given the outstanding service both Sir Richard and his son, Sir Philip, gave to their king, and given that Philip died in such exceptional and wretched circumstances, having already lost his young wife and unborn child, in the most horrific devastation of our age, and given that Sir Richard too has only recently lost *his* life, again in tragic circumstances...' He paused and bowed his head, keeping it lowered for several moments. 'In my view it is only just and honourable that Sir Richard's wishes be fulfilled, and that the de Bohun family should retain their estates through the medium of Sir Philip's son, conceived, as I understand it, prior to his marriage to the Lady Isabella.'

There was a good deal of muttering in the crowd over the earl's last comment, but Matilda thought it must be true. And the sheriff and the jurymen seemed to share her view, for they were all nodding and waggling their heads.

The earl returned to his seat, and Matilda thought that everything he'd said did sound very fair. But none of it refuted the truth that Dickon was illegitimate and therefore not strictly entitled to inherit. Glancing across at Thorkell and his father, she could see that their earlier confidence in a successful outcome had vanished. But surely the jury would still find in their favour, for theirs was the legitimate entitlement, despite the earl's fine words?

The jurymen got up from their places at the table and filed out of the hall back through the arras. Had they gone out for a breath of air? They were away for quite some time, and the villagers in the hall were becoming restless. But, at length, the men returned and retook their seats, and the sheriff asked them if they had come to a conclusion.

Each man answered, one by one, and by the time the last man spoke, it was clear that the jurymen had been convinced of the fairness of young Dickon's right to the inheritance, despite his illegitimacy.

Sir Walter nodded. 'It seems to me also a fair-minded, equitable decision, given the uniquely difficult circumstances that have afflicted the de Bohun family.' He puffed out his chest. 'I will inform the court of pleas of the jury's decision.'

Cheers of relief erupted from the villagers, whilst Thorkell leapt to his feet, shouting his objection to the verdict. But Sir Walter shook his head and went forward to speak to Thorkell and his father.

Amid the rising clamour, the earl stepped forward again, held up his hand and signalled to the sheriff for a moment's further chance to speak. At Sir Walter's nod, the earl faced him and the Bounes. 'I would make a further point. Lady de Bohun has instructed me to offer to transfer all of the de Bohun lands in Dorset to Sir Morys Boune, as a gesture of conciliation.'

Sir Walter agreed that was a fair and honourable proposal, but Matilda could see that neither Thorkell nor his father looked at all impressed by it.

The villagers, chatting happily now and still raising the occasional cheer, pushed their way out of the hall, through the door that led onto the bailey. Matilda wanted to leave too. She cast what she thought would be her last gaze at Thorkell Boune and was frightened by what she saw on his face and his father's. Both were black with anger, and she was suddenly afraid that Thorkell might think she had led him into this and find a way of blaming her.

She hadn't meant to but, as she gazed, she caught Thorkell's eye. He scowled back at her. But then he jerked his head to show he wanted to meet her outside the hall. She nodded. She would go out to talk to him, despite her fear of what he might be going to say.

Outside, Thorkell led Matilda away into the garden, to the arbour.

'Sit,' he said to her, indicating the turf seat, but did not sit himself. 'So where have you been all this time?'

Matilda looked up in surprise. 'I haven't—'

'I came to see you in April and was told by the gatekeeper you were away, visiting relatives, he said.'

She shook her head.

'Then, in July, I came again, and got the same story. So you were away for *four* months?' Thorkell sneered. 'I didn't think you had any relatives, or none who'd entertain you for so long.'

She was confused. 'I haven't been away at all. The gatekeeper must have misunderstood—'

Thorkell narrowed his eyes. 'He wouldn't have got it wrong twice, Matilda.' He raked his hair with his hand. 'No, I suppose her ladyship put him up to it. She didn't want me seeing you. And why would that be, I wonder?'

Matilda's heart was pounding, but she didn't know how to answer.

'We've just lost the case, Matilda,' Thorkell went on, his voice harsh. 'I protected you by not calling you to witness. I thought it might put you in danger, or at least embarrassment, if they knew it was *you* who told us about Dickon.'

She nodded. She hadn't thought of it as protection.

'As it was, there were enough people to admit the truth. But perhaps it was all for nothing, because you'd already told her ladyship what you'd told me. So she could get the earl on to her side for him to give a sob story about how brave and noble the de Bohuns were, and how tragic the death of Philip and his stupid little wife. So the poor de Bohuns have suffered enough, let's not take their land away from them too—'

Thorkell picked up a fallen branch and lashed out at the arbour. Matilda jumped at the crack of wood on wood, and tears welled in her eyes.

But Thorkell was not finished. 'Pah!' he cried, thrashing at the arbour once again. 'It's not justice that happened here today, but patronage and prejudice. And de Fougère had the nerve to suggest we're thrown the little sop of the Dorset lands.'

For a while, Thorkell seemed so angry that Matilda feared he might hit out at her. But he paced a while back and forth in front of her, muttering to himself, and eventually became a little calmer.

'I must go back to find my father,' he said. 'You'll come with me.'

Matilda wasn't at all sure she wanted to, for she didn't know where she stood with Thorkell now that they'd lost Meonbridge. But she didn't have much choice in the matter, for Thorkell grasped her arm and marched her back through the garden, out of the manor gate and down towards the village.

At length they arrived at Mistress Rolfe's, where he and his father were lodging. He left her in the parlour whilst he went to find Morys. She thought briefly about running back to the manor house. But when Thorkell returned, she was still there, waiting.

'My father's leaving,' he said. 'But I'm going to stay another night.'

'Why?'

'Our business with Meonbridge isn't done. My father wants it and so do I. We'll just have to find another way.' He put out a hand and rested it lightly on her arm. 'And perhaps you, my sweet, can help us. After all, you did try to bring the truth out into the open.'

Matilda was astonished at how suddenly Thorkell's mood had changed. 'It was wrong of Sir Richard to tell such lies. Even her ladyship and Lady Johanna thought so. I was only making sure the truth was known.' She bit her lip.

He took her chin gently in his hand, and kissed her. 'You weren't to know the de Bohuns would appeal to aristocratic partiality to claim that wrong is right.'

A short while later, Matilda returned to the manor, to see Margaret and Rosa, and to have supper. They were in high spirits, which she made a pretence of sharing. But, after she had picked at her food a while, she excused herself and went up to bed, claiming her headache had returned.

When it was quite dark and the household had settled down for the night, Matilda slipped out of the house, and, using an old forgotten gate she knew of that was obscured by ivy and had no lock, she escaped the manor grounds and found Thorkell waiting for her nearby.

'I know an old house,' he said in a whisper.

She queried how he could know of any such place, but then realised with chagrin that it was probably Blanche Jordan's. And when she and Thorkell arrived at the house, a good way along the road to Middle Brooking, she knew that she was right. It had been Blanche's family home until she left to marry Alain Jordan, when he came back a knight from Crécy with Sir Richard, and it was where her parents had continued to live until they died in the Mortality. Like so many houses in Meonbridge after the plague passed on, it was abandoned, left to crumble, but perhaps it hadn't crumbled away entirely, for Matilda had heard gossip that Blanche went there sometimes to "entertain" her gentlemen friends. Presumably, she had brought Thorkell here... But Matilda decided not to let the thought of that upset her. For, after all, this was what she'd been craving for months, and she was hardly going to let the thought of him with that slut stand in her way.

As a lovers' nest, the house was hardly what Matilda had dreamed of. It had once been one of the better houses in the village, but now the daub was falling from the walls, and the door was so swollen that Thorkell had to lean hard upon it to make it open. He led her inside, holding up the lantern he'd brought with him. The main room was under a collapsed part of the roof, and the floor was covered with dead leaves and other debris. But, in a corner of the house, what was perhaps once a storeroom was still sheltered by a roof and walls that seemed quite sound. There was even a small window, protected by a half-broken shutter on the outside and a tattered piece of cloth.

And there was a bed, of sorts.

It was just a straw mattress, lifted off the floor on a rough wooden frame. A thick blanket had been thrown across the mattress, and underneath it was a sheet. Matilda shuddered to think what might have found its way onto that sheet, but decided it was better not imagined.

She had to smile. 'What a delightfully comfortable trysting place you've brought me to, Sir Thorkell,' she said, tilting her head to one side, and he laughed.

'Who needs comfort when we have each other?' he said.

Then he put down the lantern and came to stand in front of her. He took her face in his hands and kissed her lips. Then he dropped his hands and untied the lacing at the front of her gown and pulled down the bodice to her waist.

Matilda thought she should surely be holding back, resisting in some way, to make it clear that she was not like Blanche Jordan. But resistance was already impossible, and she did nothing to stop him gently cupping her breasts in his hands. Or lowering his face to drop light soft kisses onto each one.

And now Matilda was afire, all hesitation gone, wanting nothing more than for him to touch her in her most private place.

'Now,' she whispered, 'now.'

But Thorkell shook his head. 'Oh, no, my sweet,' he whispered close into her ear, 'it is I who decides when the time is right, not you.'

She trembled. 'I think I might die, if it is not soon.'

He blew into her ear. 'You won't die, my sweet Matilda, but you will surely be in Paradise.'

20

CASTLE BOUNE
SEPTEMBER 1357

M orys thumped his mazer down so hard onto the table that red wine slopped onto the sleeve of his surcoat. But he didn't notice, and Thorkell knew his father couldn't care less about his surcoat, despite it being newly acquired for their appearance at the sheriff of Hampshire's court.

Gunnar was trying to calm his father, but it was clear that Morys held Thorkell wholly responsible for his humiliation at the court, before all of Meonbridge, and refused to let his anger rest. The old man just kept going on and on, reiterating the reasons why Thorkell was to blame.

'Why did I listen to you, boy?' he growled, and Thorkell gritted his teeth.

Then Morys assumed a whiny voice. '"Oh, Pa, if we get Meonbridge *legally*, I can hold the estate with honour". Pah! You really thought the de Bohuns would let us win?'

'Our case was strong, Pa. We weren't to know de Fougère would interfere—'

'Or that the court of pleas would hand our case over to the sheriff

194

of Hampshire, who'd then select the jurymen himself and sit in judgement on us,' said Gunnar, grimacing.

Morys banged his mazer once again. 'You're right, Gunnar. The Hampshire gentry ranged against us uncivilised outsiders. Patronage, that's what it was. Not justice at all. The sheriff *fixed* the jury, so they'd fall for all that trumpery spouted by de Fougère, despite Sir Dicky's lies and the falseness of the de Bohuns' claim.' He roared and spat into the rushes.

Thorkell had had enough, and kicked out at a stool, sending it spinning across the floor and almost landing in the fire. Gunnar leapt up and rescued it before it began to burn. 'Calm down, little brother.'

But Thorkell threw his hands up in the air. 'Why should I, when I'm being arraigned by my own father for trying to give this family a position in society?'

Gunnar snorted. 'You really are an idiot, Thorkell. You're pissing in the wind if you think that Hampshire society is going to welcome the likes of us.'

Thorkell scowled. 'We're as good as any of them—'

'You might think so, but they don't.'

'Anyway,' said Morys, 'we don't do things their way. We have our own ways, and I suggest we stick to them.' He grinned. 'Because we know they work.'

Gunnar nodded. 'You're right, Pa.' Then he turned to his brother. 'I see what you're after, Thorkell, but I just don't think it's going to happen. We must do what we always planned to do—'

'Kidnap the brat?' said Thorkell.

'Or worse, you said.'

And Thorkell laughed out loud. 'It will be a pleasure.'

Morys banged his mazer down a third time, but this time he accompanied the thump with a loud guffaw. 'That's more like it.'

Thorkell shrugged and, going over to the table, poured himself a cup of wine. He sat down and mused on their original plan to kidnap the boy. He hadn't considered it before, but he now realised how inconvenient it would be to mount an attack from such a distance as Castle Boune. It occurred to him that Morys should not have refused the de Bohuns' offer after all. 'What are you going to do about the de Bohuns' Dorset manors, Pa? Don't you think you should accept them?'

Morys growled. 'I'm not a cur grovelling and pawing for their scraps—'

Thorkell held up his hand. 'No, Pa, but just think. How useful it would be to have a muster point closer to Courtenay Castle, or at least to Meonbridge.'

Gunnar chortled. 'Good thinking, little brother. It must be closer to both of them than here.'

Thorkell nodded. 'I don't know how much closer... But, anyway, Pa, the de Bohuns were offering to *give* you those manors. It's surely absurd to refuse them just out of pride and umbrage, when they could be useful to us?'

Morys didn't answer but poured himself yet another cup of wine and sat in apparent contemplation, scratching at his chin. At length, he thumped his hand upon the table. 'Very well. Gunnar, you'll ride to Meonbridge tomorrow and accept Lady de Bohun's offer.' He snorted. 'She likes you, doesn't she?'

Gunnar's eyes twinkled. 'More than Thorkell, anyway. Given she's tried to ban him from visiting his little woman—'

Thorkell sprang to his brother's side and cuffed him around the head. Gunnar retaliated with a punch to Thorkell's belly, and the two men fell into a brawl just as they did when they were boys. Except that now they were laughing as well as punching. But it wasn't long before Gunnar raised his hands. For Thorkell was now a good deal taller and stronger than his older brother and, if he often lost a fight when they were younger, these days he always won.

At Gunnar's capitulation, Thorkell disentangled himself from the scrimmage and stood up, then offered his hand to his brother to haul him to his feet. 'I'm not your "little brother" any more, eh, Gunnar?' he said.

He grimaced. 'Sadly not. But I daresay I can best you in other ways.'

Thorkell shook his head and laughed. 'Now, what about this plan?'

The strategy had always been for the de Bohun brat to meet somehow with an "accident". Now he was no longer at home in Meonbridge, but living at Courtenay Castle, Thorkell thought that, maybe on one of his

196

occasional visits home, he could seem to be waylaid by bandits and kidnapped, or even killed.

'Who accompanies him when he travels?' said Gunnar. 'Did your little woman tell you?'

Thorkell grinned. 'She did. She has a wealth of information, as I always thought she would have.'

Morys grunted. 'Let's hope this time it doesn't lead us into disaster.'

Thorkell shook his head. 'She said what usually happens is that the Meonbridge bailiff, John atte Wode, accompanies the boy to Courtenay Castle, with a small band of armed men, and a friar from the de Courtenay household.'

'Why the friar?' said Gunnar.

'Apparently he tutors the boy in reading and writing and suchlike. And it was agreed that, if the brat was away from the de Courtenays for more than two or three days, the tutor would accompany him. So the friar stays at Meonbridge for as long as the boy does. Then when he's ready to return, the whole party travels with him.'

Gunnar frowned. 'Why does the boy go back to Meonbridge anyway?'

'Matilda thinks it's to learn the trappings of lordship—'

'But he's only eight.' Gunnar threw back his head in a great guffaw.

Thorkell shrugged. 'Who knows, then?'

Morys grunted. 'Can we get back to the little "accident"? Who of those men is, shall we say, pliable? The friar, perhaps?'

Thorkell nodded. 'Possibly. Matilda said he seemed a weak, sly sort of fellow.'

Gunnar guffawed again. 'A friar – sly? A man of God? Surely not!'

Morys and Thorkell shared his feigned amusement. But then Gunnar wondered out loud how they could approach the friar in order to bribe him.

And Thorkell immediately thought he knew the answer. 'The de Courtenays are seething about the court case. I ran into Baldwin afterwards.'

'Ran into?' said Gunnar, and Thorkell grinned.

'And?' said Morys, frowning.

'Lady de Courtenay was especially mortified to be forced to admit in public that something she'd appeared to assert before was in fact a lie—'

'What do you mean?' said Gunnar.

'When they agreed to accept the brat as a page, it was on the unspoken assumption that he was their grandson as well as the de Bohuns', even though they knew full well he wasn't. They agreed to maintain the fiction, without actually declaring it.'

'Then, in court, my lady had to divulge what she knew to be the truth, and show herself to have been dishonest, if not actually a liar.' Gunnar smirked.

Thorkell joined in his brother's mirth. 'Sir Hugh was evidently much aggrieved that his wife had been put into such an undignified position. And that, because of what she said, his own honesty was called into question.' He snorted. 'Baldwin was enraged that his parents had been humiliated in such a public place.'

'So everyone is furious,' said Morys, growling. 'So *what?*'

'I suggested he might like to support us, if we pursued our claim to Meonbridge.' Thorkell raised an eyebrow. 'And, when he resisted, I persuaded him to agree.'

'"Persuaded?"' Morys snorted, his eyes alight. 'So what are you thinking?'

'We'll get him to work on the friar, and to organise the little accident, as close to Courtenay Castle as possible.'

Morys nodded. 'Would he balk at murdering the boy?'

Thorkell shook his head. 'He loathes the brat.'

21

R osa was emerging from the chapel into a blustering wind and driving rain that caught her and her fellow nuns between the chapel door and the relative shelter of the cloister, when she realised there was a visitor at the gate. Running back out into the rain and across the courtyard, she hurried to the gate to find out who had come and was not surprised to find John atte Wode, once more trying to gain admittance in the face of the bad-tempered old gatekeeper.

John was soaked through from his ride, and Rosa insisted that he dry himself off and warm up a little before he related his news. She brought him some bread and cheese and a cup of small ale to fend off what she knew would be his early morning hunger.

The bailiff shivered as he sat before the rather feeble fire burning in the priory's public chamber, rubbing his hands together. 'It's hard to get warm again,' he said, and Rosa nodded.

'It is a pity I cannot offer you a change of clothes, but I am afraid we have none here.'

'No matter,' mumbled John, through a mouthful of sour bread and

199

crumbling cheese. He pointed to his mouth and Rosa nodded again, understanding.

'Finish your food, John. Whatever you have to tell me can surely wait a little longer.'

He managed a smile, then took a slurp of ale. Rosa murmured that she would leave him for a few moments and went in search of Sister Juliana.

'Can you please try to find a good warm blanket, Sister? For our chilly visitor.' Juliana nodded and ran off on her mission, and Rosa returned to see if John had finished eating.

'Thank you,' he said, when she came back into the room. He pointed to the empty bowl and cup. 'And I apologise for my ill manners, as always.' He grimaced, but Rosa laughed lightly.

'No matter. Now what is it you have come to tell me?'

'I'm afraid our nephew's been in danger,' he said. Rosa gasped, but John held up his hand. 'But he's unharmed, at least in body.'

Rosa clutched her silver cross and raised it to her lips. 'God be praised for that. What happened, John? Was anyone hurt?'

'I'm afraid so, Sister.'

And he went on to relate how the party travelling with Dickon on his journey home to Meonbridge from Courtenay Castle, for a visit to his grandmother, had been attacked on the road ten miles or so from Haslemere. 'It seemed that the friar, Dickon's tutor, led our party into an ambush—'

Rosa gasped. 'Why would he do that?'

'I'll tell you later why I think he did,' said John. 'Anyway, the ambush consisted of half a dozen armed ruffians, who tried to take Dickon from us. But my Meonbridge men made a good job of overcoming the attackers, and I managed to get away, taking Dickon and the friar with me. The rest of my men caught up with us soon after, having chased off the attackers with their greater force of arms.' He grunted. 'Whoever organised the ambush didn't assign enough, or good enough, men.'

At that moment, Juliana appeared at the door, carrying a folded woollen blanket, and Rosa took it from her and, unfolding it, placed it around John's shoulders. He smiled gratefully at both Rosa and little Juliana, who bobbed a curtsey and withdrew.

'So, you said the friar *led* the party into the ambush?' said Rosa.

John nodded. 'That's the way it seemed. When we were back in Meonbridge, I suggested to him that he'd organised the attack, though of course he denied it. But our constable, Geoffrey Dyer, persuaded the friar to talk.'

Rosa tutted. She mused upon what type of "persuasion" the constable might have used, and assumed it involved some kind of violence. 'Really, John, was that necessary?'

'I thought so, given the danger he'd put our nephew in.' Rosa nodded, though she could hardly give her approval to such methods. 'Anyway,' continued John, 'the friar gave in easily enough, confessing also Baldwin de Courtenay's part in the plot.'

'But why would Baldwin want to harm Dickon?'

'The friar didn't know, but he suggested Baldwin was angry that his parents, and in particular his mother, were so humiliated at the sheriff's court.'

Rosa nodded. 'Poor Lady de Courtenay was certainly most unhappy at having to reveal her own dishonesty, particularly when I believe she was persuaded quite against her better judgement.' She got up and paced around the room a little. 'So what will you do about Baldwin? What does my mother think?'

'I'm not sure we should do anything. We've Dickon safe in Meonbridge, but he mustn't go back to Courtenay Castle.'

Rosa shook her head. 'I now wonder why on earth we thought it right for him to stay there after the court case.'

'I agree. But her ladyship will send a message to the de Courtenays, saying we've found a different place for him to train.'

'And have you?'

'Her ladyship intends asking the earl. Given his support at the court, she's confident he'll take the boy and Dickon will be well protected at Steyning Castle.'

'That does seem a good plan.' Rosa sighed. 'Oh, John, if only my father had not tried to deceive everyone with his claim that Dickon was his legitimate heir.'

'Yet, if Sir Richard hadn't made his claim, wouldn't Meonbridge now be in the hands of Morys Boune?'

She looked up, surprised. Was he right? She considered it a

moment. Suppose her father had *not* made his claim, and had *not* introduced Dickon to the Bounes? After his death, the law might well have simply taken its natural course, and Morys would have been discovered to be the rightful heir. If her mother tried then to gainsay it, her opinion and Dickon's illegitimate claim would almost certainly have been dismissed.

'Despite all that has happened, John, I think you must be right. My father's words precipitated the Bounes into actions that have proved their undoing.'

He nodded, but then a shadow fell across his face. 'Yet, Sister, I think we mustn't assume the Bounes will now let it go. So we must hope Dickon will soon be safely in the protection of the earl.'

22

Thorkell thought he'd never again see his father any angrier than when they lost their claim for Meonbridge at the sheriff's court. But, right now, Morys's fury seemed so vehement Thorkell wondered if the old man's heart might give way.

Thorkell too was angry that Baldwin de Courtenay had failed in such a simple task as kidnapping an eight-year-old boy. But his father was raging up and down the hall, throwing at the absent Baldwin every vile defamation he could draw up from his well of calumnies, which was very deep.

Gunnar, sitting in the shadows, out of his father's rampaging path, grimaced at his brother, and Thorkell shrugged.

Gunnar got to his feet. 'Pa, it's over,' he said, raising his voice above his father's carping. 'There's nothing we can do about it.' Morys roared his displeasure, but Gunnar continued. 'We must just try again—'

Morys strode to the table and brought his fist down upon it. 'And when we do, we'll do it *our* way,' he hissed. 'With *our* men. Men we can trust. Not rely on some imbecile—' His face was crimson.

Gunnar placed a hand upon his father's shoulder and pushed him

down onto a bench next to the table. 'Sit down, Pa. And calm down...'
He poured his father a cup of wine and put it in his hand. 'Drink this.'

Morys grabbed the cup and took a long, deep draught, but coughed
as he overdid it and, spluttering, sprayed wine over the table and his
eldest son.

Gunnar yelled and jumped back. 'Was that really necessary, Pa?' He
flicked at the drops of wine spattering his tunic. 'Can we just stop all
this sound and fury?' He turned to Thorkell. 'Can you talk some sense
into him, little brother?'

Thorkell went and sat down opposite his father. 'Gunnar's right, Pa.
There's no good to be had from dwelling on what's happened. We just
need to think of a better plan than Baldwin's.'

'And the first thing you can do is get rid of that imbecile. He needs
to disappear—'

Gunnar frowned. 'Why, Pa?'

Morys grunted. 'I'd have thought that was obvious, even to you. To
make sure he doesn't blab about *our* part in the failed attack.'

'You're right, Pa,' said Thorkell. 'We'll arrange it.' He glanced across
at his brother, who shrugged. 'Soon.'

Morys took another swig of wine and snorted. 'Good. And, in the
meantime, perhaps you should spend some time with your Meonbridge
whore. See if she's got any better ideas for getting at the boy?'

Thorkell grimaced at his father's epithet for Matilda. Though why
he objected to it, he didn't know. Of course, Matilda wasn't like
Blanche Jordan, who certainly would spread her legs to anyone who
asked her. No, Matilda was devoted to just one man – him. Rather like
his faithful hounds. He grinned to himself. Perhaps it was Matilda's
staunch devotion that he valued? A pity for her that it was neither
reciprocated, nor likely to be of any further value once his ambition
had been realised.

MEONBRIDGE
NOVEMBER 1357

When Thorkell rode into Meonbridge, it was dark, the moon's light
obscured by a blanket of thick cloud. He was wearing a black cloak

with an enormous hood that could conceal his face, should anybody be abroad.

As usual, when he was getting close to Meonbridge, he'd found a rider willing to take Matilda a message, telling her where and when to meet him. There was always a possibility that his message would fail to reach her, if the messenger took his fee but didn't bother to ride to Meonbridge. Or that Matilda wouldn't be able to find a way of slipping out. But so far it had worked. He let the thought of her sensuous body play around inside his head, and the familiar stirring soon demanded to be sated.

He waited close by the old gate in the manor's outer wall that Matilda had used last time she'd slipped out to meet him. The gate was so obscured by ivy that, in the dark, it was quite hard to find, but on the outside of the wall, quite close to the gate, there was a substantial stand of saplings, where he'd concealed himself before. Tonight, it was so black he'd be quite hidden in the middle of the trees, so he dismounted and led his horse between the tree trunks and hoped Matilda would not be long.

By the time he saw the gate ease open and Matilda – or at any rate, a woman – emerge, also clad in a dark enveloping cloak, Thorkell had almost given up hope that she would come. He'd become impatient and was already thinking about leaving. But he'd come such a long way for this that he thought he might just find a way of reprimanding her instead. He smirked at the idea of it.

The woman ran lightly from the gate to join him amid the trees. He couldn't see her face.

'Matilda?' he whispered.

'Of course.' She giggled.

He was relieved it was her but irritated about his wait. 'Why were you so long?' He knew he sounded vexed, and told himself he should calm his temper, if he wanted the next few hours to be worth his journey. So he put his arms around her, and pulled her close.

'It's not easy to get away,' she said.

'What excuse did you give?'

'I didn't have to. Margaret went to her room early with a megrim. But I had to wait till Libby was asleep.'

'What'll happen if the girl wakes up and finds you gone?'

'Nothing. She's accustomed to it, for I often leave my bed at night, when I can't sleep. She'll just drift off again.'

Thorkell nodded. 'That's fortunate.' He pulled her close to him again. 'Shall we go?'

'To the house?'

He had thought they might go to an inn a couple of miles from Meonbridge, but now it was so late, the inn would be closed to visitors. 'Do you know if Blanche is likely to be there?'

Matilda shook her head against his chest. 'I don't think so. Only the other day I heard that her husband had found out about her new favourite, one of the squires.' She giggled. 'Just a boy really—'

'And he squeezed the life out of her in his jealousy?' Thorkell barely suppressed a laugh.

Matilda pulled away from him. 'No, of course not. But I think he may have curtailed her liberty.'

'Good for us, then,' said Thorkell. 'Shall we try it?'

It was freezing cold inside Blanche's' cottage.

'Shall we light a fire?' said Matilda, but Thorkell snorted.

'And let all the neighbours know we're here?'

'They'd think it was Blanche.'

'But doesn't everyone in Meonbridge know she's no longer allowed out?'

'I think only folk in the manor know.' Matilda shrugged. 'Anyway, it might not even be true.'

Thorkell snorted. He felt like slapping her. 'We'll do without the fire, Matilda. We'll just have to create enough heat of our own.' He grinned, although she couldn't see it.

But at that moment the moon must have emerged a little from behind the blanket of cloud, for a few scraps of feeble light shone through the broken shutters. A faint shaft of light fell across Matilda's face, and Thorkell cupped her head in his hands.

'That's better, I can see you now.' He kissed her, on her forehead, then her cheeks, and finally her lips. He felt her shudder.

'Shall we go and make some heat?' she whispered and, nodding, he took her hand and led her to the little room at the back of the house.

'I said we'd soon get warm,' said Thorkell in her ear. He wrapped his legs and arms around her and pulled her tight against his body. He breathed hotly into her ear.

Matilda nodded. 'I was on fire.'

'You certainly are a little demon.' He kissed her ear, then bit it lightly.

She squealed. 'Ow! That hurt.' And then she nipped his lip, a bit too hard, and Thorkell yelped like a dog.

'And so did that, you bitch.' He licked his bottom lip and tasted blood. Then, his humour changing in an instant, he unfolded his arms and pushed Matilda away so roughly that she rolled off the mattress onto the filthy floor, dragging the blanket with her. She cried out, with surprise, he supposed, for she could hardly have been hurt, and she whimpered a little, like a cur that's just been kicked.

But the sudden shiver of freezing air on Thorkell's back was an urgent, chastening reminder of the need to keep warm, and for once he decided to back down. It would be absurd to freeze to death for the sake of a bitten lip. So he leaned across the mattress and felt for Matilda's arm. But, as he found it, she pulled away. He growled but tried again.

'Matilda, I didn't mean to push you,' he said, reaching for her arm again and finding it. 'You shouldn't have bitten me like that.'

This time she didn't pull her arm away but stayed lying on the floor. Thorkell's skin was prickling with the cold. He'd have to get up and dress if she didn't let him back under the blanket soon. He ground his teeth. He had no choice but to plead guilty.

Rolling across the bed, he put his arms around Matilda and lifted her back onto the mattress. Then, disentangling her from the heavy blanket, he rewrapped it around them both, and clasped her to him once again. She was shivering, though her body still felt warm.

'I'm sorry,' he said, and kissed her head.

Matilda nodded. 'Me too.' And she nuzzled at the crook of his shoulder with her chin.

. . .

Thorkell woke up with a start. It was still dark and absolutely silent outside the house. Not even a breath of wind. He wondered if snow had fallen but was disinclined to get up to find out. The moon was still up, for a faint light shone through the half-broken shutter at the tiny window, seeping around the tattered cloth. Letting his eyes accustom to the light, he found that he could just see Matilda, sleeping peacefully in his arms. He stared down at her face, watching her eyelids flutter, her lips move quietly, the rise and fall of her lovely breasts beneath the blanket.

It *was* a pity he was merely using her. A pity she believed him when he pretended to offer marriage. A pity she would be expendable once he'd won his prize.

All a pity that he comprehended well enough but was, in truth, quite able to shrug off.

He dropped a kiss onto Matilda's forehead, and then her lips. She stirred a little and he whispered in her ear, 'Shall we warm ourselves up again?'

But she continued sleeping. He grunted. There was nothing for it but to make her. He remembered then that earlier he'd thought of punishing her for coming to him so late last night. He grinned to himself. Wasn't now the perfect moment?

He freed the arm that Matilda was lying on and, rolling her a little so she was on her back, he heaved himself on top of her and took her easily. But, moments later, she was awake, and would have screamed if he'd not been ready to clamp his hand across her mouth.

The moon's light had gone from the window, and he could no longer see her face, but Thorkell thought she might be crying. When he'd finished and rolled off her, his hand slipped off her mouth, but she stayed quiet. Laying his hand against her face again, he felt the wetness on her cheeks. She brought up her hand to his and, taking it from her face, placed it on her breasts.

'Why didn't you wake me?' she said and gave a little sob.

'I did.'

But Matilda shook her head. 'You know you didn't.' Then she moved her hand to caress the curve of Thorkell's waist and hip. 'Again?' she said. He thought briefly of denying her, but it seemed pointless also to deny himself.

. . .

Afterwards, Matilda fell asleep once more, but Thorkell lay awake. The moon was again casting a faint glimmer through the tiny window, and he would soon have to wake Matilda, if he was to fulfil the real purpose of his journey here. Yet even he, looking at her lovely face, felt the smallest pang of guilt at his duplicity towards her. But he at once dismissed it. They needed a plan, and Matilda was the source of information about life inside the manor. A source that he had to tap, or his journey would have been for nothing.

He shook Matilda's shoulder, and whispered in her ear, but it took a few attempts before her eyes half opened.

'Is it morning?' she said.

'Yes, but not yet time to rise.' He kissed her. 'Matilda, I need to talk to you.'

Her eyes then opened wide. 'What about?'

'The de Bohun brat.'

Her eyes fluttered closed again as she turned her head away. 'Oh.'

He stroked her cheek. 'We need another plan, Matilda. We haven't given up on winning Meonbridge, despite the verdict of the court.'

Matilda nodded. 'Was it you who planned the attack on Dickon? It was I who told you how he travelled between Courtenay Castle and Meonbridge...'

Thorkell didn't answer, and Matilda carried on. 'But Margaret and John atte Wode think it was Baldwin de Courtenay who planned it, in revenge for the way his parents were discomfited at the court.'

'Baldwin *was* furious and, when we suggested he might like to arrange to capture the brat, he jumped at the idea. It was simpler for him to do it – in theory, anyway. But the halfwit failed to do it properly. So now we must do something else.'

She pouted. 'I could be offended that you only brought me here to pick my brains, rather than make love to me,' she said, a tart edge to her voice. But then she let her tongue play on her lips. 'What will happen, if you do kidnap Dickon?'

Thorkell snorted. He could hardly tell her what he and his father thought. Gunnar would take a less murderous stance, but his own view and their father's would prevail. 'The plan is to spirit him away,' he said, 'out of the country, maybe. Give him a new identity.'

'That doesn't seem too bad.'

Thorkell grunted. Was she simple? Or just refusing to see the obvious? Surely she must realise that, if they let the brat live, when he grew to manhood he'd return to Meonbridge and take his revenge. But her mind was clearly set on a happier outcome.

'So what would happen if your father did inherit Meonbridge?'

He knew well enough what she was hoping he would say, so he did. 'He'll give Meonbridge to me, and of course I'll need a wife...'

She seemed to need him to say no more than that to be both thrilled and, he assumed, ripe for further questioning.

'So when is the boy most vulnerable, do you think?'

She appeared to think a little before she answered. 'Not at Steyning Castle,' she said, and Thorkell agreed. Attacking de Fougère's castle would be suicide.

'In Meonbridge would be better,' continued Matilda, 'but he's not here often, though Margaret does like him home occasionally. Of course most pages don't go home except at Christmas, but she wants to see him, and it seems the earl's agreed. But, when he is here, he's guarded closely by the squire, Piers, so he's hardly ever on his own.'

'But you've said before he's always liked running wild. Couldn't he be persuaded to slip the squire's clutches?'

She seemed to be thinking. 'I think you should wait until the weather's warmer,' she said at last. 'Say, around Easter time, when he'll surely come home for a visit? Then perhaps he and Libby could slip out together. He'd like that. I think Margaret pushes him too hard and protects him overmuch. He's only eight, and surely deserves some fun.'

Thorkell grunted. It was irritating to have to wait until the spring but capturing the boy outside the manor buildings would undoubtedly be easier than storming the place. 'You're right, Matilda.' He kissed her hair. 'Can you think of where he could be taken?'

Matilda shrugged. But then Thorkell realised that dawn was breaking, so they'd have to leave here soon. 'Matilda?'

'I'd need to think about it. Though there is a place I've taken them both before, down by the river, a pool.' She smiled. 'Dickon loves swimming. Might that be suitable?'

'Perhaps. Is it quiet?'

'Oh, yes, very. Especially in the early morning.'

Then she sat up, her eyes wide. 'You wouldn't hurt Libby, would you? When you take Dickon, Libby won't be harmed?'

Thorkell sat up too and stroked her cheek. 'Of course not, Matilda. We'll work something out.'

Matilda sighed. 'Am I really doing this? Getting involved in a kidnap plot – again...'

As dawn lightened the room a little further, Thorkell could see the frown lines on her face. 'You're not really *involved*, Matilda.' He kissed her again. 'And just think of how it will be afterwards.'

She hunched her shoulders and let out a little laugh. Her eyes were bright now. Shaking off the blanket, she took Thorkell's face in her hands and covered it in kisses. 'Yes,' she said, 'I *am* thinking of it, and I can scarcely bear to wait.'

23

MEONBRIDGE

APRIL 1358

It was early morning and barely light, before most members of the household, apart from a few servants, were awake. Dickon and Libby, excited by the prospect of a small adventure, woke early and crept quietly from their bed chambers, without seeming to rouse any of the solar's other occupants. Libby hadn't noticed that her mother was only pretending to be asleep. Mama had told her that if she and Dickon slipped off early, they wouldn't be missed for quite a while, because she was responsible for them both first thing every day, until Piers came to take over after breakfast.

Libby had jumped at her mother's suggestion, though she was surprised, and thought it rather strange, that Mama was proposing that she and Dickon go to the river on their own. For she was sure she'd heard her ladyship say to Mama that, during the two weeks Dickon was home for Easter, he wasn't to go *any*where without Piers.

But then, thought Libby, her mama wasn't much like other mothers.

The children tiptoed down the solar stairs and waited for two servants, who were tending to the fire and setting up the tables for the meal that was scarcely ever taken by most members of the household, to leave the hall. Then they ran lightly across to the door that led out onto the bailey and took a circuitous route around the building towards the garden, to avoid being spotted by the grooms or a wakeful squire.

Libby led the way, for Mama had told her of a secret, hidden gate in the manor's outer wall. Dickon was thrilled to find it, as it made escaping from the manor much easier than trying to get past that old fool in the gatehouse.

'Why's your ma helping us sneak out like this?' he said to Libby. 'Won't Grandmama be furious? And poor old Piers'll get the blame...'

Libby giggled. 'Mama feels sorry for you, being cooped up indoors or guarded by Piers all the time. She thought you'd like some fun.' She tilted her head a little. 'It's our secret though...'

Dickon grinned. 'I like your ma. Mine's always trying to keep me clinging to her skirts.'

'But you don't stay with her now, do you?'

'Sometimes. She *is* my ma.' He rolled his eyes. 'And I like seeing Jack and my brothers and little sister.'

Outside the wall, they ran through the fields down to the river and made their way along the bank to a spot where there was a deep pool overhung with willow trees. Libby's mama had brought them here before, but not for a long time, and Dickon was so pleased to be back, he wanted to leap into the water right away.

But Libby shook her head. 'Not yet, Dickon, it'll be too cold. Wait for the sun to warm it up a bit.'

'I don't think it'll get much warmer. But I'll wait a while, anyway.'

Libby opened her little scrip and took out a bundle that contained a couple of pieces of hard bread and some cheese. She handed a share to Dickon. 'Mama thought we'd like some breakfast,' she said.

Dickon chewed on the bread. 'It's very hard, and this cheese is horrible.' He wrinkled his nose.

But they didn't care at all and, breaking into fits of giggles, rolled around upon the grassy bank.

Piers's heart was thumping with panic at the thought of what her ladyship would say when she discovered he'd lost her grandson.

He'd awoken early, before dawn, and couldn't get back to sleep again. He wasn't required to attend to Dickon until after breakfast, but he thought he might as well go now. Matilda Fletcher would undoubtedly be pleased if he relieved her of her duty earlier than usual.

But she wasn't pleased at all. In truth, she seemed most annoyed with him.

He'd knocked on her door, to tell her that he was here. But when she opened it, her face at once creased into a frown. She pulled the door closed behind her and stood on the landing in her night chemise.

'Go away, Piers,' she said in a low, hissing voice. 'Dickon's still asleep. Go away and come back at the proper time.'

Piers turned to go back downstairs, but Matilda's attitude seemed so curious that, after she had gone back into her room, he crept along to Dickon's little chamber to see if his charge was really not awake. But all he found there was the old servant who slept on the narrow truckle bed, still snoring loudly. Dickon's bed was empty. Piers flew back to Matilda's room and hammered on her door.

'He's not there,' he cried, not bothering to keep his voice quiet.

Matilda's eyes were sparking. 'Shush,' she whispered. 'Do you want to wake her ladyship?'

He shook his head. 'But where *is* he?'

'How should *I* know?'

Piers didn't believe she didn't know and tried to press her. But all she would say was that he must have slipped out early. 'He's such a wild boy, disobedient and reckless...'

Piers disagreed. Dickon had in fact lost his wildness and obstinacy since he'd been away. But now was not the time to argue. 'Where might he have gone?'

Matilda refused to suggest any possibilities and, this time, Piers spun on his heel and ran, taking the narrow stairs a few at a time, then across the hall and out of the door onto the bailey. Should he try the garden or the fields?

The man gazed about as the horse beneath him stumbled and limped through the riverside vegetation. It was, he thought, a fine spring morning to be ambling through the fields and woods of Hampshire, and along the banks of this pretty, meandering river. To be sure, it was a much different view from the bleaker, more windswept one he was accustomed to.

He grinned to himself as he thought of the inn where he'd sojourned yestereve. He'd enjoyed a better than merely comfortable bed, and tasty victuals, and a whole flagon of fine Gascon wine. It was good for once to have sufficient funds to treat himself.

The horse, however, wasn't up to much. It was a low-grade palfrey, of dubious temper, but it suited his present needs. He'd be happier if the coarse woollen robe was not so itchy against his naked legs, and the ridiculous open shoes didn't let in the dirt and stones. But needs must.

The man leaned back in the saddle and the palfrey stopped. He glanced up at the sky: he'd made good time from the inn. It had been a pity to have to leave his comfortable bed, and the wench he'd shared it with, so early, but it had to be. He'd reached the river a little way upstream and thereafter kept to its banks to be sure of arriving at the location in good time.

Looking about him, he knew that he was close. He'd been here only days before.

Dickon couldn't wait to try the water. 'Come in too, Libby,' he said, pleading, but she shook her head.

'You know I can't swim,' she said, pouting. She couldn't, but it was also true that she was far too shy to take off her kirtle in front of Dickon, even though she'd got her night chemise on underneath.

But Dickon was happy enough to strip down to his braies, and sitting on the bank, he dipped his feet into the water. He squealed. 'God's blood, it's cold.'

Libby tutted. 'You shouldn't swear, Dickon. Your grandmama would scold you if she heard.'

Dickon screwed up his eyes. 'I never do it when she's around.' He shivered. 'So shall I jump?'

Libby giggled. 'You know you want to.' And he nodded and rolled forward into the water. He submerged his whole body and almost at once bobbed up again, gasping. But then he laughed and swam the few strokes towards the overhanging trees. They were just starting to come into leaf, and the branch tips dipped and dabbled in the water.

Dickon dipped and dabbled too, but then he ducked beneath the willow, and all of a sudden, he was yelling.

Piers had run all around the gardens and the orchard, but somehow knew that wherever Dickon was it wasn't inside the manor grounds. He couldn't account for his conviction, but he let himself be guided by it.

He hurried back across the bailey to the gatehouse, then made his way around the manor's outer wall until he reached the banks of the river. Dickon loved the river, and Piers often found him down here, either fishing or, in the warmer weather, swimming. He hoped that he was right, and that was where the boy had gone this morning.

Libby jumped up and ran to the water's edge. 'Where are you, Dickon?' she called. But then she saw his arms thrashing around just behind the dipping trees. They were only feet away, but the pool between her and them was deep, and Libby was fearful of the water.

But then Dickon was screaming 'Libby, help me!' and she began to sob.

'What's wrong?' she cried.

As Dickon's head bobbed up above the water, he yelled 'My leg, it's caught. Help me, Libby!'

For a moment she didn't know what to do but then, despite her fear, she plunged into the water, fully dressed. It wasn't quite as deep as she had thought, and she found she could bounce along the bottom towards the trees, though her skirt was billowing up around her, making it difficult to move forward. But shortly she reached Dickon and grabbed at his outstretched arms.

'Pull,' he cried, and she did. But Dickon screamed.

'My foot's caught in something,' he whimpered, 'and it hurts.' Then he too was sobbing.

The man leaned back again to halt the horse. He thought he'd heard a cry. He listened. Yes, there it was again. A child's cry. Perhaps his little stratagem was working? He kicked his heels against the palfrey's flanks and, as it trotted forward, he guided it towards the pool in the bend of the river that he'd visited two days before.

Libby tried again to pull on Dickon's arms, but he just screamed again, and she was so terrified of hurting him that she stopped and stood in the water, weeping.

But then a man appeared, standing on the riverbank. 'What's afoot?' he called. 'You need help in there?'

Libby turned and saw a stranger, dressed like a friar, and with the kindest of faces, looking most worried and concerned. 'He's caught his leg on something,' she cried, 'and I can't pull him free.'

The friar nodded and, tying the reins of his palfrey to a tree, ran down to the pool and leapt into the water, his robes bulging out around him. He waded across to the children and felt around under the water.

'It's some net,' he said. 'You're caught up in a net, my lad.' He gestured to Libby to go back to the bank then, taking a knife from his belt and dipping his head beneath the water, he slashed at the netting. He had to dip and slash a few times before Dickon yelled that his leg was free, then the friar put his arms around the boy and pulled him to the bank.

'Well now,' said the friar, when Dickon was sitting on the grass again. 'Let's see if I've got something to wrap round you, lad, before you catch your death.' And he went over to his horse, grazing just a few yards away, and returned with a thick woollen blanket, which he put around Dickon's shoulders.

The friar smiled at Libby. 'Are you all right, little one?' he said, and she nodded, although she was really very cold. And Mama would be furious with her for getting her kirtle so wet and dirty.

The friar turned his attention to Dickon's leg, which was bleeding, the skin torn in the struggle with the net. Fetching a bag containing various ointments and other bits and pieces, the friar applied a salve to the wound and wrapped it round with strips of cloth.

Libby thought how brave Dickon was being for, though he winced as the friar treated his leg, he wasn't crying any more. And when his leg was bound, he said thank you to the friar and he'd go home now. And he pulled himself to his feet, and Libby stood up too.

But the friar put his hand on Dickon's shoulder and pressed him down again. 'No, no, young master. It's best we go to the village, and find the barber-surgeon, Simon Hogge – you know him?' Dickon and Libby both nodded. 'He'll be able to tell if there's anything badly wrong with your leg and patch you up properly.'

'But I'm all right now you've bound it,' said Dickon.

The friar shook his head. 'You don't know that, boy. Best be on the safe side. And you, miss, you run home and tell your mother what's happened. Then she can come down to the village later to pick up your friend from Simon's.'

Libby nodded but, looking across at Dickon, she could see he wasn't happy, and she didn't know whether to obey the friar or stay with Dickon.

But now, though the friar had at first seemed kind, when she didn't leave, and Dickon struggled as he tried to pick him up to take him to his horse, the man suddenly became quite angry. He put his arms around Dickon's waist and wrenched him off his feet.

Piers ran along the river bank, stopping occasionally to catch his breath. He'd been to all the usual spots where Dickon fished, but found no sign that the boy had been there of late.

But then, a short distance away, close to the river, he saw a horse, whinnying and pulling at its reins, which were tied up to a tree. Then he heard shouting – a child's voice – and he dashed towards it.

―――――――

Dickon yelled again. 'Libby, I don't want to go with him.' He pummelled at the friar's hands to force him to let go. The friar wasn't a big man, but he seemed very strong, for he started towards his horse, still holding fast to Dickon.

Libby was sobbing again, not knowing how to help. But then she spotted a fallen branch, small enough for her to lift, yet heavy enough to be a club. She picked it up and, running after the friar, with all her strength she swung it and hit him around the legs, hard enough to make him stumble and lose his grip on Dickon. Freed at last, Dickon yelled at the top of his voice.

And, at that moment, Piers Arundale appeared, ploughing through the meadow grasses and, roaring, he sprinted towards the friar brandishing his short sword. But the friar quickly regained his balance and hobbled the few steps to his horse. Then, throwing himself up into the saddle, he galloped away before the squire could reach him.

24

MEONBRIDGE
APRIL 1358

Margaret returned to the solar after taking breakfast with her bailiff, John atte Wode, to find Matilda rushing about wailing and clearly in distress.

'Whatever is the matter?' she said, but Matilda could not answer through her sobs.

Margaret tutted. 'For Heaven's sake, Matilda, pull yourself together, and tell me what is wrong.'

Matilda let out a few more sobs, and then took a deep breath. 'It's the children—'

'What about the children?'

She let out another wail. 'They're missing.'

'Missing? What do you mean? How long have they been missing?'

'An hour or two.'

'An hour or two?' said Margaret, then upbraided herself for parroting Matilda's words. 'Why did you not you raise the alarm as soon as you saw that they had gone?'

'I did,' she said, wringing her hands together. 'But I woke up very late because I'd been lying awake for hours with a megrim, and I only fell asleep when it was almost dawn—'

'Yes, yes. And when you *did* wake up...?'

'When I saw Libby wasn't in her bed, I went to find Dickon and found he wasn't there either.'

Margaret pressed her lips together and, closing her eyes, rubbed at her forehead. 'You're supposed to *look after* Dickon in the early morning,' she said, her voice hard.

'I know,' cried Matilda. 'But I thought Piers must've come to get them earlier than usual, and that, finding me asleep, he took them off. But when Piers did come up to get them later, I realised he hadn't come earlier after all...'

Margaret sighed. Matilda was hardly a girl, but she really could not be relied upon for anything.

'...and so I told Piers the children must've run off to play, and would he go and look for them, and he went off to search the manor.' Matilda took a breath.

'So where is Piers now?'

'I don't know. Still searching, I suppose.'

Margaret sighed again, then called Agatha over and asked her to send a boy to look for Piers and bring him back here.

A short while later, Piers arrived back at the manor. Agatha came up to the solar to announce that he was here, and that he had the children with him. Both Margaret and Matilda ran downstairs, and Matilda, her distress overly fulsome in Margaret's view, threw herself at Libby and, sobbing, clasped the girl to her breast.

'What's happened to you?' she said at last, holding the bedraggled Libby at arms' length.

Margaret took Dickon in her arms, despite his wet and filthy clothes. She felt much like sobbing herself but managed to keep herself under control. 'What has happened, Dickon?' Then she turned to Piers. 'Do you know, Master Arundale?'

'Not the whole story, m'lady, but I do know a man tried to snatch young Dickon.' Margaret gasped, but Piers continued. 'But it was Dickon's own courage, and young Libby's, that stopped the villain succeeding in his treachery.'

Margaret pulled Dickon to her. 'Well done for being brave, but why were you outside the manor on your own?' She held the boy away from her. 'When you know full well that it is not allowed.'

Dickon hung his head. 'I'm sorry, Grandmama. Libby and me thought it'd be fun to go swimming in the river. Anyway, Libby's—'

Matilda let out a sudden, strained sort of laugh, and gave her daughter a little shake. 'You are so *naughty*, Libby, leading poor Dickon astray.' She laughed again, more lightly, and turned to Margaret. 'But she surely didn't think he'd be in danger so early in the morning...'

Libby opened her mouth to speak, but Matilda stifled the girl's words by crushing her once more in a tight embrace.

Dickon, too, seemed on the point of saying something else, but Margaret shook her head at him. 'I am afraid that you are in danger at any time, and I forbid you, child, to run off on your own again. Is that clear?' He nodded.

Margaret called Agatha over and asked her now to send for John atte Wode. Then she put her hand on Dickon's shoulder. 'I want you and Libby to go and put on dry clothes, then come back here and tell us everything that happened. But I want Master atte Wode to hear what you have to say, in the hope that he will be able to institute a search for this knave.'

Once the children were clean and dry, and John had come back from the fields, where he had been overseeing the sowing of the spring crops of oats and barley, peas and beans, everyone sat down, and Margaret bid Dickon tell them what had happened at the river.

Dickon told the story, with Libby piping up once or twice with something he had forgotten. At the point at which Dickon described his leg getting caught up in the net, Piers stepped forward and produced a piece of netting from his scrip.

'This is a piece of what the friar cut away.' He handed it to John. 'Looks like fishing net, don't you think, Master atte Wode?'

John nodded. 'The sort they use to trap fish swimming up the river. Perhaps it was torn from its moorings last time there was a storm? Then got caught up underneath the trees?' He frowned. 'Though it seems somewhat unlikely, your ladyship.'

Margaret nodded. 'I agree. And why did this so-called friar appear, as if from nowhere, ready to rescue Dickon?'

'And him insisting Dickon go to Simon Hogge's seemed suspicious to me, m'lady,' said Piers. 'It was obvious he planned to kidnap Dickon, once Libby had set off home.'

Margaret thanked Dickon for telling her the story but scolded him again for going off at all. 'You are precious to us, Dickon, and you *must not, ever,* go off without proper companionship. I am afraid that Libby's company is not enough. Although I am grateful to you, Libby, for being so very brave and helping him to safety.'

Later, after Matilda, Piers and the children had gone off to spend the day together in some quiet indoor pursuit, Margaret asked John to stay behind. 'Can you spare the time? I know how busy you are.'

'There's much to do, my lady, but protecting our little lord's important too. What is it you want to say?'

'Only that I am convinced that this attack, like the one back in September, was the work of those wretched Bounes.'

'It would be hard to prove, m'lady, but I do share your suspicion.'

Margaret smiled. 'I am glad you do, John. I worry that the Bounes are determined to win Meonbridge by foul means, as the fair means have plainly failed them. It is clear that the so-called friar was intent on kidnapping Dickon. Surely, the Bounes would like Dickon to disappear, so that they can then legitimately claim Meonbridge for themselves. But how could we prove that the man was in their employ?'

John shook his head. 'I don't think we can, m'lady. You can be sure they're experts at covering their tracks. After all, we thought it was Baldwin de Courtenay who arranged the first attack, but maybe he did it at the Bounes' command?' He frowned. 'By the bye, I haven't told you, my lady, that I've heard Baldwin is dead—'

Margaret gasped. 'Dead? How?'

'I heard it were a riding accident, m'lady,' said John, 'but I don't know if it really were an *accident.*' He shrugged. 'Mebbe the Bounes did ask him to do it and, because he failed, they killed him.'

Margaret sank heavily into her chair.

'Are you all right, m'lady?' He turned. 'Agatha, please bring her ladyship a cup of wine.' Agatha dropped a curtsey and hurried from the room to fetch a flagon.

'Anyone could've set the net in place,' continued John, 'if they'd been paid to by Morys Boune.'

'Is it worth investigating?' said Margaret, wearily. 'Could we perhaps find out if anyone saw the man acting suspiciously near the river?'

'To be honest, your ladyship, I think it's hopeless. That man will be long gone back to Hereford, or wherever.' He stood up. 'But I'll look into it, see if there's anything to help us.'

25

Watching his father rage and storm was commonplace – he'd observed it all his life. But seeing Morys so despairing and downcast was not. It was, Thorkell knew well enough, a sign of his father's profound frustration at yet another failure, yet another humiliation, an offence against his potency and manhood. The first ignominy, losing the court case, was perhaps the worst, being so very public, but the failure of each attempt to kidnap the de Bohun brat had compounded Morys's loss of face, and brought him to a new low.

But it wasn't just the humiliations that were making his father so morose. They'd all agreed to move to one of their new Dorset manors for the summer, as a more convenient launching place for any assault on Meonbridge. The manor house near Cranborne was small but, like Meonbridge, a good deal more comfortable than the vast and chilly Castle Boune. Yet Morys's gloomy mood had been clearly worsened by his decision to leave Alwyn and his daughters behind in Herefordshire. Thorkell did wonder if it had been a mistake for, although the house here was really too small for Morys's extensive household, his father seemed bereft without the company of his wife.

Instead of raging up and down his new hall, Morys now sat mournfully by the fire, the inevitable cup of wine clutched between his massive hands. Gunnar was sitting with him, and Thorkell went to join them. His father raised his eyes to his sons.

'Does the boy have a charmed life?' he said.

'Of course not, Pa,' said Gunnar. 'We simply have to do it ourselves and not rely on others.'

Morys nodded. 'Getting de Courtenay to do our work was clearly a miscalculation, for the man's an idiot—'

'*Was* an idiot,' said Thorkell.

Morys's eyebrows lifted and small creases appeared at the corners of his eyes. 'Ah, you hadn't said.'

Thorkell nodded. 'I hear the de Courtenays can't understand how such an expert rider as their son could simply *topple* off his horse and break his neck.'

A grin curved Morys's lips. 'Tragic, tragic. To lose a son...' He shook his head slowly, then took a draught of wine. 'So *that* worked.'

'We did it ourselves,' said Gunnar.

'Good, good.' Morys put down the cup and signalled to Gunnar for some more. 'But I was surprised that Roger Philbert failed to get the boy—'

'The "friar",' said Gunnar, grinning. 'He's usually so reliable. Perhaps he – and even we – misjudged the potential vigour of an eight-year-old boy?'

'And a little wench,' said Thorkell, shaking his head. 'Though, on reflection, sending in a friar to "rescue" the boy, when he'd already been betrayed by his tonsured tutor, was pretty witless. A knight in armour might've been a better choice?'

Gunnar twisted his mouth. 'You're right, little brother. But what now?'

Morys got up and began his usual pacing. His mood seemed to have improved a little, now he had a plan to make. 'We've transferred ourselves here to this cottage—'

'A *comfortable* cottage, Pa,' said Thorkell, winking.

'Yes, yes, Thorkell, I grant you, comfortable, if very cramped.' Morys eased his back and grimaced. 'But we came here purposefully, to make an assault on Meonbridge more easily achieved. So the "what now", Gunnar, is an assault.'

'And is the aim to capture the de Bohun boy, or kill him?' Gunnar chewed at his bottom lip.

'Capture would lead to kill, I think?' said Morys.

Thorkell nodded. 'It has to. If we leave the brat alive, once he's grown, he'll come back to Meonbridge to take his revenge.'

'Exactly.'

'And is it rape and pillage of the whole community?' said Gunnar, rubbing his hand across the back of his neck. 'Or will you let the manor's servants and retainers live?'

'It would be a pity to kill them all, when we'll need them to run the manor once we've won it for ourselves.'

Morys guffawed. 'It would. But I doubt we'll be able to extract the brat and make off with him without attracting attention. So we may have no option but wanton murder. But I think, Thorkell, we'll not ask your whore's advice this time.'

Thorkell bristled a little, still, at his father's epithet for Matilda. 'What she told me about the arrangement of the upstairs chambers will be useful,' he said, feeling peevish. But he had to admit that most of her advice had proved of little value and, good as it had been to bed her, in truth she had probably outlived her usefulness.

'Her advice hasn't been of much help, I agree.' He scowled. 'More fool me for trusting her.'

Gunnar snorted. 'Oh, come on, little brother. You can't be blamed for wanting to swive her, with her great dark eyes and shapely figure. She just hoped to win you for herself, to make you think her a valuable asset. A wife, no less. Not just another wench lusting after the contents of your braies.'

Thorkell pulled a wry face. 'I suspect she's *still* imagining I'm going to marry her and make her mistress of Meonbridge.'

Morys banged his cup down on the table. 'Enough. Let's make a plan.'

When Morys and Gunnar had gone to their beds, the plan for their assault on Meonbridge had been discussed at such length and in such detail that Thorkell felt it was imprinted upon his brain. Yet he stayed behind, before the dwindling fire, wanting to think it through again, without the distractions of his father and brother.

Matilda had told him some time ago that Sir Richard, and now Lady de Bohun, had only four armed retainers and a couple of squires, and a dozen or so male servants, none of whom were fighting men, though a few might take up arms in an emergency. So twenty trained and well-armed retainers would surely be more than a match for the de Bohuns' meagre forces.

The aim was to execute the abduction so quietly and swiftly that they could get in and out without too much risk of injury to their own men. But he wouldn't scruple to kill her ladyship's entire household, if it meant they got the brat away.

Yet it surprised him, as he sat there gazing into the dying fire, that the one person he would rather didn't die in the attack was – still – Matilda. Up to now, he'd thought that, if she was hurt or even killed, it would be unfortunate, but nothing to cause him grief. But, tonight, as he recalled her lying in his arms, her great adoring eyes looking up into his, he thought it would be a pity for her to lose her life.

26

John dipped his head as he came through the cottage door. He was inches taller than Jack, indeed than most men in the village. He removed his cloak and hung it on a hook by the door, then stepped over to Agnes, sitting at the table chopping vegetables.

'Sister,' he said softly. 'Fare you well?' He placed a hand upon her shoulder, and she put down her knife and patted his hand with hers.

'Not so bad,' she said, her voice a whisper. 'Not so bad.' She looked up at him briefly and gave him a weak smile, then picked up the knife again.

He bent down and dropped a kiss upon her head, then turned to Jack. Jack cocked his head towards the door, and John nodded.

'John and me are going for a stroll, Agnes,' Jack said. 'We'll be back for dinner.'

John demurred. 'Not me, sister. I must get back to Ma.'

'How is she?'

He shook his head. 'Not herself.'

Agnes nodded. 'I'll look in,' she said wanly, and Jack raised an eyebrow at John.

They went into the garden and sat down on the turf bench under the arbour, covered now in a mass of sweet-smelling blooms of yellow and white.

Jack sighed as he fingered the smooth-planed uprights of the arbour. 'I watch her sometimes, sitting here. She never sniffs the honeysuckle or roses, never brings out any sewing to while away a warm spring evening, never brings a blanket for the children to sit at her feet whilst she tells them stories. She did once find pleasure sitting here, but no longer.' He leaned his head against the timber. 'I don't know where my lovely girl has gone.'

John nodded. 'She *is* very melancholy. Worse, you think?'

'It seems so.' Jack shook his head. 'For years, Dickon's bad behaviour wore her out, and made her so gloomy you might have thought she'd find it easier without him here. But, in the weeks before he went away, she and the boy got closer than I have ever seen them since he was a baby. And, for a while, she became again the lovely, merry girl I married. But it didn't last. As soon as Dickon left, she at once fell into melancholy again. She cheers a little each time he comes home to visit, but when he's gone again, the misery returns. And, since the attacks, and especially the one last month at the river...' He swallowed hard, feeling his own misery welling up inside him. 'In truth, it is much worse.'

'Mebbe in time—?' began John.

'Mebbe.' But he couldn't see how time would make any difference. He leaned his elbows on his knees and rested his chin upon his hands. He stayed that way a while, not speaking, then sat up again and stretched, and clasped his hands behind his head. 'But you didn't come here, brother, to hear my woes. What did you want to talk about?'

John stood up and brought a honeysuckle floret to his nose. He sniffed and smiled, then sat down again. 'I wanted to tell you I've asked both her ladyship and Sister Rosa if they object to us telling everyone the truth about the Bounes—'

'You mean about the attacks on Dickon?'

John nodded. 'Since the court case, everyone in the village surely now accepts that Dickon is Agnes's son and Philip's, *and* that he's the de Bohuns' chosen heir. They know too that the Bounes contested Dickon's claim and lost. But what most don't know, Jack, is how fiercely the Bounes are likely to fight for Meonbridge. They won't realise the Bounes won't have just slunk back to Herefordshire and forgotten about Meonbridge.'

'Of course, after the first attack, it was put about that it was arranged by Baldwin de Courtenay, allegedly in revenge for his mother's humiliation at the court.'

'That's right. Though the Bounes were surely behind whatever Baldwin did.'

'But when Dickon moved to Steyning, all of us thought he'd then be safe.'

'Yet when he came back to Meonbridge to celebrate Easter with you and Agnes and his grandmother, somehow the Bounes *knew* he'd be here...'

Jack nodded. 'Though we don't know for sure the so-called friar was in their pay—'

'I think we *do*.' John snorted.

Jack let out a grisly sort of laugh. 'Very well, I agree. But who's the "everyone" you plan to tell?'

'The whole village.' He grinned. 'All our friends and neighbours. For I'm certain, one day, maybe soon, the Bounes will attack Meonbridge directly—'

'You mean a raid on the manor?'

He nodded. 'Sir Giles told me once that's how they've won most of their lands. By bloody assault and murder.'

Jack felt a sudden dryness in his throat. 'But her ladyship has few armed retainers...'

'Indeed. So the villagers must be prepared to fight.' John locked eyes with Jack. 'We have to win their support, for her ladyship's sake, for Dickon's and for our own.'

That evening Ellen Rolfe's ale-house was overflowing with the folk gathering together in response to the bailiff's message, delivered around the village by half a dozen lads. When Jack arrived, the racket of excited chatter was filling the main drinking room. He looked around, wondering who had answered John's call, and saw men and women from every class of Meonbridge folk: villeins and cottars, artisans and freemen, and several who were in her ladyship's direct employ.

Jack moved amongst them, thanking them for coming.

'Y'know what this is all about, then, Jack?' said Will Cole, who'd walked down from his shepherd's cot, and was standing with his employers, Eleanor and Walter Nash.

He nodded. 'I do, but I'll let John explain.'

A group of cottars were standing together, concern etched upon their faces, amongst them Will Mannering and his son Harry, and John Ward, with his son Arthur and aunt Alys. And Nick Ashdown was there with Susanna Miller, and her brother-in-law, Thomas, her stepson, Tom, and the baker Ivo Langelee. Even Adam Wragge, her ladyship's steward, had come, though he rarely these days stepped inside an ale-house. He was deep in conversation with other officials of the manor, Geoffrey Dyer, the constable, Martin Foreman, the hayward, and Simon Hogge.

Simon touched Jack's arm as he passed by. 'I've been saying this is all about those rascally Bounes. Am I right, Jack?'

He grimaced. 'We knew this time would come, but John thinks it'll likely come sooner than expected. And now Meonbridge has to work together to save ourselves from those villains.'

Adam shook his head. 'It will not be only Meonbridge, Jack.'

'Indeed. They'll want all the de Bohun domains.'

Shortly, John came through the door, accompanied by his younger brother Matthew. John went to speak to Ellen Rolfe, who fetched him a low stool that he set up at one end of the room, to give him extra height so everyone in the room could see as well as hear him.

He stepped up onto the stool and raised his hands into the air. Not everybody noticed, and he had to shout for quiet before all faces turned towards him and the clamour died.

Smiling at first, John thanked them all for coming, but then his expression became more serious. 'Neighbours, friends. What I have to tell you is troubling, but I can no longer keep the truth of our worrying situation from you.'

A few low mutterings and whisperings hissed around the room, but John held up his hands again. 'Let me explain.'

The mutterings stopped, and John nodded.

'First, you should know Lady de Bohun's agreed I should do so. And what I'm about to say to you is for her sake, and for young Dickon's, and for the sake of all of us in Meonbridge. For it's my belief – and her ladyship's – that Meonbridge is in danger.'

Many of the listeners gasped, and one or two of the women let out small cries. But John continued.

'Let me remind you, first, about young Dickon. When he came first to Meonbridge, as a baby, he was acknowledged as the son of my sister, Agnes, and her husband, our carpenter, Jack Sawyer. Jack brought the boy up as his own. But, in truth, Dickon was not Jack's son, but that of our murdered lord-in-waiting, Sir Philip de Bohun. Some of you knew that truth already, well before Sir Richard lost his life, though many didn't. Before he died, Sir Richard had named his grandson Dickon as his heir. But it was only when his lordship's cousin, Sir Morys Boune, decided to challenge Dickon's claim, on the grounds of the boy's illegitimacy, that everyone in Meonbridge understood the truth.

'I'm sure everyone here knows well enough that Sir Morys lost his case. Sir Richard's liege lord, Raoul de Fougère, spoke for Dickon, and judge and jury all agreed that the honour of the de Bohuns should be continued through the body of Sir Richard's grandson, Sir Philip's son. And now, Dickon lives in the household of the earl, learning to be a de Bohun, and a knight.'

Simon stepped forward and offered John a cup of ale. John nodded and took a long draught before continuing.

'But, my friends, that's not the end of the story for Sir Morys Boune and his two sons. For you can be sure they haven't just *accepted* the dismissal of their case. Their loss will rankle with them. They haven't simply returned to Herefordshire, giving Meonbridge no further thought. Indeed, there've been two attempts already to capture our young Dickon, perhaps even to murder him—'

The collective gasp now fairly erupted in the room.

'Capture Dickon?'

'Murder 'im?'

'Poor little lad...'

'What happened, John?' said Nick.

John then related briefly what happened in the attack last year when Dickon was coming home from Courtenay Castle.'

'Why'd we hear naught about it?' asked Will Cole, raising his hand.

'At the time, Will, her ladyship decided not to make known news of the attack, so as not to cause alarm. Only one or two in the village knew of it – the constable, and Jack of course.'

'And what of the second attack?' said Nick.

'It's what's prompted me to call this meeting,' John said. 'A few weeks ago, just after Easter, when Dickon came home to spend a little time with his family and his grandmother, another attempt was made to kidnap him. This time the attack was foiled by our little lord's own bravery, and that of Libby Fletcher, and by the heroism of her ladyship's squire, Piers Arundale, who ran headlong at the kidnapper with his sword and drove him off.'

'Good lad,' cried Simon and raised a cheer.

'An' good for the littl'uns for being so brave,' called out Ann Webb, and John agreed.

'Though what that Fletcher girl were doing wi' his lordship is anybody's guess,' said Alys, sneering, but John ignored her and instead gestured to Will, whose hand was raised again, to speak.

'How d'you know,' said Will, 'these attacks've bin down to the Bounes?'

'We don't *know*, Will, but we're sure enough. Who else'd want to kidnap Dickon?'

Will nodded. 'True.'

'So, my friends,' continued John, 'our young lord's life is in danger. He's safe at the earl's castle, but whenever he comes home to Meonbridge, he must be protected at all times.'

'Is that what you're asking of us, John?' said Simon, but John shook his head.

'More than that, Simon. You must all understand, if the Bounes take Meonbridge from the de Bohuns, our lives will be very different from what we're used to. They're a bunch of knaves, so I've heard, who've won most of their lands by bloody assault and murder. Who think nothing of putting women and children to the sword if they get in their way. Who treat their tenants worse than dogs—'

Gasps and cries filled the room.

'But,' said Geoffrey Dyer, his face gloomy, 'we do all know the lad's a bastard—' He reddened. 'Begging yer pardon, Jack.' But Jack held up

234

his hands. 'And these Bounes know it too. And so did the court. So, even though the court found in favour of the lad, in law the Bounes' case is the true one.'

Simon then took John's place on the stool. 'That may be true, Geoffrey, but the de Bohuns have been our lords for three generations. And surely we don't want Lady de Bohun turned out and young Dickon disinherited?'

There were shouts of agreement.

'Sir Richard were a good master, weren't he?' continued Simon, but this was met by a few grunts and a brief burst of laughter.

'You go' a short mem'ry, Simon 'Ogge,' said Alys. 'What 'bout in the Death when 'e closed the manor and left us all to perish? And what 'bout afterwards when 'e wouldn't pay the wages, and wouldn't give any of the spare land to us cottars, but brought in those fellows from Winchester? And what 'bout—'

Thomas Miller held up a hand. 'Yes, yes, Alys, we all recall the bad times, but his lordship weren't a cruel master. And think of how well and kindly her ladyship always ran the manor when he were away. And how well she's doing now? Surely we can't let *her* down?' He paused. 'An' what about our little lord? He ain't just a de Bohun, is he, he's one o' our own, grandson of Stephen atte Wode, nephew of our bailiff?'

'What you suggesting, Master 'Ogge?' said John Ward, frowning at his aunt to stop her butting in again.

Simon pulled himself up tall. 'That, if the Bounes come to Meonbridge to press their claim by violence, *we* must stand alongside her ladyship and her household in supporting young Dickon's claim.'

'Even if it means we have to take up arms against them?' said Nick Ashdown, his face pale.

The bailiff stood up again next to Simon. 'Yes, Nick. Even if we have to fight.'

27

M atilda was bored and miserable – again. She couldn't concentrate on anything and even walking in the garden had ceased to be a pleasure, for she was bereft. Nonetheless, she came often to her favourite arbour just to sit and think. She wished she could be alone here, but now she always had to bring her daughter with her. Dickon had been back at the earl's ever since the kidnap attempt in April, so Matilda had to occupy Libby's time entirely on her own, until such time as Dickon came home again to visit.

Matilda understood that Margaret would hardly let Piers Arundale spend time with the girl when Dickon wasn't here. It was a nuisance, for Libby wanted her mother to play with her. But playing with a little girl was the last thing Matilda wished to do.

She'd received no messages from Thorkell since April. She thought that, because the plot had failed – again – Thorkell must want nothing more to do with her. For, in this case, and the earlier one, he'd acted upon her information, and she assumed he must now think her advice inept, or worse.

Tears sprang to her eyes, as she thought of their last time together, in Blanche's house, back before Christmas, months before the incident at the river. Although, on the days leading up to the incident, she'd exchanged several messages with Thorkell about the plot, she'd not seen him, not lain in his arms, not had him kiss her cheeks or nibble at her ear. She whimpered. How she *longed* to have him touch her once again.

She recalled what Thorkell had said to her that night: "I'll need a wife". And then he'd looked into her eyes, caressed her hair and kissed her. Hadn't he?

The tears rolled down her cheeks. It was surely a deception. He hadn't meant it. It was just a ploy to get information from her. Which had of course been *her* plan too. But, in her plan, providing information to Thorkell Boune had been just a step on the way to him making her his wife. And, if once it had seemed to be working, now it clearly wasn't.

She let the tears fall thickly, not attempting to wipe them away, until Libby ran up to her, bored perhaps of bowling her hoop alone up and down the grassy paths.

'Mama, why are you crying?' the girl said in a kindly tone and, putting her hand up to her mother's face, she wiped at the tears with her thumb.

Matilda couldn't stop a final sob, then groped in the small scrip at her waist for a linen rag and rubbed it roughly at her face. 'Nothing, poppet. Just Mama being foolish.' She put her arms around her daughter's waist and drew her close. 'Just Mama being foolish,' she said again, and buried her face in Libby's soft brown hair.

But it wasn't only Thorkell. Margaret had changed towards her too.

Until not long ago, her ladyship had been as kind and solicitous towards Matilda as her own mother might have been but, since the incident at the river, she seemed to regard her with disappointment – perhaps even dislike. So Matilda had been on edge for weeks, worrying that Margaret somehow *suspected* her involvement in the two attacks on Dickon.

When John atte Wode finally admitted to Margaret that he'd found out nothing about the so-called friar who'd tried to kidnap Dickon, and thought they'd never be able to discover if the Bounes were behind the plot, her ladyship had turned her attention to Matilda.

Matilda had been almost shocked by Margaret's boldness. 'You have been seeing Thorkell Boune secretly, have you not, Matilda?'

How could her ladyship know? Perhaps she was just guessing? Yet, as it seemed Thorkell had abandoned her, was there now any point in denying the truth? She nodded miserably. 'But not since November,' she added.

Margaret seemed surprised at that, perhaps that it was so long ago. So Matilda took her chance to show she truly was no longer seeing Thorkell. Though, when Margaret murmured that perhaps she had known nothing of the river incident after all, Matilda couldn't stop her face from blushing.

'Of course I didn't, your ladyship,' she said, feigning, yet indeed also feeling, deep hurt. 'I'd do nothing to bring harm to Dickon.'

Again, as she perpetrated her lie, she felt a flush creep down her neck and spread across her breast. And she could see that Margaret doubted the truth of what she had just said.

But her ladyship didn't press her, which, in truth, made Matilda's anxiety worse, not knowing whether or not Margaret did suspect her of betrayal. For it was undoubtedly true that she'd been plotting to betray Margaret, for the sake of winning Thorkell and becoming mistress of Meonbridge herself. Indeed, plotting to throw her ladyship out of her own home.

However, if Margaret had decided, for whatever reason, to say nothing more of her suspicions, it seemed that she'd resumed her efforts to remove Matilda from her household. She told her that she'd again approached the steward, Adam Wragge, with the offer of a larger dowry, and this time he was expressing a little more interest in taking Matilda as his wife. And now, Matilda thought, a knot of misery tightening inside her, as Thorkell seemed not to be interested in her any more, if Adam offered, she would accept. It was hardly what she'd dreamed of, but it would have to do.

But only the day after she decided that she would be the wife of Adam Wragge, a messenger boy found Matilda in the garden and slipped a note into her hand.

Her heart was thumping as she unfolded the paper and scanned the few spidery words and little drawings that were typical of the notes that Thorkell sent her. She could hardly believe that, after all this time, he did want to meet her again. But it was not to be at night, or in Blanche's house. He'd bring a horse for her, he said, and they'd go for a ride together, away from Meonbridge.

In some ways it was disappointing. What she wanted more than anything was for Thorkell to strip off all her clothes and then his own, then lie down beside her and... She shook her head. She should be glad he wanted to see her at all. And, after all, a horse ride did not preclude...

This time she met him outside the village. He'd suggested in his note that a disused mill further down the river would be a suitable daytime meeting place, and it wasn't all that far for her to walk. He was waiting for her when she arrived. He'd dismounted and tied both horses to a tree, beneath which he was sitting, his back against the trunk, his eyes closed.

Despite her worry that Thorkell no longer cared for her, Matilda thought she'd test his feelings with a little tease. She crept towards him, taking the lightest of footsteps, and when she reached him, finding him apparently asleep, she knelt down by his side. If he wasn't truly asleep, he was making a good pretence of it, and she put out her hand to stroke his face. But she squealed and toppled backwards when his eyes flew open and he thrust out a hand to grab her wrist.

'God's eyes, Matilda, what do you think you're doing?' His voice was not playful, but annoyed.

She felt tears welling and wiped the heel of her other hand across her eyes. 'I just wanted to surprise you.'

'I think the time for such surprises may have passed.'

He stood up and went over to the horses. He untied them and offered the reins of the little grey palfrey to Matilda. 'I brought you a small horse, thinking you maybe don't ride much these days.'

She nodded, trying hard to keep the tears from flowing again. 'Thank you. He looks perfect.' She took the reins. 'Could you help me up, please?'

Thorkell nodded curtly and walked around the horse to stand beside her. He bent down and made a platform with his hands. She placed her foot onto his clasped hands and sprang up onto the palfrey's back. She was relieved that she did so with reasonable ease, sensing that Thorkell would be irritated if she made a mess of it.

Thorkell mounted his own horse, a fine black stallion. 'Ready?' he said to her, his eyebrows raised, then, at her nod, he clicked his tongue and turned his mount to trot across the water meadows and into the small forest that lay beyond.

Matilda followed but, for the first time, she realised her heart was thumping not from excitement but from fear. Thorkell was acting so cold and tetchy, perhaps he'd actually come here, and was leading her away from Meonbridge, in order to dispose of her? Suddenly she thought maybe she didn't want to follow Thorkell after all. Leaning back in the saddle, she relaxed the reins, and the palfrey slowed to a stop.

Thorkell carried on for several paces before he realised she was no longer close behind him. He stopped and twisted in the saddle. 'What's wrong?'

She could hardly say she was afraid of him. But what else could she say?

'Why have you come?' she said at last. 'Why did you want to see me?' She took a deep breath. 'For it's obvious that, whatever else the reason, it wasn't to make love to me.'

He turned his horse and trotted back towards her. He leaned back in his saddle and stared at her, saying nothing.

Not understanding his behaviour, Matilda trembled, and he noticed it. He gave a small grin. 'Ah, I see, you're afraid. You think maybe I've come to kill you. But why would I do that, Matilda?'

She couldn't stop her trembling. 'Because you've no further use for me?'

Thorkell shook his head. '*That* may be true...' Matilda gasped, and her hands flew to her face. 'But not that I want to kill you. Or harm you in any way.'

'What, then?'

'I came to tell you what's going to happen. I wanted you to know, Matilda, so you could prepare yourself, be ready for when it happens. So that you and your girl don't get in the way.'

Thorkell's horse then trotted round in a circle, as if impatient to get moving. Thorkell leaned forward to pat its neck. 'Come with me, just a little way. We'll find a place to stop and talk.'

Matilda's trembling eased a little. She didn't know if she could trust this man or not. She thought a moment, then she gently kicked the palfrey's flanks and he trotted on.

They rode on through the forest and out the other side of it, until they reached land that must be well beyond the Meonbridge domains. A small hamlet appeared on the horizon and Thorkell pointed to it. 'There. It's abandoned.'

'How do you know?'

'I passed it on my way to Meonbridge. It's deserted. A plague village, perhaps.'

She nodded and followed on, until they reached the settlement of half a dozen tiny cottages, all of them dilapidated, with shrubs and weeds of every kind growing up inside them. They dismounted and Thorkell led her to the largest and least broken down of the dwellings.

'Here,' he said, pushing open the door. 'There's even a couple of stools.'

It was, though, very dusty, and Matilda suggested they take the stools outside and wipe them down. The day was warm and bright, and there seemed no reason not to sit in the sunshine whilst they talked. Though Thorkell shrugged at her proposal, he did as she asked, and they sat in silence for a while before Matilda spoke.

'So, what *is* going to happen?' she asked. 'You have a plan?'

Thorkell nodded. 'Father's angry that the previous attempts failed to deliver the de Bohun brat into our hands, because we relied on other people to carry out our wishes. So now Pa wants to do what he's always done – simply attack, kidnap the brat, and kill anyone who gets in the way.'

Matilda gasped, and she was trembling again. 'Kill?' she said in a whisper.

'It will likely be violent, Matilda, so I advise you to keep yourself and the girl out of the way.' He explained how the attack was planned to happen, and when precisely she'd be in danger.

'The squire always sleeps in Dickon's room now.'

'So he'll have to be disposed of,' said Thorkell, shrugging. 'It's possible everyone upstairs will die—'

'You'd *kill* her ladyship?'

'I suppose I'd rather not murder an old lady but, if she gets in our way, tries to stop us taking her grandson—'

'Which she surely will,' said Matilda, understanding at that moment that Margaret was not the sort of woman who'd allow the Bounes simply to walk into Meonbridge and deprive her of her heir.

Matilda bowed her head. It was *she* who'd brought this horror to Meonbridge. A flood of shame washed over her, and she felt for some moments that she couldn't bear to return to Meonbridge and watch the destruction of the place she loved.

But at length she stood up. She was certain there was nothing she could do to stop it happening, but she knew now that at least she had to *be* there when it did.

28

MEONBRIDGE

JUNE 1358

Since the river incident in April, Margaret had been disinclined to allow her grandson to come home at all. But when she sent a message to the earl suggesting that he keep Dickon at Steyning permanently, Raoul replied that, although he agreed the boy was safer within the fortifications of his castle, he thought he might be so unhappy that it would be detrimental to his training.

"Of course," wrote the earl, *"it is customary for boys of his age to leave home to undergo their training but, in Dickon's case, I wonder if we should be a little kind, and not expect too much of him."*

Margaret nodded as she read. She was surprised that such a man as Raoul de Fougère was so patient and forbearing. It seemed much unlike the somewhat bellicose knight she thought she knew. She agreed with his sentiments. And yet she did not. Dickon was nine now, an age when many boys of gentle birth would have long past left their parents, with perhaps only one visit home a year at most. Yet most such boys expected it, for they had been brought up in the knowledge

243

that it would happen. But, until he was seven, Dickon had thought himself a carpenter's son, and had, Margaret supposed, assumed he would follow Jack into the trade, whether or not he had ever asked, or been told, as much.

She wanted to consult her daughter on the matter and was becoming impatient for her arrival. For Dickon had travelled home from Sussex yesterday, under the protection of Margaret's own armed retainers, and a few of the earl's, for one of his brief holidays, and Johanna – Rosa – had decided to come too, to spend a few days with her little nephew.

'Is there any sign yet of my daughter?' Margaret said to Agatha, when the servant came to help her dress.

'Oh, yes, m'lady. She's been 'ere a while since. Left the priory soon after dawn, she said, and come to Me'nbridge afore you'd even stirred, your ladyship.' She grinned. 'She settled 'erself into 'er chamber, then said she were goin' off to the chapel to say her prayers. "Terce", were it?'

Margaret nodded. 'Yes, yes, it would be Terce.' She paced up and down the room a little. 'But why did you not wake me earlier, Agatha?'

'Lady Rosa said there were no need—'

'*Sister* Rosa,' said Margaret, feeling irritation with her garrulous old maid. 'But where is she now, Agatha? She surely cannot still be praying?'

Agatha shrugged and turned to go, but she met Rosa just outside the chamber door. 'Go in, m'lady,' Margaret heard the servant say. 'Her ladyship's *awaiting* you.' The emphasis Agatha placed on "awaiting" made Margaret think her words might have been accompanied by rolling eyes. Sometimes, Agatha had the impertinence of a maid a quarter of her age. Margaret could not suppress a grin but resumed her pacing as her daughter joined her.

'Really, Mother,' said Rosa, her face serene, 'you should try to calm yourself. Whenever I see you these days, you do seem so uneasy.'

Margaret winced. Only this morning she had stared at herself in her little silver-backed mirror, and seen how drawn her face was, and how her brow seemed to have become permanently creased. 'I cannot help myself, my dear. There is so much to make me anxious.'

Margaret sat down and Rosa pulled up a stool next to her. She laid her hand upon her mother's arm and squeezed it gently. 'I do understand that, Mother. And perhaps, now I am here, I can help?'

Margaret nodded. 'Indeed. I should like to talk through with you my worries about Dickon. The second attempt to snatch him back in April has made me so very nervous...'

'Tell me.'

Margaret took a deep breath and took Rosa's hand in hers. 'I do think I should be tougher with the boy. I am sure your father would have been—'

Rosa raised her eyebrows. 'Tougher about what?'

'About him coming home. For, each time he travels, I am so fearful of the danger. And I am afraid when he is here, for it seems that he is as much as risk here as anywhere. I suspect he is safest at Steyning Castle, with its fortifications and greater numbers of men-at-arms.'

'I daresay that is true. So are you thinking, Mother, that Dickon should not come home at all?'

Margaret nodded. 'I am. Yet it seems so harsh. I am much torn between wanting to toughen the child up, so he learns what it will mean to take his place as lord here when he is grown, and wishing to see him. Even the earl suggested that Dickon might still need the comfort of his visits home, given his different background from most other boys in his position.'

'I am surprised to hear that. One might imagine a man like the earl would take the hardest line.'

'You would.' Margaret's eyes twinkled briefly. 'Yet he seems most thoughtful and tender towards our little boy.'

'But perhaps that is just for now, whilst Dickon settles fully into his new life. Until he accepts his future.'

Margaret nodded. 'Perhaps Raoul is expecting that, soon, Dickon will no longer need his visits here, but will accept Steyning entirely as his home, and the other pages as his playmates and brothers.'

'And I think, Mother, that you should assume that too. Encourage Dickon to accept what destiny has brought him, and to embrace it.'

Margaret smiled. 'I think you may find him already greatly changed.

He was undoubtedly chastened by the river incident, so he is a little more compliant now and allows Piers to accompany him everywhere. Yet he seems also very eager to grow up so that he can take revenge upon his attackers, whoever they may be.'

'And do we yet know?'

She shook her head. 'We do not *know*, but John has made his view of the matter quite clear.'

'The Bounes.'

'Indeed. Although we cannot prove it.'

'I thought that the first attack was the work of Baldwin de Courtenay?'

Margaret agreed. 'But, as you know, John and I always believed that the Bounes were somehow behind it, and two months ago John discovered that Baldwin had died, allegedly in some sort of accident. But John suspects that the Bounes disposed of him, for having let them down.'

Rosa gasped. 'Are they really so very wicked?'

'I think they might be. John tried to hunt down the so-called friar who attempted to snatch Dickon at the river, but he found absolutely nothing. He says that he imagines the Bounes are skilled at covering their tracks. So we have no way of proving, or even discovering, whether or not the Bounes were involved.'

She leaned back in her chair and pressed her fingers against her brow. 'But I am fearful that, if it *is* them, and they have not yet given up their claim to Meonbridge, they will not scruple to use the foulest means to win it, since the honest ones have failed them. The attempts on Dickon's person have already been foul enough, but I suspect that there is worse to come.'

'Goodness, Mother, do you mean that they might attack the manor?'

'Indeed. John thinks so too. Quite recently he called the villagers together to inform them of his fears, and...' She smiled wanly at Rosa, '...and they agreed to support us—'

'And so they should.'

Margaret shook her head then touched her daughter's arm. 'We might *hope* that our tenants would favour us as their lords over the Bounes. But they are farming folk, my dear, and have never been required to stand and face violence from a body of armed and vicious knaves.' She sighed. 'Yet that is what they have agreed to do.'

Rosa gasped. 'To fight?'

'If needs be.' Margaret looked down at her hands and spread her fingers. 'I have already asked Sir Alain Jordan to take charge of the manor household. To inform everyone of the possible danger, to intensify the training of our retainers and squires, and to arm those servants capable of combat.'

Rosa gasped again, and when Margaret looked up at her, her daughter's face was terror-stricken. 'Mother, I can scarcely believe it might come to our servants and our tenants engaging in combat with armed and ruthless fighters.'

'I agree. But we have to be prepared.'

'Does Dickon know of your suspicions?'

Margaret shook her head. 'I have not yet told him. Although I am inclined to do so before too long. He may still be only nine, but he is bright and intelligent, and wants to understand.'

'Soon, then.'

The two women broke their conversation, first for Rosa to go to her chamber and recite the office for Sext, and then for both to join the rest of the household for dinner. Margaret saw that, as usual, Dickon was subdued and kept close to the squire Piers. Since the incident at the river, Margaret had denied Matilda any further responsibility for Dickon, and given him entirely into the squire's care. Piers now slept in Dickon's chamber, and accompanied him everywhere when he was in Meonbridge. He was also continuing the lessons he would be learning at Steyning Castle. And, although the boy was still somewhat withdrawn, she could see that he was growing a little more confident under Piers's tutelage.

Margaret was glad of her decision about Matilda. But she noticed that Dickon no longer paid any attention to little Libby, who now sat, her face long and gloomy, with her equally disconsolate mother, at the far end of the table. Margaret knew that Dickon never now asked Libby to join them when he and Piers went off together, perhaps because what they mostly did – practising with bows and arrows, playing at fighting, and rehearsing his page's tasks – was deemed to be of neither interest nor purpose to a girl. Perhaps, too, since Dickon had been in Steyning, he had decided he no longer wanted the company of girls. Margaret was sorry that Libby had thus lost her companion, but it had to be. And she was now more determined than ever that it would be best if Matilda and her daughter left the manor house to start a different life – the life of a villein's family.

Back in the solar after dinner, Margaret told Rosa what she had been thinking. 'In truth, I am eager now for Matilda to leave here.' She sighed.

Rosa pursed her lips. 'It is unchristian of me to say so, but I think that you should get rid of her as soon as possible.'

Margaret frowned. '"Get rid of" is rather harsh, my dear. I shall not be so brutal as to evict her, particularly because of Libby. But neither can I force Adam Wragge to marry her, despite the generous dowry I am offering.'

'Indeed? Making it worth his while?'

Margaret winced, ashamed that she seemed to be selling Matilda off.

But Rosa nodded. 'I do agree that you can hardly be so unsubtle as to oust her from your household. Finding her a suitable alternative to living here is undoubtedly the kinder way. I just hope, Mother, that we do not come to rue the day that you and Father took her in.'

'That sounds as if you suspect her of some sort of collusion with the Bounes.'

'As you know, I have always thought Matilda a gossip, which is why I was so concerned when she seemed to be on the brink of an attachment to Thorkell Boune. Gossips and men with evil intent are easy bedfellows.'

Margaret shrugged. 'When Thorkell came back to Meonbridge expressly, he said, to see Matilda, and you reprimanded me for letting him in—'

'I did, and you told me the gatekeeper turned him away the next time he came.'

'Indeed. And I believe he came once more and was again refused entry.' She sat forward. 'I do not think he has tried to enter since.'

'But Matilda could meet him secretly. You can hardly imprison her. Have you asked her if she has seen him?'

Margaret nodded. 'I asked her outright only the other day, and she admitted to seeing him in secret on two or three occasions. But she insisted that she had not seen him since last November, which makes her involvement in the river incident unlikely.'

'Unless they communicate by messenger?'

'I suppose that that is possible.' Then she let out a great sigh. All of this conversation was mere baggage to the central problem. 'But the question arises, why? *Why* would Matilda wish to betray us?'

29

MEONBRIDGE
JUNE 1358

T horkell raised his eyes to the eastern horizon: a hint of light was just appearing. But heavy cloud hung over Meonbridge and it was still too dark to see the faces of his comrades.

Difficult to see, but all too easy to hear the slightest sound, even the movement of a mouse scuttling through the undergrowth, for not a breath of wind was riffling the leaves on the trees, not a single bird yet trilling its dayspring song.

His company of men dismounted and tethered their horses to the branches of the slender saplings clustered together in a thick copse close by the manor wall. All were dressed in black, and all wore masks as well as hoods.

It was so quiet that they had to tread with the lightest of footsteps, and they kept close together so they could communicate by touch and gesture, rather than in words. These men had fought together for many years and were well practised in the art of soundless conversation.

Morys and Gunnar had agreed that Thorkell should lead the operation. They would play their part, but he would be the one to give directions. With Thorkell at the front of the group, they moved together slowly, beyond the copse then along the road that followed the line of the manor's outer wall, with the narrow but fast-running tributary of the river flowing in between.

Stealth and silence were the rule.

It was not invariably so. Often, they made no effort to keep an assault a covert operation. Instead, their strategy would be surprise, accompanied by so much force and noisy clamour that panic and alarm rapidly overwhelmed their quarry. Unable to muster any sort of retaliation, their victims – men, women and children – were often slaughtered where they stood, their mouths agape in terror, with no opportunity for retribution against their attackers or for confession before their God.

But, this time, they had agreed, they would aim to find the boy and snatch him as quickly, and with as little fuss, as possible. They would kill whomever they must, but quietly and swiftly. They would not linger in the fight unless forced to do so. A rapid, silent entrance and an equally rapid and silent departure were what they hoped to achieve.

Arriving at the manor gatehouse, Thorkell crossed the short bridge that spanned the stream between road and wall, the company following close behind. He directed most to crouch down in the shadows to one side of the gate, whilst two men scaled the wall with a grappling hook and rope. Dropping down the other side, the pair would make their way into the gatehouse. Thorkell could hear nothing of what was happening, but he imagined the surly old gatekeeper would put up a brief struggle before his throat was cut.

Shortly, the gate was unlocked, and the body of masked and hooded men pushed through into the manor's bailey.

Thorkell stood fast a moment, making certain of his bearings in the dark.

He had only ever been inside the manor's hall, so finding his way around upstairs in the solar depended upon the accuracy of Matilda's information. She had said that the boy's chamber was at the top of the solar stairs. Sleeping alongside him would be his guardian, a squire still young and green enough to present no problem. It was true that the squire had been stalwart at the river, rushing at the "friar", Roger Philbert, with his sword. But Roger had been too quick for him, and the eager squire was denied the chance to prove his mettle. He'd not have the chance to do so this time either.

A short distance from the boy his grandmother and her old servant would be sleeping, according to Matilda. To save any confrontation, Thorkell hoped they'd not be roused. He had killed many old women in his time, but the idea of thrusting a sword into the belly of Lady de Bohun whilst her eyes pleaded with him for mercy was repugnant, even to him. He was confident he could deal quickly with a just-roused squire and, provided the two old women stayed asleep, making off with the brat should be easy.

Just up, in, stab, grab and go.

Thorkell gestured towards the entrance to the great hall. To reach the solar, they had to pass through the hall, where the few men-at-arms and household servants would presumably still be asleep, on pallets clustered around the fire. They had debated earlier whether they could slip across the hall with such speed and stealth that none of the sleepers heard them. But it was a risk, for someone might be awake. So they agreed it would be a lesser risk to draw at least some of them out of the hall, to investigate some incident, such as a fire.

Through the gloom, Thorkell could see what looked like a towering pile, standing in the middle of the bailey. He wondered at it for a moment then realised it must be a bone-fire, a mound of timber, bones and debris, built in preparation for the Midsummer celebrations, in a week or so. How helpful of her ladyship to provide the means of her own undoing...

He directed two men to fire the pile. The timber must have been tinder dry, for it ignited easily and flames were soon surging upwards through the tower. Once the fire was burning fiercely enough, Thorkell sent four men into the hall, one to raise the alarm, the others to hide as best they might until the hall began to empty, to deal with any servants left behind, whether roused or still asleep.

Moments later, four men ran from the hall and down the steps onto the bailey.

Thorkell glanced up at the sky. Dawn was just beginning to break beyond the forest in the distance, but the heavy cloud still hung over the manor, keeping the bailey in sufficient gloom to make it hard to tell if any of those spewing from the hall were armed. But half of

Thorkell's men, crouching at the base of the steps, sprang up, taking the servants unawares, and dispatched all but one man quickly and quietly with a knife across the throat.

The one who dodged the knife took to his heels across the bailey, towards the gardens. His would-be killer started to give chase but Thorkell stayed his flight. 'Leave him,' he whispered. 'Let's get the de Bohun brat.'

He hurried forward, leading the rest of the company up the steps into the hall. Inside, through the darkness, he could just see some of his men who'd gone in earlier crouching over a few bodies – dead, he assumed – lying on the floor around the empty hearth. He tapped one of the men on the shoulder.

'Was he armed?' he said, keeping his voice low.

The man nodded. 'With a knife, m'lord. He put up a bit of a fight, but I were too strong for him.'

'A servant, d'you think?'

'Yes, m'lord. Don't seem to be any fighting men here—'

Thorkell looked about him. There were in fact only three bodies. So where were all the others? He expected there to be twice the number of servants and retainers than the nine they had so far encountered. He shook his head, then sprang up and sought out his brother, whom he recognised by his mask.

'Shouldn't there be more than this?' whispered Gunnar the moment Thorkell approached him. 'Where are they all?'

Thorkell detected a note of alarm in his brother's voice. 'No idea,' he said. 'Matilda must have got it wrong again.'

Gunnar grunted.

'No matter,' continued Thorkell. 'Let's get the brat and go. You all stay down here, spread out and keep watch, and I'll take Hywel and Madoc upstairs as we agreed. We're not likely to be long.' He winked, though of course Gunnar couldn't see it.

30

MEONBRIDGE

JUNE 1358

Jack awoke with a start. Agnes's fingers were prodding him in the ribs. 'Jack, listen,' she whispered in his ear. 'Can you hear the church bell?'

He sat up sharply and listened. 'You're right, Agnes. It's what we agreed for the signal if Meonbridge was in danger. Either Sire Raphael's seen danger himself, or someone's alerted him.'

'What danger, Jack?' said Agnes, clutching at his arm.

He could have shouted at her but didn't want to wake the boys. 'You *know* what danger, Agnes,' he hissed. 'The Bounes.' He shrugged off her hand. 'Mebbe they're in Meonbridge.'

He leapt up from the bed and pulled on his hose and shirt and surcoat, then ran over to the door to put on his boots. 'I must go and see if John's awake, then we must raise the hue and cry.'

Agnes scrambled from the bed and, running over to him, plucked at his sleeve. 'Jack, be careful,' she whimpered.

He had no time for this, but he wrapped his arms around her and held her close. 'I will. Stay here, and don't venture out until I'm back.'

He kissed the top of her head. 'I don't know how long I'll be.' She lifted her face, her eyes wide with fear, and he bent down and placed a firm kiss upon her lips. Then he pushed her gently away, threw open the door, and hurried out into the early morning.

The atte Wodes' croft was only a short distance away. He ran up the road and hammered on the cottage door. John must've been standing just behind it, for he opened the door at once.

'Ah, Jack. You've heard it too.' He fastened the final toggle on his surcoat and stepped through the door. He pointed across to the manor. 'Have you seen it?'

'What?' said Jack then, following John's finger, saw smoke rising from what seemed to be the manor's bailey. 'Fire?'

John nodded. 'Thomas Miller was here moments ago. It was him who roused me. He was up and ready to start milling when he saw the light of fire coming from the manor. I reckon Sire Raphael must've seen it too.'

'Where's Tom now?'

'I sent him down into the village to raise the hue and cry. We must go and help him.'

Jack frowned. 'Though we don't know what the fire signifies—'

'Why'd there be a fire in the bailey before dawn? Summat's amiss, Jack, even if it's not the Bounes.'

They ran down into the village, the clanging of the bell getting louder as they neared the church. 'I'll find Thomas,' shouted John. 'I said he should start down in Meonvale, so we can—'

But, as they reached the green they saw, in the growing light, that a crowd of men was already gathered.

Jack ran to the church and slipped inside. Sire Raphael was at the bottom of the tower, pulling on the bell rope. The elderly curate, Godfrey Cuylter, was pacing up and down the nave, mumbling and wringing his hands. Jack approached the priest and nodded to him.

'Should I continue?' said Sire Raphael, pausing a moment.

'Maybe a while longer. Is it for the fire in the manor?'

The priest nodded. 'I rose late for Matins and, as I hurried to Saint Peter's, something made me look north towards the manor and I saw the tops of flames.' He pulled on the rope again. 'I could not imagine why there would be a fire out of doors at such an hour. Perhaps it is a sign of the havoc we had feared?'

Jack nodded. 'The bailiff thinks it might be.' He darted outside again and looked across the green. The crowd of village men had grown, and John was standing in their midst, calling on them to follow him. Jack went back into the church. 'I think you can stop now, Father. The hue and cry's been gathered and they're on their way up to the manor. Thank you for your help—'

But Sire Raphael shook his head. 'I will come with you.' He hurried over to a table and, picking up a few items, put them into a scrip. 'For the last rites.' He grimaced. 'In case of havoc.'

Jack and Raphael had to run to catch up the company of marching villagers. Jack could see that every man was armed with something – axes, knives, a few swords, several sickles and some scythes, flails and pitchforks.

Maybe it wasn't the Bounes who'd set the fire. When they reached the manor, they might find some other reasonable explanation for the smoke and flames. But Jack felt in his bones there *was* no other explanation. What was going on at the manor was what the village had been preparing for, he was certain of it.

They'd been preparing for it, and they were ready.

31

H is two longest-serving henchmen, Hywel and Madoc, close behind him, Thorkell ran lightly across the hall towards the narrow staircase that led up to the solar. They moved with stealthy footsteps, still hoping to accomplish their mission fast and without too much of a fight, so the company could get away unscathed.

Upstairs, fingers of light were just beginning to seep through the shutter of the small window that lit the solar passage. Matilda had said that the chamber the brat occupied with his minder was the first one on the left close to the staircase head. At the chamber door, Thorkell signalled to his men to stand on either side, pressed tight against the passage wall. Then, lifting the latch as softly as he could, he leaned against the door. Before he could take even one step inside the chamber, someone hurtled towards the open door, a short sword held outstretched. But Madoc lunged sideways and stabbed the sword-bearer in the shoulder. With a cry, the young squire dropped his weapon and toppled forward, collapsing to the passage floor.

Thorkell stepped over the squire's squirming body and ran into the room, intending to pluck the de Bohun brat from his bed. But a man

257

dressed in a servant's tunic leapt up and dashed forward, a cudgel in one hand.

'You leave be my little lord,' he cried out, but Thorkell lunged at him, thrusting his knife into the servant's chest. The brat was already yelling and making for the door. But Thorkell twisted around and, too quick for him, pulled from his surcoat the rag he'd brought for the purpose and forced it into the boy's mouth. Madoc secured it with another piece of rag, then Hywel too ran forward, pulling a long sack from his scrip. He threw it over the boy's head and down towards his feet, then tied a rope around his ankles and another around the middle. Thorkell nodded and, grasping the flailing bundle, hefted it over his shoulder. The brat wriggled but to no avail: Thorkell was too strong to lose his grip.

The three men turned to go back down the stairs, but were halted by the sight of two women, standing at the staircase head, dressed only in their night chemises. One was Lady de Bohun, holding a small shield before her. Alongside her stood a younger woman Thorkell took to be a servant, her hair covered in a close-fitting cap. She was brandishing a short sword.

Astonished at the sight, Thorkell could not suppress a laugh. But his astonishment at once turned to anger that Lady de Bohun had not stayed asleep and was now forcing him to confront her. And, of course, he realised with a sudden snort, the "servant" must be her daughter. Did he have to kill her too? He'd killed many women in his time, but never a nun...

Damn them both to Hell!

He hissed at Hywel and Madoc to get the women out of his way, but both men hesitated. Thorkell's head began to pound and he swallowed to moisten his dry throat. He took a step forward, but so did Lady de Bohun, holding her shield aloft. In the growing light, she was close enough for him to see a bright gleam in her eyes.

'You will not take my grandson!' she cried, and the brat squirmed. Thorkell punched at his head and he went still, at which Lady de Bohun screamed. 'I *demand* that you put him down.'

'Ha!' hooted Thorkell, momentarily diverted by the old woman's bravado. But then he sneered. 'I don't answer to old women's demands.'

Madoc guffawed. 'Quite right, m'lord.' Then he and Hywel edged past Thorkell, their knives held out before them. 'Move, m'lady,' he growled, flourishing his knife at her.

She flinched, but stood her ground. 'You will not take him! *He* is lord of this manor, not you.'

'Not for much longer, your *lady*ship,' said Thorkell. He took another step towards the stairs.

But then a cry behind him made him spin around. A young girl was standing in the passage just by the door to Dickon's chamber. She glanced down at the squire, lying on the floor, then up at Thorkell and his men, all three now standing quite close to the stairs. Then, emitting a piercing shriek, she hurtled forward and launched herself at Thorkell.

The assault was so unexpected that, unbalanced as he was with the brat over his shoulder, Thorkell teetered. But Madoc twisted on the spot and, grabbing hold of the girl's hair, yanked her aside, and swung her hard against the passage wall. She slammed into the stone and slumped onto the floor.

At that moment Matilda too appeared in the passage, just beyond where the squire lay unmoving. Thorkell groaned: the stupid bitch had ignored his advice. And presumably the girl Madoc had perhaps just murdered was her daughter? So be it. He had tried to warn her.

Matilda saw her daughter lying insensible on the floor and, screaming, darted forward. But Madoc seized her before she reached the girl, and Thorkell, furious at being thwarted by all these women, roared.

'You turds,' he bellowed to his men. 'Must I repeat myself? Get these *whores* out of my way.'

Madoc grunted and thrust Matilda away from him so forcefully that she stumbled against the wall. Hywel lunged at Lady de Bohun, knocking her off balance, and she toppled into the nun.

'Deal with them,' Thorkell hissed. 'Then follow.'

Madoc nodded, and Thorkell took his chance. Pushing past the women, he hurtled down the narrow staircase, bumping his writhing hostage against the curving wall at every step.

At the bottom of the stairs, he halted. Why was everyone just standing around? Why weren't they fighting? Where *were* all the de Bohuns' men?

He spotted Gunnar's distinctive mask. 'Brother, what's afoot?' he called out.

'We were waiting for you—'

Thorkell didn't understand, but it wasn't the time to ask. 'We're leaving,' he said. 'I'll go the way we planned. You deal with any opposition. But don't delay.' Then, behind him, he heard Matilda's shrill voice, calling him. Damn the woman! He cocked his head towards the stairs. 'Bring her with you.'

Gunnar nodded. 'Go quickly, brother. We'll follow on.'

Thorkell lurched across the hall, his hostage squirming on his shoulder, towards the cross passage that led, he knew, towards the kitchens.

32

M atilda flew down the stairs, yelling Thorkell's name. Why she was calling him, she didn't know... To beg him not to kidnap Dickon? To take her with him?

Neither made a scrap of sense.

But, in the hall, there was sign of neither Thorkell nor Dickon, just other masked and black-clad men, seemingly about to leave, and a few prostrate bodies of what looked like manor servants.

'Where's Thorkell?' she cried and was answered with silence and shaking heads.

She remembered telling Thorkell of a back route to the bailey, out through the kitchens, and started across the hall towards the cross passage. But her way was blocked almost at once, as a huge man loomed before her, his thick arms folded across his chest.

'An' where'd you think you're going, missy?' His mouth stretched into a wide grin, showing a good number of missing teeth.

What was the answer? If she was even considering going after Thorkell, she was mad. And when her befuddled brain conjured up the image of Libby, lying senseless on the solar floor, she knew she was not only mad, but wicked. She'd abandoned her child, for Heaven's sake, without even knowing how badly hurt she was... Had she truly put Thorkell before her own child? A sob rose in her throat, and she tried to turn, to run back up the staircase. But another grabbed her from behind, hard fingers digging into the flesh of both her arms.

'Oh, no, you're coming with us, Mistress Fletcher,' he hissed into her ear, and tightly gripped her arms. He and his comrade both guffawed.

Another man, standing close by, came forward. 'So *this* is Thorkell's whore?'

She gasped. 'I'm no whore!'

The man shook his head. 'Given what I've heard about you, madam, I doubt your word.' He chuckled, and the man holding her laughed too.

'Yes, Pa, this is Matilda. Thorkell said to take her with us.'

Matilda cried out.

'Why?' said the man Matilda now knew must be Sir Morys.

And her captor, Thorkell's brother, snorted. 'For our sport, I warrant.'

Matilda let out another cry. For their sport? How dare they! She tried to kick out at Gunnar's legs, but he side-stepped her thrusting foot, and she toppled against his chest. Her heart was thumping now so wildly she thought that she might faint. Her stomach roiled at the thought of what they might do to her. But she had no more time to think, as Gunnar shoved her roughly towards his monstrous comrade, whose massive fists crushed her arms so hard she thought her little bones might snap.

'Right, missy,' the huge man snarled. 'Time to go.' She struggled a moment, but it was hopeless.

The black-clad men all surged towards the door and out onto the bailey steps. Her captor dragged her behind him, ignoring it when her shoulder struck the doorframe, making her cry out.

Outside, it was light enough to see the faces of seven or eight men standing, weapons raised, at the bottom of the bailey steps. Matilda could see they were de Bohun men: some were manor servants, unaccustomed to wielding knives against a practised foe, but a couple at least were men-at-arms, including Alain Jordan. She was close enough to see a frown upon his face, as he scanned the company of Boune men. Was he expecting one of them to be carrying Dickon?

She called out to him. 'Alain! Dickon... That way...' She wrenched one arm from her captor's grip and pointed a shaking finger towards the garden.

Alain nodded, then turned as if to run, but a Boune man at once leapt upon his back and brought him down, punching him hard upon the head.

Matilda screamed but her captor slapped her face. 'Quiet, you,' he growled and dragged her forward to descend the steps, where each de Bohun man was now fighting hand to hand with a black-clad Boune. Matilda quailed. Surely it was hopeless? Brave as her ladyship's serving men might be, there were more than twice as many Bounes and all of them skilled fighters.

The huge man crushed her arm again, dragging her away towards the manor gate, along with those Boune men who weren't fighting. But, as they neared the gate, Matilda heard the clamour of men shouting and, looking up, saw a crowd surging through the gate towards them. They were village men, all brandishing a weapon of some sort – knives and axes, pitchforks and sickles. She cried out in relief, but at the same time her chest felt tight. Most of those men too would be no match for the Bounes' vicious henchmen...

Then came more shouts, this time from behind her. Matilda twisted her head and all the de Bohun men looked to be cut down, whilst the triumphant Bounes were running forward to join their comrades. But, in the distance, at the far end of the bailey, she could just make out a lurching figure who surely must be Thorkell, with Dickon on his shoulder, and he was, as she'd suspected, heading for the garden and, she assumed, the hidden gate.

Turning back again, she saw John atte Wode at the front of the village men. Ignoring her captor, she yelled to him, 'John, look. He's running off with Dickon.' And thrusting out her free hand, she pointed frantically towards the lurching figure.

'Who?' John shouted back, raising his voice above the mounting din.

'Thorkell – Thorkell Boune.' She pointed again, her finger

quivering with urgency. 'There – the hidden gate. Head him off the other side of the wall.'

John nodded and, tapping the shoulders of the two men closest to him, he ran back through the manor gate.

Matilda's heart was pounding now with terror, for Dickon and for herself. But then she found herself amidst a frenzy of slashing blades and stabbing spikes, as Meonbridge men fell upon those trying to flee the manor. Her captor was forced to let go of her arm as three village men leapt upon him, two slicing at him with their knives, the other pounding at his head with a heavy mason's hammer. The huge man sank helpless to the ground and Matilda turned to run.

But, from behind, her arm was grasped yet again. He pulled her sharp towards him. 'Not so fast, whore,' he growled, and took a few steps sideways. It was Morys.

Then Simon Hogge was there before them, a short sword in his hand.

'Free her,' he yelled and lunged at Morys. The old man parried Simon's thrust but, in Matilda's struggles to wriggle from his grip, he was thrown off balance. Simon thrust again and, this time, his sword tip found the soft flesh of Morys's belly. He fell forward, pulling Matilda over. But almost at once he lost his grip on her and she was free.

'Go,' cried Simon, and she spun around, looking for a gap between the fighting men. But she was hemmed in on every side, as every Boune man seemed under attack from two or three from Meonbridge. She whimpered, thinking she was about to die, caught between the slicing swords and cruel axes.

But then she saw her chance. A Boune man went down and his Meonbridge assailants lowered their weapons. But, as she stepped around them, she felt a sharp pain in her back and toppled sideways. Dizzy with pain and shock, she was aware of a pair of strong arms catching her, whilst another man lunged forward, wielding an axe. A man screamed and collapsed to the ground just behind her. But Geoffrey Dyer was leaning over her, his arm reaching down. Then she was lifted up and borne away.

Matilda sobbed as the image of her daughter swam into her head.

Certain now that her own life was ebbing away, she'd never see her little girl again, nor even know if she was still alive.

33

F rom the corner of his eye, Jack saw movement at the bailey door. He glanced across to see Sister Rosa standing at the top of the steps.

'God's eyes!' he muttered, then nudged Geoffrey's arm. 'Look.' He gestured towards the nun: she was holding a short sword in her hand.

The constable snorted. 'God's eyes indeed. Not every day you see a nun wielding a sword.'

'Not that she's exactly *wielding* it.'

He watched Rosa's eyes scan the scene before her: several bodies lay around the bailey steps, some writhing, some quite still. Other men sat with their heads resting in their hands. And a few were on their feet but leaning limply against a wall or parapet. Jack, Geoffrey and the constable's men were examining the fallen, checking to see who was dead and who alive.

As Jack continued to stare at Rosa, the sword slipped from her grasp. She gasped and brought both hands up to her face. Then she saw Jack and ran down the steps towards him.

'Have you seen Dickon?' she cried out as she approached. 'Or Thorkell Boune?'

He shook his head. 'John's already in pursuit. Matilda told him the villain had run off towards the garden and the hidden gate—'

'Matilda?'

Jack pointed to where Matilda was lying on the ground, Simon kneeling at her side.

Rosa gasped. 'Is she badly hurt?'

'Knife in her back.'

Her hand flew to her mouth. 'Will she live?'

Jack shrugged. 'Dunno, m'lady.' He jerked his head towards the hall. 'What happened inside?'

'Thorkell snatched Dickon—From his chamber—He ran downstairs—'

'He didn't come this way...' Alain Jordan limped across. His arm was bleeding, but it seemed not to bother him over much. 'M'lady,' said Alain, bowing his head to Rosa. 'We waited by the steps, assuming that, if the knaves attempted to snatch young Dickon, they'd come out through the bailey door. But, when they did, he wasn't with them.'

'So Thorkell must have escaped another way,' she said.

'Through the kitchens?' said Jack.

She frowned. 'How did he—?' But then she shook her head. 'No matter. But John has gone after him?'

Jack nodded. 'With some others. Let's hope they come back soon, with Thorkell, *and* with Dickon.'

Rosa fingered the cross hanging on a cord around her neck. 'Oh, sweet Virgin, keep our little lordling safe,' she whispered. Then she spun around, taking in the numbers of injured and uninjured men around them. She was shivering, despite the gentle warmth of the early morning sun.

'Whilst we wait for John's return,' she said, 'will you both please tell me what has happened?'

Alain repeated how, with his fellow men-at-arms and a few brave serving men, he'd lain in wait for the attackers to emerge from the hall, and how surprised he'd been to see they didn't have young Dickon with them. 'Then Matilda Fletcher was dragged out onto the bailey steps, and she yelled at me that Dickon was being borne off through the garden. I was about to follow, when I was set upon by one of the Bounes' churls. Then all of us were grappling with the devils and my chance to chase after the lad was lost.' He grunted. 'I'm sorry, my lady.'

Rosa shook her head. 'You did your best, Sir Alain.' She turned to Jack. 'But then you arrived?'

Jack told her about the hue and cry, and how the village men had come together on the green, armed and ready to support her ladyship and protect young Dickon. 'They agreed to it weeks ago, when it were clear that Dickon, and Meonbridge, were in danger from the Bounes—'

'My mother told me that the tenants had agreed to fight for us.'

'For Dickon, and her ladyship. And our home.'

Rosa bit her lip. 'In truth, I did not agree with her when, after Father died, she wanted to throw herself upon the mercy of the village, as she put it.' She sighed. 'I feared they might not think we merited their support.'

'It's complicated, m'lady,' said Jack. 'Everyone thinks of Dickon as one of *us*, as well as a de Bohun.' He rubbed at his neck. 'And Lady de Bohun's always treated the tenants fairly, even if Sir Ri—'

She held up her hand. 'I understand.' She moved away and gestured to him to follow. 'What is happening now?'

Jack pointed to some black-clad men being guarded by a group of villagers. 'They're the uninjured, or only slightly injured, Bounes. We'll get them down to the manor cells, then let the sheriff play his part.' He gestured towards another group of black-clad men lying on the ground. 'Those are either dead or badly injured.'

'And do we have many dead?' she whispered.

He rubbed at his neck. 'Your servants and men-at-arms, and the villagers, did well to overcome the Bounes. We villagers made up for our lack of fighting skill with our force of numbers.' He let out a long breath. 'But I'm afraid many of the manor servants died. In the first attack, I think. One man-at-arms too is dead.'

'And the villagers?'

Jack turned his face away. 'We lost a few. Brave men, doing what they're not accustomed to.'

'Who, Jack?'

He shook his head. 'You mightn't know of them, m'lady. Nick

Ashdown, Martin Foreman… Others…'

She let out a long sigh. 'I do know both those names, Jack.' She touched the cross again, and her lips moved with silent words.

'And many more are injured,' Jack continued. 'Some of them men you mightn't think would fight for the de Bohun cause. Will Cole and John Ward amongst them. Cottars, but good men, and as loyal as any to Meonbridge.'

Rosa looked up at Jack and her eyes were damp. She touched his arm. 'We shall be forever in their debt.'

As she spoke, Jack heard a sudden commotion behind them, on the bailey steps. He turned to see Lady de Bohun emerging from the hall, her greying hair uncovered and awry. Two serving men came after her, together with the squire Piers Arundale, and between them they were man-handling two Boune men, both dazed and unsteady on their feet. Sir Alain hobbled over and suggested the men were taken to join their comrades.

Rosa ran to her mother and put her arm around her ladyship's waist. 'How are you, Mother?' she said. 'And how is little Libby?'

Her ladyship gave a weak smile. 'I am well enough, my dear.' She twisted around and gestured at the bailey door. 'And Libby is just coming…'

At that moment her ladyship's elderly maid, Agatha, appeared, holding Libby's hand. The child looked pale, but her mouth was set in a defiant line.

Jack arched his eyebrows. Thorkell Boune's escape with Dickon had clearly met with some opposition. 'What *did* happen up there, m'lady?' he said to Rosa.

She told him how she and her mother had tried to stop Thorkell from taking Dickon, and she had wounded his two men with a wild sword swing. Jack couldn't help but grin. 'That was brave.'

But she shook her head. 'They had killed one of our serving men, stabbed Piers Arundale, then tried to smash poor Libby's head against the wall. Then they jostled my mother so roughly that she fell over.' She sighed. 'I was so very angry that I just wielded the sword that was in my hands. In truth, I scarcely expected to hit anyone.'

'But you did.'

She gave a sheepish grin. 'Sufficient to disable them both, at least.

Then Piers, albeit he was injured, and two more servants who were with us, all stepped forward to keep the Boune men pinned to the floor. But, in the mayhem, Thorkell took his chance.'

'And got away,' said Jack. 'And, if he didn't come out through the door, as Sir Alain had expected, he must have reached the bailey through the kitchens.' He scratched his head. 'I wonder how he knew?'

Rosa frowned. 'Perhaps Matilda told him.'

When John returned, he had neither Thorkell nor Dickon with him. Lady de Bohun and Sister Rosa both cried out when they saw him coming through the gate with only the two village men he'd gone with. Her ladyship sank down at the top of the bailey steps, her face clutched in her hands. She seemed to be holding back her tears. But Rosa was almost wild with anger.

'How *dare* he,' she said, her voice shrill. 'How dare he kidnap his own cousin, and a child!'

'The man's a villain,' said John. 'But I'm not sure he's left Meonbridge.'

'Why so?' said Jack.

'We found a string of horses tied up in that copse close to the hidden gate. They must belong to the Bounes. We thought at first Thorkell might've got away on one, but the beasts were so quiet and unperturbed, somehow it didn't seem possible he could've lurched up to them, only moments earlier, with a flailing hostage on his shoulder. That surely would've made them skittish?'

Jack nodded. 'So he's still on foot, you reckon, and somewhere in the village?'

'Must be. I'll organise a search party.'

'Where will you look? Where might a stranger hide in Meonbridge?'

Lady de Bohun eased herself up from the step. 'Matilda will undoubtedly know the answer to that question,' she said, her nostrils flaring, and Jack saw her and Rosa exchange a nod.

'I don't think Matilda's awake,' he said.

Rosa shrugged. 'So let us rouse her.'

Simon had dressed Matilda's wound, and she was sleeping. 'It looks

270

worse than I think it is,' he said, as Jack and Rosa looked down at her.

'So she is not about to die?' Rosa's voice was cold.

Simon stared wide-eyed at Jack but agreed Matilda didn't seem to be on the point of death. 'Shall I try to wake her, Sister?' Rosa nodded, and he took a small bottle from his scrip and, uncorking it, wafted it beneath Matilda's nose. She sneezed and then her eyes flew open. At once, Rosa leaned down and shook her roughly by the shoulder, making her cry out.

But Rosa ignored her cries. 'Wake up, Matilda. Tell us where Thorkell might take Dickon.'

Matilda stared at Rosa, her eyes unfocussed.

Rosa seized her shoulder again and jerked it. 'Tell us.'

Matilda struggled to sit up a little then shook her head. 'How would I kn—?'

John then bent forward and thrust his face close into hers. 'You knew Thorkell was heading for the hidden gate, Matilda,' he hissed. 'How was that?'

'She knows well enough,' said her ladyship, now angry too. 'She must have told him precisely where he would find Dickon's chamber.'

Matilda began to weep.

'Well?' said John.

Her face crumpled and, through her sobs, she admitted telling Thorkell about Dickon's chamber and how to find the gate.

Rosa cried out and raised her hand, seemingly about to strike Matilda, but her mother caught her wrist in mid-air. 'No, daughter, we must not resort to the tactics of our enemies.' Rosa's mouth fell open and, sinking to her knees on the bailey's hard, dusty ground, she clasped her hands together and bowed her head.

It was shocking sight, Jack thought, to see such a serene and gentle lady as Sister Rosa so overwhelmed.

Lady de Bohun, her face now dark with fury, took a deep breath before leaning forward and grasping Matilda's arm. 'Tell us now, Matilda, where that knave has taken Dickon.' Her tone carried a harshness Jack had never heard before. 'You might save the child from injury, or worse—' she continued. 'Surely you would not want his death upon your conscience? Especially if you are yourself about to enter Purgatory?'

Matilda cried out at that. 'No, I didn't mean—'

'Oh, I think you *did*, Matilda,' said her ladyship. 'But at least try to save the child.'

'And quickly,' added John, 'before Thorkell does his worst.'

Tears flooded Matilda's cheeks, and it was difficult to hear her answer.

'Say that again,' said John, and she repeated it. Blanche Jordan's house.

Everyone exchanged astonished looks, but John shrugged. 'Now's not the time to ask. Let's just go and find them.'

Jack insisted that, as Dickon's stepfather, he should go with John. Simon was chosen too, in case the boy needed urgent care, and John asked the constable to join them, with a couple of his men.

'Take two of my men-at-arms as well,' said Lady de Bohun. 'Thorkell Boune may only be one man but he will be desperate. Trained soldiers will be useful.'

The sun was up as the well-armed party ran down into the village and out along the road that led to Middle Brooking. Jack thought Blanche Jordan's house was no longer fit to live in, though gossips in the village had it that she sometimes went there for secret trysts, and he often wondered why Sir Alain, a fine soldier, didn't take his wife in hand.

The house was set well back from the track. It had two doors, front and back, connected by a cross passage that separated the main rooms. One of the de Bohun men-at-arms led John, Simon and one of the constable's men round to the rear door, whilst Sir Preston Aldbury directed Jack and the others to approach the front, treading as softly as they could across the junk-strewn yard. They lined up either side of the door, against the crumbling walls, and listened. Matilda had been right: or at any rate *someone* was inside.

Jack put his ear against the edge of a small window, its outer shutter broken. A man was grunting, a child whimpering. What was happening? Jack glared at Sir Preston, his eyes pleading for action. The soldier nodded and held up his hand, five fingers raised.

Suddenly they heard the child cry out, and then the scream was quickly stifled. Sir Preston nodded again, then slammed his shoulder against the door and burst it open, the others falling in behind him. They turned from a passage into the hall, its floor strewn with debris from where the roof had partially collapsed. A couple of small windows made it just light enough to see the room's extent, and in the far corner Jack could see a door. Leading to another room perhaps?

Then the sound of scuffling and whimpering came from that direction and the child cried out again. That's where they are, thought Jack, and grinned: Thorkell was trapped.

At that moment, John and the others burst in through the back door and joined them in the hall. And Dickon – if it was Dickon, yet it surely was – must have realised he was no longer alone with his captor, for he yelled for help. But, at the same time, the sound of pounding and hammering came from behind the door.

'I reckon he's trying to break out,' said Geoffrey, and returned to the passage to run outside again, his men behind him.

'They'll stop him getting away,' said Sir Preston, cocking his head to where Geoffrey and the others had gone. 'Time for us to force the issue here.'

'But he might hurt Dickon,' said Jack, his heart thumping now.

The soldier shrugged. 'We have to risk it,' he said and lunged at the door, his sword raised.

Terrified as Jack was for his boy, he didn't know what else to do. So, as Sir Preston heaved the door open with his shoulder, Jack tumbled in behind him, and the others followed.

Thorkell Boune was standing by a gaping hole in the back wall, where he had, Jack assumed, been attacking the already broken daub. But the hole was not yet large enough for a child to crawl through, let alone a man. Thorkell held Dickon by his hair and had a knife pressed to the child's throat. Dickon's eyes were huge, his face shiny with snot and tears.

But, when he saw Jack, he cried out 'Pa!', and struggled to free himself. Squirming, he aimed a sudden backwards kick at Thorkell's shins, and found his mark. Thorkell stumbled but, as he lurched sideways, still holding onto Dickon's hair, he pulled the boy over, his knife hand flailing.

Dickon shrieked, and Jack ran towards him. He threw himself at

Thorkell, smashing with his own strong fist at the hand grasping Dickon's hair. Thorkell was forced to let go, and Dickon crumpled to the floor.

Then Jack was on top of Thorkell, punching him in the head and face. John fell upon him too, holding Thorkell down, whilst Jack continued his assault. Jack felt the bones of Thorkell's nose crumble beneath his knuckles and relished the sound of Thorkell's screams as his fist pounded the villain's mouth, smashing at his teeth. Blood spattered onto Jack's shirt and hose, mixed with splinters of bone and particles of flesh, but he didn't – couldn't – stop...

But then, above the thumping in his head, he heard Simon urging him to let Thorkell be.

'Jack! Dickon's hurt,' he cried. 'We must get him home—'

Jack heard, but his outrage kept him pummelling at Thorkell's face.

Simon shouted at him again to stop, then Jack realised John was no longer at his side. Moments later, two men pulled him away and he staggered back, his knuckles on fire and bleeding, his head pounding. But then, understanding what Simon had just said, he spun around. The surgeon was kneeling at Dickon's side.

Jack dropped down beside him. 'Is he badly hurt?'

'A knife wound,' said Simon. 'We must get him back to the manor, so I can dress it properly.'

Jack lunged to his feet and threw himself at Thorkell once again. 'You stabbed him,' he growled. 'My boy—'

Thorkell's face was so damaged he couldn't speak, but Jack was certain a faint smirk passed his lips. He wanted to wipe the leer away, but John grasped his arm. 'Leave it, Jack. Let the soldiers deal with him. We must look to Dickon.'

Jack looked into his brother-in-law's eyes.

'We have to look to Dickon now,' said John again. 'Justice can come later—'

'Justice?' Jack snorted. 'That villain has no right to "justice". Retribution, more like—'

But John rested a hand lightly on his shoulder and shook his head. 'Jack, that's not you talking—'

Jack shrugged him off. 'It is now.'

34

The late afternoon sun streamed through the open windows of the solar, but its cheerful brightness could not lift their mood. Rosa and her mother had recovered something of their equilibrium. They had put on fresh clothes, taken a little food, and were now sipping at their second or third cup of reviving wine. But they were barely speaking, each lost in her own grief and worry about Dickon, and the deaths of so many Meonbridge men.

It was a couple of hours since Jack and John had brought Dickon back, alive but badly injured. He was lying in his chamber now. Simon had dressed his wound. It was deep, but he thought the knife had not entered any major organ.

'Are you not confident of a favourable outcome?' said Margaret, her face grey, making her look much older than she was.

Simon had shrugged. 'Our little lord is tough, m'lady – his grandfather's heir, to be sure. With good care, he might pull through.'

'Only "might", Simon?'

He had shrugged again, but Rosa could see in his eyes that he was not willing to be optimistic about Dickon's future.

Soon after the men had returned with Dickon, Agnes had arrived at the manor in an utter panic, not knowing that Dickon was home again and still alive. But, when she discovered how badly hurt he was, she seemed to lose her wits completely, flailing up and down the chamber, sobbing and pulling at her hair. She was convinced her boy was going to die.

Rosa thought Agnes's behaviour most undignified, but reminded herself that, years ago, when Philip died, her own conduct had been anything but restrained. She should not judge her former friend. Poor Agnes! Rosa often wondered if Agnes would have been happier if she had never returned to Meonbridge but had lived out her life with Jack and their children in some place where the true identity of her first-born son was never known. Of course, that would have meant that Rosa's own parents would never have known they had a grandchild, and an heir, but a great deal of difficulty and heartache, not to say falsity and mayhem, might have been avoided.

But she would not say any of this to her mother, who adored her grandson, despite his obstinate and mischievous nature, partly because, she often said, he reminded her so much of Philip.

At length, Agnes calmed down sufficiently for Jack to let her sit in Dickon's chamber, and help him nurse the boy. Piers Arundale, already much recovered from his injury, had been detailed to look after their younger children, whilst Simon had gone off to tend to those lying on trestles downstairs in the hall.

Suddenly Margaret broke the silence. 'I shall have to help the families who lost their menfolk in the battle,' she said. 'And those men who have been injured.'

Rosa smiled. Despite her anxiety about her grandson, her mother did not let herself forget her responsibilities towards her tenants. 'Help in what way, Mother?'

'Ask John to organise work parties to help those who cannot manage their own land? Provide a little food, perhaps? What do you think?'

'That seems fair. Those men risked a lot to stand by us.'

'They did.' Her mother dabbed her kerchief at her eyes. She had rarely been one for tears, but these last few months had tested her severely, and even the formidable Margaret de Bohun was permitted to show a degree of strain.

Rosa rose from her chair and, going over to her mother, took her hand and squeezed it. 'The village will recover,' she said. Even if Dickon does not, she thought, but did not say.

The two women had retreated once more into fitful, but not uncompanionable, silence when Agatha knocked on the chamber door and announced Sir Giles Fitzpeyne.

Giles strode over to Margaret, who started to rise from her chair. But he shook his head and gestured her to sit again. Rosa got up and invited him to sit by her mother, whilst she crossed to the small table and took a stool.

Earlier, Sir Giles had ridden at speed through the manor gate, accompanied by his fine entourage, moments after John, Jack and the others had gone off in search of Thorkell Boune and Dickon. There had been much shouting and whinnying as the riders were forced to rein in their horses swiftly to avoid collision between men and beasts.

Giles had dismounted almost before his horse came to a stop and ran over to the bailey steps, where Rosa and her mother, still dishevelled in their nightwear, and distressed that Dickon might be lost, were just turning to go back into the hall.

'Margaret,' he called out. 'Am I too late?'

And he had discovered, to his anger and distress, that he had indeed not come in time to prevent the Bounes' attack.

Rosa had seen despair in his eyes when he realised that he had failed in his mission. She had gestured towards Sir Alain Jordan and Piers Arundale who, despite their wounds, had just started directing operations to get the captured Bounes down into the manor's dungeons, and to give what aid they could to all the injured.

'With their own injuries, they are struggling, I think,' she had said. 'Perhaps you could help?'

'Gladly, gladly,' and immediately Giles had taken charge, bidding Sir Alain and Piers go have their wounds attended to, whilst he detailed some of his own men to deal with the prisoners, and others to give help to those in need of succour.

A while later, John, Jack and Simon returned with Dickon, and Rosa's and her mother's attention had turned towards him. Then Agnes came and the whole manor seemed to be in a state of uproar and panic over Dickon's fate.

Not long afterwards, the two men-at-arms, with Geoffrey and his henchmen, came back with Thorkell. They had not bothered to make a litter, but simply dragged him, despite his injuries and drifting consciousness, up through the village to the manor. Giles had ordered him to be thrown into a cell, without troubling to let his wounds be tended.

Now it seemed that Giles had asked to see Rosa and her mother because he wanted to explain himself. He sat for a few moments without speaking, then shook his head and raised his eyes. 'I am so sorry, Margaret, that I have failed you. Because I knew what was going to happen—'

Both women gasped as one.

'You knew?' said Rosa.

He nodded, tears in his eyes. 'Yet I couldn't decide what to do. It was hard for me to go against my wife's father and brothers. Gwynedd begged me – again – not to get involved, and I argued with her, and with myself, back and forth, trying to decide whether my loyalty to Richard and to you, Margaret, was stronger than my duty to my wife.' He got up from the chair and paced about the room. 'In the end, I knew that I had no choice, for the sake of what Richard and I had once been to each other, and for the debt I owed you, Margaret, for my part in his death. I had to come and stop those villains seizing Meonbridge. For I knew that their methods would be violent, and that your resources here might not be sufficient to defend yourselves.'

He sank down again into the chair, and he seemed on the point of weeping. 'I am so sorry for leaving my decision too late to save you from this dreadful assault.'

'At least you came,' said Margaret. 'And you are helping now.'

Giles nodded, but seemed not at all convinced that he was absolved of blame. Rosa came across and, pouring a cup of wine, handed it to him. He took it and downed the cup in one. Then he held the cup out to Rosa, a weak smile on his lips, and she refilled it. She did the same to her own cup and her mother's then, picking up her three-legged stool, she brought it over and sat down again.

'What now?' she said.

Giles grimaced. 'One thing I should say, although I hardly wish to, is that Thorkell Boune probably needs the surgeon's attention if he is to survive long enough to stand trial for his crimes.'

'What do you think, Mother?' said Rosa.

She nodded. 'Let him have it. I want him to be judged, and to be seen to pay.'

Giles put down his cup and spread his hands. 'I agree. For I think that his father will not face earthly justice.'

'Morys Boune is *here*?' said Margaret, her eyebrows raised.

'Indeed,' said Giles. 'As is his other son, Gunnar. Did you not realise?'

Rosa and her mother shook their heads.

'Gunnar is uninjured,' continued Giles, 'but I have separated him from his men and put him in a cell alone for later questioning. But Morys is in the hall, lying amongst the injured and the dying. He is very badly hurt.'

Rosa gasped. 'I had not realised that all three had come.'

'Perhaps,' said Giles, 'they thought that, with all of them here, they would be more likely to succeed.'

'I wish to speak with him,' said Margaret, almost springing to her feet.

'But why, Mother?' said Rosa. 'What can you possibly have to say to him?'

Giles shrugged. 'I too wish to speak with my father-in-law.' He grimaced. 'I always knew he was a knave, but I never thought he would resort to violence against his own kin.' He stood up. 'Perhaps, Margaret, we should both take our chance now to say our piece before he is called to whatever fate next awaits him?'

In truth, Rosa did not want to meet the man who had perpetrated such mayhem against them, but her mother seemed so set upon it, she reluctantly agreed.

In the hall, Giles approached the trestle on which Morys lay, Rosa and her mother following a little behind him. He did not hold back

279

castigating Morys for his actions, although it was clear that Morys was scarcely able to respond. Only flickering eyelids and twitching fingers suggested that he could even hear what Giles was saying.

'I want to know what happened to Richard,' said Margaret. 'I daresay he knows?'

'Almost certainly,' said Giles. 'But I think he is no longer capable of saying anything to you, or me.'

Rosa shook her head. Her time, and her mother's, would be better spent tending to those men of Meonbridge who had risked their lives for their family, rather than trying to coax a confession from a dying brigand. Nonetheless, she had to let her mother do as she wished. But she moved away herself, thinking she would visit each of the injured Meonbridge men. She would tell them of her mother's promise of practical help to them and their families and say a prayer for their recovery or salvation.

Some hours later, Agatha came with a message from Matilda. Matilda was confined to her own chamber, with one of Giles's men standing guard outside her door, but she had apparently recovered sufficiently from her injury to be able to stand up and walk around, if cautiously.

Agatha frowned as she relayed the message to her mistress. 'Missus Fletcher says she wants to speak to that Thorkell. I told her you'd not allow it—'

Rosa turned to her mother. 'I agree with Agatha. I am not sure that Matilda has any right to make demands.'

Agatha grunted. 'Indeed, m'lady. That treach'rous strumpet should be in the dungeons along with the other felons.'

Margaret shook her head. 'No, no, Agatha,' she said, then rubbed at her temples with her fingers. 'Yet, she *has* betrayed us utterly...' She raised her eyes, full of hurt, to Rosa. 'She must have plotted with Thorkell more than once to throw Dickon into danger, so that the Bounes could claim Meonbridge after Dickon's death.' Her eyes filled with unaccustomed tears. 'How could she be so traitorous? After all that Richard and I have done to help her?'

Rosa felt unseemly fury rising in her breast. It was hard to maintain a saintly calm. 'As you know, Mother, I have always thought you treated Matilda with more kindness than she deserved. And you should have insisted that she marry one of those men Father found for her, instead of permitting her to pick and choose.'

Margaret nodded. 'I agree, but what we know now we did not know then. Matilda has indeed been very foolish. I assume she believed that Thorkell Boune would marry her, and make her mistress of Meonbridge, if he succeeded in killing Dickon and driving me from here.'

'That is not foolish but wicked,' said Rosa, her temper rising still. 'She deserves nothing more than to be driven from here herself, to make a future by her own devices instead of benefitting from your too generous support.'

'My head tells me you are right, yet I am afraid my heart still grieves for the misery that Matilda endured as Robert Tyler's daughter and Gilbert Fletcher's wife. And I cannot bear to abandon little Libby to her mother's fate, if I do as you suggest and drive her out of here.'

'Keep Libby here then,' said Rosa. 'Let the mother shift for herself but nurture the child and make her some man's useful wife. And trust that she is not so tainted by her blood that she turns out as wicked as her forebears.'

Her mother looked shocked. 'I understand your anger, my dear, but your words are anything but Christian.'

Rosa looked away. Her mother was right. Indeed, she herself scarcely recognised the Rosa she had become in recent weeks. She was not acting, nor even thinking, like the joyous, life-affirming Sister Rosa she had grown into during her happy years at the priory. 'I am not at all myself,' she said, turning back. 'I must go and pray. For Dickon, for Matilda, for our injured men, and for myself.'

Her mother nodded. 'We still have to decide whether or not to grant Matilda's request.'

'Later.' She kissed her mother's cheek and left the room. She would go downstairs to the chapel and ask God to forgive her.

It was early morning, not quite sunrise, when Rosa emerged from the chapel. She had spent all night in prayer, by turns kneeling at the *prie-dieu* that had been her father's and lying prostrate on the cold hard floor before the great golden cross. Before she even considered breaking her fast, the first thing she must do was take a tour around the hall, checking on the state of the injured Meonbridge men.

But the first trestle she came to was the one on which lay Sir Morys Boune. She stopped, and crossed herself, for the sight of him was shocking. His arms were hanging over the table's edge and his body lay quite still, but in a contorted pose as if he had died in agony. His face too suggested it, for his mouth was agape, his eyes fixed open, as if he had seen a fearful vision at the moment of his death.

Yesterday, she might have rejoiced at Sir Morys's demise but, today, after a night recovering her customary piety and compassion, her bitterness had faded. She wondered if he had been given absolution before he died. In case he had not, she knelt down and prayed for his soul, although in truth she doubted such a man had much possibility of redemption.

Rosa then walked around the rest of the injured men, and returned to Sir Morys's corpse. She was about to go upstairs to see her mother when Sire Raphael entered the hall. She hailed him. 'What losses have there been during the night?' she asked. 'I saw another Meonbridge man had died.'

Raphael nodded. 'I gave him absolution only an hour or two ago. We will move him shortly.' Then he pointed to Sir Morys. 'And I see that this man here has now passed on.'

'Indeed,' said Rosa. 'Do you know who he is?'

He shook his head. 'Only that he is one of the villains who attacked us.'

Rosa nodded. 'It is Sir Morys Boune, my father's cousin, the man who sought to kill our little lord and deprive him and our family of Meonbridge.'

The priest's eyebrows lifted. 'I did not realise it was he.' He looked down at him. 'It seems that he may have come to a terrifying end.'

'I thought that too. Had you or Master Cuylter shriven him?'

'Not I, nor Godfrey neither, I believe.'

Rosa thought he looked a little shame-faced. She felt guilty too. 'We best pray for him now then,' she said.

But Raphael shrugged. 'I fear that, because of the magnitude of his sins, he will have died without God's friendship, and so will not have entered the state of purification from which he might at length ascend to Paradise.'

Rosa gasped. 'You mean that he is already—?'

The priest spread his hands. 'We might presume so.'

Rosa went upstairs to see her mother, who was taking a small breakfast in her chamber. Libby was with her. Rosa smiled at the girl. 'Have you seen your mama this morning, child?' Libby shook her head. 'Well, pop along to see how she is. I wish to have a private word with her ladyship.'

Libby seemed unsure, but Margaret nodded at her to do as Rosa asked, and the girl ran off.

'Sir Morys is dead,' said Rosa, without preamble.

Her mother gasped. 'I did not know.'

'I think it was quite recent, for Sire Raphael did not know until I drew his attention to it a few moments ago.' She poured herself a cup of small ale. 'And it seems he died in terror, and unshriven.'

Her mother almost spilt her ale and, putting the cup down, covered her mouth with her hand. 'How do you know?'

Rosa explained what she had seen and her conversation with the priest.

'I would not wish such an end on anyone, however wicked they were on earth,' said Margaret, her voice a whisper.

'I agree, Mother.' She took a sip of ale. 'Sire Raphael believes our prayers can no longer help Sir Morys, but I shall pray for him withal.'

'I too,' said Margaret, picking up her cup again.

'Have you seen Dickon yet this morning?' asked Rosa. She picked up a small sweetmeat from the dish Agatha had brought, trying to tempt her ladies into eating.

Margaret raised her eyes to her daughter. 'I am afraid to.'

'That is not like you, Mother, to be fearful in the face of what is dire and difficult.'

'I know. But this is somehow more difficult than anything I have had to face before, even Philip's murder, even Richard's...' Her eyes were damp. 'For, if Dickon dies, what will happen to the family, what will happen to Meonbridge, and all of your father's other domains? When I think of it, my mind becomes such a whirl of doubt and worry, I cannot imagine what I am going to do.'

Rosa sat down opposite her mother and reached out to squeeze her hand. 'We will work it out together.'

Margaret gave her a wan smile. 'Before Agnes brought baby Dickon home to Meonbridge,' she went on, 'we had thought – your father and I – that Meonbridge might indeed be lost, with Philip dead and you sequestered in the priory. But, in the end, I persuaded Richard to agree to entrust Meonbridge to Northwick, so that the priory could run and benefit from the estate, along with your other lands. We never really decided what to do with the other estates in Sussex and Dorset, but at least Meonbridge's destiny was agreed. Then Dickon came into our lives. And, although he was not legitimate, Richard always said he would find a way of ensuring that the boy would inherit all the de Bohun lands. He thought he had time to make all the arrangements... As you know, he always intended sending the boy away to train, just as any legitimate heir would do, and, when he was old enough, he would tell Dickon of his destiny.'

'But it did not work out quite as he had planned,' said Rosa. 'He died untimely, and Sir Morys and his beastly sons thought they could easily outwit you, and me, and our little boy.'

'They did, but they were wrong. For they did not reckon with the support of our tenants.'

Rosa nodded. 'I was wrong to doubt your faith in them.'

Margaret leaned across the table and patted Rosa's arm. 'You have not known them for as long as I have. Anyway, let us go to see my grandson.' She drew herself up tall and pressed her lips together, then marched boldly to the door.

In Dickon's chamber, everyone was quiet. Even Agnes, who Margaret said she had heard weeping on and off throughout the night, was sleeping, lying on the truckle bed usually occupied by Piers Arundale. Piers was playing quietly in a corner with Agnes's younger children and Libby Fletcher.

Jack came forward to greet them.

'How is he?' Rosa asked.

He shrugged. 'Simon's just left. The wound got filled up with some foul-smelling yellow stuff. He's cleaned it away but—'

'Is that not considered a sign of healing?' said Rosa.

But her mother shook her head. 'I have heard Simon say it is best to remove it, then douse the wound with wine, and smear it again with honey or one of his healing salves.'

Jack nodded. 'That's what Simon said to me. But he's worried now that Dickon has a fever. He thinks it's related to the foul matter. He's bid me and Piers bathe him constantly with water to keep him cool.'

'Will he live?' said Margaret, her face stricken.

Jack's eyes were damp. 'Simon's not certain that he will... Indeed...'

'What?' said Rosa.

He shook his head.

'Oh, Jack,' cried Margaret, unable to suppress a sob.

'We must pray, Mother,' said Rosa. 'Let us leave Jack to care for the boy's body, and we will pray that God will spare him. But that, if he cannot, then at least he will welcome his little soul soon into Paradise.'

Jack laid his hand on Rosa's sleeve. 'Please, Sister, don't let Agnes hear you speak so. She's beside herself with terror.'

Rosa nodded. 'I am sorry, Jack. It was unthinking of me to speak so in your presence. But I shall go now and do my part.'

Her mother spun around and lurched from the room, and Rosa hurried after her. They returned to Margaret's chamber, where she poured herself another cup of wine, though Rosa shook her head.

'Will you come with me to the chapel, Mother?'

'I shall,' said Margaret, but then slumped into her chair. 'If Dickon dies, it will surely be God's punishment for all our lies. For Richard's untruth, and our complicity in his deception.'

Rosa shook her head. 'Mother, we have not been complicit. We were compelled to be evasive, for Dickon's sake and the future of our family but you and I, Mother, have not, since Father's death, made any claim that we knew to be a lie.'

Yet her mother seemed unable to shake off her melancholy. 'Oh, Rosa, Rosa, what shall we do if Dickon dies?'

Rosa went to stand before her mother and bowed her head. 'Perhaps I shall give up the priory after all?'

She said it to give her mother comfort, yet she did not even know if she *could* renounce her vows. And, in truth, the very idea of giving up her calling made her feel her heart might break.

35

T he warmth of the summer sunshine touching Margaret's cheeks
    did nothing to relieve the chill clutching at her heart, as she and
Rosa stood amongst her servants and her tenants in what they still
thought of as the "new" graveyard. It was nine years ago that Stephen
atte Wode, the then reeve, had ordered it to be dug, when the
Mortality was spawning more bodies than the churchyard had space to
bury. But not since that dreadful year had so many needed to be buried
all at once as did today.

Despite the churchyard's lack of space, many still wished to see
their loved ones buried close to the church. Few were laid to rest there
now, although occasionally a family member would be tucked in above
or alongside earlier remains. But the relatives of Meonbridge's most
recent dead had agreed that the new graveyard, which now had trees
for shade and flowering plants for consolation, was a fitting resting
place for those who had given their lives for their little lord and for
their home.

Moreover, they had agreed that they would all be laid together.

Margaret had waited at the church porch for the sad processions to arrive. Sire Raphael had planned a mass and service of remembrance for the dead before they were all taken the short distance down the rutted lane that ran alongside the church on their final journey in this world.

Carts bearing coffins or simply shrouded bodies had trundled through the village from every corner of Meonbridge. Cottars came from Meonvale, and villeins from village crofts or farms beyond the village bounds, and Margaret's own servants were brought down from the manor house.

Following each cart were grieving friends and relatives.

First to arrive had been the cart bearing the body of Nick Ashdown, laid in a fine oak coffin, and occupying the cart alone. Behind it walked Susanna Miller, at her side her son Tom and brother-in-law, Thomas, once more the miller. Susanna was burying her third love. She and Nick had not yet tied the knot, but Margaret had heard that they had planned to do so soon. But, now, Susanna was alone again. Yet, as she approached the church, she held her head high, proud perhaps of the sacrifice her Nick had made. Walking with Susanna were Eleanor and Walter Nash, taking charge of her younger children. Margaret recalled how, two years ago, Eleanor – so distraught at Susanna's arraignment for the supposed murder of her husband, Henry – had persuaded Richard to take Susanna's part in court. And, between them, they had succeeded in winning Susanna's freedom.

But, Margaret suspected, Eleanor was not following Nick's coffin only to support Susanna, but also on her own account. For had she not, for years, been courted eagerly by Nick, although in the end she had chosen Walter to be her husband?

The next cart to arrive came from Meonvale and bore three shrouded bodies, including those of William Mannering, and Fulke Collyere, who, with his brother, worked for Thomas at the mill. From what she knew of William, he was honest and stout-hearted, and had been grief-stricken at being forced to admit at the court, when the Bounes brought their case against Dickon's right to Meonbridge, that Agnes was the child's mother. Others were compelled to say it too, but Margaret recalled the misery on William's face when he blurted out the words, knowing that they denied his little lord's legitimacy. And now he had given his life for that same boy, whilst his own son, Harry, was clutching fast to the side of the cart that bore the corpse of his only parent. He was no longer a child – fifteen, perhaps? – but he was now alone, and his desolation was etched into his face. She resolved to ensure the boy had work, and perhaps too she could find him a guardian, someone to help him through the next few years to adulthood.

An adult already, yet scarcely seeming so, was young Warin Collyere, gripping the other side of the cart on which his older brother lay. Warin was not exactly simple but slow of thought and lazy and he had relied on Fulke for getting him through life. He still had his job at the mill, but could he manage living on his own? Margaret doubted it, from the little that she knew of him. She sighed deeply at the sight of those two boys, set adrift now without a family's support.

It reminded her again of what had happened nine years ago, when the Mortality left so many orphaned children in its wake. Some of them not only survived but made the best of their situation – Eleanor Titherige and her stepbrother, Roger Stronge, were two such who did. Others could not manage alone and were taken in by families who had lost their own children. But a few boys had formed themselves into a gang of mischief-makers and left Meonbridge in search of the rich pickings they had heard might be had easily in the villages emptied by the slaughter. She had never heard if those boys had thrived or ended their lives swinging on a gibbet. But she was determined that would not happen to Harry or to Warin. It was her duty to ensure they remained in Meonbridge as useful tenants.

More carts came, but it was the one bearing her own servants that had grieved her most.

For these brave men – one or two of them hardly more than boys – had been ill equipped to fight. They were kitchen hands, servers, gardeners – none of them trained, or expected, to engage in combat with skilled swordsmen. Although, in recent months, Sir Alain Jordan had been giving instruction in self-defence to the entire household, in dread anticipation that the Bounes might one day mount a direct attack. But, for these men, the Bounes' henchmen had proved too strong, or simply too numerous.

Now, in the middle of the new graveyard, Margaret stood before the row of thirteen neatly excavated pits. Behind her and on every side, the whole of Meonbridge seemed to have gathered, men, women and children, come to offer thanks to those who died so that Meonbridge might not be brought to ruin.

Men staggered forward, bearing the coffins and the shrouded bodies from the carts left in the lane, and lowered them gently to the ground, each into their allotted place.

As Sire Raphael gave the final blessing, '...for thou art dust, and thou shalt return to dust...', relatives picked up a few crumbs of Meonbridge soil from the excavated piles and dropped them onto their loved one's corpse.

Margaret stepped forward and did the same, for every one of her tenants and servants. Rosa followed her example, as then did every villager, halting at each grave to pluck some loamy fragments from the heap and throw them atop the body of their friends and neighbours, their lips moving in silent prayer.

There was, Margaret realised, no wailing. She had seen tears in Susanna's eyes, and in young Harry's but, although weeping might follow in the privacy of cottages and chambers, for now, gravity and resignation prevailed.

But, in truth, Margaret could readily have thrown herself bodily to the ground and howled for the untimely loss of all these lives. Death was commonplace and frequent. God ordained how each person lived and died, and when their allotted span had run. Sometimes His ways seemed bewildering and cruel, as they had nine years ago. But what had happened here and now in Meonbridge was man-made, a conflict caused by the telling of a lie.

Somewhere in the Bible, she knew not exactly where, it said, "*Lying lips are an abomination to the Lord*". Sir Raphael had once said so in a sermon. Margaret bit her lip. She recalled that sermon now, though not quite when it was. Sometime after Richard's death? She had not thought it at the time, but was Sire Raphael then somehow alluding to Richard's lie about Dickon's legitimacy? She shook her head. Surely no one beyond the family knew of it then?

But she remembered too another of the priest's biblical sayings that day in church. "*For nothing is secret that shall not be made manifest; nor anything kept hidden that shall not be known and come abroad.*" She gasped at the memory of those portentous words. Did Sire Raphael know all along of Richard's falsehood, and that it would at length lead to disaster?

Back in her chamber, Margaret asked to be left alone.

Rosa nodded. 'I will go to the chapel, Mother. To pray for the souls of all those buried today, and for us, who brought this mayhem to Meonbridge.' She sighed. 'I may not return for supper.'

Rosa was right of course. Richard had told the lie whilst, as his wife and the one left to deal with the outcome, Margaret had tried to counter it with the truth. Yet the result had still been disaster for many, if not – God willing – for their little lord. Could she have dealt with it better? She would never know. Her task now was to ensure that Meonbridge and her tenants prospered and to put her trust in God to allow Dickon to recover and, in time, assume his responsibilities as lord.

Margaret insisted that Matilda was kept confined to her room. Giles had suggested that she might be locked up, perhaps to stand trial alongside Thorkell and Gunnar Boune, but Margaret did not want that. She no longer wanted Matilda's company, but still found it in her heart to feel pity for the girl, despite her treachery.

She repeated to Giles what she had said to Rosa. 'I cannot stop grieving for the ill treatment that Matilda suffered at the hands of her father and wicked husband. She was such a lively girl, with great hopes and expectations, albeit she was headstrong. But all her yearnings came to naught.'

'Yet I understand that you and Richard tried to find her a fitting husband?' said Giles.

'We did. But Matilda harboured an ambition of being more than a mere villein's wife, and could not be persuaded to accept any of the good, if dull, men that we offered her.' Margaret's eyes narrowed. 'She might now much regret her obstinacy.'

It was clear that Matilda did at least *wonder* if she had been foolish not to accept one of those men, unappealing as they might have been. Since the attack on Meonbridge, she was behaving quite differently from the wilful, selfish young woman she had been. Indeed, she seemed chastened, remorseful, even contrite. But her contrition made her listless, and she spent her days lying on her bed, not bothering to occupy herself with anything, nor even to play with Libby.

But Margaret thought it was time she prepared Matilda for her future. She did not yet know quite what that would be, but it was no longer as her companion. Matilda's wound had proved to be scarcely more than skin deep, and there was now no reason for her to claim she needed "rest".

'Why do you not take a turn about the gardens, Matilda?' said Margaret, one particularly bright and sunny morning. 'Now your injury is healing, you would surely benefit from some fresh air and exercise.'

Matilda raised her, now usually downcast, eyes. 'I thought you expected me to stay in here.' Her words might have suggested her former petulance, but her tone was quite disconsolate.

Margaret nodded. 'It is true that I want to ensure you are no longer able to take liberties with my hospitality. But you are not a prisoner and, as long as you are accompanied, I am content for you to walk the manor grounds as you used to do.'

'Can I take Libby with me?'

'Of course. She too needs time outdoors.' Then a thought occurred to Margaret, and she wondered why she had not done it years before. 'Perhaps I should instruct you both in tending vegetables and herbs? It is a skill that will undoubtedly be useful.'

Matilda shrugged, and seemed not to have noticed the implication behind Margaret's remark. An implication that was, in truth, only just beginning to form in Margaret's head, an idea she intended to discuss with Giles when he next came to Meonbridge.

'Well,' said Margaret, 'shall we go?'

'We?'

'Indeed. I shall come with you this morning. We shall examine the herb garden together.'

Matilda nodded feebly. 'Shall I fetch Libby?'

'I have already said so. One day she will marry, and gardening is an essential skill for a married woman.'

Matilda did tilt her head at that, her eyes perplexed. 'But only if she is a country wife.'

'Which is what of course she will be.' She spun around and strode to the door of the chamber. 'I shall await you in the hall, Matilda. Do not dally.' She swept out into the passage. So Matilda had still not surrendered her ambitions, even if she had transferred them to her daughter. She was incorrigible... Hopefully, Giles would come back soon, and Matilda's future could be decided.

The gardening lessons did not prove a great success, at least as far as Matilda was concerned. Libby, Margaret thought, was eager enough to learn. Perhaps she needed occupation? But Matilda appeared indifferent to everything.

Every thing, that is, except one.

Margaret was demonstrating how onions need to be lifted and left to dry before they could be carried away for storage. She worked along the rows with her little mattock, gently easing the yellow bulbs away from their bed. Libby and Matilda were supposed to be following on behind, shaking off the soil and bending the leaves over. Libby seemed to be enjoying it, but Matilda kept stopping and, pressing her hand against her back, gazed about her, leaving her daughter to do the work.

Margaret strove to maintain her composure, but Matilda was trying her patience. 'Matilda, this lesson is for you as well as Libby.'

'But it pains my back,' said Matilda, 'and I really don't enjoy it.' She pouted.

Margaret shook her head. The old Matilda still lurked inside that limp exterior. 'Nonetheless, it is a valuable task to learn.' She waved her mattock in the air. 'I suggest that you make a better effort.'

But, after only a few more onions, Matilda stood up again and was staring at the manor buildings. Following her gaze, Margaret realised that she was looking towards the undercroft, where some of the storerooms had, years ago, been converted into a few cells, intended to keep village miscreants in custody before they came before a court, or were taken away to Winchester by the sheriff. The cells were rarely used but, now, they housed the Boune brothers and their henchmen.

Margaret eased herself to her feet and went over. 'Matilda?'

'*Can* I see him?' she said, her eyes glittering and her tone querulous.

And Margaret then recalled that it was several days ago that Agatha had brought a message from Matilda, asking if she could see her former lover. 'Why should you want to see him?' she said. 'Such an outright villain?'

'I did love him. And I thought that he loved me.' Her eyes glistened.

Margaret shook her head. 'I doubt, Matilda, that Thorkell Boune has ever loved anyone. He is a thorough-going knave...'

Matilda nodded. 'I know that now, my lady.' She chewed at her lip. 'But can I?'

The next morning, Thorkell was brought up from his cell. His hands bound, and with one of Giles's retainers standing guard, he was placed in a corner of the great hall. Margaret decided to accompany Matilda, curious herself to see how he was faring as a prisoner.

It was two weeks after the assault on Meonbridge, yet Thorkell's wounds had scarcely begun to heal, despite Simon's attentions. She supposed the surgeon had done only the minimum to keep the man alive. It was astonishing how much devastation Jack had inflicted, in what she heard had been a frenzied beating. Jack was normally such a mild-tempered man. She supposed that Thorkell's assault on Dickon had unleashed in Jack a parent's instinct to defend and to avenge his child, just as a sow becomes ferocious when her piglets are being threatened.

Jack certainly had wreaked violent retribution.

In truth, despite her loathing of the man, Margaret was almost saddened to see how Thorkell's once handsome face was now so ruined. But she soon turned away, not wanting him to observe how much his condition shocked her. Not that he looked at her, but rather kept his gaze directed at his feet.

But Matilda seemed almost gleeful to see the man she had apparently once loved so much destroyed. She stared at his face and did not look away. And then she giggled.

'A moment, my lady,' she said. 'I want to fetch something.'

Matilda dashed across the hall to the solar stairs, her listlessness seemingly forgotten. She quickly returned with a battered metal mirror that Margaret had not seen before. Matilda thrust the mirror before

Thorkell's eyes, seemingly relishing the chance to show him how he looked.

But Thorkell would not look, either at himself or at Matilda, keeping his eyes firmly directed towards the floor. And, because she could not see his face properly whilst standing up, Matilda crouched down, so that she could stare up at his disfigurement.

It was a strange meeting. Margaret had imagined that Matilda might scream, or maybe even hit out at him, for all along deceiving her and then not caring what happened to her during the attack. But she did neither. She simply stared, and laughed at what she saw, and laughed again when he refused even to respond to her taunts.

It was surprising too how broken Thorkell was in spirit as well as in his body. Margaret thought he might be pugnacious or defiant. But it seemed as if the failure of all his operations, as well as the loss of his father, of his aspiration to be lord of Meonbridge, perhaps even of Matilda's adoration, had brought him to despair. And Giles had said that the judgement against Thorkell would almost certainly mean death, so perhaps too, he had lost hope of any sort of future.

But, if Thorkell had no future, the boy he had hoped to destroy had shown his de Bohun mettle, fighting against the powers of darkness that sought to drag him from the world. Margaret awoke one morning to find her grandson standing by her bedside. She rubbed at her eyes, thinking she must still be dreaming, but then the boy leaned forward and kissed her cheek.

'Good morning, Grandmama,' he said, and kissed her again. And she sat up and, throwing her arms around the boy, hugged him to her breast.

'Oh, my darling boy, how happy I am to see you.' She stretched out her arms to hold him at a better distance to see him clearly. 'You look so well. How do you feel?'

The child shrugged. 'My legs are a bit floppy, and it still hurts here...' He twisted around and pointed to his side, where Thorkell's knife had pierced him. 'But Master Hogge says I will mend.'

'And how glad I am to hear it.' She gestured him to move away so that she could swing her legs out of the bed and stand up. 'Does your mother know?'

He shook his head. 'Ma's at home with my brothers and sister. And

I reckon Pa will be already in his workshop. It's only Master Hogge and you who know.' He giggled. 'Ma and Pa will be ever so surprised, won't they, Grandmama?'

Margaret laughed along with him. 'They will indeed. And very, very pleased.' She took his hand and drew him over to the big chairs by the hearth, though the fire in it was barely alight. 'As will all of Meonbridge.'

He nodded. 'So am I lord of Meonbridge now, Grandmama?'

Margaret was startled, yet why should she be? It was only three months short of two years ago that she had told Dickon who he was and what that meant. He understood that the Bounes had come to court seeking to take Meonbridge from him and had gone away empty-handed. And he was only too well aware that someone – unspecified, but surely he knew it was the Bounes – had threatened his life. Young as he was, she was certain that he did now fully understand exactly *why* he was training to be a page at Raoul de Fougère's castle, and what the future held for him. But perhaps she had not made it quite clear enough that he needed to be rather older than nine to take up the mantle of his destiny.

She smiled. 'Well, dear, at the moment *I* am lord of Meonbridge—'

He giggled again. 'You can't be a lord, 'cause you're a lady.' His eyes were bright.

She grinned. 'Yes, that is very true. But I am allowed to be the lord, to stand in for you and look after Meonbridge and all your domains, whilst you are so little—'

'I'm not *little*,' he said, pouting. 'I'm nine!'

She ruffled his dark hair, reminding herself of how confident and self-assured Philip had been at this age. Then, she had found Philip an impossible handful but, now, she was grateful for *this* little boy's strong-mindedness, and the knowledge that he would surely grow into a man – a knight – as fine and noble as his father and his grandfather.

'And nine is a great age, my darling boy,' she said, hugging him to her once again. 'But not yet great enough for you to manage your domains all by yourself. And, anyway, you have all that training still to do. You enjoy that, do you not?'

He shrugged. 'Sometimes. I'm unhappy to be away from here, but it's fun with the other boys, and I love learning to ride and fight.'

'And, as soon as you feel fully strong enough, you must go back and carry on with it. I shall take good care of your domains, my little lord, with the help of our faithful friend, Sir Giles Fitzpeyne.'

Dickon nodded. 'I think he's nice.'

'He is *very* nice, Dickon. He was your grandpapa's greatest friend, and he will forever be *your* friend and mentor.'

A few days after Dickon's wonderful recovery, Giles came back to Meonbridge. His second child – another daughter – was just three months old, and Margaret had insisted, despite her wish for his help with the impending trial of the Bounes, that Gwynedd too deserved a little of his time.

Giles had beamed. 'And I am eager to spend time with all my girls.' But then he pushed out his bottom lip, just like a disappointed boy. 'It was so hard last month leaving Gwynedd when she had so recently birthed our little Nesta.'

'Especially when she did not want you to come here at all,' said Margaret.

'Indeed. But I am glad I did.'

'As am I.'

Margaret marvelled at Giles's stamina, for the ride from Shropshire to Hampshire was long and arduous. When she married Richard and first came to Meonbridge, she had to travel even further, from Cheshire, and she remembered how dreadfully exhausting and uncomfortable she had found the journey. She had never repeated it. It had taken weeks to recover her strength, and she was then a young woman. Whereas Giles was now quite old, and had been back and forth—How many times? She could not quite recall...

But Giles was a good friend. Despite his aching remorse at his failure to prevent the Bounes' attack, she trusted him and his counsel absolutely.

The morning after his return, Giles came up to the solar to consult Margaret about a request made by Gunnar Boune. Margaret and Rosa were breaking their fast together, Margaret wishing to be with her daughter as much as possible in the last few days before Rosa returned to Northwick.

'Shall I stay, Sir Giles?' said Rosa. 'Or would you prefer to speak to my mother in private?'

Margaret had noticed that Rosa seemed now to be withdrawing again from Meonbridge affairs. This had happened only in the last few days. It was as if she was consciously relinquishing any responsibility she might have held for Meonbridge during the past few weeks, so that she could fully resume her duties at the priory. She had, after all, only come to Meonbridge for a brief visit, to see her nephew, but that was three weeks ago, and Margaret knew how anxious Rosa was to return to what she now considered her true home.

'No, no,' said Giles, 'do stay, Sister. You might be interested...'

Then he told them that Gunnar Boune had asked to speak to them, because he wanted to tell the truth about everything that had happened.

'Everything?' said Margaret.

'In truth, Margaret, I am suspicious of his motives. I imagine he thinks that he might be absolved of his part in the attack on Meonbridge, and the earlier attacks on Dickon, if he confesses all.'

Rosa tutted. 'How can he be absolved? He is surely as guilty of the crimes of assault and murder as are his father and his brother?'

Giles shrugged. 'I suspect he may not be *quite* as guilty—'

Rosa laughed at that. 'Not "quite"?'

'Only in that I think, from the little I know of the three men, it is likely that Morys and Thorkell were the principal plotters behind everything that has happened. And that Gunnar rather went along with it—'

'Even so,' said Rosa. 'That does not *absolve* him.'

Margaret was quiet throughout this exchange, but wondered how much of "what had happened" Gunnar might want to divulge. 'I must admit that, if he plans to tell us how Richard died, and why, I would much like to hear it.'

'That will surely all come out at the trial?' said Rosa.

Giles shook his head. 'It might not. The sheriff's tourn might well focus only on the known crimes perpetrated by the Bounes.'

'So let us hear him,' Margaret said.

. . .

Gunnar was brought up to the hall and sat down in a corner with a guard. His hands were not bound. When Margaret, Rosa and Giles approached, Gunnar stood up.

'I am grateful—' he began, but Giles held up his hand.

'It is not for *your* benefit that her ladyship has agreed to listen to what you have to say.' Giles knit his brows. 'What is it you want to tell her?'

'I wanted to explain,' said Gunnar. 'First, about Sir Richard—'

Margaret could not suppress a gasp and she nodded at Gunnar. 'Continue.'

Gunnar admitted that Richard's death had been planned to hasten the inheritance going his father's way. 'However, the plan was not my father's,' he said, 'but my brother's. And neither my father nor I knew anything of it until quite recently. It *was* my father who decided to give you the gift of horses, Sir Giles, but the so-called groom who came with the beasts, as a seeming afterthought, was in fact one of Thorkell's own retainers, not a groom at all, but an expert archer.'

Giles grunted. 'I was told the man could not bear to be parted from the horses—'

'It seemed a plausible enough explanation. And Thorkell's man was skilled at making murder look like an unlucky accident.'

'Which was how it seemed,' said Giles. 'Even though I must say I was suspicious.'

'But why did your brother want to murder Richard?' said Margaret.

Gunnar raised an eyebrow. 'I would have thought that obvious, your ladyship. My little brother is impatient. Once Sir Richard was dead, it would in theory be easier to get rid of Dickon.'

Margaret gasped. '"Get rid of" him?'

'Of course,' said Gunnar. 'We had already been planning to remove the boy, so that our father became the legal heir. But Thorkell thought it likely many years before Sir Richard died naturally, and he wanted to hasten the event, knowing that my father was proposing to vest Meonbridge in him.'

Giles shook his head. 'But he did not know that I would visit Meonbridge, and that Richard and I would go out hunting.'

'On the contrary, Sir Giles. For, after you had shared your reminiscences of Sir Richard with my father, you did, I understand, speak of visiting him, and mentioned the splendid hunting available in the forests here. Shortly afterwards, you took delivery of my father's gift of horses.' He bit his lip. 'And, believe me, Sir Giles, they were a genuine gift, from my father to his new son-in-law. My father then knew nothing of Thorkell's plans.'

Giles nodded.

'But,' continued Gunnar, 'you were so delighted with the beasts that you at once proposed a hunting trip to Meonbridge, and Thorkell saw the opportunity he'd been waiting for and, at the last moment, offered you the services of the groom. It was a plan that simply fell into place.'

Margaret saw Giles turn away. He would now truly believe that he *had* caused Richard's death. For, if he had not been so delighted with his new horses, he might not have so hastily proposed the hunting trip and given Thorkell the chance he wanted to wreak mayhem in Meonbridge.

But, after a few moments, Giles turned back to Gunnar. 'I might accept that neither you nor your father knew of the plot against Sir Richard. But am I to take it that you *did* know of the plots to, as you put it, "get rid of" Dickon? I am assuming that all the attempts on the boy's life were your doing?'

Gunnar shrugged. 'Again, not really mine, Sir Giles. I was never very keen on the plan to kidnap Dickon, and certainly not to kill him.' He grimaced. 'I always went along with my father's plans rather than being truly party to them.'

'And you think that absolves you from blame?' said Rosa, her voice rising.

'Partly, perhaps. After all, my future lay in Herefordshire. I had no reason to seek the inheritance of Meonbridge. It was my father, and in particular my brother, who wanted it.'

'But you enjoyed the game of pursuit withal?' said Giles.

'Not that either. As I say, I rather collaborated, out of filial duty to my father, and in the interests of the family.'

'Which makes you simply a spineless knave instead of an outright wicked one,' said Margaret, tossing her head and making her headdress quiver.

'I'll not dispute that, your ladyship,' he said, his eyes betraying a fear that she had not seen until then. 'But do I have your permission to continue?'

'The court case, perhaps?' she said.

Gunnar nodded. 'You might be surprised to learn that bringing the lawsuit against you was actually Thorkell's attempt to do things properly.'

Margaret guffawed. '"Properly"?'

'Indeed. He wanted us to be seen to win Meonbridge legally, so that he could come here as lord and hold the estate with integrity and honour—'

Giles nearly exploded. 'Integrity? Honour? The man is an utter villain.'

'But how,' said Rosa, 'did he know you had a legal case?'

'Because he learned of the boy's bastardy. We realised then we didn't have to go to the trouble of disposing of him, because he had no entitlement to Meonbridge after all. The way was clear for our father to make a legitimate claim. And so we did.'

'But how did Thorkell obtain this information?'

'The woman Matilda Fletcher told him,' said Gunnar. 'I rather thought you might have realised that.'

Margaret nodded. 'We have suspected all along that it was she who betrayed us.'

Gunnar snorted. 'I feel almost sorry for her. She pursued my faithless brother, thinking he might make her his wife and the mistress of Meonbridge, but in truth he never would have done so.'

'We assumed that,' said Margaret. She would not confess to this man that she also felt sorry for Matilda, although her well of sympathy for her had now just about dried up at this final confirmation of how far she had betrayed them. Matilda had of course told the truth about Dickon, rather than the lies that Richard, and then she herself, had perpetrated. But she must have known what would happen if the Bounes won their case and the right to hold Meonbridge. It was a wicked act from a woman who had received such succour from the very ones she was betraying. 'Anyway, the court decided against you.'

'You can imagine how much that decision enraged and humiliated Thorkell, and my father.'

Margaret nodded. 'What of the assaults upon my grandson?'

Gunnar grimaced. 'None of which succeeded. Almost as if you de Bohuns were blessed with supernatural powers.'

'Or rather,' said Rosa, 'that God knew the rightness of our position and thwarted you at every turn.'

He spread his hands. 'You may well be right, Sister.' Then he told them about the first two plots to kidnap Dickon, accusing Baldwin de Courtenay for the first failure and the incompetent "friar" for the second. He admitted too that Baldwin's "accident" was indeed punishment for his failure.

Margaret gasped. 'Poor Hildegard.'

Gunnar shook his head. 'Relying on others to carry out our plans has never worked,' he said, gloomily. But then he grimaced. 'Not that the final one worked either. Thorkell was so sure the assault on Meonbridge could be easily accomplished with just twenty men. He even thought—' He looked up at Margaret. 'This is the *truth*, my lady. We hoped to accomplish the boy's removal without causing much, if any, bloodshed to your household. We understood you had few armed retainers—'

'Four,' said Margaret.

He shrugged. 'But we hadn't reckoned on the bravery of your servants, or that your tenants would rise up in your support, or that they would be so fierce.'

Margaret smiled. 'I suppose you would understand very little of courage, steadfastness and loyalty.'

She was glad she knew why Richard had been killed, even if the knowledge hardly eased the pain of losing him. But, if Gunnar hoped, as Giles had suggested, that by his confession he would be absolved of his part in his family's crimes against their cousins, she could not think that such an outcome would be just.

Back upstairs in the solar, she, Rosa and Giles all sat in silence. The others were, she presumed, mulling over Gunnar's testimony, just as she was.

At length, Rosa broke the silence. 'He must not be absolved,' she said to Giles.

'I understand your point of view, but I think the court might well allow Gunnar his liberty, upon certain conditions.'

'What conditions?'

302

'Morys has of course already paid the ultimate price, with no possibility of redemption, from what you say, Sister?' Rosa nodded. 'And it is likely that Thorkell will too.'

'You mean he will die?'

He nodded. 'They will want to make him an example, to show that such contemptible crimes cannot be seen to pay. But Gunnar may be spared, allowed to go home, to provide for his stepmother and her brood of daughters.' He grinned. 'However, he will, I am certain, be deprived of most of his property, reducing his holding perhaps just to Castle Boune and its immediate demesne. And he will, I suspect, be required to swear fealty to the king and to keep the king's peace henceforth, on pain of surrendering *all* his property to the crown.'

'But who will monitor his peace-keeping? The Hampshire sheriff has no jurisdiction in Herefordshire.'

'Arrangements will be made,' said Giles. 'And I shall not be so far away...'

Yet Margaret still felt apprehensive. 'But might he not, some years in the future, decide to try again to claim Meonbridge?'

Giles shook his head. 'You heard the man, Margaret. He is different from his father and brother. He is, as you said...' he grinned, '...a spineless knave rather than an entirely wicked one. I suspect he may be looking forward to a quiet life. And if he is deprived of most of his property, and he has already lost his entire retinue of henchmen, he will not have the power – and he has never really had the drive – to act the brigand.'

'Lost his henchmen?' said Rosa.

'Ah, yes,' said Giles. 'You did not know? It has already been decided. All are to be banished across the sea to France, in the expectation that they will likely join up with bands of *routiers*—' Rosa raised a questioning eyebrow, and Giles nodded. 'Companies of mercenaries, who roam the countryside, rioting and pillaging. Sometimes, they provide valuable support to the king's campaigns, but they are for the most part not honourable men. It should suit those Boune knaves well.'

'So Gunnar will have no forces to call upon?'

'Well, he could build up another force, but that would go counter to the order to keep the peace. I doubt that he will risk it.' Giles then beamed, his old good-naturedness once more shining through. 'Anyway, it will not be so very long before young Dickon is a man, and strong enough himself to fight for Meonbridge and his other domains.'

'Ten years, at least?' said Margaret.

'Less,' said Giles. 'And, in the meantime, Margaret, let you and I undertake to build him a fine retinue of good and loyal men.'

It was the last day before Rosa was to return permanently to Northwick. Margaret had so enjoyed her daughter's company, she was loath to let her go. But she had no power to make her stay. Nor should she try. Rosa's life was in Meonbridge no longer.

They strolled together in the garden. Rosa admired the roses, blooming profusely and with an astonishingly sweet scent in the arbour with its delightful babbling fountain. But she admired much more her mother's herb garden and her splendid potagers and orchards, all burgeoning with cabbages, beans and onions, plums and apples, pears and grapes.

'I am looking forward to seeing our potagers again,' she said. 'I do hope they are thriving as abundantly as yours.' She smiled, then turned to see the puckered expression on Margaret's face. 'I am sorry I have to leave you, Mother, but you do understand that I must?'

'Of course, my dear. How could I keep you from your calling?'

They strolled some more then sat down on a seat with a view across the fields beyond the manor walls towards the forest. It was a good spot to take in the breadth of Meonbridge's domain.

'So have you decided, Mother, what is to happen with Matilda?' asked Rosa. 'You have not yet arranged a marriage for her, have you?'

'I have not. After we learned that Matilda was indeed as perfidious as we had suspected, I could no longer bring myself to ask any of our good Meonbridge men to take on such a woman as a wife. Nicholas Cook, for example, gave us such noble service in the battle for Meonbridge, I did not think he should be saddled with such a disloyal, faithless woman. And how could I possibly foist her upon such a man as Adam Wragge?'

'I agree entirely, Mother.'

But, perversely almost, Margaret was still sad. 'Yet Matilda is quite broken. She understands the enormity of what she has done and that she must leave Meonbridge. She must now go and live her life as best she might amongst strangers. I have told her that I shall care for Libby, as you suggested. She should be grateful enough for that.'

'Where will Matilda go?'

'I do not yet know for sure. The Dorset manors we passed to the Bounes have reverted now to us, but I asked Giles to sell them. He has already arranged the sale to a knightly acquaintance of his. A good soldier, Giles says, if rather a rough and ready sort of man. It will take a while for all the deeds and such to be drawn up, but I am proposing to ask him to take Matilda as a servant.'

'Does he know of Matilda's background?'

'Not yet, but Giles says he knows how to deal with miscreants and traitors.' Margaret lowered her eyes a moment. 'I do hope that, if he agrees to take her, he will not mistreat her.'

Rosa nodded. 'I hope it proves a satisfactory solution. It will be far beneath Matilda's hopes and expectations, but all – more than – in truth she now deserves.'

'That is my view. And at least I shall not have abandoned her entirely.'

They rose from the seat and walked back towards the house.

'I am glad that Giles is giving you so much help,' said Rosa. 'He is a good man.' She pressed her lips together.

'I always said so,' said Margaret. 'But you refused to believe me.'

'I know. And I know *now* that, if I had wanted to marry, I could hardly have done better for myself than Sir Giles Fitzpeyne.'

Margaret gasped. 'Then why—'

Rosa held up her hand. 'Because I *didn't want* to marry, Mother. I was certain of it then. And surely you can see now how it was very much the right decision for me to enter the priory? I have never been so happy and contented with my life as I am there.'

Margaret nodded. She knew that Rosa was right. Her daughter had truly blossomed from a pale, unhappy girl into a strong, resourceful woman. Who would surely one day – perhaps not before too long? – be prioress.

She took her daughter's hand and squeezed it. 'I do know that, and I could not be more delighted.'

36

MEONBRIDGE
SEPTEMBER 1358

Matilda hardly wanted to attend the sheriff's tourn. She wasn't certain she even wanted to find out what fate awaited Thorkell. And yet...

Surprisingly, Lady de Bohun decided not to go. Though Matilda did know her ladyship was heartsick of the whole affair and simply wished it to be over.

'Anyways,' said Margaret's maid, old Agatha, the morning of the trial, when she brought the news that Margaret would not attend the court in person, but leave Sir Giles to represent her, 'her ladyship says the trial's just a formality. The fate of those knaves has already been decided.' The old servant grinned.

Matilda gasped. 'What do you mean?'

Agatha tapped her nose. 'You'll 'ave to find out for yourself.' And she hobbled out of Matilda's chamber and fairly slammed the door.

Matilda slumped down upon her bed and held her head between her hands. Agatha had never been warm towards her, in all the years Matilda had been here. It was as if the old servant resented her and Libby living in the manor, as if they had no right to share accommodation with her lady. But, since Thorkell's attack on Meonbridge, and the rumours of Matilda's own part in it all had spread throughout the manor and the village, Agatha treated her with contempt, as did all the other manor servants, and any villagers Matilda might chance to meet on one of her rare outings.

Agatha still brought her her meals, to be taken in her room, as Margaret no longer allowed her to dine in the hall. But, when Agatha came, the door would be flung open by the Shropshire man who continued to stand guard outside her chamber. The old woman would totter in with the victuals on a tray and bang it down upon the small chest in which Matilda kept her own and Libby's clothes. Agatha usually said nothing, but always gave Matilda a fleer before shuffling from the room again and banging the door shut behind her.

Matilda scarcely left her room at all. The gardening lessons Margaret had attempted to give her and Libby a month or two ago had stopped – for Matilda, at any rate – and her ladyship no longer suggested accompanying her on a walk outside. When Matilda did go out for a breath of air, she was escorted only by the Shropshire man, who didn't refuse to speak to her but said little, keeping his conversation to the weather, or how well or otherwise this or that flower or tree or vegetable was thriving.

She was, too, deprived of Libby's company, for the girl had replaced her mother as her ladyship's companion. Matilda grieved for Libby – and perhaps also for her own failure to be a proper mother to her daughter. Margaret had already made it clear that she intended to keep Libby with her until she was old enough to marry, and then, Matilda assumed, she would be rid of her. Rid of the girl who no doubt reminded her ladyship of the years of misery Matilda's family had brought to the de Bohuns.

Matilda stood up and stepped over to the tiny window that had a view across the manor garden. Not that she could see out without standing on the small stool that was her only seat. She climbed up and, pushing open the shutter, peered out. Her eyes filled with tears at the knowledge that she would soon leave this place, a place she loved despite the unhappiness of so much of her life here.

She did wonder why she was still here at all, why Margaret hadn't already sent her packing. What was her ladyship waiting for? Was she making some arrangement for her? Otherwise, there surely was no reason for her not to have simply banished her, to shift entirely for herself? Perhaps, after the trial, her ladyship would say what she had in mind for her...

In the end, Matilda decided to follow Margaret's example and not go to the trial. She supposed there might be revelations that would help her to understand why Thorkell had so misused her, but in truth she didn't want to know. Anyway, if Agatha was right, and the trial was simply a formality, the outcomes already agreed, perhaps there would be very little in the way of evidence. And she suspected, too, that Thorkell would decline to say much, if anything, in his defence.

A week or so ago, she had asked the Shropshire man what he knew of Thorkell's present health and state of mind. Nothing, he had said, but he would enquire. The next morning, when he resumed his post, having exchanged a few words with the man who usually took his place when he needed rest or a measure of recreation, he opened the door to Matilda's chamber and stepped inside.

'I've information for you, miss,' he said. His face was gloomy, and Matilda didn't know what exactly she hoped he might be about to tell her. Indeed, she wasn't sure why she'd even asked him to find out.

She stood up and clasped her hands together. 'Well?' she said, her voice a whisper.

'I saw him,' said the man. 'God's eyes, he were ugly. With his nose laid open and still black with blood, his jaw smashed, his mouth full of broken teeth.'

'His injuries still haven't healed?' said Matilda. She thought Simon Hogge had attended him, but perhaps his only purpose was to keep Thorkell alive so he could come to trial.

He shrugged. 'Rather they seem fixed upon his face. But I suppose it hardly matters now.'

'What do you mean?'

'They'll surely hang him for his crimes.'

She surprised herself by realising she really didn't care what happened to Thorkell now. She nodded at the man and thanked him for his information.

He turned to go. 'Will you attend the trial?'

She shook her head. 'I think not. Perhaps you can bring me news of the verdicts?'

He nodded. 'I'll not be going myself, but I'll find out.' Then he left the room, closing the door quietly, presumably to resume his station outside in the passage.

Matilda felt sure that, when the man brought her the news, she would be able to accept it with equanimity. Her love of Thorkell had died completely and she was glad that it would soon be all over, and she could get on with her life, whatever it was that Margaret was planning for her. She felt a little aggrieved that Thorkell's brother, Gunnar, seemed to have got away with his part in it all, sent back to Herefordshire to resume his life, to marry, have children perhaps. But her guard did say Gunnar would lose all of the family's property apart from Castle Boune, and that he would no longer have a retinue of retainers, so perhaps Gunnar's life in future would be one of peace and moderation.

At the early morning hour of Thorkell's execution, she lay in her bed awake, by turns holding her breath and weeping, until she thought his end might have come. She had thought she didn't care, but it seemed that she did. Or rather, what she cared about was the loss of what she had thought *might be*, even though she now knew the reality of it had only ever been within her imagination.

When the Shropshire man knocked on her door and entered the room an hour or so later, Matilda was not as composed as she had hoped to be. She was exhausted from lack of sleep and from the turmoil of confused emotions in her heart. Nonetheless, she stood and clasped her hands together at her waist, attempting to show her self-control. But, when she raised her eyes to his, she knew her composure was about to fail, for she could see at once from his expression that Thorkell's end had not been easy.

'What have you to tell me?' she said.

He cleared his throat. 'That Thorkell Boune is dead.'

She nodded. 'And how was his death?' she whispered. 'Were you told?'

He shook his head. 'I went myself. So I could tell you true, should you want to know.'

She twisted her mouth. Did she?

The man coughed. 'So do you want to know what happened, miss?'

If he didn't tell her, she would always wonder. Just knowing Thorkell was dead was somehow not enough. She needed to know how... 'Was it a noble death?' she said at length.

The man bit his lip. 'I wouldn't say so.'

She gasped and slumped down onto the edge of her bed. 'Tell me.'

He sat down on the room's only stool. 'It weren't pretty, miss...'

He hesitated still, yet she might as well hear what he had to say. She gestured to him to continue.

'When he were brought to the hanging place in the cart, the knave could scarcely stand. He were so weak, the Hundred gaoler and his henchman had to drag him across towards the rope...'

Nausea rose in Matilda's throat. Could she bear to hear this? Her strong, handsome man brought so low...? But she didn't demur.

'They pulled him to his feet,' the man continued, 'but had to hold him upright, to bring his head close to the noose...'

Matilda groaned.

'Usually they tie the legs but, this time, they couldn't, for the henchman had to hold onto him whilst the gaoler slipped the noose over his head. It were all done hastily, and I reckon the knot weren't sat properly on his neck.'

She looked up. 'What do you mean?'

'It were a mess. The cart were driven forward, the henchman still holding on to stop the villain collapsing in a heap. Then, at the last moment, the henchman jumped off the back of the cart, letting the man go. The rope's supposed to break the neck, but it didn't... He were just dangling there, being throttled... You could hear him gurgling and wheezing, even above the cheering of those who'd come to watch...'

Matilda cried out at that.

'Shall I stop, miss?' he said, but she shook her head.

'Did it take long?' she whispered.

'Too long,' he said, and grimaced. 'His arms and legs, they twitched and jerked like he were doing some sort of demonic dance. And his eyes were rolling, and his tongue lolled from his mouth, as he gasped for air and couldn't catch it.'

Matilda looked up at him. Was he *enjoying* telling her all this? But, no, she could see in the pallor of his face that he wasn't.

'It were truly shocking, miss. Even for me. And, God knows, I've seen some grim sights in my time.'

'So Thorkell said nothing before he died?' she said.

'Naught at all.' He gave a rueful grin. 'He couldn't really, could he? The priest said the usual words, you know, "May God have mercy on your soul." But, to be honest, miss, I can't think God'll have much mercy for such a knave as he.'

Her heart quailed. 'Had he been shriven?'

'Truly, I dunno, miss. I been here, not in the dungeons.'

Unbidden, tears filled Matilda's eyes. 'Perhaps his sins were anyway too great to be forgiven?'

The Shropshire man stood up. 'I wouldn't know about that, miss.' He stepped forward and touched her lightly on the shoulder. 'Anyway, it's over. Wherever he is now, he can't harm you.'

She nodded and thanked the man for taking the trouble to bring her the news.

But, when he had gone, closing the door quietly behind him, she threw herself prostrate onto the bed and wept. Even if her love for Thorkell had now withered away, how could she forget how strong and handsome he had been, what delicious pleasure he had brought her, and how much she *had* once loved him – and thought that he loved her?

And, remembering, she wished that, after all, she hadn't asked the Shropshire man to paint the grisly picture she now had in her head of how her handsome Thorkell met his ignominious end.

Lady de Bohun had summoned Matilda to her chamber and, as she stood now before the lady who had shown her such kindness for so many years, Matilda was sick with terror at what she now intended. She understood how wicked she had been, how treacherous and deceitful. She knew she deserved to be entirely abandoned, to shift as best she could in a world of strangers. But would her ladyship do that to her? Would she be so cruel?

Matilda trembled. 'My lady?'

Margaret nodded. 'I must tell you what I have decided about your future.' She gestured to a chair. 'Please sit, Matilda.'

Matilda sat down, perching on the edge of the seat and gripping the chair's arms.

Margaret sat in the other chair and straightened her back. 'I have not abandoned you entirely, Matilda. For what you did, I think I would have been within my rights to do so. But—' She sighed. 'For all that has happened in past years,' she whispered, 'I cannot.'

Matilda nodded. So was her ladyship not going to banish her after all? She said nothing, but bowed her head and waited for Margaret to continue.

'We had a manor in Dorset, which Sir Giles has sold for me, to an acquaintance of his. You will go there as a servant.' So she *was* leaving Meonbridge...

Matilda could not stop the tears. 'Will Libby be coming with me?' she whispered.

Margaret shook her head. 'As I have already said, I shall keep Libby here as my companion and, when she is fifteen, I shall find her a good, but suitable, husband. Libby will learn to be a villein's wife.'

Matilda looked up, flicking at her cheeks.

'I shall brook no argument about the match,' continued Margaret. 'Libby will do as I say. But I shall treat her well and will do my best for her.'

Matilda nodded. 'Thank you, my lady.' How could she be anything but glad that her daughter would at least have a future, albeit not the future she had hoped for her?

'What sort of servant will I be?' she asked, her lips trembling.

'A general servant. It is a small household, and you will undertake a variety of tasks.'

'Who is the owner, and does he have a wife?'

Margaret's eyebrows lifted. 'He is a knight, and his wife is dead.'

'A knight?' Perhaps it would not be so bad to work in the household of a gentleman? Who knew what opportunities there might be...

But her ladyship seemed to have read her mind. 'Oh, Matilda,' she cried out, then shook her head. 'Yes, he is a knight, and a well-respected one, but he is old enough to be your grandfather, and a veteran of many of the king's wars. In truth, I understand he bears even more battle scars than Sir Giles. But he is not, Giles tells me, an unkind man.'

Matilda nodded. So, a servant in the household of an ageing soldier. It sounded very dull.

Then Margaret coughed. 'You will be the only woman in the household. So whatever service your master asks of you, it will be your duty to provide it.'

Matilda's head snapped up. 'Might he marry me?'

But her ladyship laughed out loud. 'Really, Matilda, you never do give up. No, he will not marry you. He has sons and daughters, and grandchildren, and no need of another wife.'

Matilda turned away, but Margaret must have known that she was weeping. 'I am sorry, Matilda, but you have brought this upon yourself. Sir Richard offered you several suitable matches, but you rejected them all, thinking you somehow deserved a man of higher rank. But, now, no man in Meonbridge will have you, and I am no longer willing to ask on your behalf. This...this is the result of your deceit and treachery, against me and my grandson, and indeed against the whole of Meonbridge. You have to leave the place from which you sought to banish *me*, where you plotted to let your friends and neighbours be invaded by murderous villains, just to fulfil your own selfish desire to be a lady. But you are no lady, Matilda. You are a Jezebel...'

Matilda's tears flowed freely, knowing that her ladyship was right.

'I shall do my best for your daughter,' continued Margaret, 'but I no longer wish to look upon your face, Matilda. Go and make the best of the rest of your life. Be grateful that you were not brought to trial for your treachery. Be grateful too that I have not simply turned you out to shift entirely for yourself. In Dorset, you will have a roof over your head, food and the opportunity to serve a noble knight. Be satisfied with that.'

At length, Matilda nodded. She had no choice but to accept what she was offered.

'I shall bring Libby to you now,' said Margaret, 'and I shall leave you two together to say your farewells. Then, be gone. Sir Alain Jordan will accompany you to Dorset, but then he will return, and you will no longer have any connection with this place.'

Margaret swept from the room and Matilda was left alone, to grieve for what she had done and what she had now to endure. But Thorkell was dead. At least she had been spared a traitor's end. For that at least she should be grateful. She awaited Libby, and braced herself for those farewells, knowing that thereafter she would possibly never see her little girl again.

EPILOGUE

FITZPEYNE CASTLE, SHROPSHIRE
OCTOBER 1358

Giles rode with Gunnar Boune on the long journey north from Hampshire. He had invited Gunnar to spend a few days at Fitzpeyne Castle, so that he could see his sister Gwynedd and his two little nieces.

As they rode together, they talked. It was the first time Giles had spent any significant time in Gunnar's company. And he discovered that he rather liked the man. He was mild-mannered and droll-humoured and, his own scepticism withal, Giles did at length believe him when Gunnar said he simply wanted to marry and settle down to a quiet life.

'I'm not sure you trust my word, Sir Giles,' said Gunnar, 'when I say that I truly did not agree with my father's and brother's plans to kill Sir Richard, and then to kidnap and murder Dickon. Indeed, I never agreed with any of their schemes to increase our domains by pillaging those of others and murdering their occupants.'

He grinned. 'When Lady de Bohun called me spineless, she hit the nail on the head, for that is – I now realise – *exactly* what I've always been. Never bold enough to stand up to my father, to tell him that

315

what he did was evil, to refuse to play a part. Instead, I simply collaborated out of duty and, I suppose, for a quiet life.'

'Hardly "quiet", given the mayhem you caused.'

Gunnar guffawed. 'No, but quiet in the sense of not constantly arguing with my father and brother, a task for which I was quite ill equipped. They are – were – much stronger-willed than I ever was.'

Giles nodded, although it occurred to him that Gunnar might be being deliberately untruthful, or simply deceiving himself. On the other hand, he did seem to have lost most of the spirit he had when Giles first met him. Although perhaps Gunnar's seeming spirit then had been merely a pretence, intended to fool his father, at least, that he shared his outlook and agreed with his schemes, even though he did not.

Standing behind an arras with a view into the solar chamber, Giles watched Gunnar with his stepsister and nieces. He could not imagine Thorkell ever bouncing baby Nesta on his knee or crawling around the floor pretending to chase little Angharad, then picking her up and throwing her up into the air, making her squeal with pleasure. Gwynedd laughed at her brother's antics, her warmth towards him palpable.

Giles coughed and slid into the room. He smiled. 'The little ones are a delight, are they not?'

'I'd no idea they could be,' said Gunnar. 'Angharad is certainly a most engaging child.'

The nurse came then to take the children to their beds. Giles took his wife's arm and led her downstairs to the small supper that had been prepared, and Gunnar followed. Afterwards, Gwynedd retired, claiming fatigue.

'But you two,' she said, 'continue by the fire and take more wine. I am sure you have much knowledge still to share.' She dropped a light kiss onto Giles's greying head, touched her brother's arm and slipped away upstairs.

'*Do* we?' Gunnar said, as Giles refilled his cup.

Giles sat down and drank some of his wine. Then he nodded. 'I am intrigued to know how it is that you are so different from your brother.'

'You doubt it?'

'Not at all. I am just curious as to why Thorkell turned out so like your father, whilst you—'

'Are perhaps more like my angelic mother?' Gunnar grinned.

'Indeed. Can you find a reason for it?'

Gunnar emptied his mazer, and Giles picked up the flagon and filled it once again. Then Gunnar nodded. 'There may be an explanation.'

Giles leaned back in his chair. 'Are you willing?'

Gunnar took another swig. 'I had a happy childhood at least till I was four. When Thorkell was born. Till then I'd spent my days by my mother's side—'

'A woman who Morys told me was an angel.'

'She *was* beautiful, and loving and sweet-natured. Every boy's imagining of the perfect mother. In some ways, a quite unsuitable wife for my bellicose father. Though I am sure that Pa adored her. When she died, giving birth to Thorkell, Pa was desolate. He and I clung together in our misery.'

'I recall Morys telling me how she died. But what of Thorkell?'

'I only realised it much later, but I think my father *blamed* Thorkell for our mother's death. I, too, hated him for "killing" her, yet I also pitied him for never knowing her. But my father treated Thorkell harshly, as did the women he employed to nurse him.'

Giles raised a questioning eyebrow.

'Pa put him, a newborn baby, into the so-called "care" of a wet-nurse. But she was a cruel woman, who often denied my little brother food when he cried. She remained in charge of Thorkell till he was almost three. Then, at length, Pa remarried.' Gunnar snorted. 'He brought another cold-hearted woman into the household. A woman who was unable to bear children, and took out her grief on me and my brother. But it was Thorkell who bore the brunt of it for, by then, I was spending most of my days with Pa or my tutor, whilst Thorkell was still confined to the women's quarters. By the time he was released into the tutor's charge, he had, it seemed, learned that women were heartless, untrustworthy creatures. And he never changed his mind.'

Giles got up to pour more wine. 'Yet I thought your brother did love women?'

Gunnar shook his head. 'He could be charming, but he always had to master them. He took his pleasure from their bodies but, as with Matilda Fletcher, he also used them in whatever way appropriate to further his own ends.'

Giles nodded. 'Poor Matilda...' He put the flagon back onto the table.

'Anyway,' continued Gunnar, 'after another few years, it seemed Pa had had enough of his barren, sharp-tongued wife, and he arranged for her to have an "accident"—'

'God's blood, man!' cried Giles, spinning around. 'How can you say it as if it was nothing?'

Gunnar spread his hands. 'I apologise. In truth, I only heard of it much later, for I was then away at Sir Henry Blandefordde's. One of the household servants told me.' He screwed up his face as he mimicked the serving woman's voice. '"That woman were a wicked besom," she said, "'oo made your litt'l brother's life a mis'ry." It seemed that all the household staff loathed their mistress, so nobody bothered to question her disappearance. And it wasn't long afterwards that my father married Alwyn.'

Giles shook his head. 'I knew Morys was a knave, but to murder his own wife...' He drained his cup and poured himself another.

'He was never reluctant to take savage action, if it brought him what he wanted. And Thorkell learned to be the same, whereas I...' Gunnar shrugged then, cradling the mazer in his hands, leaned forward and let out a deep breath. It was several moments before he looked up. 'There is no reason why you should already know this, but my father was not the first Boune to further his own interests through treachery and violence. His grandfather – Sir Richard's grandfather too...' He arched his eyebrows. 'Henry, his name was. He was just the same, an arrant knave. Many of the estates he held, throughout middle England, the Welsh borders and across the south, were won *il*legitimately.'

Giles had been leaning forward, poking at the fire, already annoyed that he had let it burn too low. Confounded by Gunnar's news of Richard's – apparently dishonourable – forebears, Giles made a stab at the glowing embers, and a shower of sparks flew upward. He leapt back, alarmed that his hair or clothing had come close to singeing. Then, throwing a few more logs into the reviving blaze, he returned to his chair.

'So,' he said, 'Meonbridge and Richard's other domains were not all gained by honest means?'

'Indeed. However, *Richard's* father subsequently held his estates with honour and, when he expanded, he did so lawfully. Whereas Richard's uncle perpetuated the violent methods of his father.'

'And Morys saw no reason not to follow his father's dubious example?'

'But it's all over now, Sir Giles. Indeed, I'm relieved no longer to have to live that kind of life. I'm looking forward to settling down on my little domain with a wife and maybe a scion or three.'

'You'll be asking for your Welsh princess's hand?'

'I doubt she will want me now, in my ignominious state, or at least her father won't. So I will have to find myself another bride. Of good birth, I hope, but...' He spread his hands.

Giles shook his head. Gunnar might well have to make do with a bride of lesser rank. But that would surely be no bad thing? 'There is no rule that says a woman of lower rank will make you a worse wife and mother of your children than one of higher birth.'

'Do you believe that?'

'How can it not be true? There are surely good people everywhere, of every station in life, just as there are villains...' He winked, and Gunnar smiled.

'A good woman,' said Gunnar. 'And children. And the chance to lead a quiet life. I rather relish the idea of learning to run my estate and engaging in some gentler pursuits. Maybe I will even learn to read?' He shook his head. 'I can scarce believe I am saying it, but it is the truth.'

When Giles had travelled back to Shropshire, it was not only Gunnar who had joined his entourage, but also Dickon, riding pillion behind one or other of Giles's retainers.

Giles had almost begged Margaret to let Dickon come to Shropshire, to stay for a few years to complete his page training, before returning to the earl in Sussex to continue as a squire.

'Will the earl not think it strange, or even ungrateful, if Dickon does not return to him now?' she had said.

Giles did not know for sure, but Raoul de Fougère was his liege lord as well as Richard's and he was confident he could persuade him of the plan. Although he would not tell Raoul his motives for wanting to counsel the grandson of his dearest friend – to assuage his guilt at both being party to Richard's murder, and failing to prevent, or even mitigate, the assault on Meonbridge.

By the time the trial was over, and Gunnar was ready to return to Herefordshire, the earl had agreed to let Giles be Dickon's lord until the boy was twelve, when he would return to Sussex to make the transition from page to squire. But the earl wrote later:

"My dear Giles, I agree to this plan with some disappointment, for I much like the boy, and know that he was beginning to enjoy, and benefit from, his life here in Steyning. Nonetheless, I appreciate that you might feel you have some sort of obligation towards the de Bohuns, for all that has befallen them at the hands of your relatives by marriage..."

Giles had blushed as he read that. The earl was nothing if not perceptive. He would have to ensure that Dickon's training here in Shropshire was the very best he could provide.

───────────

Gunnar was quite apprehensive when he left to ride the thirty miles or so west to Castle Boune, accompanied by a small party of Giles's own retainers. 'I wonder what reception I shall receive from my stepmother? And how shall I break the news to her of our enormous change in fortunes?'

'It will not be a comfortable conversation, I warrant,' said Giles.

Gunnar was mournful too about having to let Giles's retainers return to Shropshire. 'I'll have to learn to manage as a country gentleman, with unweaponed servants and no sword arms at my disposal.' Yet, beneath the frown of disappointment on Gunnar's face, Giles fancied he could see a lurking grin, of genuine relief, perhaps.

He nodded. 'It will be different. But I am sure you will make the best of it.'

They parted with a promise to maintain contact, if only for the sake of Alwyn and Gwynedd and their many daughters.

When Giles then went in search of Dickon, he found him in Gwynedd's chamber, playing happily with the little girls.

Giles was wistful at the sight of the boy. He so much hoped for a son of his own but, so far, Gwynnie had borne him only girls, and females were her mother's only surviving offspring. It occurred to him that perhaps the "strong Welsh border stock" Morys had claimed that Alwyn, and therefore Gwynedd, came from, was not so robust after all. Recalling Morys's words, "And she's borne me many a fine filly", Giles wondered if maybe fillies were indeed all he could look forward to himself.

He laughed and shook his head. So be it. He was lucky to be married at all at his ripe old age, and to be producing heirs, be they fillies *or* colts. For now, at least, he would make do with a temporary son, or perhaps, rather, a nephew.

'Tell me, Dickon,' he said, ruffling the boy's hair. 'What do you think that you should call me?'

The boy shrugged.

'Well, of course,' continued Giles, 'whilst you are pursuing your page training, I am your lord and master. So, when we are outside, with the other boys and the servants and retainers, I think you should call me "my lord". But, indoors, or here with Gwynnie and the children, that seems a little formal. Do you not agree?'

Dickon nodded.

'So I wondered if you thought that "Uncle" might be fitting?'

Dickon giggled. 'But you're too old to be my uncle. John and Matthew are my uncles and they're much younger than you.'

Giles guffawed. 'Ah, but they are your real uncles, your mother's brothers. Whereas I am just an old trusted friend of your grandmama's and, once, your grandfather's greatest friend. And such a trusted friend can sometimes be thought of as a *sort of* uncle, as a kindly counsellor. I should like to think, Dickon, that you will always feel you can come to me for encouragement and guidance, even when you are a man.'

Dickon nodded again. 'I'd like that too.'

'So it is agreed?'

Dickon grinned. 'Yes, Uncle.'

Giles could scarcely have been happier – happier even than when he had fought beside his king in the wars against the Scots, and at Sluys and Caen, and the glorious battle of Crécy. He had always considered himself a fine soldier and had thought his long years of service to the English throne, and others, were the zenith of his life. But now, as he strolled the grounds of Fitzpeyne Castle, with Gwynedd on his arm, and their girls and Dickon with them, he wondered if, after all, *now* was that zenith, even for such a man as he.

He shared Gunnar's admission that he now wanted a quiet life, although Gunnar was still a young man who might grow bored with interminable tranquillity. Whereas Giles was no longer youthful and could, he thought, quite permissibly and cheerfully live out his days managing his estates with his family around him. If he craved excitement, he could join in the training of his squires but, for the most part, the orchards and the gardens and the fields and forests would be his principal domain...

And it occurred to him that, alongside the archery and wrestling, the weapon skills and horsemanship, Dickon would surely do well to learn a little about managing an estate.

As their route took them to edges of the home grounds, beyond which lay meadows and, beyond them, some of the arable land, Giles gestured towards the fields, then raised his arm and pointed towards the more distant woodland. Then, as they strolled back through the orchards and the gardens, he tried to draw Dickon's attention to all that was growing there.

'Meonbridge has fine grounds, Dickon,' he said, 'much finer still than here.' Dickon nodded but turned away, thrashing at the tall grasses that edged the path.

'Whilst you grow to be a man,' continued Giles, 'your grandmama will take good care of all your domains and keep them in good heart. But one day, you will be lord of Meonbridge, and all those lands will be your responsibility. Do you not think that, when the time comes for you to take them over from her ladyship, it would be best if you already understood what you were taking on?'

They came to the flower garden that Gwynedd had only this year created. Giles looked about him with a delighted grin. He was so impressed with the improvements his dear little wife had made.

But Dickon stared at the cascades of fading roses dripping from the arches ranged behind a bed of long dead irises and still thriving if bedraggled daisies. At length he pouted. 'Flowers are boring,' he said, and gave a swipe at a tall daisy growing too close to the path.

'Haha!' cried Giles. 'I can understand that sweet-smelling flowers might not interest a boy. But I warrant you like eating, eh? And it is important, Dickon, that you understand your land, what crops grow in its fields and gardens, what animals graze its meadows, what creatures inhabit its forests. Its strengths and its weaknesses. That way you can ensure that your lands thrive and prosper.'

But Dickon shrugged and, turning, stared across to where the training ground was situated beyond the castle walls.

Gwynedd squeezed Giles's arm. 'I think Dickon is still a little young, my dear, to have much interest in farming. Bowmanship and horse-riding are probably more to the taste of nine-year-olds.' Her eyes were shining.

And of course she was quite right.

Giles gently withdrew his arm from hers, and put his hand upon Dickon's shoulder. 'Perhaps you would prefer it if I told you about the adventurous exploits of your father and your grandfather? They were the most gallant and most noble of King Edward's knights...'

Dickon looked up then, slipping his little hand into Giles's big one, he beamed.

GLOSSARY

Bailey – A courtyard of a castle or fortified house, enclosed by an outer wall.

Bailiff – The lord's chief official on the manor.

Braies – The equivalent of men's underpants, braies were a loose garment, usually made of linen and held up by a belt, and which might hang below the knees or be short to mid-thigh.

Barber-surgeon – A medical practitioner who, unlike many physicians of the time (who were more interested in the imbalance of *humours*), carried out surgical operations, often on the battlefield. Many had no formal training, and were often illiterate. Alongside surgery, their tasks also included bloodletting, teeth extraction, performing enemas, treating all manner of ailments and selling medicines (as well as, presumably, cutting hair).

Canonical hours – The specified times for prayer but also used to mark the times of day:

- **Matins**: Midnight or sometime during the night
- **Lauds**: Dawn or 3 a.m.
- Prime: The first hour, about 6 a.m.
- **Terce**: The third hour, about 9 a.m.
- **Sext**: The sixth hour, about noon

- Nones: The <u>ninth</u> hour, about 3 p.m.
- **Vespers**: The "lighting of the lamps", about 6 p.m.
- **Compline**: The last hour, just before retiring, around 9 p.m.

Cotehardie – A fitted tunic worn by both men and women, the male version often quite short, the female's trailing on the ground. It was worn over an undergarment of some sort, a shirt for a man, perhaps a chemise and a thin kirtle for a woman.

Cottar – The tenant of a cottage, usually holding little or no land, on the bottom rung of village society.

Crécy, battle of – One of the decisive battles of the Hundred Years War, fought in August 1346, the first of three notable English victories against the French.

Croft – The garden plot of a village house.

Demesne – The part of the lord's manorial lands reserved for his own use and not allocated to his tenants or freeholders.

Freemen – Free tenants were not only personally free, but had no obligation to do regular work on the demesne land of the lord.

Frumenty – A sort of porridge, typically made from wheat and milk. Sometimes, in wealthier households, it might contain dried fruit or nuts, or be sweetened, and was often served as an accompaniment to meat.

Garderobe – A small chamber inside a prosperous house containing the privy.

Hue-and-cry – A way of apprehending a criminal, in which everyone within earshot of a person calling out for help was required to chase, and hopefully catch, any sort of malefactor.

Humours – Ancient medical theory held that the human body encompassed four humours, which needed to be kept in balance. Illness of whatever kind supposedly arose from an excess or deficit of one of the humours. The four humours were black bile, yellow bile, blood and phlegm, and corresponded to the four "temperaments", respectively, melancholic, choleric, sanguine, and phlegmatic. The physician's task was to attempt to correct any imbalance between the humours to restore a person to sound health.

Leman – A man's mistress.

Manor – A small-holding, typically 1200-1800 acres, with its own court and probably its own hall, but not necessarily having a manor house. The manor as a unit of land was generally held by a knight or managed by a bailiff for some other holder.

Mazer – A type of drinking cup made from hardwood.

Megrim – Migraine.

Melancholy – Generally speaking, a depressive state of mind. See *Humours*

Prie-dieu – A small desk for private prayer, with a kneeling platform and a sloping top for a Bible or book of prayer.

Routier – A mercenary soldier, typically organised into bands, but free of any association with governments or kings. The term is most associated with the companies of men who, during the Hundred Years War, roamed the French countryside terrorising the inhabitants.

Sheriff's tourn – The circuit made by the sheriff of a county twice a year, in which he presided at the court in each Hundred, an Administrative division of an English shire or county, in theory equalling one hundred hides though it rarely did.

Solar – In a manor house or castle, the private living and sleeping quarters of a wealthy family, usually, though not always, on an upper floor.

Surcoat – An outer garment, much like a sleeveless coat, worn by both men and women.

Villein – The wealthiest class of peasant. Villeins usually cultivated 20-40 acres of land, often in isolated strips.

A MESSAGE FROM THE AUTHOR...

If you've enjoyed reading *De Bohun's Destiny*, please do consider leaving a brief review on your favourite site. Reviews are of enormous help to authors, both in terms of providing feedback and in building readership. Thank you!

And, if you enjoy my writing, perhaps you'd like to join "Team Meonbridge"?

In return for your support, I will send you updates on my books and my writing, and periodically ask for your help or feedback.
As a small "thank you" for joining the team, I will send you FREE novellas featuring some of the Meonbridge characters.

If you are interested, please visit my website at www.carolynhughesauthor.com and select **JOIN THE TEAM!** to open the sign up form.

I look forward to your company!

ACKNOWLEDGEMENTS

I am so grateful to the many people who continue to help me along my writing and publishing journey. I wouldn't have made the journey without them.

For *De Bohun's Destiny*, I must again thank my small group of "beta readers", who read an early version of the manuscript to help ensure the story was coherent and, hopefully, enjoyable. So, Alan, Rhonwen and David, thank you so much for your feedback – it really was of enormous help.

Again heartfelt thanks to my lovely editor, Hilary, for once more assuring me that the story I've written about these long-ago people is worth the telling. And, finally, thank you so much, Cathy Helms, at www.avalongraphics.org, for designing such a stunning cover.

ABOUT THE AUTHOR

CAROLYN HUGHES has lived much of her life in Hampshire. With a first degree in Classics and English, she started working life as a computer programmer, then a very new profession. But it was technical authoring that later proved her vocation, as she wrote and edited material, some fascinating, some dull, for an array of different clients, including banks, an international hotel group and medical instruments manufacturers.

She has written creatively for most of her adult life, but it was not until her children flew the nest several years ago that writing historical fiction took centre stage, alongside gaining a Master's degree in Creative Writing from Portsmouth University and a PhD from the University of Southampton.

De Bohun's Destiny is the third MEONBRIDGE CHRONICLE.

You can connect with Carolyn through her website www. carolynhughesauthor.com and social media:

facebook.com/CarolynHughesAuthor

twitter.com/writingcalliope

ALSO BY CAROLYN HUGHES

FORTUNE'S WHEEL: The First Meonbridge Chronicle

How do you recover when half your neighbours are dead from history's cruellest plague?

1349. In Meonbridge, the Black Death has killed half its population, among them Alice atte Wode's husband and Eleanor Titherige's entire family. Even the manor's lord and his wife, Margaret de Bohun, did not escape the horror.

Now the plague is over, it's a struggle to return to normal life. When tensions between the de Bohuns and their tenants deepen into violence and disorder, the women must step forward to find the way out of the conflict that is tearing Meonbridge apart.

"Exceptionally well written...astoundingly well researched...grab yourself a copy and get list in an altogether different time."
Brook Cottage Books @BrookCottageBks

"This is probably in my top 5 favorite books this year...The writing in this novel blew me away! a wonderful spin on history. Overall I give this book 10 out of 5 stars." Laura H., NetGalley & The Reading Wolf

"Completely intriguing, fascinating and surprisingly emotional...more please!" The Book Magnet @thebookmagnet

"An accomplished, fascinating historical fiction novel – and an impressive debut." What Cathy Read Next, @Cathy_A_J

"Well written, gripping and satisfying. I loved this book." Kate O., NetGalley

"Historical fiction at its best!" Jeannette S., NetGalley

"Would be a great book for a book group!" Ruth M., NetGalley

ALSO BY CAROLYN HUGHES

A WOMAN'S LOT: The Second Meonbridge Chronicle

How can mere women resist the misogyny of men?

1352. In Meonbridge, a resentful peasant rages against Eleanor Titherige's efforts to build up her flock of sheep. Susanna Miller's husband, grown melancholy and ill-tempered, succumbs to idle talk that his wife's a scold. Agnes Sawyer's yearning to be a craftsman is met with scorn. And the village priest, fearful of what he considers women's "unnatural" ambitions, is determined to keep them firmly in their place.

Not all men resist women's desire for change – indeed, they want it for themselves. Yet it takes only one or two misogynists to unleash the hounds of hostility and hatred...

"I didn't so much feel as if I were reading about mediaeval England as actually experiencing it first hand." Linda's Book Bag @Lindahill50Hill

"The dialogue is very well done. I certainly felt I was right there." Chill with a Book @ChillwithaBook

"I adored this book! A highly recommended read for lovers of historical fiction." Brook Cottage Books @BrookCottageBks

"It's a great tribute to Carolyn's wonderful writing and her ability to recreate the era and its people that I slipped back in time quite effortlessly." Being Anne @Williams13Anne

"Another fantastic piece of completely immersive historical fiction from Carolyn Hughes...I'll definitely be at the front of the queue for her next book." The Book Magnet @thebookmagnet

"An absorbing account of the times." Historical Novel Society @histnovsoc